"MY DEAR WATSON, YOU WOULD CONFER
A GREAT FAVOUR UPON ME BY COMING.
AND I THINK THAT YOUR TIME WILL NOT BE
MISSPENT, FOR THERE ARE POINTS ABOUT
THE CASE WHICH PROMISE TO MAKE IT
AN ABSOLUTELY UNIQUE ONE . . ."

This is the kind of opening that has made readers
shiver with delicious anticipation ever since Sherlock
Holmes began the great tradition of the British detective story.

Now you can witness the finest moments of Arthur
Conan Doyle's Holmes and such worthy successors as
G. K. Chesterton's modest and marvelous Father
Brown, Grand Allan's roguish Colonel Clay, Agatha
Christie's irresistible Hercule Poirot, and all the others
who take a proud place in the front ranks of—

THE GREAT
BRITISH DETECTIVE

ABOUT THE EDITOR:

RON GOULART is the editor of the detective anthology *The
Hardboiled Dicks* and author of *Cheap Thrills*, a history of
pulp magazines, as well as the author of over 100 mystery
and science fiction novels. He has also written several dozen
mystery yarns for *Ellery Queen's Mystery Magazine* and
Alfred Hitchcock's Mystery Magazine and won an Edgar
Allan Poe Award from the Mystery Writers of America.

A lifelong mystery fan, Goulart lives in Connecticut with his
wife and two sons.

MENTOR Anthologies You'll Want to Read

(0451)

- [ ] **GREAT ACTION STORIES edited and with an Introduction by William Kittredge and Steven M. Krauzer.** A brilliantly designed collection of spellbinding tales by such writers as Dashiell Hammett, Raymond Chandler, Mickey Spillane, Damon Runyon, Dorothy Johnson, John Sayles, and many others. (619153—$1.95)

- [ ] **THE EXPERIENCE OF THE AMERICAN WOMAN: 30 Stories edited and with an Introduction by Barbara H. Solomon.** A century of great fiction about the place and the role of women in America. Works by Kate Chopin, William Faulkner, Toni Cade Bamabra, Katherine Anne Porter, and many other fine writers are included. (621158—$3.95)

- [ ] **STORIES OF THE AMERICAN EXPERIENCE edited by Leonard Kriegel and Abraham H. Lass.** These stories, by some of the greatest writers America has produced, give vivid insight into both our complex national character and our rich literary heritage. Authors included range from such nineteenth-century masters as Nathaniel Hawthorne and Herman Melville to such moderns as Richard Wright and Nelson Algren. (620224—$2.25)

- [ ] **21 GREAT STORIES edited by Abraham H. Lass and Norma L. Tasman.** The stories in this volume have been selected to represent the full spectrum of the storyteller's art. Includes such great writers as "Saki," Edgar Allan Poe, Jack London, James Joyce, Mark Twain, and others. (620666—$2.25)

- [ ] **THE SECRET SHARER and Other Great Stories edited by Abraham H. Lass and Norma L. Tasman.** Complete with biographical data and informative commentary, this anthology stands out as a worthy companion to 21 Great Stories. It includes brilliant stories by such writers as John Updike, Katherine Anne Porter, Flannery O'Connor, Isaac Babel, and others. (620844—$1.95)

THE GREAT
BRITISH
DETECTIVE

*Edited and with an
Introduction by*

RON
GOULART

A MENTOR BOOK
NEW AMERICAN LIBRARY
TIMES MIRROR
New York and Scarborough, Ontario

Library of Congress Catalog Card Number: 82-81665

ACKNOWLEDGMENTS

ALLINGHAM, Margery: "The Magic Hat." Reprinted by permission of Paul R. Reynolds, Inc. Copyright by Margery Allingham.

BAILEY, H. C.: "The Violet Farm" from *Mr. Fortune, Please*. Reprinted by permission of the author. Copyright H. C. Bailey 1927.

CARR, John Dickson: "The Incautious Burglar" from *The Men Who Explained Miracles*. Reprinted by permission of Harold Ober Associates Inc. Copyright 1940 by John Dickson Carr.

CHRISTIE, Agatha: "The Disappearance of Mr. Davenheim" from *Poirot Investigates*. Reprinted by permission of The Bodley Head and by permission of Dodd, Mead & Co., Inc. Copyright 1923, 1924, 1925 by Dodd, Mead & Co., Inc. Copyright renewed 1951, 1952, 1953 by Agatha Christie Mallowan.

CHESTERTON, G. K.: "The Invisible Man" from *The Innocence of Father Brown*. Reprinted by permission of Miss D. E. Collins and Cassell Ltd., and by permission of Dodd, Mead & Co., Inc. Copyright 1911 by Dodd, Mead & Co., Inc. Copyright renewed 1938 by Frances B. Chesterton.

FREEMAN, R. Austin: "A Case of Premeditation." Reprinted by permission of the Estate of R. Austin Freeman and Hodder & Stoughton Ltd.

RENDELL, Ruth: "Means of Evil" from *Means of Evil*. Reprinted by permission of Hutchinson Publishing Group Ltd. and by permission of Doubleday & Co., Inc. Copyright 1979 by Kingsmarkham Enterprises, Ltd.

SAYERS, Dorothy: "The Abominable History of the Man with Copper Fingers." Reprinted with the permission of A. Watkins, Inc. and by permission of David Higham Associates. Copyright © 1928 by Dorothy Leigh Sayers.

VICKERS, Roy: "The Rubber Trumpet" from *The Department of Dead Ends*. Reprinted by permission of Curtis Brown Ltd., London, on behalf of the Estate of Roy Vickers. Copyright 1935 by Roy Vickers.

(The following page constitutes an extension of the copyright page.)

MENTOR TRADEMARK REG. U.S. PAT. OFF. AND FOREIGN COUNTRIES
REGISTERED TRADEMARK—MARCA REGISTRADA
HECHO EN CHICAGO, U.S.A.

SIGNET, SIGNET CLASSICS, MENTOR, PLUME, MERIDIAN AND NAL
Books are published *in the United States* by
The New American Library, Inc.,
1633 Broadway, New York, New York 10019,
in Canada by The New American Library of Canada Limited,
81 Mack Avenue, Scarborough, Ontario M1L 1M8

First Printing, August, 1982

1 2 3 4 5 6 7 8 9

PRINTED IN THE UNITED STATES OF AMERICA

Acknowledgments

I'm appreciative of the help given me by Barbara Bayzn of Davis Publications, Bill Dunn of Dunn's Mysteries of Choice and Steve Lewis of *The Fatal Kiss*. And a tip of the bowler to Denis Gifford and J. Randolph Cox for coming to my aid in the matter of Sexton Blake.

Now a few words about some of the books that were helpful.

The Bibliography of Crime Fiction: 1749–1975 (1979), compiled by Allen J. Hubin, was indispensable. Hubin, of course, lists every American mystery novel and short story collection published in the more than two centuries covered. Books are indexed under author, title, and series characters. Even 112 of the authors who contributed to the saga of Sexton Blake are mentioned.

A Catalogue of Crime (1971), by Jacques Barzun and Wendell Hertig Taylor, was also useful, although Barzun and Taylor loathe several authors I admire. The book lists and comments on well over two thousand British and American detective novels and short story collections.

The Detective Short Story (1942, 1969), a bibliography by Ellery Queen, helped, as did *Queen's Quorum* (1951), by Ellery Queen, which provides an annotated listing of EQ's choice of the 106 best short story collections in the field.

Finally, for background information on writers as well as their detectives, I found the next two volumes could be depended on: *Encyclopedia of Mystery & Detection* (1976), edited by Chris Steinbrunner and Otto Penzler, and *Twentieth Century Crime and Mystery Writers* (1980), edited by John M. Reilly.

Contents

Introduction

In writing a history of anything, the thorniest problem is selecting the point at which to begin. To some historians there is no difficulty in dating the birth of the detective story, since they are convinced it all began in 1841 when Edgar Allan Poe created the first private detective of fiction in his short story "The Murders in the Rue Morgue." There are others, however, who maintain that elements of the detective yarn can be found much earlier in the literature of Western man. To them, Adam's concern over Eve and the apple, for instance, has all the aspects of the classic whodunit. Keeping these opposing views in mind, we won't attempt to pinpoint the day and the hour upon which the British detective story began.

Crime, violence, and murder have long been popular staples in English fiction. Even before these intriguing topics found their way into the three-decker novels of the nineteenth century, they were flourishing in the street literature. Before Victoria assumed the throne, the shilling shockers and the penny dreadfuls (akin to our present-day paperbacks, although smaller, slimmer, and much more wretchedly printed), were ladling out bloody sensations to the ever-growing number of lower class citizens who were able to read. Early in Queen Victoria's reign, and on a somewhat higher plane, novelists like G. W. M. Reynolds and G. P. R. James offered their readers mystery and intrigue in numerous works. The fascination with the underworld and crimes of violence spread to such writers as Charles Dickens and Wilkie Collins, both of whom featured detectives in their novels. Anthony Trollope was also often preoccupied with crime and its consequences, though usually on a middle class and higher level.

While developing out of this British tradition, most of the

detectives you'll meet in this book owe their existence more to the advent of Sherlock Holmes late in the nineteenth century. Sometime in 1886, Arthur Conan Doyle, a barely successful young doctor who dabbled in fiction, decided to write a detective novel. *A Study in Scarlet* was not a particularly well-wrought book and when it appeared in *Beeton's Christmas Annual* in 1887, after having been rejected by a half dozen or more publishers, it caused little stir. When the second novel about Sherlock Holmes, *The Sign of Four*, emerged in 1890, it did not exactly set the Thames afire either. But when Doyle's eccentric, arrogant, drug-taking, violin-playing investigator began appearing in a series of short stories in *The Strand* magazine, the reading public suddenly discovered Holmes. A later editor of the magazine tells of "people fighting at the bookstalls for the new Holmes story on the first of every month." Doyle, who would much rather have devoted all his time to writing historical novels, found himself famous, rich, and stuck with Sherlock Holmes and Dr. Watson for the remainder of his life.

After Holmes came the deluge. The years from 1891, when the first Holmes short story showed up in *The Strand*, until 1914, when the First World War killed for good and all the gaslit era in which Holmes thrived, formed an especially rich period for the detective short story. Besides *The Strand*, there were *Pearson's*, *The Windsor*, *Cassell's*, *The Ludgate Monthly*, *The Idler*, and many other relatively well-paying magazines all anxious to provide their readers with tales of mystery and detection. Across the sea in America periodicals like *Collier's*, *McClure's* and *The Saturday Evening Post* were vying to reprint the latest adventures of Sherlock Holmes and his increasing number of rivals. The 1890s saw the coming of Arthur Morrison's Martin Hewitt; of C. L. Pirkis's Loveday Brooke, Lady Detective; of Grant Allen's pioneering rogue Colonel Clay; and of E. W. Hornung's better remembered rascal Raffles. L. T. Meade (the initials masked Mrs. Elizabeth Thomasina Meade), in collaboration with assorted gentleman friends, turned out several series, including one about a villainous lady known as the Sorceress of the Strand. After the turn of the century came Baroness Orczy's Old Man in the Corner, R. Austin Freeman's Dr. Thorndyke, Robert Barr's Eugène Valmont, G. K. Chesterton's Father Brown, and Ernest Bramah's Max Carrados.

The mystery novel did not thrive as well as the shorter form in the years immediately after the debut of Holmes. There were of course the two early Holmes novels, followed by *The Hound of the Baskervilles* in 1902 and *The Valley of Fear* in 1915. And there had been Fergus Hume's *The Mystery of a Hansome Cab* in 1887, a "melodramatic and badly written tale of secret marriage and threatened respectability" in the words of *A Catalogue of Crime*, that had early sales much more impressive than those of the first Holmes novel. In 1892 there was Israel Zangwill's *The Big Bow Mystery*, one of the early locked room puzzles (and many years later the basis of a Sydney Greenstreet-Peter Lorre movie). The 1890s also saw E. W. Hornung, Conan Doyle's brother-in-law, turning out several Australian-based novels dealing with crime in a fairly realistic manner. A less exotic note was struck in the first years of the twentieth century with R. Austin Freeman's first Dr. Thorndyke novel, *The Red Thumb Mark*, published in 1907, an innovative work dealing with the possibility of faking fingerprints. The prolific Edgar Wallace's *The Four Just Men* burst forth in 1906, the first of his nearly ninety novels of crime and detection, with a very early use of the notion of a gang of vigilante-like crimefighters that was to prove so appealing to many later British and American pulp writers. In 1910, A. E. W. Mason's *At the Villa Rose* was published. Although its detective, M. Hanaud, is with the French Sûreté, no one could be more British than Mason, who is also the author of that classic of stiff-upper-lip-ism, *The Four Feathers*. In the last year before England entered World War I, *Trent's Last Case*, by E. C. Bentley, appeared. A dull, drab book, it is one about which historians differ. Some find it a breakthrough for realism, others consider it a spoof of detective novels. E. Phillips Oppenheim (the E stands for nothing more exotic than Edward) was born nine years before Edgar Wallace and outlived him by fourteen, thus obtaining a lead of close to a quarter century in which to beat Wallace's record for productivity. Oppenheim produced, from 1892 to 1943, 109 novels of detection, crime, and international intrigue, as well as over forty books of short stories, almost all of them dealing with one series character or another. Despite such a monumental body of mystery works, Oppenheim is remembered today chiefly for his 1920 espionage novel, *The Great Impersonation*.

While all this ratiocination was going on in slick paper

periodicals and hardcover books, a slightly different kind of
detective was developing in the cheap paper markets appealing
to the less sophisticated reader. The champ of this new breed
was Sexton Blake, who came along in 1893 and quite soon
thereafter had set up shop in a boys' fiction weekly with the
stirring name of *Union Jack*. "Those who take detective fiction seriously claim that his successes are due less to pure
deduction than to calculated coincidence," comments E. S.
Turner in *Boys Will Be Boys*, "an ability to recover almost instantly from concussion, and such specialized attainments as
the power to out-stare cobras." Quite early in his career, Blake
moved into chambers in Baker Street and took to sitting
around clad in a dressing gown and smoking a pipe. Closer to
America's original Nick Carter (in fact, some of the Blake
yarns were reprinted in this country with his name changed
to Nick Carter), Blake was a man of action, a master of disguise, and the scourge of criminal conspiracies worldwide.
Turner, surely the best historian of junk literature in the Western world, gives a glowing account of the sort of villainy Sexton Blake overcame in his long and successful career. Blake
combatted "the Brotherhood of Silence; the Brotherhood of
the Yellow Beetle; . . . George Marsden Plummer, the Scotland Yard renegade, and his beautiful accomplice Vali Mata
Vali; Huxton Rymer and his equally beautiful female accomplices Mary Trent and Yvonne; . . . Waldo the Wonder Man;
Mr. Mist, the invisible man; Dr. Ferraro, who demanded
£1,000,000 for not blowing up London; . . . King Karl II of
Serbovia, director of the Double Four gang (which included
a female impersonator, a circus strongman, and a baby-faced
midget); Zenith the Albino; . . . mad scientists, hooded ter-
rors, fraudulent Atlantic flyers, crooked lawyers, rascally
rajahs, American racketeers, and human bats." Hordes of
other penny-paper detectives followed in Blake's illustrious
wake. Among them were Nelson Lee, Dixon Brett (who specialized in outwitting a sinister Oriental named Fan Chu Fang,
the Wizard Mandarin), Falcon Swift ("the only detective to
play international soccer wearing a monocle"), and Martin
Track.

The novel became the dominant form of the mystery in
England in the 1920s. "The decline of the short story's popu-
larity, which became sharply noticeable after World War I,
corresponded to the novel's rise," says Julian Symons. The

Twenties are almost always labeled the Golden Age of the English mystery novel, even by those who, like Symons, consider a good deal of the books of the decade to be dull, unconvincing, and silly. The period commenced with the publication in 1920 of Agatha Christie's very first book, *The Mysterious Affair at Styles*, and Freeman Wills Crofts' *The Cask*. Crofts, an engineer by trade, introduced his best known detective, Inspector French, in 1924. Anthony Boucher, many years after its first publication, called *The Cask* "the most completely competent first novel in the history of crime fiction." Symons, on the other hand, finds Crofts "plodding," adding that he knew "nothing about Scotland Yard, and did not think it important that he should learn the details of police procedure." I would tend to side with Symons, never having been able to get through a Crofts novel yet. Quite a bit livelier is H. C. Bailey's Reggie Fortune, another sleuth who was introduced in book form in 1920. *Call Mr. Fortune* is a collection of short stories and Bailey didn't get around to trying a novel about his plump police surgeon detective until 1934. Yet another 1920 debutant was H. C. "Sapper" McNeile's Bulldog Drummond (in the book of the same name). Major Hugh Drummond led a band of stalwart chaps who dealt out their own swift brand of conservative justice to crooks, foreigners, and all other low types. A. A. Milne, the Winnie-the-Pooh man, entered the mystery field in 1922 with *The Red House Mystery*, a tale of murder and impersonation which greatly annoyed Raymond Chandler (see *The Simple Art of Murder*). Dorothy L. Sayers published her first Lord Peter Wimsey novel, *Whose Body?*, in 1923, John Rhode's first of too many Dr. Priestly novels came along in 1925, Leslie Charteris gave us that suave rogue, the Saint, in 1928, and Margery Allingham introduced Albert Campion in *The Crime at Black Dudley* in 1929. The Thirties brought Michael Innes's Inspector Appleby, Nicholas Blake's Nigel Strangeways, and Ngaio Marsh's Inspector Roderick Alleyn. Among the many other new mystery and suspense writers who emerged in the years just before World War II were Eric Ambler, Geoffrey Household, and John Dickson Carr.

In recent years there's been a concerted effort, especially in England itself, to topple many of the 'tec idols of the Golden Age. Julian Symons attacks several revered names in *Mortal Consequences* (1972). Most of them he labels members of "what may be called the Humdrum school of detective novelists." Such writers as Crofts, John Rhode, and J. S. Fletcher had, in Symons' view, little talent for fiction. "They had some skill in constructing puzzles, nothing more." He is none too fond of Miss Sayers either, concluding that her later mystery novels "show . . . an increasing pretentiousness, a dismal sentimentality, and a slackening of the close plotting that had been her chief virtue."

More serious than the charges of ineptness and dullness are those accusing many British mystery writers of the first decades of our century with class and race prejudice. The best presentation of the case is *Snobbery with Violence* (1971), by Colin Watson, himself a mystery novelist. "Thrillers were packed with despicable and evil-intentioned foreigners," Watson writes of the novels of the Golden Age, "while even writers of the more sedate detective stories devoted some of their talents to remarkably splenetic portraiture of characters with dark complections or guttural accents. Foreign was synonomous with criminal in nine novels out of ten." Watson assumes that the attitudes involved in many of the detective stories of the day did not particularly disturb the publishers or the majority of English readers. "Huge sales continued to be enjoyed by Sapper, a rabid racialist; by John Buchan, whose characters frequently make disparaging remarks about Jews and Negroes; by the anti-Semitic G. K. Chesterton; and by other equally famous and equally psychotic authors."

Keeping in mind the flaws as well as the strengths of the great British detectives and their creators, I've put together a collection intended to show them for the most part at their best. Although this is a relatively plump collection, not every major English investigator could be fit in. I've also limited my choices to the 1890s and the first half of this century, operating on the notion that it's easier to pick greats when looking back across a gulf of at least a couple of decades. Even so, you'll find a diverting group of detectives herein, both clever eccentrics and self-effacing everyday types, along with some cunning rascals. All in all, a fair sampling of what British detectives have been up to in the years since Sherlock Holmes first announced that the game was afoot.

—RON GOULART

SHERLOCK HOLMES

In the fall of 1894, Robert Barr interviewed his friend and colleague Arthur Conan Doyle for McClure's Magazine. Seated in two comfortable wicker chairs on the broad lawn of the Doyle residence, the two somewhat portly authors, Doyle in his middle thirties and Barr nearly ten years his senior, talked of many things. The state of fiction, the comparative merits of assorted British and American authors, even the mystery of the ship Marie Celeste. Toward the end of their exchange Barr got around to asking, "By the way, is Sherlock Holmes really dead?" "Yes," Doyle replied. "I shall never write another Sherlock Holmes story." This was only seven years after Sherlock Holmes and Dr. Watson had been introduced to the world in the pages of Beeton's Christmas Annual in the novel A Study in Scarlet and a little over three years after the first Holmes short story, "A Scandal in Bohemia," appeared in The Strand magazine. That story and the five more Doyle then did for the magazine began the craze for Holmes and Watson that has never abated. Celebrity touched Doyle, the public cried for more adventures of the Baker Street sleuth, Doyle's prices began to rise from a modest thirty-five pounds per Holmes yarn to an eventual eight hundred pounds each. All this made Dr. Doyle unhappy and as early as 1892 he was contemplating ways of getting rid of Sherlock Holmes. "He takes my mind off better things," explained Doyle, who believed his best work was to be found in historical novels like The White Company. The pleas of his editors, along with the increasing fees, kept him going until he had done a total of one less than two dozen short stories about Holmes. But in that twenty-third, "The Final Prob-

*lem," he kept his promise to have Holmes vanish forever,
"never to return." Or at least he tried to. As it turned out,
however, he was not to be allowed to get away with this particular murder. He held out for eight years against a worldwide public outcry. Then in 1901 he wrote* The Hound of
the Baskervilles, *a novel supposedly set in the period before
Holmes and the sinister Professor Moriarty took their fatal
plunge over the Reichenbach Falls. Finally Doyle capitulated
completely and in 1903 he brought Sherlock Holmes back
officially from the dead in the story entitled "The Adventure
of the Empty House." For nearly the rest of his life Conan
Doyle kept returning to his desk, hoping that each new
Holmes adventure would be the last.*

Silver Blaze
by Arthur Conan Doyle

"I am afraid, Watson, that I shall have to go," said Holmes
as we sat down together to our breakfast one morning.

"Go! Where to?"

"To Dartmoor; to King's Pyland."

I was not surprised. Indeed, my only wonder was that he
had not already been mixed up in this extraordinary case,
which was the one topic of conversation through the length
and breadth of England. For a whole day my companion had
rambled about the room with his chin upon his chest and his
brows knitted, charging and recharging his pipe with the
strongest black tobacco, and absolutely deaf to any of my
questions or remarks. Fresh editions of every paper had been
sent up by our news agent, only to be glanced over and
tossed down into a corner. Yet, silent as he was, I knew perfectly well what it was over which he was brooding. There
was but one problem before the public which could challenge
his powers of analysis, and that was the singular disappearance of the favourite for the Wessex Cup, and the tragic
murder of its trainer. When, therefore, he suddenly an-

nounced his intention of setting out for the scene of the drama, it was only what I had both expected and hoped for.

"I should be most happy to go down with you if I should not be in the way," said I.

"My dear Watson, you would confer a great favour upon me by coming. And I think that your time will not be misspent, for there are points about the case which promise to make it an absolutely unique one. We have, I think, just time to catch our train at Paddington, and I will go further into the matter upon our journey. You would oblige me by bringing with you your very excellent field-glass."

And so it happened that an hour or so later I found myself in the corner of a first-class carriage flying along en route for Exeter, while Sherlock Holmes, with his sharp, eager face framed in his ear-flapped travelling-cap, dipped rapidly into the bundle of fresh papers which he had procured at Paddington. We had left Reading far behind us before he thrust the last one of them under the seat and offered me his cigarcase.

"We are going well," said he, looking out of the window and glancing at his watch. "Our rate at present is fifty-three and a half miles an hour."

"I have not observed the quarter-mile posts," said I.

"Nor have I. But the telegraph posts upon this line are sixty yards apart, and the calculation is a simple one. I presume that you have looked into this matter of the murder of John Straker and the disappearance of Silver Blaze?"

"I have seen what the *Telegraph* and the *Chronicle* have to say."

"It is one of those cases where the art of the reasoner should be used rather for the sifting of details than for the acquiring of fresh evidence. The tragedy has been so uncommon, so complete, and of such personal importance to so many people that we are suffering from a plethora of surmise, conjecture, and hypothesis. The difficulty is to detach the framework of fact—of absolute undeniable fact—from the embellishments of theorists and reporters. Then, having established ourselves upon this sound basis, it is our duty to see what inferences may be drawn and what are the special points upon which the whole mystery turns. On Tuesday evening I received telegrams from both Colonel Ross, the owner of the horse, and from Inspector Gregory, who is looking after the case, inviting my coöperation."

"Tuesday evening!" I exclaimed. "And this is Thursday morning. Why didn't you go down yesterday?"

"Because I made a blunder, my dear Watson—which is, I am afraid, a more common occurrence than anyone would think who only knew me through your memoirs. The fact is that I could not believe it possible that the most remarkable horse in England could long remain concealed, especially in so sparsely inhabited a place as the north of Dartmoor. From hour to hour yesterday I expected to hear that he had been found, and that his abductor was the murderer of John Straker. When, however, another morning had come and I found that beyond the arrest of young Fitzroy Simpson nothing had been done, I felt that it was time for me to take action. Yet in some ways I feel that yesterday has not been wasted."

"You have formed a theory, then?"

"At least I have got a grip of the essential facts of the case. I shall enumerate them to you, for nothing clears up a case so much as stating it to another person, and I can hardly expect your coöperation if I do not show you the position from which we start."

I lay back against the cushions, puffing at my cigar, while Holmes, leaning forward, with his long, thin forefinger checking off the points upon the palm of his left hand, gave me a sketch of the events which had led to our journey.

"Silver Blaze," said he, "is from the Somomy stock and holds as brilliant a record as his famous ancestor. He is now in his fifth year and has brought in turn each of the prizes of the turf to Colonel Ross, his fortunate owner. Up to the time of the catastrophe he was the first favourite for the Wessex Cup, the betting being three to one on him. He has always, however, been a prime favourite with the racing public and has never yet disappointed them, so that even at those odds enormous sums of money have been laid upon him. It is obvious, therefore, that there were many people who had the strongest interest in preventing Silver Blaze from being there at the fall of the flag next Tuesday.

"The fact was, of course, appreciated at King's Pyland, where the colonel's training stable is situated. Every precaution was taken to guard the favourite. The trainer, John Straker, is a retired jockey who rode in Colonel Ross's colours before he became too heavy for the weighing-chair. He has served the colonel for five years as jockey and for seven as trainer, and has always shown himself to be a zealous and honest servant. Under him were three lads, for the establishment was a small one, containing only four horses in all. One of these lads sat up each night in the stable, while the others slept in the loft. All three bore excellent characters. John Straker, who is a married man, lived in a small villa about two hundred yards from the stables. He has no children, keeps one maidservant, and is comfortably off. The country round is very lonely, but about half a mile to the north there is a small cluster of villas which have been built by a Tavistock contractor for the use of invalids and others who may wish to enjoy the pure Dartmoor air. Tavistock itself lies two miles to the west while across the moor, also about two miles distant, is the larger training establishment of Mapleton, which belongs to Lord Backwater and is managed by Silas Brown. In every other direction the moor is a complete wilderness, inhabited only by a few roaming gypsies. Such was the general situation last Monday night when the catastrophe occurred.

"On that evening the horses had been exercised and watered as usual, and the stables were locked up at nine o'clock. Two of the lads walked up to the trainer's house, where they had supper in the kitchen, while the third, Ned Hunter, remained on guard. At a few minutes after nine the maid, Edith Baxter, carried down to the stables his supper, which consisted of a dish of curried mutton. She took no liquid, as there was a water-tap in the stables, and it was the rule that the lad on duty should drink nothing else. The maid carried a lantern with her, as it was very dark and the path ran across the open moor.

"Edith Baxter was within thirty yards of the stables when a man appeared out of the darkness and called to her to stop. As she stepped into the circle of yellow light thrown by the lantern she saw that he was a person of gentlemanly bearing, dressed in a gray suit of tweeds, with a cloth cap. He wore gaiters and carried a heavy stick with a knob to it. She was most impressed, however, by the extreme pallor of his face and by the nervousness of his manner. His age, she thought, would be rather over thirty than under it.

" 'Can you tell me where I am?' he asked. 'I had almost made up my mind to sleep on the moor when I saw the light of your lantern.'

" 'You are close to the King's Pyland training stables,' said she.

" 'Oh, indeed! What a stroke of luck!' he cried. 'I understand that a stable-boy sleeps there alone every night. Perhaps that is his supper which you are carrying to him. Now I am sure that you would not be too proud to earn the price of a new dress, would you?' He took a piece of white paper folded up out of his waistcoat pocket. 'See that the boy has this tonight, and you shall have the prettiest frock that money can buy.'

"She was frightened by the earnestness of his manner and ran past him to the window through which she was accustomed to hand the meals. It was already opened, and Hunter was seated at the small table inside. She had begun to tell him of what had happened when the stranger came up again.

" 'Good evening,' said he, looking through the window. 'I wanted to have a word with you.' The girl has sworn that as he spoke she noticed the corner of the little paper packet protruding from his closed hand.

" 'What business have you here?' asked the lad.

" 'It's business that may put something into your pocket,' said the other. 'You've two horses in for the Wessex Cup—Silver Blaze and Bayard. Let me have the straight tip and you won't be a loser. Is it a fact that at the weights Bayard could give the other a hundred yards in five furlongs, and that the stable have put their money on him?'

" 'So, you're one of those damned touts!' cried the lad. 'I'll show you how we serve them in King's Pyland.' He sprang up and rushed across the stable to unloose the dog. The girl fled away to the house, but as she ran she looked back and saw that the stranger was leaning through the window. A minute later, however, when Hunter rushed out with the hound he was gone, and though he ran all round the buildings he failed to find any trace of him."

"One moment," I asked. "Did the stable-boy, when he ran out with the dog, leave the door unlocked behind him?"

"Excellent, Watson, excellent!" murmured my companion. "The importance of the point struck me so forcibly that I sent a special wire to Dartmoor yesterday to clear the matter up. The boy locked the door before he left it. The window, I may add, was not large enough for a man to get through.

"Hunter waited until his fellow-grooms had returned, when he sent a message to the trainer and told him what had occurred. Straker was excited at hearing the account, although he does not seem to have quite realized its true significance. It left him, however, vaguely uneasy, and Mrs. Straker, waking at one in the morning, found that he was dressing. In reply to her inquiries, he said that he could not sleep on account of his anxiety about the horses, and that he intended to walk down to the stables to see that all was well. She begged him to remain at home, as she could hear the rain pattering against the window, but in spite of her entreaties he pulled on his large mackintosh and left the house.

"Mrs. Straker awoke at seven in the morning to find that her husband had not yet returned. She dressed herself hastily, called the maid, and set off for the stables. The door was open; inside, huddled together upon a chair, Hunter was sunk in a state of absolute stupor, the favourite's stall was empty, and there were no signs of his trainer.

"The two lads who slept in the chaff-cutting loft above the harness-room were quickly aroused. They had heard nothing during the night, for they are both sound sleepers. Hunter was obviously under the influence of some powerful drug, and as no sense could be got out of him, he was left to sleep it off while the two lads and the two women ran out in search of the absentees. They still had hopes that the trainer had for some reason taken out the horse for early exercise, but on ascending the knoll near the house, from which all the neighbouring moors were visible, they not only could see no signs of the missing favourite, but they perceived something which warned them that they were in the presence of a tragedy.

"About a quarter of a mile from the stables John Straker's overcoat was flapping from a furze-bush. Immediately beyond there was a bowl-shaped depression in the moor, and at the bottom of this was found the dead body of the unfortunate trainer. His head had been shattered by a savage blow from some heavy weapon, and he was wounded on the thigh, where there was a long, clean cut, inflicted evidently by some very sharp instrument. It was clear, however, that Straker had defended himself vigorously against his assailant, for in his right hand he held a small knife, which was clotted with blood up to the handle, while in his left he clasped a red-and-black silk cravat, which was recognized by the maid as having been worn on the preceding evening by the stranger who had visited the stables. Hunter, on recovering from his stupor, was also quite positive as to the ownership of the cravat. He was equally certain that the same stranger had, while standing at the window, drugged his curried mutton, and so deprived the stables of their watchman. As to the missing horse, there were abundant proofs in the mud which lay at the bottom of the fatal hollow that he had been there at the time of the struggle. But from that morning he has disappeared, and although a large reward has been offered, and all the gypsies of Dartmoor are on the alert, no news has come of him. Finally, an analysis has shown that the remains of his supper left by the stable-lad contained an appreciable quantity of powdered opium, while the people at the house partook of the same dish on the same night without any ill effect.

"Those are the main facts of the case, stripped of all surmise, and stated as baldly as possible. I shall now recapitulate what the police have done in the matter.

"Inspector Gregory, to whom the case has been committed, is an extremely competent officer. Were he but gifted with imagination he might rise to great heights in his profession. On his arrival he promptly found and arrested the man upon whom suspicion naturally rested. There was little difficulty in finding him, for he inhabited one of those villas which I have mentioned. His name, it appears, was Fitzroy Simpson. He was a man of excellent birth and education, who had squandered a fortune upon the turf, and who lived now by doing a little quiet and genteel book-making in the sporting clubs of London. An examination of his betting-book shows that bets to the amount of five thousand pounds had been registered by him against the favourite. On being arrested he volunteered the statement that he had come down to Dartmoor in the hope of getting some information about the King's Pyland horses, and also about Desborough, the second favourite, which was in charge of Silas Brown at the Mapleton stables.

He did not attempt to deny that he had acted as described upon the evening before, but declared that he had no sinister designs and had simply wished to obtain first-hand information. When confronted with his cravat he turned very pale and was utterly unable to account for its presence in the hand of the murdered man. His wet clothing showed that he had been out in the storm of the night before, and his stick, which was a penang-lawyer weighted with lead, was just such a weapon as might, by repeated blows, have inflicted the terrible injuries to which the trainer had succumbed. On the other hand, there was no wound upon his person, while the state of Straker's knife would show that one at least of his assailants must bear his mark upon him. There you have it all in a nutshell, Watson, and if you can give me any light I shall be infinitely obliged to you."

I had listened with the greatest interest to the statement which Holmes, with characteristic clearness, had laid before me. Though most of the facts were familiar to me, I had not sufficiently appreciated their relative importance, nor their connection to each other.

"Is it not possible," I suggested, "that the incised wound upon Straker may have been caused by his own knife in the convulsive struggles which follow any brain injury?"

"It is more than possible: it is probable," said Holmes. "In that case one of the main points in favour of the accused disappears."

"And yet," said I, "even now I fail to understand what the theory of the police can be."

"I am afraid that whatever theory we state has very grave objections to it," returned my companion. "The police imagine, I take it, that this Fitzroy Simpson, having drugged the lad, and having in some way obtained a duplicate key, opened the stable door and took out the horse, with the intention, apparently, of kidnapping him altogether. His bridle is missing, so that Simpson must have put this on. Then, having left the door open behind him, he was leading the horse away over the moor when he was either met or overtaken by the trainer. A row naturally ensued. Simpson beat out the trainer's brains with his heavy stick without receiving any injury from the small knife which Straker used in self-defence, and then the thief either led the horse on to some secret hiding-place, or else it may have bolted during the struggle, and be now wandering out on the moors. That is the case as it appears to the police, and improbable as it is, all other explanations are more improbable still. However, I shall very quickly test the matter when I am once upon the spot, and until then I cannot really see how we can get much further than our present position."

It was evening before we reached the little town of Tavistock, which lies, like the boss of a shield, in the middle of the huge circle of Dartmoor. Two gentlemen were awaiting us in the station—the one a tall, fair man with lion-like hair and beard and curiously penetrating light blue eyes; the other a small, alert person, very neat and dapper, in a frock-coat and gaiters, with trim little side-whiskers and an eyeglass. The latter was Colonel Ross, the well-known sportsman; the other, Inspector Gregory; a man who was rapidly making his name in the English detective service.

"I am delighted that you have come down, Mr. Holmes," said the colonel. "The inspector here has done all that could possibly be suggested, but I wish to leave no stone unturned in trying to avenge poor Straker and in recovering my horse."

"Have there been any fresh developments?" asked Holmes.

"I am sorry to say that we have made very little progress," said the inspector. "We have an open carriage outside, and as you would no doubt like to see the place before the light fails, we might talk it over as we drive."

A minute later we were all seated in a comfortable landau and were rattling through the quaint old Devonshire city. Inspector Gregory was full of his case and poured out a stream of remarks, while Holmes threw in an occasional question or interjection. Colonel Ross leaned back with his arms folded and his hat tilted over his eyes, while I listened with interest to the dialogue of the two detectives. Gregory was formulating his theory, which was almost exactly what Holmes had foretold in the train.

"The net is drawn pretty close round Fitzroy Simpson," he remarked, "and I believe myself that he is our man. At the same time I recognize that the evidence is purely circumstantial, and that some new development may upset it."

"How about Straker's knife?"

"We have quite come to the conclusion that he wounded himself in his fall."

"My friend Dr. Watson made that suggestion to me as we came down. If so, it would tell against this man Simpson."

"Undoubtedly. He has neither a knife nor any sign of a wound. The evidence against him is certainly very strong. He had a great interest in the disappearance of the favourite. He lies under suspicion of having poisoned the stable-boy; he was undoubtedly out in the storm; he was armed with a heavy stick, and his cravat was found in the dead man's hand. I really think we have enough to go before a jury."

Holmes shook his head. "A clever counsel would tear it all to rags," said he. "Why should he take the horse out of the stable? If he wished to injure it, why could he not do it there? Has a duplicate key been found in his possession? What chemist sold him the powdered opium? Above all, where could he, a stranger to the district, hide a horse, and such a horse as this? What is his own explanation as to the paper which he wished the maid to give to the stableboy?"

"He says that it was a ten-pound note. One was found in his purse. But your other difficulties are not so formidable as they seem. He is not a stranger to the district. He has twice lodged at Tavistock in the summer. The opium was probably brought from London. The key, having served its purpose, would be hurled away. The horse may be at the bottom of one of the pits or old mines upon the moor."

"What does he say about the cravat?"

"He acknowledges that it is his and declares that he had lost it. But a new element has been introduced into the case which may account for his leading the horse from the stable."

Holmes pricked up his ears.

"We have found traces which show that a party of gypsies encamped on Monday night within a mile of the spot where the murder took place. On Tuesday they were gone. Now, presuming that there was some understanding between Simpson and these gypsies, might he not have been leading the horse to them when he was overtaken, and may they not have him now?"

"It is certainly possible."

"The moor is being scoured for these gypsies. I have also

examined every stable and outhouse in Tavistock, and for a radius of ten miles."

"There is another training-stable quite close, I understand?"

"Yes, and that is a factor which we must certainly not neglect. As Desborough, their horse, was second in the betting, they had an interest in the disappearance of the favourite. Silas Brown, the trainer, is known to have had large bets upon the event, and he was no friend to poor Straker. We have, however, examined the stables, and there is nothing to connect him with the affair."

"And nothing to connect this man Simpson with the interests of the Mapleton stables?"

"Nothing at all."

Holmes leaned back in the carriage, and the conversation ceased. A few minutes later our driver pulled up at a neat little red-brick villa with overhanging eaves which stood by the road. Some distance off, across a paddock, lay a long gray-tiled outbuilding. In every other direction the low curves of the moor, bronze-coloured from the fading ferns, stretched away to the sky-line, broken only by the steeples of Tavistock, and by a cluster of houses away to the westward which marked the Mapleton stables. We all sprang out with the exception of Holmes, who continued to lean back with his eyes fixed upon the sky in front of him, entirely absorbed in his own thoughts. It was only when I touched his arm that he roused himself with a violent start and stepped out of the carriage.

"Excuse me," said he, turning to Colonel Ross, who had looked at him in some surprise. "I was day-dreaming." There was a gleam in his eyes and a suppressed excitement in his manner which convinced me, used as I was to his ways, that his hand was upon a clue, though I could not imagine where he had found it.

"Perhaps you would prefer at once to go on to the scene of the crime, Mr. Holmes?" said Gregory.

"I think that I should prefer to stay here a little and go into one or two questions of detail. Straker was brought back here, I presume?"

"Yes, he lies upstairs. The inquest is to-morrow."

"He has been in your service some years, Colonel Ross?"

"I have always found him an excellent servant."

"I presume that you made an inventory of what he had in his pockets at the time of his death, Inspector?"

"I have the things themselves in the sitting-room if you would care to see them."

"I should be very glad." We all filed into the front room and sat round the central table while the inspector unlocked a square tin box and laid a small heap of things before us. There was a box of vestas, two inches of tallow candle, an A D P brier-root pipe, a pouch of sealskin with half an ounce of long-cut Cavendish, a silver watch with a gold chain, five sovereigns in gold, an aluminum pencil-case, a few papers, and an ivory-handled knife with a very delicate, inflexible blade marked Weiss & Co., London.

"This is a very singular knife," said Holmes, lifting it up and examining it minutely. "I presume, as I see blood-stains upon it, that it is the one which was found in the dead man's grasp. Watson, this knife is surely in your line?"

"It is what we call a cataract knife," said I.

"I thought so. A very delicate blade devised for very delicate work. A strange thing for a man to carry with him upon a rough expedition, especially as it would not shut in his pocket."

"The tip was guarded by a disc of cork which we found beside his body," said the inspector. "His wife tells us that the knife had lain upon the dressing-table, and that he had picked it up as he left the room. It was a poor weapon, but perhaps the best that he could lay his hands on at the moment."

"Very possibly. How about these papers?"

"Three of them are receipted hay-dealers' accounts. One of them is a letter of instructions from Colonel Ross. This other is a milliner's account for thirty-seven pounds fifteen made out by Madame Lesurier, of Bond Street, to William Derbyshire. Mrs. Straker tells us that Derbyshire was a friend of her husband's, and that occasionally his letters were addressed here."

"Madame Derbyshire had somewhat expensive tastes," remarked Holmes, glancing down the account. "Twenty-two guineas is rather heavy for a single costume. However, there appears to be nothing more to learn, and we may now go down to the scene of the crime."

As we emerged from the sitting-room a woman, who had been waiting in the passage, took a step forward and laid her hand upon the inspector's sleeve. Her face was haggard and thin and eager, stamped with the print of a recent horror.

"Have you got them? Have you found them?" she panted.

"No, Mrs. Straker. But Mr. Holmes here has come from London to help us, and we shall do all that is possible."

"Surely I met you in Plymouth at a garden-party some little time ago, Mrs. Straker?" said Holmes.

"No, sir; you are mistaken."

"Dear me! Why, I could have sworn to it. You wore a costume of dove-coloured silk with ostrich-feather trimming."

"I never had such a dress, sir," answered the lady.

"Ah, that quite settles it," said Holmes. And with an apology he followed the inspector outside. A short walk across the moor took us to the hollow in which the body had been found. At the brink of it was the furze-bush upon which the coat had been hung.

"There was no wind that night, I understand," said Holmes.

"None, but very heavy rain."

"In that case the overcoat was not blown against the furze-bushes, but placed there."

"Yes, it was laid across the bush."

"You fill me with interest. I perceive that the ground has been trampled up a good deal. No doubt many feet have been here since Monday night."

"A piece of matting has been laid here at the side, and we have all stood upon that."

"Excellent."

"In this bag I have one of the boots which Straker wore, one of Fitzroy Simpson's shoes, and a cast horseshoe of Silver Blaze."

"My dear Inspector, you surpass yourself!" Holmes took the bag, and, descending into the hollow, he pushed the matting into a more central position. Then stretching himself upon his face and leaning his chin upon his hands, he made a careful study of the trampled mud in front of him. "Hullo!" said he suddenly. "What's this?" It was a wax vesta, half burned, which was so coated with mud that it looked at first like a little chip of wood.

"I cannot think how I came to overlook it," said the inspector with an expression of annoyance.

"It was invisible, buried in the mud. I only saw it because I was looking for it."

"What! you expected to find it?"

"I thought it not unlikely."

He took the boots from the bag and compared the impressions of each of them with marks upon the ground. Then he clambered up to the rim of the hollow and crawled about among the ferns and bushes.

"I am afraid that there are no more tracks," said the inspector. "I have examined the ground very carefully for a hundred yards in each direction."

"Indeed!" said Holmes, rising. "I should not have the impertinence to do it again after what you say. But I should like to take a little walk over the moor before it grows dark that I may know my ground to-morrow, and I think that I shall put this horseshoe into my pocket for luck."

Colonel Ross, who had shown some signs of impatience at my companion's quiet and systematic method of work, glanced at his watch. "I wish you would come back with me, Inspector," said he. "There are several points on which I should like your advice, and especially as to whether we do not owe it to the public to remove our horse's name from the entries for the cup."

"Certainly not," cried Holmes with decision. "I should let the name stand."

The colonel bowed. "I am very glad to have had your opinion, sir," said he. "You will find us at poor Straker's house when you have finished your walk, and we can drive together into Tavistock."

He turned back with the inspector, while Homes and I walked slowly across the moor. The sun was beginning to sink behind the stable of Mapleton, and the long, sloping plain in front of us was tinged with gold, deepening into rich, ruddy browns where the faded ferns and brambles caught the evening light. But the glories of the landscape were all wasted upon my companion, who was sunk in the deepest thought.

"It's this way, Watson," said he at last. "We may leave the

question of who killed John Straker for the instant and confine ourselves to finding out what has become of the horse. Now, supposing that he broke away during or after the tragedy, where could he have gone to? The horse is a very gregarious creature. If left to himself his instincts would have been either to return to King's Pyland or go over to Mapleton. Why should he run wild upon the moor? He would surely have been seen by now. And why should gypsies kidnap him? These people always clear out when they hear of trouble, for they do not wish to be pestered by the police. They could not hope to sell such a horse. They would run a great risk and gain nothing by taking him. Surely that is clear."

"Where is he, then?"

"I have already said that he must have gone to King's Pyland or to Mapleton. He is not at King's Pyland. Therefore he is at Mapleton. Let us take that as a working hypothesis and see what it leads us to. This part of the moor, as the inspector remarked, is very hard and dry. But it falls away towards Mapleton, and you can see from here that there is a long hollow over yonder, which must have been very wet on Monday night. If our supposition is correct, then the horse must have crossed that, and there is the point where we should look for his tracks."

We had been walking briskly during this conversation, and a few more minutes brought us to the hollow in question. At Holmes's request I walked down the bank to the right, and he to the left, but I had not taken fifty paces before I heard him give a shout and saw him waving his hand to me. The track of a horse was plainly outlined in the soft earth in front of him, and the shoe which he took from his pocket exactly fitted the impression.

"See the value of imagination," said Holmes. "It is the one quality which Gregory lacks. We imagined what might have happened, acted upon the supposition, and find ourselves justified, Let us proceed."

We crossed the marshy bottom and passed over a quarter of a mile of dry, hard turf. Again the ground sloped, and again we came on the tracks. Then we lost them for half a mile, but only to pick them up once more quite close to Mapleton. It was Holmes who saw them first, and he stood pointing with a look of triumph upon his face. A man's track was visible beside the horse's.

"The horse was alone before," I cried.

"Quite so. It was alone before. Hullo, what is this?"

The double track turned sharp off and took the direction of King's Pyland. Holmes whistled, and we both followed along after it. His eyes were on the trail, but I happened to look a little to one side and saw to my surprise the same tracks coming back again in the opposite direction.

"One for you, Watson," said Holmes when I pointed it out. "You have saved us a long walk, which would have brought us back on our own traces. Let us follow the return track."

We had not to go far. It ended at the paving of asphalt which led up to the gates of the Mapleton stables. As we approached, a groom ran out from them.

"We don't want any loiterers about here," said he.

"I only wished to ask a question," said Holmes, with his finger and thumb in his waistcoat pocket. "Should I be too early to see your master, Mr. Silas Brown, if I were to call at five o'clock to-morrow morning?"

"Bless you, sir, if anyone is about he will be, for he is always the first stirring. But here he is, sir, to answer your questions for himself. No, sir, no, it is as much as my place is worth to let him see me touch your money. Afterwards, if you like."

As Sherlock Holmes replaced the half-crown which he had drawn from his pocket, a fierce-looking elderly man strode out from the gate with a hunting-crop swinging in his hand.

"What's this, Dawson!" he cried. "No gossiping! Go about your business! And you, what the devil do you want here?"

"Ten minutes' talk with you, my good sir," said Holmes in the sweetest of voices.

"I've no time to talk to every gadabout. We want no strangers here. Be off, or you may find a dog at your heels."

Holmes leaned forward and whispered something in the trainer's ear. He started violently and flushed to the temples.

"It's a lie!" he shouted. "An infernal lie!"

"Very good. Shall we argue about it here in public or talk it over in your parlour?"

"Oh, come in if you wish to."

Holmes smiled. "I shall not keep you more than a few

minutes, Watson," said he. "Now, Mr. Brown, I am quite at your disposal."

It was twenty minutes, and the reds had all faded into grays before Holmes and the trainer reappeared. Never have I seen such a change as had been brought about in Silas Brown in that short time. His face was ashy pale, beads of perspiration shone upon his brow, and his hands shook until the hunting-crop wagged like a branch in the wind. His bullying, overbearing manner was all gone too, and he cringed along at my companion's side like a dog with its master.

"Your instructions will be done. It shall all be done," said he.

"There must be no mistake," said Holmes, looking round at him. The other winced as he read the menace in his eyes.

"Oh, no, there shall be no mistake. It shall be there. Should I change it first or not?"

Holmes thought a little and then burst out laughing. "No, don't," said he, "I shall write to you about it. No tricks, now, or—"

"Oh, you can trust me, you can trust me!"

"Yes, I think I can. Well, you shall hear from me to-morrow." He turned upon his heel, disregarding the trembling hand which the other held out to him, and we set off for King's Pyland.

"A more perfect compound of the bully, coward, and sneak than Master Silas Brown I have seldom met with," remarked Holmes as we trudged along together.

"He has the horse, then?"

"He tried to bluster out of it, but I described to him so exactly what his actions had been upon that morning that he is convinced that I was watching him. Of course you observed the peculiarly square toes in the impressions, and that his own boots exactly corresponded to them. Again, of course no subordinate would have dared to do such a thing. I described to him how, when according to his custom he was the first down, he perceived a strange horse wandering over the moor. How he went out to it, and his astonishment at recognizing, from the white forehead which has given the favourite its name, that chance had put in his power the only horse which could beat the one upon which he had put his money. Then I described how his first impulse had been to lead him back to

King's Pyland, and how the devil had shown him how he could hide the horse until the race was over, and how he had led it back and concealed it at Mapleton. When I told him every detail he gave it up and thought only of saving his own skin."

"But his stables had been searched?"

"Oh, an old horse-faker like him has many a dodge."

"But are you not afraid to leave the horse in his power now, since he has every interest in injuring it?"

"My dear fellow, he will guard it as the apple of his eye. He knows that his only hope of mercy is to produce it safe."

"Colonel Ross did not impress me as a man who would be likely to show much mercy in any case."

"The matter does not rest with Colonel Ross. I follow my own methods and tell as much or as little as I choose. That is the advantage of being unofficial. I don't know whether you observed it, Watson, but the colonel's manner has been just a trifle cavalier to me. I am inclined now to have a little amusement at his expense. Say nothing to him about the horse."

"Certainly not without your permission."

"And of course this is all quite a minor point compared to the question of who killed John Straker."

"And you will devote yourself to that?"

"On the contrary, we both go back to London by the night train."

I was thunderstruck by my friend's words. We had only been a few hours in Devonshire, and that he should give up an investigation which he had begun so brilliantly was quite incomprehensible to me. Not a word more could I draw from him until we were back at the trainer's house. The colonel and the inspector were awaiting us in the parlour.

"My friend and I return to town by the night-express," said Holmes. "We have had a charming little breath of your beautiful Dartmoor air."

The inspector opened his eyes, and the colonel's lip curled in a sneer. "So you despair of arresting the murderer of poor Straker," said he.

Holmes shrugged his shoulders. "There are certainly grave difficulties in the way," said he. "I have every hope, however, that your horse will start upon Tuesday, and I beg that you will have your jockey in readiness. Might I ask for a photograph of Mr. John Straker?"

The inspector took one from an envelope and handed it to him.

"My dear Gregory, you anticipate all my wants. If I might ask you to wait here for an instant, I have a question which I should like to put to the maid."

"I must say that I am rather disappointed in our London consultant," said Colonel Ross bluntly as my friend left the room. "I do not see that we are any further than when he came."

"At least you have his assurance that your horse will run," said I.

"Yes, I have his assurance," said the colonel with a shrug of his shoulders. "I should prefer to have the horse."

I was about to make some reply in defence of my friend when he entered the room again.

"Now, gentlemen," said he, "I am quite ready for Tavistock."

As we stepped into the carriage one of the stable-lads held the door open for us. A sudden idea seemed to occur to Holmes, for he leaned forward and touched the lad upon the sleeve.

"You have a few sheep in the paddock," he said. "Who attends to them?"

"I do, sir."

"Have you noticed anything amiss with them of late?"

"Well, sir, not of much account, but three of them have gone lame, sir."

I could see that Holmes was extremely pleased, for he chuckled and rubbed his hands together.

"A long shot, Watson. a very long shot," said he, pinching my arm. "Gregory, let me recommend to your attention this singular epidemic among the sheep. Drive on, coachman!"

Colonel Ross still wore an expression which showed the poor opinion which he had formed of my companion's ability, but I saw by the inspector's face that his attention had been keenly aroused.

"You consider that to be important?" he asked.

"Exceedingly so."

"Is there any point to which you would wish to draw my attention?"

"To the curious incident of the dog in the night-time."

"The dog did nothing in the night-time."

"That was the curious incident," remarked Sherlock Holmes.

Four days later Holmes and I were again in the train, bound for Winchester to see the race for the Wessex Cup. Colonel Ross met us by appointment outside the station, and we drove in his drag to the course beyond the town. His face was grave, and his manner was cold in the extreme.

"I have seen nothing of my horse," said he.

"I suppose that you would know him when you saw him?" asked Holmes.

The colonel was very angry. "I have been on the turf for twenty years and never was asked such a question as that before," said he. "A child would know Silver Blaze with his white forehead and his mottled off-foreleg."

"How is the betting?"

"Well, that is the curious part of it. You could have got fifteen to one yesterday, but the price has become shorter and shorter, until you can hardly get three to one now."

"Hum!" said Holmes. "Somebody knows something, that is clear."

As the drag drew up in the enclosure near the grandstand I glanced at the card to see the entries.

Wessex Plate [it ran] 50 sovs. each h ft with 1000 sovs. added, for four and five year olds. Second, £300. Third, £200. New course (one mile and five furlongs).

1. Mr. Heath Newton's The Negro. Red cap. Cinnamon jacket.
2. Colonel Wardlaw's Pugilist. Pink cap. Blue and black jacket.
3. Lord Backwater's Desborough. Yellow cap and sleeves.
4. Colonel Ross's Silver Blaze. Black cap. Red jacket.
5. Duke of Balmoral's Iris. Yellow and black stripes.
6. Lord Singleford's Rasper. Purple cap. Black sleeves.

"We scratched our other one and put all hopes on your word," said the colonel. "Why, what is that? Silver Blaze favourite?"

"Five to four against Silver Blaze!" roared the ring. "Five to four against Silver Blaze! Five to fifteen against Desborough! Five to four on the field!"

"There are the numbers up," I cried. "They are all six there."

"All six there? Then my horse is running," cried the colonel in great agitation. "But I don't see him. My colours have not passed."

"Only five have passed. This must be he."

As I spoke a powerful bay horse swept out from the weighing enclosure and cantered past us, bearing on its back the well-known black and red of the colonel.

"That's not my horse," cried the owner. "That beast has not a white hair upon its body. What is this that you have done, Mr. Holmes?"

"Well, well, let us see how he gets on," said my friend imperturbably. For a few minutes he gazed through my field-glass. "Capital! And excellent start!" he cried suddenly. "There they are, coming round the curve!"

From our drag we had a superb view as they came up the straight. The six horses were so close together that a carpet could have covered them, but halfway up the yellow of the Mapleton stable showed to the front. Before they reached us, however, Desborough's bolt was shot, and the colonel's horse, coming away with a rush, passed the post a good six lengths before its rival, the Duke of Balmoral's Iris making a bad third.

"It's my race, anyhow," gasped the colonel, passing his hand over his eyes. "I confess that I can make neither head nor tail of it. Don't you think that you have kept up your mystery long enough, Mr. Holmes?"

"Certainly, Colonel, you shall know everything. Let us all go round and have a look at the horse together. Here he is," he continued as we made our way into the weighing enclosure, where only owners and their friends find admittance. "You have only to wash his face and his leg in spirits of wine, and you will find that he is the same old Silver Blaze as ever."

"You take my breath away!"

"I found him in the hands of a faker and took the liberty of running him just as he was sent over."

"My dear sir, you have done wonders. The horse looks very fit and well. It never went better in its life. I owe you a thousand apologies for having doubted your ability. You have done me a great service by recovering my horse. You would do me a greater still if you could lay your hands on the murderer of John Straker."

"I have done so," said Holmes quietly.

The colonel and I stared at him in amazement. "You have got him! Where is he, then?"

"He is here."

"Here! Where?"

"In my company at the present moment."

The colonel flushed angrily. "I quite recognize that I am under obligations to you, Mr. Holmes," said he, "but I must regard what you have just said as either a very bad joke or an insult."

Sherlock Holmes laughed. "I assure you that I have not associated you with the crime, Colonel," said he. "The real murderer is standing immediately behind you." He stepped past and laid his hand upon the glossy neck of the thoroughbred.

"The horse!" cried both the colonel and myself.

"Yes, the horse. And it may lessen his guilt if I say that it was done in self-defence, and that John Straker was a man who was entirely unworthy of your confidence. But there goes the bell, and as I stand to win a little on this next race, I shall defer a lengthy explanation until a more fitting time."

We had a corner of a Pullman car to ourselves that evening as we whirled back to London, and I fancy that the journey was a short one to Colonel Ross as well as to myself as we listened to our companion's narrative of the events which had occurred at the Dartmoor training-stables upon that Monday night, and the means by which he had unravelled them.

"I confess," said he, "that any theories which I had formed from the newspaper reports were entirely erroneous. And yet there were indications there, had they not been overlaid by other details which concealed their true import. I went to Devonshire with the conviction that Fitzroy Simpson was the true culprit, although, of course, I saw that the evidence against him was by no means complete. It was while I was in the carriage, just as we reached the trainer's house, that the immense significance of the curried mutton occurred to me. You may remember that I was distrait and remained sitting after you had all alighted. I was marvelling in my own mind how I could possibly have overlooked so obvious a clue."

"I confess," said the colonel, "that even now I cannot see how it helps us."

"It was the first link in my chain of reasoning. Powdered opium is by no means tasteless. The flavour is not disagreeable, but it is perceptible. Were it mixed with any ordinary dish the eater would undoubtedly detect it and would probably eat no more. A curry was exactly the medium which would disguise this taste. By no possible supposition could this stranger, Fitzroy Simpson, have caused curry to be served in the trainer's family that night, and it is surely too monstrous a coincidence to suppose that he happened to come along with powdered opium upon the very night when a dish happened to be served which would disguise the flavour. That is unthinkable. Therefore Simpson become eliminated from the case, and our attention centres upon Straker and his wife, the only two people who could have chosen curried mutton for supper that night. The opium was added after the dish was set aside for the stable-boy, for the others had the same for supper with no ill effects. Which of them, then, had access to that dish without the maid seeing them?

"Before deciding that question I had grasped the significance of the silence of the dog, for one true inference invariably suggests others. The Simpson incident had shown me that a dog was kept in the stables, and yet, though someone had been in and had fetched out a horse, he had not barked enough to arouse the two lads in the loft. Obviously the midnight visitor was someone whom the dog knew well.

"I was already convinced, or almost convinced, that John Straker went down to the stables in the dead of the night and took out Silver Blaze. For what purpose? For a dishonest one, obviously, or why should he drug his own stable-boy? And yet I was at a loss to know why. There have been cases before now where trainers have made sure of great sums of money by laying against their own horses through agents and then preventing them from winning by fraud. Sometimes it is

a pulling jockey. Sometimes it is some surer and subtle
means. What was it here? I hoped that the contents of h
pockets might help me to form a conclusion.

"And they did so. You cannot have forgotten the singula
knife which was found in the dead man's hand, a knife whic
certainly no sane man would choose for a weapon. It was, a
Dr. Watson told us, a form of knife which is used for th
most delicate operations known in surgery. And it was to b
used for a delicate operation that night. You must know, wit
your wide experience of turf matters, Colonel Ross, that it
possible to make a slight nick upon the tendons of a horse
ham, and to do it subcutaneously, so as to leave absolutely n
trace. A horse so treated would develop a slight lameness
which would be put down to a strain in exercise or a touc
of rheumatism, but never to foul play."

"Villain! Scoundrel!" cried the colonel.

"We have here the explanation of why John Straker wishe
to take the horse out on to the moor. So spirited a creatur
would have certainly roused the soundest of sleepers when i
felt the prick of the knife. It was absolutely necessary to do i
in the open air."

"I have been blind!" cried the colonel. "Of course that wa
why he needed the candle and struck the match."

"Undoubtedly. But in examining his belongings I was fo
tunate enough to discover not only the method of the crim
but even its motives. As a man of the world, Colonel, yo
know that men do not carry other people's bills about in thei
pockets. We have most of us quite enough to do to settle ou
own. I at once concluded that Straker was leading a double
life and keeping a second establishment. The nature of th
bill showed that there was a lady in the case, and one wh
had expensive tastes. Liberal as you are with your servants
one can hardly expect that they can buy twenty-guinea walk
ing dresses for their ladies. I questioned Mrs. Straker as t
the dress without her knowing it, and, having satisfied mysel
that it had never reached her, I made a note of the milliner's
address and felt that by calling there with Straker's photograph I could easily dispose of the mythical Derbyshire.

"From that time on all was plain. Straker had led out the
horse to a hollow where his light would be invisible. Simpson
in his flight had dropped his cravat, and Straker had picked it

up—with some idea, perhaps, that he might use it in securing the horse's leg. Once in the hollow, he had got behind the horse and had struck a light; but the creature, frightened at the sudden glare, and with the strange instinct of animals feeling that some mischief was intended, had lashed out, and the steel shoe had struck Straker full on the forehead. He had already, in spite of the rain, taken off his overcoat in order to do his delicate task, and so, as he fell, his knife gashed his thigh. Do I make it clear?"

"Wonderful!" cried the colonel. "Wonderful! You might have been there!"

"My final shot was, I confess, a very long one. It struck me that so astute a man as Straker would not undertake this delicate tendon-nicking without a little practice. What could he practice on? My eyes fell upon the sheep, and I asked a question which, rather to my surprise, showed that my surmise was correct.

"When I returned to London I called upon the milliner, who had recognized Straker as an excellent customer of the name of Derbyshire, who had a very dashing wife, with a strong partiality for expensive dresses. I have no doubt that this woman had plunged him over head and ears in debt, and so led him into this miserable plot."

"You have explained all but one thing," cried the colonel. "Where was the horse?"

"Ah, it bolted, and was cared for by one of your neighbours. We must have an amnesty in that direction, I think. This is Clapham Junction, if I am not mistaken, and we shall be in Victoria in less than ten minutes. If you care to smoke a cigar in our rooms, Colonel, I shall be happy to give you any other details which might interest you."

LOVEDAY BROOKE

The great wave of private detectives that swept across England in the wake of Sherlock Holmes included quite a few lady sleuths. The end of the nineteenth century saw the advent of Dorcas Dene, Miss Van Snoop, Hagar Stanley, Florence Cusack, Hilda Wade, and Dora Myrl. Probably the best of the lot was Loveday Brooke, a "sensible and practical woman," who began her career in the pages of The Ludgate Monthly in 1893. Loveday was the employee of a male-dominated London detective agency and her chief once paid her the compliment of saying she possessed "the faculty—so rare among women—of carrying out orders to the very letter." When we meet Loveday, she has been working for the Fleet Street detective agency almost a half dozen years and is just past thirty. "Her features were altogether nondescript," we are told, and "she was neither handsome nor ugly."

Hiding behind the C. L. initials was Mrs. Catherine Louisa Pirkis. Married to a naval officer, C. L. Pirkis wrote romantic novels in the 1870s and 80s. The magazine stories about her female investigator were collected together in 1894 as The Experiences of Loveday Brooke, Lady Detective. This was Mrs. Pirkis's final book. The exact year of her birth remains a mystery, but she died in 1910.

Drawn Daggers
by C. L. Pirkis

"I admit that the dagger business is something of a puzzle to me, but as for the lost necklace—well, I should have thought a child would have understood that," said Mr. Dyer irritably. "When a young lady loses a valuable article of jewellery and wishes to hush the matter up, the explanation is obvious."

"Sometimes," answered Miss Brooke calmly, "the explanation that is obvious is the one to be rejected, not accepted."

Off and on these two had been, so to speak, "jangling" a good deal that morning. Perhaps the fact was in part to be attributed to the biting east wind which had set Loveday's eyes watering with the gritty dust, as she had made her way to Lynch Court, and which was, at the present moment, sending the smoke in aggravating gusts, down the chimney into Mr. Dyer's face. Thus it was, however. On the various topics that had chanced to come up for discussion that morning between Mr. Dyer and his colleague, they had each taken up, as if by design, diametrically opposite points of view.

His temper altogether gave way now.

"If," he said, bringing his hand down with emphasis on his writing-table, "you lay it down as a principle that the obvious is to be rejected in favour of the abstruse, you'll soon find yourself launched in the predicament of having to prove that two apples added to two other apples do not make four. But there, if you don't choose to see things from my point of view, that is no reason why you should lose your temper!"

"Mr. Hawke wishes to see you, sir," said a clerk, at that moment entering the room.

It was a fortunate diversion. Whatever might be the differences of opinion in which these two might indulge in private, they were careful never to parade those differences before their clients.

Mr. Dyer's irritability vanished in a moment.

"Show the gentleman in," he said to the clerk. Then he

turned to Loveday. "This is the Reverend Anthony Hawke, the gentleman at whose house I told you that Miss Monroe is staying temporarily. He is a clergyman of the Church of England, but gave up his living some twenty years ago when he married a wealthy lady. Miss Monroe has been sent over to his guardianship from Pekin by her father, Sir George Monroe, in order to get her out of the way of a troublesome and undesirable suitor."

The last sentence was added in a low and hurried tone, for Mr. Hawke was at that moment entering the room.

He was a man close upon sixty years of age, white-haired, clean-shaven, with a full, round face, to which a small nose imparted a somewhat infantine expression. His manner of greeting was urbane but slightly flurried and nervous. He gave Loveday the impression of being an easygoing, happy-tempered man who, for the moment, was unusually disturbed and perplexed.

He glanced uneasily at Loveday. Mr. Dyer hastened to explain that this was the lady by whose aid he hoped to get to the bottom of the matter now under consideration.

"In that case there can be no objection to my showing you this," said Mr. Hawke; "it came by post this morning. You see my enemy still pursues me."

As he spoke he took from his pocket a big, square envelope, from which he drew a large-sized sheet of paper.

On this sheet of paper were roughly drawn, in ink, two daggers, about six inches in length, with remarkably pointed blades.

Mr. Dyer looked at the sketch with interest.

"We will compare this drawing and its envelope with those you previously received," he said, opening a drawer of his writing-table and taking thence a precisely similar envelope. On the sheet of paper, however, that this envelope enclosed, there was drawn one dagger only.

He placed both envelopes and their enclosures side by side, and in silence compared them. Then, without a word, he handed them to Miss Brooke, who, taking a glass from her pocket, subjected them to a similar careful and minute scrutiny.

Both envelopes were of precisely the same make, and were each addressed to Mr. Hawke's London address in a round,

school-boyish, copy-book sort of hand—the hand so easy to
write and so difficult to bring home to any writer on account
of its want of individuality. Each envelope likewise bore a
Cork and a London postmark.

The sheet of paper, however, that the first envelope enclosed bore the sketch of one dagger only.

Loveday laid down her glass.

"The envelopes," she said, "have, undoubtedly, been
addressed by the same person, but these last two daggers have
not been drawn by the hand that drew the first. Dagger number one was, evidently, drawn by a timid, uncertain and inar-
tistic hand—see how the lines wave and how they have been
patched here and there. The person who drew the other daggers, I should say, could do better work: the outline, though
rugged, is bold and free. I should like to take these sketches
home with me and compare them again at my leisure."

"Ah, I felt sure what your opinion would be!" said Mr.
Dyer complacently.

Mr. Hawke seemed much disturbed.

"Good gracious!" he ejaculated; "you don't mean to say I
have two enemies pursuing me in this fashion! What does it
mean? Can it be—is it possible, do you think that these
things have been sent to me by the members of some Secret
Society in Ireland—under error, of course—mistaking me for
someone else? They can't be meant for me; I have never, in
my whole life, been mixed up with any political agitation of
any sort."

Mr. Dyer shook his head. "Members of secret societies
generally make pretty sure of their ground before they send
out missives of this kind," he said. "I have never heard of
such an error being made. I think, too, we mustn't build any
theories on the Irish post-mark: the letters may have been
posted in Cork for the whole and sole purpose of drawing off
attention from some other quarter."

"Will you mind telling me a little about the loss of the
necklace?" here said Loveday, bringing the conversation suddenly round from the daggers to the diamonds.

"I think," interposed Mr. Dyer, turning towards her, "that
the episode of the drawn daggers—drawn in a double
sense—should be treated entirely on its own merits, considered as a thing apart from the loss of the necklace. I am

inclined to believe that when we have gone a little further into the matter we shall find that each circumstance belongs to a different group of facts. After all, it is possible that these daggers may have been sent by way of a joke—a rather foolish one, I admit—by some harum-scarum fellow bent on causing a sensation."

Mr. Hawke's face brightened. "Ah! now, do you think so—really think so?" he ejaculated. "It would lift such a load from my mind if you could bring the thing home, in this way, to some practical joker. There are a lot of such fellows knocking about the world. Why, now I come to think of it, my nephew, Jack, who is a good deal with us just now, and is not quite so steady a fellow as I should like him to be, must have a good many such scamps among his acquaintances."

"A good many such scamps among his acquaintances," echoed Loveday; "that certainly gives plausibility to Mr. Dyer's supposition. At the same time, I think we are bound to look at the other side of the case, and admit the possibility of these daggers being sent in right-down sober earnest by persons concerned in the robbery, with the intention of intimidating you and preventing full investigation of the matter. If this be so, it will not signify which thread we take up and follow. If we find the sender of the daggers we are safe to come upon the thief; or, if we follow up and find the thief, the sender of the daggers will not be far off."

Mr. Hawke's face fell once more.

"It's an uncomfortable position to be in," he said slowly. "I suppose, whoever they are, they will do the regulation thing, and next time will send an instalment of three daggers, in which case I may consider myself a doomed man. It did not occur to me before, but I remember now that I did not receive the first dagger until after I had spoken very strongly to Mrs. Hawke, before the servants, about my wish to set the police to work. I told her I felt bound, in honour to Sir George, to do so, as the necklace had been lost under my roof."

"Did Mrs. Hawke object to your calling in the aid of the police?" asked Loveday.

"Yes, most strongly. She entirely supported Miss Monroe in her wish to take no steps in the matter. Indeed, I should not have come round as I did last night to Mr. Dyer, if my

wife had not been suddenly summoned from home by the
serious illness of her sister. At least," he corrected himself
with a little attempt at self-assertion, "my coming to him
might have been a little delayed. I hope you understand, Mr.
Dyer; I do not mean to imply that I am not master in my
own house."

"Oh, quite so, quite so," responded Mr. Dyer. "Did Mrs.
Hawke or Miss Monroe give any reasons for not wishing you
to move in the matter?"

"All told, I should think they gave about a hundred reasons—I can't remember them all. For one thing, Miss Monroe said it might necessitate her appearing in the police
courts, a thing she would not consent to do; and she certainly
did not consider the necklace was worth the fuss I was making over it. And that necklace, sir, has been valued at over
nine hundred pounds, and has come down to the young lady
from her mother."

"And Mrs. Hawke?"

"Mrs. Hawke supported Miss Monroe in her views in her
presence. But privately to me afterwards, she gave other reasons for not wishing the police called in. Girls, she said, were
always careless with their jewellery, she might have lost the
necklace in Pekin, and never have brought it to England at
all."

"Quite so," said Mr. Dyer. "I think I understood you to
say that no one had seen the necklace since Miss Monroe's
arrival in England. Also, I believe it was she who first discovered it to be missing?"

"Yes. Sir George, when he wrote apprising me of his
daughter's visit, added a postscript to his letter, saying that
his daughter was bringing her necklace with her and that he
would feel greatly obliged if I would have it deposited with as
little delay as possible at my bankers', where it could be easily got at if required. I spoke to Miss Monroe about doing
this two or three times, but she did not seem at all inclined to
comply with her father's wishes. Then my wife took the matter in hand—Mrs. Hawke, I must tell you, has a very firm,
resolute manner—she told Miss Monroe plainly that she
would not have the responsibility of those diamonds in the
house, and insisted that there and then they should be sent off
to the bankers. Upon this Miss Monroe went up to her room,

and presently returned, saying that her necklace had disappeared. She herself, she said, had placed it in her jewel-case and the jewel-case in her wardrobe, when her boxes were unpacked. The jewel-case was in the wardrobe right enough, and no other article of jewellery appeared to have been disturbed, but the little padded niche in which the necklace had been deposited was empty. My wife and her maid went upstairs immediately, and searched every corner of the room, but, I'm sorry to say, without any result."

"Miss Monroe, I suppose, has her own maid?"

"No, she has not. The maid—an elderly native woman—who left Pekin with her, suffered so terribly from sea-sickness that, when they reached Malta, Miss Monroe allowed her to land and remain there in charge of an agent of the P. and O. Company till an outward bound packet could take her back to China. It seems the poor woman thought she was going to die, and was in a terrible state of mind because she hadn't brought her coffin with her. I dare say you know the terror these Chinese have of being buried in foreign soil. After her departure, Miss Monore engaged one of the steerage passengers to act as her maid for the remainder of the voyage."

"Did Miss Monroe make the long journey from Pekin accompanied only by this native woman?"

"No; friends escorted her to Hong Kong—by far the roughest part of the journey. From Hong Kong she came on in the *Colombo,* accompanied only by her maid. I wrote and told her father I would meet her at the docks in London; the young lady, however, preferred landing at Plymouth, and telegraphed to me from there that she was coming on by rail to Waterloo, where, if I liked, I might meet her."

"She seems to be a young lady of independent habits. Was she brought up and educated in China?"

"Yes; by a succession of French and American governesses. After her mother's death, when she was little more than a baby, Sir George could not make up his mind to part with her, as she was his only child."

"I suppose you and Sir George Monroe are old friends?"

"Yes; he and I were great chums before he went out to China—now about twenty years ago—and it was only natural, when he wished to get his daughter out of the way of young Danvers's impertinent attentions, that he should ask me to take charge of her till he could claim his retiring pension and set up his tent in England."

"What was the chief objection to Mr. Danvers's attentions?"

"Well, he is only a boy of one-and-twenty, and has no money into the bargain. He has been sent out to Pekin by his father to study the language, in order to qualify for a billet in the customs, and it may be a dozen years before he is in a position to keep a wife. Now, Miss Monroe is an heiress—will come into her mother's large fortune when she is of age—and Sir George, naturally, would like her to make a good match."

"I suppose Miss Monroe came to England very reluctantly?"

"I imagine so. No doubt it was a great wrench for her to leave her home and friends in that sudden fashion and come to us, who are, one and all, utter strangers to her. She is very quiet, very shy and reserved. She goes nowhere, sees no one. When some old China friends of her father's called to see her the other day, she immediately found she had a headache and went to bed. I think, on the whole, she gets on better with my nephew than with anyone else."

"Will you kindly tell me of how many persons your household consists at the present moment?"

"At the present moment we are one more than usual, for my nephew, Jack, is home with his regiment from India, and is staying with us. As a rule, my household consists of my wife and myself, butler, cook, housemaid and my wife's maid, who just now is doing double duty as Miss Monroe's maid also."

Mr. Dyer looked at his watch.

"I have an important engagement in ten minutes' time," he said, "so I must leave you and Miss Brooke to arrange details as to how and when she is to begin her work inside your house, for, of course, in a case of this sort we must, in the first instance at any rate, concentrate attention within your four walls."

"The less delay the better," said Loveday. "I should like to attack the mystery at once—this afternoon."

Mr. Hawke thought for a moment.

"According to present arrangements," he said, with a little hesitation, "Mrs. Hawke will return next Friday, that is the day after to-morrow, so I can only ask you to remain in the house till the morning of that day. I'm sure you will understand that there might be some—some little awkwardness in——"

"Oh, quite so," interrupted Loveday. "I don't see at present that there will be any necessity for me to sleep in the house at all. How would it be for me to assume the part of a lady house decorator in the employment of a West-end firm, and sent by them to survey your house and advise upon its re-decoration? All I should have to do, would be to walk about your rooms with my head on one side, and a pencil and note-book in my hand. I should interfere with no one, your family life would go on as usual, and I could make my work as short or as long as necessity might dictate."

Mr. Hawke had no objection to offer to this. He had, however, a request to make as he rose to depart, and he made it a little nervously.

"If," he said, "by any chance there should come a telegram from Mrs. Hawke, saying she will return by an earlier train, I suppose—I hope, that is, you will make some excuse, and—and not get me into hot water, I mean."

To this, Loveday answered a little evasively that she trusted no such telegram would be forthcoming, but that, in any case, he might rely upon her discretion.

Four o'clock was striking from a neighbouring church clock as Loveday lifted the old-fashioned brass knocker of Mr. Hawke's house in Tavistock Square. An elderly butler admitted her and showed her into the drawing-room on the first floor. A single glance round showed Loveday that if her rôle had been real instead of assumed, she would have found plenty of scope for her talents. Although the house was in all respects comfortably furnished, it bore unmistakably the impress of those early Victorian days when aesthetic surroundings were not deemed a necessity of existence; an impress which people past middle age, and growing increasingly indifferent to the accessories of life, are frequently careless to remove.

"Young life here is evidently an excrescence, not part of the home; a troop of daughters turned into this room would speedily set going a different condition of things," thought Loveday, taking stock of the faded white and gold wall paper, the chairs covered with lilies and roses in cross-stitch, and the knick-knacks of a past generation that were scattered about on tables and mantelpiece.

A yellow damask curtain, half-festooned, divided the back drawing-room from the front in which she was seated. From the other side of this curtain there came to her the sound of voices—those of a man and a girl.

"Cut the cards again, please," said the man's voice. "Thank you. There you are again—the queen of hearts surrounded with diamonds, and turning her back on a knave. Miss Monroe, you can't do better than make that fortune come true. Turn your back on the man who let you go without a word and——"

"Hush!" interrupted the girl with a little laugh; "I heard the next room door open—I'm sure someone came in."

The girl's laugh seemed to Loveday utterly destitute of that echo of heart-ache that in the circumstances might have been expected.

At this moment Mr. Hawke entered the room, and almost simultaneously the two young people came from the other side of the yellow curtain and crossed towards the door.

Loveday took a survey of them as they passed.

The young man—evidently "my nephew, Jack"—was a good-looking young fellow, with dark eyes and hair. The girl was small, slight and fair. She was perceptibly less at home with Jack's uncle than she was with Jack, for her manner changed and grew formal and reserved as she came face to face with him.

"We're going downstairs to have a game of billiards," said Jack, addressing Mr. Hawke, and throwing a look of curiosity at Loveday.

"Jack," said the old gentleman, "what would you say if I told you I was going to have the house re-decorated from top to bottom, and that this lady had come to advise on the matter."

This was the nearest (and most Anglicé) approach to a fabrication that Mr. Hawke would allow to pass his lips.

"Well," answered Jack promptly, "I should say, 'not before its time.' That would cover a good deal."

Then the two young people departed in company.

Loveday went straight to her work.

"I'll begin my surveying at the top of the house, and at once, if you please," she said. "Will you kindly tell one of your maids to show me through the bed-rooms? If it is possible, let that maid be the one who waits on Miss Monroe and Mrs. Hawke."

The maid who responded to Mr. Hawke's summons was in perfect harmony with the general appearance of the house. In addition, however, to being elderly and faded, she was also remarkably sour-visaged, and carried herself as if she thought that Mr. Hawke had taken a great liberty in thus commanding her attendance.

In dignified silence she showed Loveday over the topmost story, where the servants' bed-rooms were situated, and with a somewhat supercilious expression of countenance, watched her making various entries in her note-book.

In dignified silence, also, she led the way down to the second floor, where were the principal bed-rooms of the house.

"This is Miss Monroe's room," she said, as she threw back a door of one of these rooms, and then shut her lips with a snap, as if they were never going to open again.

The room that Loveday entered was, like the rest of the house, furnished in the style that prevailed in the early Victorian period. The bedstead was elaborately curtained with pink lined upholstery; the toilet-table was befrilled with muslin and tarlatan out of all likeness to a table. The one point, however, that chiefly attracted Lovelady's attention was the extreme neatness that prevailed throughout the apartment—a neatness, however, that was carried out with so strict an eye to comfort and convenience that it seemed to proclaim the hand of a first-class maid. Everything in the room was, so to speak, squared to the quarter of an inch, and yet everything that a lady could require in dressing lay ready to hand. The dressing-gown lying on the back of a chair had footstool and slippers beside it. A chair stood in front of the toilet table, and on a small Japanese table to the right of the chair were placed hair-pin box, comb and brush, and hand mirror.

"This room will want money spent upon it," said Loveday, letting her eyes roam critically in all directions. "Nothing but Moorish wood-work will take off the squareness of those corners. But what a maid Miss Monroe must have. I never before saw a room so orderly and, at the same time, so comfortable."

This was so direct an appeal to conversation that the sour-visaged maid felt compelled to open her lips.

"I wait on Miss Monore, for the present," she said snappishly; "but, to speak the truth, she scarcely requires a maid. I never before in my life had dealings with such a young lady."

"She does so much for herself, you mean—declines much assistance."

"She's like no one else I ever had to do with." (This was said even more snappishly than before.) "She not only won't be helped in dressing, but she arranges her room every day before leaving it, even to placing the chair in front of the looking glass."

"And to opening the lid of the hair-pin box, so that she may have the pins ready to her hand," added Loveday, for a moment bending over the Japanese table, with its toilet accessories.

Another five minutes were all that Loveday accorded to the inspection of this room. Then, a little to the surprise of the dignified maid, she announced her intention of completing her survey of the bed-rooms some other time, and dismissed her at the drawing-room door, to tell Mr. Hawke that she wished to see him before leaving.

Mr. Hawke, looking much disturbed and with a telegram in his hand, quickly made his appearance.

"From my wife, to say she'll be back to-night. She'll be at Waterloo in about half an hour from now," he said, holding up the brown envelope. "Now, Miss Brooke, what are we to do? I told you how much Mrs. Hawke objected to the investigation of this matter, and she is very—well—firm when she once says a thing, and—and——"

"Set your mind at rest," interrupted Loveday; "I have done all I wished to do within your walls, and the remainder of my investigation can be carried on just as well at Lynch Court or at my own private rooms."

"Done all you wished to do!" echoed Mr. Hawke in amazement; "why, you've not been an hour in the house, and do you mean to tell me you've found out anything about the necklace or the daggers?"

"Don't ask me any questions just yet; I want you to answer one or two instead. Now, can you tell me anything about any letters Miss Monroe may have written or received since she has been in your house?"

"Yes, certainly. Sir George wrote to me very strongly about her correspondence, and begged me to keep a sharp eye on it, so as to nip in the bud any attempt to communicate with Danvers. So far, however, she does not appear to have made any such attempt. She is frankness itself over her correspondence. Every letter that has come addressed to her, she has shown either to me or to my wife, and they have one and all been letters from old friends of her father's, wishing to make her acquaintance now that she is in England. With regard to letter-writing, I am sorry to say she has a marked and most peculiar objection to it. Every one of the letters she has received, my wife tells me, remain unanswered still. She has never once been seen, since she came to the house with a pen in her hand. And if she wrote on the sly, I don't know how she would get her letters posted—she never goes outside the door by herself, and she would have no opportunity of giving them to any of the servants to post except Mrs. Hawke's maid, and she is beyond suspicion in such a matter. She has been well cautioned, and, in addition, is not the sort of person who would assist a young lady in carrying on a clandestine correspondence."

"I should imagine not! I suppose Miss Monroe has been present at the breakfast table each time that you have received your daggers through the post—you told me, I think, that they had come by the first post in the morning?"

"Yes; Miss Monroe is very punctual at meals, and has been present each time. Naturally, when I received such unpleasant missives, I made some sort of exclamation and then handed the thing round the table for inspection, and Miss Monroe was very much concerned to know who my secret enemy could be."

"No doubt. Now, Mr. Hawke, I have a very special request to make to you, and I hope you will be most exact in carrying it out."

"You may rely upon my doing so to the very letter."

"Thank you. If, then, you should receive by post to-morrow morning one of those big envelopes you already know the look of, and find that it contains a sketch of three, not two, drawn daggers——"

"Good gracious! what makes you think such a thing likely?" exclaimed Mr. Hawke, greatly disturbed. "Why am I to be persecuted in this way? Am I to take it for granted that I am a doomed man?"

He began to pace the room in a state of great excitement.

"I don't think I would if I were you," answered Loveday calmly. "Pray let me finish. I want you to open the big envelope that may come to you by post tomorrow morning just as you have opened the others—in full view of your family at the breakfast-table—and to hand round the sketch it may contain for inspection to your wife, your nephew and to Miss Monroe. Now, will you promise me to do this?"

"Oh, certainly; I should most likely have done so without any promising. But—but—I'm sure you'll understand that I feel myself to be in a peculiarly uncomfortable position, and I shall feel so very much obliged to you if you'll tell me— that is if you'll enter a little more fully into an explanation."

Loveday looked at her watch. "I should think Mrs. Hawke would be just at this moment arriving at Waterloo; I'm sure you'll be glad to see the last of me. Please come to me at my rooms in Gower Street to-morrow at twelve—here is my card. I shall then be able to enter into fuller explanations I hope. Good-bye."

The old gentleman showed her politely downstairs, and, as he shook hands with her at the front door, again asked, in a most emphatic manner, if she did not consider him to be placed in a "peculiarly unpleasant position."

Those last words at parting were to be the first with which he greeted her on the following morning when he presented himself at her rooms in Gower Street. They were, however, repeated in considerably more agitated a manner.

"Was there ever a man in a more miserable position!" he exclaimed, as he took the chair that Loveday indicated. "I not only received the three daggers for which you prepared me, but I got an additional worry, for which I was totally unprepared. This morning, immediately after breakfast, Miss Monroe walked out of the house all by herself, and no one knows where she has gone. And the girl has never before been outside the door alone. It seems the servants saw her go out, but did not think it necessary to tell either me or Mrs. Hawke, feeling sure we must have been aware of the fact."

"So Mrs. Hawke has returned," said Loveday. "Well, I suppose you will be greatly surprised if I inform you that the young lady who has so uncermoniously left your house is at the present moment to be found at the Charing Cross Hotel, where she has engaged a private room in her real name of Miss Mary O'Grady."

"Eh! What! Private room! Real name O'Grady! I'm all bewildered!"

"It is a little bewildering; let me explain. The young lady whom you received into your house as the daughter of your old friend, was in reality the person engaged by Miss Monroe to fulfil the duties of her maid on board ship, after her native attendant had been landed at Malta. Her real name, as I have told you, is Mary O'Grady, and she has proved herself a valuable coadjutor to Miss Monroe in assisting her to carry out a programme, which she must have arranged with her lover, Mr. Danvers, before she left Pekin."

"Eh! what!" again ejaculated Mr. Hawke; "how do you know all this? Tell me the whole story."

"I will tell you the whole story first, and then explain to you how I came to know it. From what has followed, it seems to me that Miss Monroe must have arranged with Mr. Danvers that he was to leave Pekin within ten days of her so doing, travel by the route by which she came, and land at Plymouth, where he was to receive a note from her, apprising him of her whereabouts. So soon as she was on board ship, Miss Monroe appears to have set her wits to work with great energy; every obstacle to the carrying-out of her programme she appears to have met and conquered. Step number one was to get rid of her native maid, who, perhaps, might have been faithful to her master's interests and have proved troublesome. I have no doubt the poor woman suffered terribly from sea-sickness, as it was her first voyage, and I have equally no doubt that Miss Monroe worked on her fears, and persuaded her to land at Malta, and return to China by the next packet. Step number two was to find a suitable person, who, for a consideration, would be willing to play the part of the Pekin heiress among the heiress's friends in England, while the young lady herself arranged her private affairs to her own liking. That person was quickly found among the steerage passengers of the *Colombo* in Miss Mary O'Grady, who had come on board with her mother at Ceylon, and who, from the glimpse I had of her, must, I should conjecture, have been absent many years from the land of her birth. You know how cleverly this young lady has played her part in your house—how, without attracting attention to the matter, she has shunned the society of her father's old Chinese friends, who might be likely to involve her in embarrassing conversations; how she has avoided the use of pen and ink lest——"

"Yes, yes," interrupted Mr. Hawke; "but, my dear Miss Brooke, wouldn't it be as well for you and me to go at once to the Charing Cross Hotel, and get all the information we can out of her respecting Miss Monroe and her movements—she may be bolting, you know?"

"I do not think she will. She is waiting there patiently for an answer to a telegram she despatched more than two hours ago to her mother, Mrs. O'Grady, at 14, Woburn Place, Cork."

"Dear me! dear me! How is it possible for you to know all this."

"Oh, that last little fact was simply a matter of astuteness on the part of the man whom I have deputed to watch the young lady's movements to-day. Other details, I assure you, in this somewhat intricate case, have been infinitely more difficult to get at. I think I have to thank those 'drawn daggers,' that caused you so much consternation, for having, in the first instance, put me on the right track."

"Ah—h," said Mr. Hawke, drawing a long breath; "now we come to the daggers! I feel sure you are going to set my mind at rest on that score."

"I hope so. Would it surprise you very much to be told that it was I who sent to you those three daggers this morning?"

"You! Is it possible?"

"Yes; they were sent by me, and for a reason that I will presently explain to you. But let me begin at the beginning. Those roughly-drawn sketches, that to you suggested terrifying ideas of blood-shedding and violence, to my mind were open to a more peaceful and commonplace explanation. They appeared to me to suggest the herald's office rather than the armoury; the cross fitchée of the knight's shield rather than the poniard with which the members of secret societies are supposed to render their recalcitrant brethren familiar. Now, if you will look at these sketches again, you will see what I mean." Here Loveday produced from her writing-table the missives which had so greatly disturbed Mr. Hawke's peace of mind. "To begin with, the blade of the dagger of common life is, as a rule, at least two-thirds of the weapon in length; in this sketch, what you would call the blade, does not exceed the hilt in length. Secondly, please note the absence of guard for the hand. Thirdly, let me draw your attention to the squareness of what you considered the hilt of the weapon, and what, to my mind, suggested the upper portion of a crusader's cross. No hand could grip such a hilt as the one outlined here. After your departure yesterday, I drove to the British Museum, and there consulted a certain valuable work on heraldry, which has more than once done me good service. There I found my surmise substantiated in a surprising manner. Among the illustrations of the various crosses borne on armorial shields, I found one that had been taken by Henri d'Anvers from his own armorial bearings, for his crest when he joined the Crusaders under Edward I., and which has since been handed down as the crest of the Danvers family. This was an important item of information to me. Here was someone in Cork sending to your house, on two several occasions, the crest of the Danvers family; with what object it would be difficult to say, unless it were in some sort a communication to someone in your house. With my mind full of this idea, I left the Museum and drove next to the office of the P. and O. Company, and requested to have given me the list of the passengers who arrived by the *Colombo*. I found this list to be a remarkably small one; I suppose people, if possible, avoid crossing the Bay of Biscay during the Equinoxes. The only passengers who landed at Plymouth besides Miss Monroe, I found, were a certain Mrs. and Miss O'Grady, steerage passengers who had gone on board at Ceylon on their way home from Australia. Their name, together with their landing at Plymouth, suggested the possibility that Cork might be their destination. After this I asked to see the list of the passengers who arrived by the packet following the

Colombo, telling the clerk who attended to me that I was o
the look-out for the arrival of a friend. In that second list c
arrivals I quickly found my friend—William Wentwort
Danvers by name."

"No! The effrontery! How dared he! In his own nam
too!"

"Well, you see, a plausible pretext for leaving Pekin cou
easily be invented by him—the death of a relative, the illnes
of a father or mother. And Sir George, though he might di
like the idea of the young man going to England so soon a
ter his daughter's departure, and may, perhaps, write to yo
by the next mail on the matter, was utterly powerless to pre
vent his so doing. This young man, like Miss Monroe and th
O'Gradys, also landed at Plymouth. I had only arrived so fa
in my investigation when I went to your house yesterday af
ternoon. By chance, as I waited a few minutes in you
drawing room, another important item of information wa
acquired. A fragment of conversation between your nephev
and the supposed Miss Monroe fell upon my ear, and on
word spoken by the young lady convinced me of her nation
ality. That one word was the monosyllable 'Hush.' "

"No! You surprise me!"

"Have you never noted the difference between the 'hush' o
an Englishman and that of an Irishman? The former begin
his 'hush' with a distinct aspirate, the latter with as distinct a
W. That W is a mark of his nationality which he never loses
The unmitigated 'whist' may lapse into a 'whish' when he i
transplanted to another soil, and the 'whish' may in course o
time pass into a 'whish' but to the distinct aspirate of the En
glish 'hush,' he never attains. Now Miss O'Grady's was a
pronounced a 'whush' as it was possible for the lips of a
Hibernian to utter."

"And from that you concluded that Mary O'Grady wa
playing the part of Miss Monroe in my house?"

"Not immediately. My suspicions were excited, certainly
and when I went up to her room, in company with Mrs.
Hawke's maid, those suspicions were confirmed. The order
liness of that room was something remarkable. Now, there is
the orderliness of a lady in the arrangement of her room,
and the orderliness of a maid, and the two things, believe me,
are widely different. A lady, who has no maid, and who has

the gift of orderliness, will put things away when done with, and so leave her room a picture of neatness. I don't think, however, it would for a moment occur to her to put things so as to be conveniently ready for her to use the next time she dresses in that room. This would be what a maid, accustomed to arrange a room for her mistress's use, would do mechanically. Now the neatness I found in the supposed Miss Monroe's room was the neatness of a maid—not of a lady, and I was assured by Mrs. Hawke's maid that it was a neatness accomplished by her own hands. As I stood there, looking at that room, the whole conspiracy—if I may so call it—little by little pieced itself together, and became plain to me. Possibilities quickly grew into probabilities, and these probabilities once admitted, brought other suppositions in their train. Now, supposing that Miss Monroe and Mary O'Grady had agreed to change places, the Pekin heiress, for the time being, occupying Mary O'Grady's place in the humble home at Cork and vice versa, what means of communicating with each other had they arranged? How was Mary O'Grady to know when she might lay aside her assumed role and go back to her mother's house. There was no denying the necessity for such communication; the difficulties in its way must have been equally obvious to the two girls. Now, I think we must admit that we must credit these young women with having hit upon a very clever way of meeting those difficulties. An anonymous and startling missive sent to you would be bound to be mentioned in the house, and in this way a code of signals might be set up between them that could not direct suspicion to them. In this connection, the Danvers crest, which it is possible that they mistook for a dagger, suggested itself naturally, for no doubt Miss Monroe had many impressions of it on her lover's letters. As I thought over these things, it occurred to me that possibly dagger (or cross) number one was sent to notify the safe arrival of Miss Monroe and Mrs. O'Grady at Cork. The two daggers or crosses you subsequently received were sent on the day of Mr. Danvers's arrival at Plymouth, and were, I should say, sketched by his hand. Now, was it not within the bounds of likelihood that Miss Monroe's marriage to this young man, and the consequent release of Mary O'Grady from the onerous part she was playing, might be notified to her by the sending of three such crosses or daggers to you? The idea no sooner occurred to me than I determined to act upon it, forestall the sending of this latest communication, and watch the result. Accordingly, after I left your house yesterday, I had a sketch made of three daggers or crosses exactly similar to those you had already received, and had it posted to you so that you would get it by the first post. I told off one of our staff at Lynch Court to watch your house, and gave him special directions to follow and report on Miss O'Grady's movements throughout the day. The results I anticipated quickly came to pass. About half-past nine this morning the man sent a telegram to me saying that he had followed Miss O'Grady from your house to the Charing Cross Hotel, and furthermore had ascertained that she had since despatched a telegram, which (possibly by following the hotel servant who carried it to the telegraph office), he had overheard was addressed to Mrs. O'Grady, at Woburn Place, Cork. Since I received this information an altogether remarkable cross-firing of telegrams has been going backwards and forwards along the wires to Cork."

"A cross-firing of telegrams! I do not understand."

"In this way. So soon as I knew Mrs. O'Grady's address I telegraphed to her, in her daughter's name, desiring her to address her reply to 115a Gower Street, not to Charing Cross Hotel. About three-quarters of an hour afterwards I received in reply this telegram, which I am sure you will read with interest."

Here Loveday handed a telegram—one of several that lay on her writing table—to Mr. Hawke.

He opened it and read aloud as follows:

Am puzzled. Why such hurry? Wedding took place this morning. You will receive signal as agreed to-morrow. Better return to Tavistock Square for the night.

"The wedding took place this morning," repeated Mr. Hawke blankly. "My poor old friend! It will break his heart."

"Now that the thing is done past recall we must hope he will make the best of it," said Loveday. "In reply to this telegram," she went on, "I sent another, asking as to the movements of the bride and bridegroom, and got in reply this":

Here she read aloud as follows:

"They will be at Plymouth to-morrow night; at Charing Cross Hotel the next day, as agreed."

"So, Mr. Hawke," she added, "if you wish to see your old friend's daughter and tell her what you think of the part she has played, all you will have to do will be to watch the arrival of the Plymouth trains."

"Miss O'Grady has called to see a lady and gentleman," said the maid at that moment entering.

"Miss O'Grady!" repeated Mr. Hawke in astonishment.

"Ah, yes, I telegraphed to her, just before you came in, to come here to meet a lady and gentleman, and she, no doubt thinking that she would find here the newly-married pair, has, you see, lost no time in complying with my request. Show the lady in."

"It's all so intricate—so bewildering," said Mr. Hawke, as he lay back in his chair. "I can scarcely get it all into my head."

His bewilderment, however, was nothing compared with that of Miss O'Grady, when she entered the room and found herself face to face with her late guardian, instead of the radiant bride and bridegroom whom she had expected to meet.

She stood silent in the middle of the room, looking the picture of astonishment and distress.

Mr. Hawke also seemed a little at a loss for words, so Loveday took the initiative.

"Please sit down," she said, placing a chair for the girl. "Mr. Hawke and I have sent for you in order to ask you a few questions. Before doing so, however, let me tell you that the whole of your conspiracy with Miss Monroe has been brought to light, and the best thing you can do, if you want your share in it treated leniently, will be to answer our questions as fully and truthfully as possible."

The girl burst into tears. "It was all Miss Monroe's fault from beginning to end," she sobbed. "Mother didn't want to do it—I didn't want to—to go into a gentleman's house and pretend to be what I was not. And we didn't want her hundred pounds——"

Here sobs checked her speech.

"Oh," said Loveday contemptuously, "so you were to have a hundred pounds for your share in this fraud, were you?"

"We didn't want to take it," said the girl, between hysterical bursts of tears; "but Miss Monroe said if we didn't help her someone else would, and so I agreed to——"

"I think," interrupted Loveday, "that you can tell us very little that we do not already know about what you agreed to do. What we want you to tell us is what has been done with Miss Monroe's diamond necklace—who has possession of it now?"

The girl's sobs and tears redoubled. "I've had nothing to do with the necklace—it has never been in my possession," she sobbed. "Miss Monroe gave it to Mr. Danvers two or three months before she left Pekin, and he sent it on to some people he knew in Hong Kong, diamond merchants, who lent him money on it. Decastro, Miss Monroe said, was the name of these people."

"Decastro diamond merchant, Hong Kong. I should think that would be sufficient address," said Loveday, entering it in a ledger; "and I suppose Mr. Danvers retained part of that money for his own use and travelling expenses, and handed the remainder to Miss Monroe to enable her to bribe such creatures as you and your mother, to practise a fraud that ought to land both of you in jail."

The girl grew deadly white. "Oh, don't do that—don't send us to prison!" she implored, clasping her hands together. "We haven't touched a penny of Miss Monroe's money yet, and we don't want to touch a penny, if you'll only let us off! Oh, pray, pray, pray be merciful!"

Loveday looked at Mr. Hawke.

He rose from his chair. "I think the best thing you can do," he said, "will be to get back home to your mother at Cork as quickly as possible, and advise her never to play such a risky game again. Have you any money in your purse? No—well then here's some for you, and lose no time in getting home. It will be best for Miss Monroe—Mrs. Danvers I mean—to come to my house and claim her own property there. At any rate, there it will remain until she does so."

As the girl, with incoherent expressions of gratitude, left the room, he turned to Loveday.

"I should like to have consulted Mrs. Hawke before arranging matters in this way," he said a little hesitatingly; "but still, I don't see that I could have done otherwise."

"I feel sure Mrs. Hawke will approve what you have done when she hears all the circumstance of the case," said Loveday.

"And," continued the old clergyman, "when I write to Sir George, as, of course, I must immediately, I shall advise him to make the best of a bad bargain, now that the thing is done. 'Past care should be past care;' eh, Miss Brooke? And, think! what a narrow escape my nephew, Jack, has had!"

SEXTON BLAKE

Virtually unknown in America, Sexton Blake is famous through the British Empire. Indeed, he has been called "the most famous Englishman in the world," and more novels and stories have been written about him than about any other detective character ever. Unkindly dubbed "the office boy's Sherlock Holmes," Blake first appeared on the scene in 1893 in the pages of a boys' weekly paper. In 1894 a new story paper, the Union Jack, was started, and this became the master sleuth's chief home until the early 1930s. Although he wasn't initially a Holmes type, Sexton Blake soon began taking on some Holmesian characteristics. He even moved into lodgings in Baker Street. "At some early stage he became hawk-like, incisive, and acquired the habit of putting on a dressing-gown in order to think," cultural historian E. S. Turner has observed. "Probably it was sheer pressure of public opinion which forced him into Baker Street." While he was certainly a rival of Sherlock Holmes, Blake leaned oftener toward the more flamboyant methods of our own Nick Carter. He liked action, disguise, and the unmasking of sinister plots. "Show Blake a sheet of writing in which the fist is alternately regular and irregular, and he will be unable to tell you, from the incidence of the palsied patches, that it was written in a train traveling between Norwood and London Bridge," comments Turner. "But nail him down in a crate and throw him off the bridge at Westminster and while you are still dusting your hands and saying 'That's that' you will feel his automatic in your back." Sexton Blake was aided by a boy assistant named Tinker and a bloodhound named Pedro.

The man credited with creating the redoubtable Blake was

a prolific Scot named Harry Blyth. Blyth died of typhoid in 1898 and the character passed on into many other hands. It is estimated that over two hundred authors contributed to the saga, from the penny dreadfuls of the 1890s to the paperbacks of the 1960s. The writers included bank clerks, sheep farmers, actors, a boxer, an orange picker in South Africa, a British Secret Service agent, a laundryman, a clerk in a glassblowing factory, and sundry full-time hacks. There have been several Blake movies, both silent and sound, a television show, and various comic books. Our novelette, involving Blake in action and intrigue in both London and mysterious India, was written by William Murray Graydon. Graydon was an American who resettled in England and turned out over two hundred Sexton Blake stories and novels. This one, in somewhat longer form, originally appeared in the Union Jack *in 1906.*

The Rajah's Bodyguard

The First Chapter.
At the Foreign Office—Sexton Blake's Commission.

At ten o'clock one morning, while flaring placards and shouting new boys were acquainting the London public with such a sensation as had not been known since the time when a Chinaman was decoyed into the Chinese Legation in Portland Place and held a prisoner there, Sexton Blake drove to the Foreign Office, and was at once ushered into the private-room of Mr. Godfrey Bellingham, the Under-Secretary. The official rose to greet the famous detective, who was no stranger to him.

"Good-morning, Mr. Blake," he said. "I understand that you have been performing marvels again."

"If you refer to my little affair last night, Mr. Bellingham——"

"Little affair? My dear sir, how can you call it that. But as yet I am in the dark. I don't know what to believe or think. I have had no private information. I refer, of course, to the Rajah of Jazelpur, who is paying a visit to London. First of all, having received a vague warning yesterday afternoon to the effect that his Highness was in danger from Russian intrigue, I wrote to you asking for an interview. At a late hour last night I was startled to hear that the rajah had mysteriously disappeared, which was a terrible shock to me; and at four o'clock this morning, as I was tossing in bed, one of my secretaries came to me with the news that you had rescued his Highness and brought him back to the Hanover Hotel."

"So I did," drawled Sexton Blake, with a smile. "You are quite right, sir. The facts are very simple. Night before last, after dark, the Rajah Kumar Beg was kidnapped—drugged and carried off in a closed carriage—by two men. They took him——"

"Could one of them have been his brother?" broke in the Under-Secretary.

"One was, Mr. Bellingham! The two scoundrels were Heera Beg and Serge Zouroff, the Russian."

"By heavens, Zouroff as well! But, go on!"

"There is little more to tell," continued the detective. "Yesterday morning the rajah's servants came to me for help, begging that I would find their master. I set to work on the case, and last night I discovered his Highness Kumar Beg, bound and gagged, in a river-side shed at Wapping. I got him away just in time, within five minutes of midnight. At that hour he was to have been put on board a vessel in the Thames, by which, he would have been transported to some Russian port, and, doubtless, thence overland to Siberia. And he would never have been heard of again."

"Never!" exclaimed the Under-Secretary, who was greatly agitated. "He would have been dead to the world, beyond all aid. I am staggered by this revelation, but not surprised. I had been warned of it. You have made no arrests, I hope?"

"None, sir. I purposely allowed the scoundrels to escape."

"I am glad to hear it—very glad! I don't want the truth to leak out, for diplomatic reasons, and I have given rigorous instructions to that effect. There are some crimes—and this is one of them—that are better suppressed. The newspapers merely state that the rajah has been kidnapped and rescued. They suggest that he was to have been held for ransom; and the public will believe that. You have put this department of the Government heavily in your debt, Mr. Blake. You have performed an inestimable service. Had the plot succeeded— had the Rajah of Jazelpur been carried off to Russia—a grave peril would have threatened the British Empire."

"I can partly understand that," said Sexton Blake. "I am aware of the object of the plot. It was to get rid of Kumar Beg, to establish a belief in his death, so that his brother Heera Beg might succeed to the throne of Jazelpur. And Heera Beg is a tool of Russia, a puppet who would dance to the strings of Russian intrigue. But why is Russia so anxious to have him on the throne?"

"I will tell you in strict confidence," replied Mr. Bellingham. "The rajah's little State is on the northern frontier, between Kashmir and the Punjaub, and Russian engineers have discovered a new pass through the mountains, by which an army might be hurled over the borders of Jazelpur and down into lower India. There is the secret in a nutshell. Russia wants to have the State of Jazelpur open to her, with a view to a future invasion of India. And that would only be possible should Heera Beg succeed his brother, which he would naturally do, by Hindu law, in the event of the death or complete disappearance of Kumar Beg."

"I see. It is all clear to me now. Happily the attempt has failed."

"But the danger still exists while Heera Beg and Serge Zouroff are at large, and in London. They must be watched."

"I meant to keep an eye on them," said the detective. "And before coming here went to Zouroff's lodgings. But he and the Hindu have taken alarm and vanished. They spent the night in Connaught Square, where the Russian has been living, and before daybreak they left in great haste. It is certain that they will not return. They are afraid of arrest, and they will hide for a time."

"I am sorry to hear this," said the Under-Secretary. "However, it is worth knowing; it strengthens my resolve of yesterday—the plan that I had already arranged when I wrote to you."

"What was that?" inquired Sexton Blake.

"I will explain in a few words. The Foreign Office, you will believe, is anxious to get the rajah back to his own country.

When he left India, on his European tour, he travelled as far as Marseilles by the *Darjeeling,* a steamer of the British-India Line. To-day is Wednesday, and the *Darjeeling* is now in the Thames. She starts on her return voyage to Calcutta on Friday, and the Rajah Kumar Beg must sail with her. I have secured passages for his Highness and suite, and they will board the boat, as secretly as possible, late to-morrow night. Every precaution will be taken to prevent this from being known."

"And what do you wish me to do?" asked the detective.

"I want you to accompany the rajah to Calcutta," replied Mr. Bellingham. "I fear his life may be attempted on the way. Serge Zouroff and Heera Beg may learn of his departure, and contrive to sail with him. It is not likely that they will—the news can hastily leak out—but there is, at least, a chance of it. Will you accept this commission, Mr. Blake?"

"I will, sir. The rajah is not to be aware of my presence on board, I presume."

"No, it would be wiser not. I suggest that you should go in the disguise of a steward, and I have already settled that with the steamship company, trusting that you would accept my proposal."

"I have a sharp boy who helps me in most of my cases," said Sexton Blake. "I shall want to take him with me, and also my bloodhound Pedro. I may need them both."

"Very well; you know best," assented the Under-Secretary. "The lad can have a berth as cabin-boy, and a hiding-place can be found for the dog. I will give you a letter to the chief steward, and no doubt he will arrange all to your satisfaction, at the request of the Government. Your duties will be to keep as close a watch as possible on the rajah during the voyage, to guard his safety. When he lands at Calcutta, a military escort will be waiting to take him up-country to Jazelpur. It is important, you understand, that nobody should learn that you are to leave England by the *Darjeeling.*"

"I will see to that. At what ports does the steamer touch on her voyage?"

"At Marseilles, Port Said, Suez, Aden, Colombo, and Madras."

"The first one you mention will bear watching," said the detective. "I admit, Mr. Bellingham, that, in my opinion,

your fears are justified. Serge Zouroff and Heera Beg are
cunning and daring men. They are in London, and they will
not be idle between now and Friday; but if they are on the
Darjeeling when she sails, or if they come aboard at Marseilles, you may be sure that I will penetrate their identity."

"Suppose they send somebody else?—in case they discover
my plans, that is."

"They can send anybody they please," declared Sexton
Blake. "No Russian spy or hired assassin will elude my vigilance. But have you settled all this with the rajah, may I ask?
Will he consent to be shipped home at such short notice like
a naughty child?"

"He will consent through fear. I will give him an exagger-
ated idea of his danger, telling him that the Government cannot protect his life while he is in London, and that he must
leave secretly and at once. Yes, it will be all right, Mr. Blake.
But his Highness may cause some trouble on board the vessel.
On the voyage from India he insisted on having the head of a
steward who innocently offended him, and he could not understand why his demand was refused. He is really a barbarian, a simple-minded despot and tyrant, who orders
executions in Jazelpur as he would order his dinner. Yet he
has his good points, and his subjects both love and dread
him."

"That is just the estimate I formed of his character,"
laughed the detective. "It is half a pity he did not get Serge
Zouroff and Heera Beg into his power. He might have nailed
their heads to the outer wall of the Hanover Hotel."

"I wish he had," muttered Mr. Bellingham, as he sat down
to his desk. He wrote for a few minutes, and then handed an
envelope to Sexton Blake. "Here is the letter to the chief
steward of the *Darjeeling*," he said. "You will find him at
your service. You can be ready to sail on Friday, I presume?"

"I could be ready this afternoon, if it was necessary," replied the detective, as if he was talking of a trip to Margate
instead of a voyage of thousands of miles. "I won't see you
again until my return from India."

"You had better call to-morrow."

"I prefer not to. It might not be wise for me to pay another visit to the Foreign Office. The safety of the rajah of

Jazelpur will be in my care, Mr. Bellingham, and I shall be true to my trust."

And with that, having lit a cigar that was offered to him, Sexton Blake shook hands with the Under-Secretary, bade him farewell, and departed.

The Second Chapter.
Steward and Cabin-boy—The Deadly Serpent—
Danger in the Air.

"Turn out!" rang the unwelcome summons. "Five o'clock, boys. Turn out, and be sharp about it!"

Heads were reluctantly raised, drowsy eyes were rubbed, and soon the "boys," as the staff of stewards on a big liner are called, were having their early breakfast of coffee and bread-and-butter, attired in old clothing suitable for the tasks they had to perform. Joe Mason, the new steward, who was a slim, wiry-looking man, finished before the others, and went up to the main-deck, where he was shortly joined by Billie Smith, the cabin-boy. They nodded to each other, after a wary glance around, and then stepped over to the rail.

It was nearly half-past five o'clock in the morning, and on the half-hour the day's work would begin. No land was visible, and no craft was in sight but a red-sailed fishing smack that was lazily beating against the wind. The golden glow of the September sun was flashing out of the limitless waste of sea, and the *Darjeeling* was ploughing swiftly through the blue waters of the Mediterranean. There was something impressive about the great steamer, something to stir the imagination at this early hour. Only the throb of the machinery and the wash of the creaming waves broke the peaceful silence. The captain was already on the bridge with one of his officers, but the passengers were sleeping soundly, dreaming perhaps of friends and relatives, of wives and children, who had been left behind in England, or were waiting and longing for them in far-off places of the globe.

"Well, are you getting used to it?" Joe Mason inquired of the cabin-boy. "Are you glad you came?"

"It's not all beer and skittles, guv'nor," replied the lad, with a laugh. "The princely wages of two quid a month, and pay for your uniform and kit. One might do better—eh? I never worked so hard in my life, but I rather like it, all the same. I'd like it more, though, if there was a bit of excitement, for a change. Even his Illustrious Nobility hasn't kicked up a row yet, or wanted anybody's head chopped off."

"He hasn't had a chance," replied Sexton Blake. "The Bay of Biscay was too much for him, and he has been seasick ever since. But he is to be about to-day, I understand, and I imagine he won't be in the best of tempers. As to the excitement, that may come in time."

"Where is it to come from? We're five days out from London, and you've had a good look round. Serge Zouroff is not here, and neither is Heera Beg."

"I don't think they are, Tinker; nor, so far as I can tell, is there anybody else on board with hostile designs against the Rajah of Jazelpur. But I can't be certain of that; I may be wrong. Possibly there is a spy among the passengers or the crew, some stranger who is so cleverly disguised that I won't be able to spot him until he shows his hand. And there lies the danger. That is why you and I must be unceasingly vigilant and watchful."

"What is there to watch when the rajah has been cooped up in his state-room all the time? Aren't we getting near to Marseilles, guv'nor?"

"We should touch at that port to-day—in a few hours."

"I shouldn't wonder if Heera Beg and the Russian were to come aboard there," said Tinker.

"If they do—and it is not unlikely—I'll keep my eye on them," vowed the detective.

As he spoke, a white-clad figure, wearing a turban set with jewels, came strolling along the deck. It was Mervanji Singh, the dewan, the chief of the rajah's attendants, and he glanced indifferently at the steward and the cabin-boy, little suspecting that it was they who had rescued his master from the kidnappers.

"Will the Honoured One kindly deign to inform us of the health of the Illustrious Prince of Jazelpur?" said Sexton Blake, touching his cap.

"The good heart of the table-waiting sahib deserves an answer," the Hindu replied pompously. "The Most High has been very ill, near to death, of the ship sickness that is like swords tearing two ways in his stomach. But he finds himself greatly better, and to-day it is his will to come forth from the bed of much pain and squirms."

"You take my tip, old cock," Tinker said irreverently, "and give your master a breakfast of fat, juicy pork."

Luckily the dewan did not grasp the meaning of the words; and at that moment, as Sexton Blake frowned at the lad, the gang of stewards came tumbling up from below. A pail of water that stood on the deck was accidentally knocked over in the rush, splashing Mervanji Singh to his knees and with an angry exclamation he beat a hasty retreat, skipping away like an old goat. The chief steward appeared, issuing orders right and left.

"Stir yourselves, boys," he cried. "No skulking!"

"I'm off," said Tinker. "I'll see you later, guv'nor!"

And he hurried towards the captain's cabin, the care of which was one of his numerous duties. The lad was at everybody's beck and call, and he had shown himself so willing to oblige, and so quick to learn, that he was in constant demand.

The sun was peeping above the horizon, streaking the water with molten gold, and another day's arduous toil had begun on board the *Darjeeling*. There were two gangs, saloon-stewards, and bed-room stewards, and Sexton Blake belonged to the former. He helped to sweep and dust the saloon, to lay the carpets and clean the brass, and while this was being done, the bed-room stewards were scrubbing the alleys that divided off the sleeping-rooms.

All having been made shipshape, the boys went below to change, and at 8:30, when the gong was sounded for breakfast, they appeared again in the saloon in their neat uniforms. They were now in the capacity of waiters—each man had five or six passengers to look after—and Tinker shared in this work, carrying dishes to and from the pantry, where the bed-room stewards were helping to carve and to pour out coffee and tea.

Neither the Rajah of Jazelpur nor any of his suite were present at this meal, but the tables were well-filled with passengers, some gloomy and quiet, others keeping up a flow of laughter and conversation. A large proportion of them were Anglo-Indians—officers returning from furlough to duty, officer's wives and children, tea and indigo planters, Civil Service men, Indian magistrates, and merchants from Madras and Calcutta. Among the others were subalterns and missionaries going for the first time to their posts of duty, tourists on pleasure bent, and plucky young Britishers going out to seek their fortunes or to help along the good work of empire-building. There was not one, however, whom Sexton Blake felt he could regard with the slightest shadow of suspicion.

After the breakfast had been run, as it is called, the boys had their own breakfast, and then they divided into small squads—the glass gang, crockery gang, and plate gang—in order to clear the tables and do the washing-up. More labour followed, and for a couple of hours the bed-room stewards were busy with the passengers' room, while the saloon and other stewards polished paint and brass-work. At eleven o'clock came inspection, when the captain, the doctor, and the chief steward went round certain parts of the ship. From the galley and the pantries they entered the saloon, where the stewards were lined up at attention, and there was a twinkle in the eye of the chief steward, Mr. Perks, as he stopped before Sexton Blake. He and Captain Binney—and those two alone—were aware of the new steward's identity, and knew why he was filling a menial position on board the *Darjeeling.*

"You are doing well, Mason, and I am pleased with you," said Mr. Perks. "You will get on, my man."

"Thank you, sir," the disguised detective answered gravely, touching his forehead. "It is my wish to please."

Tinker was not present, for his various duties—he was expected to do anything and everything—had called him elsewhere after breakfast. From the saloon the inspection party passed on to the bed-rooms, where they finished, and this left the stewards free for half an hour, from eleven-thirty to twelve. Some lingered in the saloon, Sexton Blake among them, while others went below to their own quarters.

On deck the passengers were fixed comfortably in reclining chairs, or strolling to and fro under the awnings, watching for the first glimpse of the French coast. The ship's writer, who had risen with the other hands, had printed the day's menus at an early hour, and at ten o'clock he had opened the library, of which he had charge. He was now seated at his desk in the main-deck office, which was a small cabin. Here prior to sailing, and when the vessel touched at ports, he would have been found busy with mail-bags, passenger-lists, and cargo-manifestos; but at other times during the voyage he had little to do in the office except deliver such letters and notes as might be given to him, or put through the slit in the door; for it is not uncommon for passengers on a big liner to correspond with one another.

"Here, Smith, I want you!" he called, as the cabin-boy passed.

"Yes, sir," said Tinker, raising his hand to his cap.

"Take this to the Rajah of Jazelpur," bade the writer.

A flat parcel was handed to the lad, who set off on his errand. Several minutes later, above the hum of voices, rang a howl of fright, followed by a loud commotion. Sexton Blake, who had not yet gone below, at once dashed to the main-deck, and thence to the promenade-deck adjoining, where passengers were jumping wildly about, screaming and shouting. The detective had a brief glimpse of Tinker, surrounded by a circle of Hindoos, and the next instant, gliding rapidly towards him, he saw a tiny green and purple serpent no more than seven inches long. He crushed the reptile's head under his heel, lifted it gingerly, and uttered a startled exclamation. Then he hastened forward into the thick of the turmoil, where the Rajah Kumar Beg and his retainers had risen from their deck-chairs near the bridge. Tinker was in the midst of them, white and terrified.

"It wasn't my fault, your Highness!" he protested. "I had nothing to do with it. You ask the——"

"The sahib boy lies!" cried Mervanji Singh, clapping a hand to the dagger that was in his kummerbund. "Had we not eyes to see?"

"Kill the infidel dog!" raved the rajah, who was pale with fright and anger. "Off with his head, trusty ones! Slay him, as he would have slain me!"

"I tell you I don't know anything about it!" vowed the lad. "Mr. Jones, the writer, gave me the parcel to deliver to his Highness. If you don't believe me ask him——"

He broke off at sight of Sexton Blake, who now rushed into the group, having delayed to pick up, from beside one of the chairs, several bits of cord, a crumbled sheet of brown paper, and a shallow tin box about eight inches square. The captain and the chief steward had also appeared, and were trying to pacify the enraged Hindoos, which gave Tinker a chance to slip out of harm's way. Mervanji Singh turned to the detective, who was still holding the dead snake.

"Here is the evil thing!" he cried, recoiling. "By the beard of Brahma, it is the carinata!"

"I knew that," murmured the detective. "I knew I was right."

"It is the most poisonous snake of our native land of India," put in Sikander Jung, the rajah's juggler. "The Most High has been spared from a terrible fate. Had he been bitten, death would have followed in three minutes."

"Away with it!" exclaimed Mervanji Singh.

And, with a shudder, he seized the reptile and flung it into the sea.

The excited passengers, who did not understand the meaning of what had happened, had recovered from their alarm. The coast of Southern France, now in sight, occupied their attention, and meanwhile the rajah and his suite had hastily retired, whispering among themselves. A little procession, including the captain and the chief steward, Sexton Blake and Tinker, marched off to the main-deck office, where Mr. Jones, the writer, told them all he knew.

"I opened the office at eleven o'clock as usual," he said, "and I didn't see the parcel at first, for it was lying under my desk. I found it a few minutes ago, and sent the cabin-boy with it to the rajah, to whom it was plainly addressed. I have no idea where it came from. It must have been dropped through the door in the night, or in the course of the morning."

"You didn't recognise the writing?" inquired Captain Binney.

"No, sir, I didn't," replied Mr. Jones.

"It was a deliberate and dastardly attempt at murder!" declared the captain, who had, of course, suspected the motive of the crime.

"We must get to the bottom of this,". the chief steward said, in a low voice to the detective.

"I hope we shall, and without delay," Sexton Blake whispered. "Take these and examine them, Mr. Perks," he added, giving the chief steward the things he had picked up from the deck. "I want a few words with you at the first opportunity."

The Third Chapter.
The Rajah at Lunch—Sexton Blake's Mishap—
The New Passenger.

It was now twenty minutes to twelve o'clock. The passengers had forgotten the exciting incident, and were gazing towards the French coast, which was looming near on the horizon. The captain had prudently avoided speech with Sexton Blake, and the latter had gone below to the private apartments of the chief steward. He had two small rooms, and in one of them, it may be said, the bloodhound was a reluctant but obedient prisoner, ready in case he should be needed. Pedro had been smuggled on board by night, and not by a single bark or whimper—he knew better than that—had he betrayed his presence.

Having caressed his faithful dog, and conversed for a few minutes with Mr. Perks, the detective made his way to the glory hole, as the stewards' general-room is called, where he found a number of the "boys" taking their ease and smoking. He lit his pipe, and sat down beside Tinker, apart from the others. They could talk without fear, owing to the buzz of voices around them.

"Have you discovered anything?" asked the lad.

"I have discovered enough to cause me serious alarm," whispered Sexton Blake. "This has been a rude shock to my feeling of security. That deadly snake belonged to India, and it must have been brought over by a native of that land. The tin box in which it was enclosed offers no clue, nor does the cord with which it was tied, but the coarse paper in which it was wrapped, the chief steward tells me, comes from a pound packet of coarse tobacco such as the sailors of the *Darjeeling* are accustomed to buy in foreign ports. Therefore, it seems conclusive that the would-be assassin is among the crew of this vessel; and one of the crew could easily have slipped the parcel through the door of the main-deck office during the night or early this morning. One thing is certain. In spite of all precautions, some daring foe of the rajah is actually on board the *Darjeeling*."

"He will try again, that is the worst of it," said Tinker.

"But you ought to be able to spot the scoundrel if he belongs to the crew."

"It don't look much like it. No new hands have been shipped for weeks, since the last homeward voyage from India. Half a dozen of the sailors are lascars, natives of India, and I imagined that Heera Beg might have been one of them. Indeed, that is possible, for the chief steward informs me that all of the crew, including the lascars, were absent from the vessel, on shore-leave in London, during the time that the rajah was kidnapped. That supports my suspicion, but if Heera Beg is on board it will be difficult to locate him. His disguise would probably baffle me."

"I believe you are right," declared Tinker. "Either Heera Beg is a false lascar, or Serge Zouroff is playing the part of a sailor."

"One or both may be among the crew, and they may not. It is just as likely, if not more so, that they have bribed a genuine lascar to murder the Rajah of Jazelpur."

"What about the handwriting on the parcel, guv'nor? If you were to show that to the rajah and his servants they might——"

"The address was in a disguised hand; I saw that at a glance," interrupted the detective. "It could not be identifed, even by any person familiar with the writing of Heera Beg, or of Serge Zouroff, should the Russian have sent the parcel. Moreover, it would be unwise to have anything to do with Kumar Beg and his suite. I don't want to reveal myself to them, or ask them any questions, for that might betray me to the spy, who probably has an idea that I am on board the *Darjeeling*. I am sure that he does not know, else he would hardly have made such a clumsy attempt at murder."

"He would certainly have tried to get rid of you first, if he knew you were here," said the lad. "We shall have to be more vigilant than ever, guv'nor."

"We shall, my boy," replied Sexton Blake; "at least, by day. There won't be any danger at night, for Mervanji Singh and Sikander Jung sleep in the passage outside the door of the rajah's state-room. His Highness has been badly frightened; and, of course, he is well aware that the serpent was sent to him by some scoundrel in the pay of Russia. But he has made no complaint, and it is evident that he and his retainers intend to hush the matter up and be on their guard. That will be an advantage to us, and if we are sharp we may—"

"Here comes the chief steward!" broke in Tinker.

"Twelve o'clock, boys!" exclaimed Mr. Perks, thrusting his head into the room. "Time to run the lunch. Move lively, now!"

The glory hole was quickly deserted for the saloon, where some of the stewards laid the tables, while others "passed in" the food from the cooks' galley to the pantry; and at twelve-thirty, when the gong rang for lunch, the Rajah of Jazelpur and five of his suite made their first appearance in the saloon since the vessel encountered the turbulent waves of the Bay of Biscay.

A special table was reserved for his Illustrious Highness— the law of caste made that imperative—and he alone sat down to it. His servants stood around him, even the dewan, ready to anticipate his wishes; and his food was brought to him by cook Holkar, for whom a part of the galley and pantry were set aside. The group attracted considerable attention, as well they might, for after the event of the morning they had armed themselves, as if they feared another attempt at assassination. The rajah, with a fierce scowl, had calmly placed a naked sword beside him on the table, and each of the five Hindus had a dagger and a tulwar in his kummer-bund. Such a sight, in the saloon of a big ocean liner, was most curious and barbaric.

"I'm sure we'll all be murdered in our beds—I mean, in our chairs!" squeaked a maiden lady of fifty to a missionary who sat opposite to her.

"It is an outrage!" growled a white-moustached old colonel. "Why should this fat savage be allowed to insult us, as if we were a lot of Thugs? I shall complain to the captain."

"If I had my——" loudly began a dandified young subaltern. And he promptly shut up as the rajah glanced at him and reached for his sword.

But for the most part the passengers, knowing nothing of the Russian intrigue that was in the very air, were highly amused by the spectacle. The lunch went merrily on, while the waiters passed to and fro in their smart uniforms. Sexton Blake had charge of a table adjoining and beyond the one occupied by the rajah, and as he was coming from the pantry, carrying a basin of hot soup, he encountered Tinker inside the doorway of the saloon.

"Watch his Illustrious Highness," murmured the lad, who was helping the stewards. "He isn't enjoying himself a little bit. I pity that poor devil Holkar, the cook. The rajah makes him taste first of every dish, to see if it is poisoned."

"A very wise precaution," murmured the detective, wondering if the unknown spy could have access to the galley. "But I wouldn't want to be in the cook's shoes," he added.

"Nor I," said Tinker. "Not for Joseph."

Shortly before, the order to shut off steam had been flashed from the bridge to the engine-room by electric bell, and now the vessel was moving of her own impetus with decreasing speed. Sexton Blake hurried on after the brief conversation with the lad, and as he was passing through one of the narrow spaces to reach his own table, the pocket of his jacket was caught by the hilt of Mervanji Singh's tulwar. The jerk caused the detective to trip, and disaster was swift and sudden. He lurched to one side, pitched half over the seated Rajah of Jazelpur, and poured the basin of steaming soup into his capacious lap. Up jumped Kumar Beg in a fury, drenched to the skin through his flimsy garments.

"Son of a burnt father!" he yelled, dancing about like a cat on a hot griddle. "Infidel dog! Feringhee of much clumsiness!"

He snatched his sword, and aimed a terrific blow that would have cleft Sexton Blake's skull, had he not quickly dodged the hissing steel. The rajah was overbalanced by the force of the stroke, and as he bumped the floor with his shoulders, crushing his face into the carpet, he grabbed hold of Mervanji Singh, who in turn clutched at the tablecloth and capsized the table, deluging himself and his master with plates, glasses, and food.

"*Ballaji bong, japper sera!*" cried the dewan, which was doubtless some awful imprecation in Hindustani.

He rolled off the rajah, who was a ludicrous sight when he rose, for he was plastered with ginger curry from his hair to his lips, and a fish had been squashed on the breast of his silken tunic.

"Murder! Help! Preserve me!" shrieked the maiden lady, as she threw herself into the arms of the missionary.

"Cut it, guv'nor!" urged Tinker, from a safe distance.

The detective, chagrined by the disaster, was trying to apologise. Kumar Beg was dabbing at his eyes with one hand and brandishing his sword with the other. With a whoop he leapt in the air, and his elbow caught Sikander Jung in the stomach, doubling him up with pain.

"Most High, forgive your poor slave!" begged Sexton Blake. "Be graciously pleased to——"

"Where are you, descendant of pigs?" howled the rajah, who had been nearly blinded by the curry. "Where is the defiling dog of wickedness? Seize him, my trusty ones!"

"The Most High shall be obeyed," vowed Mervanji Singh.

The detective retreated a little farther, and with that, as the five Hindus were about to rush at him, Captain Binney and several stewards barred the way. Some of the passengers had fled in terror. All the rest were on their feet, and for a moment there was noise and confusion.

"Enough of this!" exclaimed the captain. "Don't shake those ugly toothpicks at me, your Highness! Tell your servants to put up their weapons. I am sorry for what has happened; but it was an accident and no offence was intended."

"Can I forgive such an insult!" spluttered the rajah. "Behold how the table-waiting sahib has wet my garments with the broth that steams and burns! If it is made from the flesh of the cow or the pig I am defiled—I have lost caste. Lay hold of the infidel, slaves! Off with his head!"

"Stand back!" commanded Captain Binney.

"Seize the dog!" raved Kumar Beg.

"We cannot, Most High," said Mervanji Singh. "The captain sahib will not let us."

The dewan staggered, uttering a startled gasp as the hand of his Royal master boxed him on one ear and then on the other.

"I will have the infidel's head!" shouted the rajah. "Am I not the Lord of Jazelpur? In my own country my word is law. I command those who displease me to be slain, and it is done."

"You Highness cannot do that sort of thing here," cried

Captain Binney, "and the sooner you understand that the better!"

"Does the captain sahib defy me?" yelled Kumar Beg, who was nearly choked with rage. "Does he dare to refuse to——"

The boat's whistle gave a screech, ear-splitting and deafening, and his Illustrious Highness jumped fairly off his feet with fright, while the other Hindus flopped to their knees. Then the rajah fled from the saloon, gathering his drenched skirts around him, and after him went his five retainers.

"Thank goodness!" muttered Captain Binney, with a significant glance at the detective. "I shall be heartily glad when we land those fellows at Calcutta. Be more careful in future, Mason," he added.

"Yes, sir," Sexton Blake answered meekly.

The maiden lady was still clinging to the missionary, and it was with difficulty that he was relased from her embrace. The motion of the vessel had now ceased, and the rattle of chains and tramp of feet, followed by a splash, told that the anchor was with difficulty that he was released from her embrace. The while the rest went on with their lunch, talking of what had occurred.

"That was a near thing, guv'nor," whispered Tinker. "I thought your head was going to roll on the floor."

"Be careful of yours, my lad," replied the detective. "That's my advice to you."

The Fourth Chapter.
The Man with the Limp—The English Mall—Saved by a Monkey.

When the passengers were all out of the saloon, the stewards had their own lunch, and after they had "strapped up" they would ordinarily have been free for the afternoon, as it was the duty of another watch to run the tea at four o'clock; but on this occasion there was some special work for them, and instead of going below to the glory hole, they went on deck as soon as they had finished.

The *Darjeeling* was at anchor in a calm sea a short distance outside the port of Marseilles, and the old French city, with its tall, white buildings, looked very beautiful against a background of hills clothed with olive-trees. A little steam tender, coughing a trail of smoke, was ploughing lazily towards the big liner. The gangway of the *Darjeeling* had been lowered, and at the top of it Mr. Jones the writer was standing by a pile of mail-bags.

"Why don't they hurry?" grumbled Captain Binney. "They have kept us waiting long enough as it is!"

"The boat-train from Paris was probably late, sir," suggested the chief steward.

"There are passengers coming, guv'nor!" said Tinker.

"Passengers and mails," replied Sexton Blake; "but they don't concern us. We have one Russian spy on board, and I hardly expect another."

The tender was soon made fast alongside the vessel, and three passengers ascended to the deck. All were apparently English. One was a middle-aged lady, another was a young man with a military air, and the third was an elderly gentleman, plainly dressed in tweeds, who walked with a slight limp. He had a sallow complexion, brown hair, and tawny beard and moustache streaked with silver.

The chief steward, who had a slip of paper in his hand, took the three in charge and led them below. Several mailbags that followed the new passengers were removed to the main-deck office, and after a quantity of luggage had been hoisted up—to be hurried into the hold by the stewards—the mail-bags for England were lowered to the tender under the watchful eye of Mr. Jones.

"Clear away!" shouted the captain.

The little craft put back towards shore; then the gangway was drawn up, the anchor was raised, and, with a farewell hoot of her whistle, with throbbing engines, the *Darjeeling* resumed her voyage and went churning out to sea.

"That didn't take long," Tinker said to the detective. "What do you think of the new passengers? A harmless lot, I call them."

"Did you observe the man with the limp?"

"What of him, guv'nor?"

"The limp is a fraud, to the best of my belief," declared Sexton Blake. "It is probably caused by a pebble or some other object under the sole of the foot. I imagine that the lame gentleman will be worth watching!"

"I wonder if his beard and moustache are false?"

"They may be, though I confess that they looked real."

"Do you suppose the man can be Serge Zouroff?" asked the lad in a low voice.

"I don't suppose anything as yet," was the reply.

The detective exchanged a few words with Mr. Perks, and then he and Tinker went below to the glory hole, where they took their ease for the rest of the afternoon. It was not until towards six o'clock that the chief steward came down, and as soon as he had entered his private room he was joined there by Sexton Blake, who had been waiting for this opportunity.

"I wish I had a dog like that," said Mr. Perks enviously, when the door had been closed.

"There isn't another like him," answered the detective, who was fondling Pedro, "and I wouldn't part with him for a million. But what have you got to tell me?" he added.

"Nothing of importance," was the reply. "Those three new passengers are all right. Mrs. Gordon is the wife of a tea planter in Assam, and Lieutenant Perry, of the Bengal Lancers, is returning from furlough to his regiment. Those two were expected—they secured their berths before the *Darjeeling* sailed from London; as for the third passenger—I have had some conversation with him—he hurried overland at short notice to catch the boat at Marseilles. His name is Basil Sheppard, and he has been summoned to the bedside of his brother who is lying ill at Pagan, in Upper Burma. The brother is a civil magistrate."

"Could not Mr. Sheppard have taken a more direct route?" inquired Sexton Blake.

"Yes, if he had waited," said the chief steward; "as it is, he will have to take another line from Calcutta to Rangoon. By the by, Mr. Jones gave me a letter for you; it was enclosed in an outer envelope that was addressed to me."

The detective opened the letter, and with an inscrutable countenance he read the following brief communication, unsigned, that was in the handwriting of the Under-Secretary of the Foreign Office:

"I have had one of our Secret Service men at work, and he reports that yesterday—two days after you sailed—a lame man made inquiries at the London office of the British-India line concerning the time of the *Darjeeling*'s arrival at Marseilles. He gave the name of Sheppard, and stated that his brother was a civil magistrate in Upper Burma. I cabled to Rangoon, and am informed, in reply, that no such person is on the Civil List. This looks suspicious, at the least!"

Sexton Blake struck a match and set fire to letter and envelope consuming both to ashes.

"Any news?" asked Mr. Perks.

"Rather!" replied the detective. "Whatever the lame passenger may be, he is not the brother of a civil magistrate in Burma. We must regard Mr. Basil Sheppard as a suspicious character."

"I should never have believed it—never!" said the chief steward. "I'll help you to keep an eye on him, though. It is six o'clock," he added, glancing at his watch. "Come along, Mason, it is time for the boys to turn out."

Dinner was served at seven o'clock. The Rajah of Jazelpur was conspicuous by his absence. And after the final clear-up the evening wore on quietly until eleven o'clock, when the lights were put out in the saloon and the night watchman relieved the gang of stewards who had been on duty until that hour, and thus ended the ordinary routine of a day on board the *Darjeeling*.

It was hard work for Sexton Blake and Tinker, but they found much in the life to interest them, and the grave task with which they were entrusted—the charge of a human life that was valuable to the British Empire—served to banish monotony.

For two days the rajah sulked in seclusion, and when at length he came forth he had apparently forgotten his burst of anger, though he and his suite were never seen without a formidable array of weapons. They were aware of their danger; they knew that a Russian spy was on board, and they were on their guard against him.

As for Mr. Basil Sheppard, he mingled freely with the passengers, spending most of the time on deck with a pipe and a novel, and he was soon a general favourite.

On Sunday—it was the second Sunday out from London—there was a muster of all hands on the promenade deck, where they were inspected by the captain and chief officers. The detective was present, and his keen gaze studied the crew, including the six lascars; but he could not fix on anybody who might be Heera Beg, nor was he by any means certain as yet that Basil Sheppard was Serge Zouroff.

After a short stay at Brindisi the blue Mediterranean was left behind. The *Darjeeling* coaled at Port Said and touched at Suez, ran through the Suez Canal and steamed down the hot waters of the Red Sea, the furnace of the maritime world. Day succeeded day, but nothing happened. No further attempt was made on the life of the rajah, and it was difficult to conceive that such a thing could be attempted, much less succeed, without the certainty of immediate discovery, and Sexton Blake was satisfied that the unknown foe would take no risk.

By day the detective and Tinker were alert and vigilant in their furtive way. Kumar Beg and his retainers occupied all of the state-rooms on both sides of one of the ship's alleys, and in this alley, which the watchman had particular instructions to guard, Mervanji Singh and Sikander Jung slept at night outside their master's door—or, rather, they slept by turns, for one or the other was always awake. Nor were other possible sources of danger overlooked. Any letter or parcel that might be addressed to the rajah would be stopped by Mr. Jones, and one of the rooms in the alley had been turned into a galley on a small scale and assigned to Holkar, the Hindu cook. He alone had a key to the room, and here he kept all the materials that he used for his master's food and drink. These precautions, it might be supposed were sufficient to protect his Highness from subtle peril; they satisfied Sexton Blake, at all events.

"There is not much cause for fear," he told Tinker. "We know that there is one secret assassin on board. I am still in doubt about Basil Sheppard; but the man has probably abandoned his designs for the voyage, trusting that he will find a better opportunity on land while the rajah is travelling up-country from Calcutta to Jazelpur, and that will be a matter for the military escort."

At ten o'clock on a sultry, breathless night, while the *Darjeeling* was rippling quietly through the Red Sea, Sexton Blake, in linen suit, was enjoying a pipe on the almost deserted promenade deck while he waited for the rajah to retire—as he had done on previous nights. He was there by special permission, and in the guise of a passenger, not as a steward; furthermore, he wore a false beard and moustache.

At intervals the detective could hear laughter and conversation from the smoke-room, and in that little place of luxury, with its soft carpet and leather-covered couches and chairs, half a dozen passengers were lounging, discussing the vessel's run. One of them was his Highness Kumar Beg, who liked to hear the talk of the Europeans. He was quite at his ease, feeling safe in the present company, though his jewelled tulwar was buckled to his kummerbund.

His fat body filled one of the seats, and diamonds and rubies worth a fortune glittered in his silken turban and tunic. He was sucking at the amber mouthpiece of a hookah that rested on the marble table in front of him, and on his lap was huddled his pet monkey, Tirza.

"I am willing to bet," declared Colonel French, an elderly officer, as he pressed an electric button beside him—"I am willing to bet we shall reach Aden by this time to-morrow."

"I'll lay you a five that we don't!" replied Mr. Brenton, an indigo planter of the Central Provinces, as he patted a small terrier that lay at his feet.

"Done!" said the colonel. "Bring me a whisky-peg," he added, to the cabin-boy, who had promptly answered the bell. "What's yours, Brenton?"

"A brandy-peg for me," said the planter.

Two other passengers ordered drinks, and as Tinker hurried off the rajah clapped his hands and nodded to Mervanji Singh, who stood in the doorway in attendance, grave and dignified. The dewan departed, coming back shortly. Then Tinker returned with a tray, and when the lad had distributed the glasses, Holkar entered the smoke-room, bearing a silver salver on which was a golden goblet of sherbet.

With a bow the cook handed the drink to his master, and the rajah was about to raise it to his lips when the monkey playfully seized the stem of the goblet, tilted it half over, and sniffed at the contents. The next instant, with a chattering cry, the little animal had dashed the goblet to the floor. Kumar Beg uttered an angry imprecation as he cuffed his pet, and with that Mervanji Singh sprang forward, his eyes dilated with terror.

"Poison, Most High—poison!" he gasped, knowing full

well that a monkey has an infallible instinct for detecting anything harmful in food or drink.

"It is impossible," declared the rajah.

"Truly it cannot be!" vowed Holkar.

Just then the indigo planter's little terrier put out his tongue and lapped twice at the stream of sherbet that was pouring sluggishly over the carpet. There was a yelp of agony, stifled by a throaty wheeze, and the dog rolled over. He squirmed convulsively, kicked a few times, and lay quite still, with a greenish froth oozing from his lips.

The Fifth Chapter.
The Mystery Is Solved—Tinker's Adventure.

For a moment nobody spoke. The occupants of the smoke-room were petrified, struck dumb, while the startling meaning of the tragedy dawned upon them. Sexton Blake, having heard the excited voices of the Hindus, had appeared in the doorway. The silence was broken by a shrill chattering from Tirza the monkey, who dropped off his master's lap, seized the goblet, and threw it under one of the seats.

"By heavens, my dog is dead!" Mr. Brenton exclaimed huskily, as he picked up the terrier. "Poor Rolf! Poor old fellow! How I shall miss him."

"He has been poisoned," said Colonel French. "That was the quickest thing of the kind I ever saw."

"I have been saved from death!" cried Kumar Beg, as he rose to his feet. "But for Tirza I should have tasted the poisoned cup and perished. Holkar, you dog of evil, you are a traitor in the pay of my enemies. That serpent was sent by you, and now you would have slain me thus, by putting poison in my drink!"

Spluttering with rage, he clutched the cook by the throat with one hand, and with the other he whipped a dagger from his kummerbund. The weapon was at once snatched from him by Tinker, and, as quickly, Mervanji Singh thrust himself in front of the terrified Holkar.

"Slay not, your Highness!" he entreated. "Let this slave speak first. Long have I known him, and I cannot believe that he is guilty of so foul a deed."

"I am innocent!" wailed the cook, falling to his knees.

"Hear me, Most High. I know nothing of the poison. I swear it. I alone have had the key to the room where I prepare the food and drink, and never have I parted with it. The door was locked when I entered, at the bidding of Mervanji Singh, to mix the sherbet-and-water."

"Dog, you lie!" thundered the rajah. "Rise, that I may plunge my dagger into your heart!"

But now Captain Binney had come on the scene, and when the affair had been explained to him he glanced furtively at Sexton Blake.

"This must be looked into, your Highness," he said to Kumar Beg. "I will try to get to the bottom of the mystery."

"Let the sahib do so!" replied Kumar Beg, as he fondly caressed the monkey that had saved his life.

The rest of the Hindus had appeared, and they and their master, with the captain, Tinker, and the detective, went quietly to the alley that was occupied by the Royal party. The occupants of the smoke-room followed, and also several other passengers—Mr. Basil Sheppard was among them—who had left their rooms; but these were not allowed to come farther than the top of the passage. Sexton Blake, who felt by no means certain of Holkar's loyalty, stopped at the door of the cabin that was used as a galley. Having scraped a match, he closely scrutinised the lock, and found traces of wax. Then he stepped into the little room, and searched it thoroughly under the watchful eyes of the rajah and his retainers. He closed the door, and whispered a few words to Captain Binney, who turned to Kumar Beg.

"The cook is innocent, your Highness," he said. "You have an unknown foe on board the vessel, and this man—he is not one of your servants—made a false key to the lock of the galley, and thus was able to put some deadly poison into the sherbet."

"I must have his head!" the rajah declared fiercely. "Let the captain sahib find him for me."

"He shall be found, sooner or later," was the reply. "Meanwhile, I will have another lock put on the door, and send you fresh supplies from the store-room. And hereafter it will be well for your Highness to taste nothing, either food or drink, until it has been first offered to your monkey."

Kumar Beg and his retainers nodded to one another—they

had been convinced of Holkar's innocence—and then the rest withdrew from the alley. The passengers willingly promised to keep the affair quiet, at the request of Captain Binney. Some went back to the smoke-room, others to their berths, while Sexton Blake slipped below unseen. He changed his clothes in the chief-steward's room, and half an hour later, when the lights had been put out above, he and Tinker had a brief conversation in the glory hole.

"That is the second narrow escape for the rajah," he said. "I believed that he would be safe until the end of the voyage, but I was wrong. Having obtained a wax impression of the lock, and filed a key to fit, the spy slipped into the galley—probably in the course of the evening—and mixed poison with the sherbet."

"Pedro might have tracked him," suggested the lad.

"I don't think so. As I had nothing that the man had worn, his scent could hardly have been picked out and followed. Moreover, I would have drawn suspicion upon myself making use of the dog. I won't do that until I am sure of success."

"Do you suspect Basil Sheppard, guv'nor?"

"Not of this crime," replied the detective. "Mr. Sheppard may be Serge Zouroff, and he needs watching. But the poison that nearly killed Kumar Beg came from India, and no doubt it was put in the sherbet by the same hand that sent the serpent. I believe that the guilty man is Heera Beg, the rajah's brother, and that he is on board the ship in the guise of a lascar. Another attempt may be made at any time, so we must be more vigilant than ever, by night as well as by day."

"The rajah will be safe enough at night!" declared Tinker.

"Unless the spy should succeed in drugging the two Hindus who sleep in the alley," said Sexton Blake. "That is not likely, however. Come, my boy," he added, "it is time to turn in!"

Another day dawned, with its round of toil for the new steward and the cabin-boy, and the scorching sun beat fiercely down on the waters of the Red Sea. Kumar Beg took his meals in the saloon, and the monkey Tirza, huddled on his lap, sniffed at every dish before it was touched by his Highness. A cloud seemed to have settled on the passengers, who were aware that a secret assassin was among them, and that the life of the Rajah of Jazelpur had been twice attempted. They gravely discussed the mystery, and their low spirits were shared by Mr. Basil Sheppard, who limped about the deck, or sat for hours with his pipe and a book.

Late that night the *Darjeeling* dropped anchor off the grim rock-fortress of Aden, in the shadow of the Arabian hills and King Solomon's tanks, and on the following morning she set her course south-east for the distant port of Colombo.

For several days, while the big liner ploughed through the torrid wastes of the Gulf of Aden and the Arabian Sea, all went well. The unknown spy did not show his hand again, nor did Mr. Sheppard's conduct justify the close watch that was kept upon him.

"We must not relax our vigilance," Sexton Blake said to Tinker, when the two were together in the glory hole; "but all the same, I believe that the assassin has abandoned his designs, and that he won't run any further risk during the voyage."

"That's just what I think, guv'nor!" replied the lad. "I'll be glad when we get to Calcutta, though."

But much was to happen before either of them was to see Calcutta, and it was well that they could not read the future. The next day not a breath of air was stirring, and the *Darjeeling* steamed over an ocean that was like a millpond. The heat was intense, and later in the afternoon, clouds of a peculiar colour massed on the horizon. Passengers and crew looked anxious, and Captain Binney did not stir from the bridge.

"I am afraid we are going to have a typhoon, Parrish," he said, to the second-officer.

"There is one brewing, sir," was the reply, "but it may not come this way."

The threatened storm held off, and dinner was enlivened by the antics of the rajah's monkey. He bit Holkar in the arm, and when rebuked for that he pulled Mervanji Singh's hair and threw a ripe peach that squashed on the spotless shirt-bosom of the young subaltern, who jumped up in a fury and fled to his cabin. About nine o'clock, when night had fallen and most of the passengers were on deck, Sexton Blake was tidying the smoke-room, and Tinker was helping the gang of stewards who were on "strap-up" duty. Kumar Beg had gone into seclusion; and Tirza, who had been in charge of Sikander Jung, had escaped from him and was roaming below, while the worried Hindu sought elsewhere for him.

The monkey had taken a liking to the cabin-boy, and as Tinker was making his way from the saloon to the pantry, carrying a pile of plates, the little animal caught sight of him, and skipped furtively and noiselessly at his heels. In blissful ignorance of this the lad went on, and just as he entered the pantry Tirza jumped upon his back. With a yell of fright he dropped the plates, which were smashed to fragments.

"Clumsy young idiot!" exclaimed Pogson, the crockery steward. "Here's a nice mess, and you'll have to pay the damage. You'll be sorry, my boy, when you find your wages docked to the tune of——"

With that the monkey leapt upon his head, gave his ear a vigorous tweak, and slapped him on the cheek.

"Drat the brute!" howled the steward. "Knock him off! Take him away or he'll bite me!"

"Keep quiet, will you?" urged Tinker. "How can I do anything while you're hopping about?"

"Pull him off!" cried Pogson, dancing more wildly than ever. "You'll laugh at me, will you? You did this a-purpose, Smith. I'll wring your neck. Ouch! Murder! The beast is clawing my face. Why don't you——"

He swayed against a stack of dishes, bringing them down with a crash; and then Tirza bounded back to Tinker's shoulder, chattering with glee. The lad took to his heels, with the angry steward in hot chase; but he eluded his pursuer by turning from passage to passage, and when he reached the saloon, still afraid of being caught, he swerved sharply and rapidly, without observing where he was going, into the alley that led to the rajah's apartments.

The alley was dark and at that instant, as ill-luck would have it, his Highness Kumar Beg and suite were approaching the saloon. Tinker saw them, but not in time to avoid disaster. Bang he went into the fat figure of the rajah, who gave a loud grunt as he was thrown flat on his back. The lad sprawled on top of him, and the monkey seized the opportunity to nip his master in the ankle. Up jumped Kumar Beg, and with that Sikander Jung trod on his toes.

"Dog of clumsiness!" he yelled, hopping about on one foot. "I am stabbed! I felt the steel in my leg!"

"The Most High is stabbed!" cried Mervanji Singh. "But we have the assassin. He is here!"

"Lay hold of him, slaves!" spluttered the rajah. "Fetch him hither!"

Tinker tried to escape, but it was too late. The dewan pinned him by the throat, others gripped his arms, and he was quickly dragged into Kumar Beg's state-room, where the electric light was switched on. The monkey, who was the cause of all the trouble, climbed sedately to a table and began to scratch his ear.

"It is the young sahib of the table-waiting and the smoke-room drinks," declared the rajah, his eyes rolling with fury.

"He is a spy of Russia, and twice before he has sought my life. By Mahadera, he shall die!"

"Help, help!" shouted the lad, who realised his dreadful peril.

"There is no help for thee, Feringhee!" hissed the dewan, as he tightened his grip on the prisoner's throat.

"Silence his tongue, that we may not be disturbed!" said Kumar Beg. "And then prepare him for the steel!"

Tinker fought desperately, but he was powerless against such odds; nor did he get another chance to cry out. His struggles having been subdued, and a handkerchief tied over his mouth, he was forced to his knees on the floor, with his face resting on a stool. Three of the Hindus held him in this position, while Holkar tugged at his hair and stretched his neck over the stool.

"Now strike!" bade the infuriated despot. "Off with his head!"

Mervanji Singh drew a tulwar, felt the edge of it, and hesitated.

"Is the Illustrious One wise?" he said timidly. "The young sahib may be innocent."

"If we slay him," put in Sikander Jung, "the captain sahib may have us seized and punished."

"Am I not the Lord of Jazelpur?" cried the rajah. "Would any Feringhee dare to lay hands upon me? The dog is certainly guilty! He is a spy of Russia! Off with his head," he added, whipping out his sword. "Do my bidding, slaves, or your own heads shall roll upon the floor!"

"The Most High shall be obeyed," said Mervanji Singh.

He raised his tulwar, and Tinker, writhing in horror, believed that his last moment had come. For an instant the
gleaming steel hovered in air, above the bared neck of the
helpless lad. Then, jumping from the table with an angry
scream, the monkey leapt upon the dewan and clutched his
descending wrist; and with that, as the door was thrown
open, Sexton Blake and two other stewards dashed into the
state-room.

"Just in time!" gasped Pogson. "Look what they're doing to
him!"

The tulwar fell from the grasp of Mervanji Singh, to whose
wrist Tirza was still holding. The rajah recoiled with a fiery
imprecation, raised his sword, and slowly lowered it as he
found himself staring into the muzzle of a revolver.

"Is your Highness mad?" the detective said fiercely, keeping the weapon levelled. "What right had you to seize this
boy? He is innocent; he must not be harmed. Bid your servants release him at once!"

The Hindus, more prudent than their master, were quick to
relax their grip of Tinker, who struggled to his feet, with a
strangled sob, hardly realising yet that he was saved. He
made a blind rush through the doorway, and after him went
the three stewards, Sexton Blake closing the door as he
brought up the rear. They sped along the alley, with the
wrathful voice of Kumar Beg ringing in their ears.

"I have been defiled by the Feringhees—I, the Lord of
Jazelpur!" he yelled. "They have mocked me to my face!
They shall all die! I will have their heads! Dogs, why did you
suffer this? Why did you not——"

The wild ravings were muffled by distance. At the top of
the passage the two stewards turned and fled towards the
pantry, while the detective and the lad slipped into the empty
saloon. Tinker was white and trembling, unnerved by the ordeal he had gone through.

"They were going to cut off my head," he panted. "They
would have done it, guv'nor, if you hadn't come. It was horrible. I can't tell you how I felt. The sword was over me,
ready to fall."

"You were in terrible danger," said Sexton Blake. "That
cold-blooded barbarian is capable of anything. He can't understand that there is a higher authority than his. Thank

Heaven I arrived in time, my boy. Pogson saw you seized and dragged into the state-room, and he was too terrified to give an alarm. He did not realise your peril. But, fortunately, I happened to come along just then."

"What do you suppose the rajah will do about it?" asked the lad.

"I don't think he will do anything. He will see that the matter had better be hushed up. But you must be careful hereafter to keep out of his way——"

"Listen! What's that?" broke in Tinker.

As he spoke a roaring noise was swelling loud and near, and a sudden lurch almost threw him off his feet. He staggered against a table and recoiled into a chair. The ship was now rocking to and fro, and overhead was a clamour of strange and alarming sounds—the rattle of cordage and the shriek of a violent gale, the rush and tramp of feet, the bawling of men.

"It must be the typhoon!" cried Tinker.

"It is," declared Sexton Blake. "It has caught us, and without warning."

Above the tumult the voice of Captain Binney ran through a speaking trumpet.

"All passengers below!" he shouted.

The China Sea is the home of the dreaded typhoon; but they are frequently encountered in the Indian Ocean, and it was one of the worst kind that had burst now. The stars were blotted out, and the heavens were inky black. Amid thunder and lightning, lashed by tremendous waves, the *Darjeeling* was driving madly, blindly through the storm, a frail and puny thing at the mercy of the elements. Passengers and stewards had sought shelter below, and in their state-rooms the Rajah of Jazelpur and his servants were cowering in fear, invoking the aid of their heathen gods.

"It is a sign that the Feringhee boy was innocent," said Mervanji Singh. "It is well for us that he escaped."

Kumar Beg had forgotten his frustrated vengeance.

"The evil sickness, it comes upon me again!" he groaned, pressing his hands to his fat stomach. "Alas, it gnaws and bites! It makes my head to swim. Put me to bed, slaves, and pray to great Brahma that he will quieten the motion of the ship!"

The Sixth Chapter.
A Narrow Escape—Heera Beg Captured.

For three days the *Darjeeling* was tossed about by the typhoon, and by the furious tropical storm which followed in its wake, and in consequence she was a day late in arriving at Colombo. Her stay there was to be a brief one; but a significant incident occurred as soon as she touched. Mr. Basil Sheppard received a cablegram, purporting to come from his brother in Burma, reporting that he was out of danger. Whereupon Mr. Sheppard decided that it was not worth while to continue the voyage, so he landed at Colombo with all his baggage, and forthwith disappeared. The same evening a new passenger came aboard, giving the name of Dr. Lambrick, and bound, according to his own story, for a hill station up in the Punjaub. Dr. Lambrick did not resemble Mr. Basil Sheppard in a single detail, but Sexton Blake regarded him with the deepest suspicion. If his surmise was correct, that Mr. Sheppard had been none other than Serge Zouroff in disguise, he thought it more than likely that the cunning Russian fearing that his first disguise had been pierced had decided to change it; and the detective determined to keep Dr. Lambrick under the closest observation.

Accompanied by Tinker and Pedro, Sexton Blake went ashore for a ramble through the town on the evening that the *Darjeeling* was due to leave Colombo. Wandering through the streets, and passing occasionally one or other of the brilliantly-lit cafes, they obtained a glimpse of the life of that strange and beautiful city before turning their steps once more towards the quay. The *Darjeeling* was due to sail at midnight, and they had not left themselves too much time, so they hurried on till they reached the quay. Not wishing to attract unwelcome attention by coming aboard together at such a late hour, they separated, Sexton Blake striding on a hundred yards or so in front of Tinker and Pedro. He was within a few yards of the *Darjeeling*'s gangway, when something—it might have been only a shadow—caught the tail of his eye, and the detective pulled up short and looked over his shoulder. There was no one in sight; even Tinker, whom he knew could not be far behind, was concealed by the darkness.

He went on for a couple of yards, stopped again, and with that swung round on his heel at the sound of a light, furtive step. His promptness saved his life. He saw close upon him the dusky figure of a man—a man who held a glittering knife, and was in the very act of striking.

"You scoundrel!" gasped the detective.

As he sprang aside, the weapon, missing its murderous aim, ripped down his sleeve from shoulder to elbow. He felt a hot, burning pain, and at once, with quick presence of mind, he grasped his assailant's wrist with one hand and fastened the other on his throat. They began to struggle, heaving and writhing, and for a moment it looked as if the stranger would wrench free and escape, for he was as agile as an eel. Sexton Blake whistled twice, and the next instant Tinker and Pedro came swiftly on the scene.

With a low growl of fury the dog bounded upon his master's foe, dragging him to the ground, and as he fell the lad tore the knife from his hand. The prostrate man uttered a gurgling cry, and before he could repeat it the detective rapped him on the skull with the butt of a revolver. The blow settled him, and he lay motionless. All was quiet, the brief scuffle having raised no alarm.

"That was a close shave, guv'nor," whispered Tinker. "I saw the fellow dodging among the trees, and I thought he might be after you, so Pedro and I ran as fast as we could. But look at his sailor's dress. He is surely one of the crew of the *Darjeeling?*"

"Yes, and he is a lascar," declared Sexton Blake, as he gazed closely at his assailant. "This is a stroke of luck."

"If he is a lascar, guv'nor, he must be the spy you want."

"I have no doubt that he is; he can't be anybody else. He must have been ashore. He saw me in the town, recognised me, and crept after us to the quay. Wait here, my boy, with the dog. The man is stunned, and he won't give you any trouble."

With that the detective glided away, and five minutes later he returned with a sheet of canvas.

"It is all right," he said. "The coast is clear, and the chief steward is ready for us. Now is our chance, Tinker. Lend me a hand—quick!"

The canvas was thrown over the slim body of the prisoner,

and Sexton Blake and the lad picked him up, carrying him as if he was a bundle of merchandise. They hurried forward, and a moment later, with Pedro at their heels, they were calmly mounting the gangway. At the top of it they passed Mr. Perks, who made a furtive sign, and then came the trying part of the ordeal. But it passed off well. Unseen, though some of the officers and crew were moving about, the little group hastened over the deck of the *Darjeeling*, through the dark saloon and the corridors beyond, and then down to the chief steward's private rooms, where the electric light was switched on. With a sigh of relief Sexton Blake closed the door, and he and Tinker placed their burden on the floor.

"I'm glad that's over," said the lad. "I was afraid we would be stopped on the way."

"It is fortunate that we were not," answered the detective, as he examined the slight cut on his arm; "for I want this affair to be kept quiet, especially from the Russian. I don't know yet how it is going to turn out."

Having removed the sheet, he quickly clapped a pair of irons on his prisoner's wrists, and bound his ankles with rope. By then the man was conscious and glaring at his captors; but before he could speak the door opened and Mr. Perks stepped into the room.

"That worked all right," he said. "You are safe here, and in a few minutes we shall be putting out to sea. The gangway has been already cast off. This is one of our crew," he added; "but have you got the man you wanted?"

"I have!" declared Sexton Blake, with a gleam of satisfaction in his eyes. "This is the identical scoundrel who has tried to assassinate the Rajah of Jazelpur, I have no doubt!"

"It is false!" snarled the lascar. "I am innocent—I try to kill nobody."

"Not so loud," bade the detective. "If you make any outcry, Heera Beg, I will send for his Highness your brother, and confront you with him."

The shot struck home. By the sudden pallor of his cheeks, by his wild, fleeting look of terror, the man betrayed beyond a doubt that he was indeed the wicked brother of the Rajah of Jazelpur.

"By Jove, you've hit the mark!" muttered Mr. Perks.

"It is a lie!" declared the lascar, as he mastered his agitation. "The sahibs must be mad. Who is Heera Beg? I do not know the name. I am a poor sailor, and I have done no wrong. Let me go, you dogs of Feringhees! Why you bring me here?"

"Well, of all the cheek!" exclaimed Tinker. "As if he didn't try to stab my guv'nor a bit ago!"

"My cunning fellow," Sexton Blake told the man, "I will let you off—or rather, I will let you down easily—on one condition. You can guess what it is."

"I know not what the sahib means," was the sullen reply.

"I think you do," said the detective. "Listen to me, and be wise. I know everything. You and Serge Zouroff are spies in the pay of Russia. You kidnapped the Rajah of Jazelpur in London, and after I rescued him from your clutches you plotted a worse crime—that of murder. The two of you sailed on the *Darjeeling*—you as a lascar, and Zouroff as an Englishman named Sheppard. You made more than one attempt on the life of the rajah, and you believed that you had got rid of me. When the vessel arrived at Colombo the Russian went ashore, but he returned soon afterwards in a fresh disguise, and he is now known as Dr. Lambrick."

The prisoner changed colour and bit his lip. Another shot had struck home.

"You see that the game is up," continued Sexton Blake. "Unless you are a fool you will save yourself. If you will make a full confession, and swear that Dr. Lambrick is Serge Zouroff, your punishment will be a light one. I promise that, and I have the power to keep my word."

"I am Heera Beg, but I am not a traitor," replied the Hindu, with a mocking laugh. "If Serge Zouroff is on the vessel, if you are fool enough to believe that, find him yourself. You will get no help from me nor will all your skill be able to save the Rajah of Jazelpur, who will surely perish before his eyes can behold the green shores of India. I have spoken, dog! I will not confess. I defy you—do your worst! I will tell you nothing—nothing!"

"It's no good," whispered Mr. Perks. "He means what he says."

The Seventh Chapter.
The Dead Rajah—Dr. Lambrick's Visit—
What the Detective Saw.

So it proved to be. Trapped and identified though he was, with the certainty of heavy punishment for his crimes hanging over him, Heera Beg would not betray his accomplice, who was the more guilty of the two. He would not even speak. Threats and persuasion failed alike to move him, and in the end Sexton Blake gave up the task as hopeless.

"I have wasted my breath," he said. "I was afraid he would be obstinate."

A gag was thrust into the prisoner's mouth and then, bound hand and foot, he was stowed away in the inner room, with Pedro to guard him. The machinery was now throbbing; from the deck above came the sound of voices and trampling feet. The *Darjeeling* was moving through the water.

"We are off—off for Calcutta!" declared Mr. Perks. "I wonder if your Russian is really on board?"

"I have no apprehension about that," said the detective. "Dr. Lambrick is certainly Serge Zouroff."

"But can you arrest him?"

"Not at present. I have no proof, nor can I swear to his identity."

"Why not set a trap for him," suggested Tinker, "by telling him that we have the lascar and that he has confessed?"

"That's not a bad idea, my boy, though I doubt if it would deceive Zouroff," replied Sexton Blake. "I must think it over, however, and meanwhile—for to-night, at least—we may regard the rajah as safe. But Heera Beg's disappearance must be accounted for in the morning," he added. "You must arrange that, Perks."

"I'll do it," said the chief steward. "I'll give the crew to understand that he was left behind on shore. And now you will be wanting to turn in. You look like ghosts, and I don't wonder at it, considering what you've gone through. You take my berth, Mr. Blake."

But the detective refused to do that, so beds were improvised on the floor for him and Tinker. They fell asleep at once, and knew nothing more until they woke in the morning to find the sun shining through the porthole and Mr. Perks missing. Sexton Blake rose and entered the inner room to greet Pedro and see that the prisoner was all right, and as he stepped out again the chief steward made his appearance. His face was agitated, and his eyes were big with excitement.

"I have news for you—terrible news!" he exclaimed.

"What is it?" asked the detective.

"His Highness the Rajah of Jazelpur—he is dead! He died suddenly during the night!"

"Dead?" gasped Tinker. "What a distressing thing, guv'nor! There will be trouble for the British Government in Jazelpur now. And we have the new rajah a prisoner in the next room!"

"Was Kumar Beg murdered—killed by poison?" inquired Sexton Blake.

"No; he died a natural death," declared Mr. Perks. "He has been ill since yesterday morning. The ship's doctor reports it as a case of heart disease."

"The body has been examined, then?"

"Yes, a couple of hours ago, as soon as the servants spread the news. It is now after ten o'clock. I let you sleep on, as I knew you must be tired."

"Very considerate of you, Mr. Perks; but I am sorry you did not waken me before. However, it does not make any difference."

"You take it very calmly."

"I do. I am inclined to doubt this tale."

"What? You don't believe the rajah is dead?"

"I don't know what to believe as yet."

"But I have seen the corpse of his Highness myself, and it is cold and rigid. There can be no doubt at all."

"I am not satisfied," said the detective.

Tinker was staggered and curious, scenting a mystery. Sexton Blake lit his pipe, sat down, and smoked in thoughtful silence for a few moments.

"I am going above," he quietly announced, as he drew from under the chief steward's berth a box in which he kept spare clothing.

"I had better bring your breakfast first," said Mr. Perks.

"Not now," was the reply. "That can wait."

Breakfast had been over for some time, and in the bright sunshine of the tropical morning, as the *Darjeeling* was ploughing northward in sight of the green coast of Ceylon, the passengers were assembled in groups on the promenade deck, excitedly discussing the terrible event that had taken place in the night. They did not like it, and still less did they like the attitude of the rajah's servants, who had insisted from the first that their master should be buried in the tomb of his ancestors at Jazelpur. The drift of the conversation was all one way, and strongly against the proposal, when Sexton Blake sauntered forward, wearing a suit of blue serge, and disguised by a false beard and moustache. He moved to and fro, listening and observing keenly.

"Of course, I don't doubt your word, Fraser," a grizzled officer was saying to the ship's doctor. "But these Hindus are a tricky lot, you know, and, under the circumstances, after the various attempts on the life of his Highness——"

"The rajah is certainly dead—as dead as a doornail!" broke in the medical man. "There was never a clearer case, sir."

"Heart trouble—eh? Did you see him while he was ill?"

"No, I did not. He was treated by his servants, who refused to——"

The two speakers strolled on, and a man standing by the rail turned to gaze after them. He attracted the notice of the detective, who spotted him as the new passenger that had come on board at Colombo. Dr. Lambrick was an elderly man, of medium height, and he looked what he claimed to be. His moustache and pointed beard were black, streaked with silver, and he wore gold-rimmed eyeglasses.

A shade of doubt crept into Sexton Blake's mind, puzzling and disturbing him.

"Can it be possible that I am wrong?" he asked himself. "He has not one point in common with the Russian. If this fellow is Serge Zouroff—and I am no longer sure of it—he is most admirably disguised."

Captain Binney now came forward, and he was immediately surrounded by the passengers, all wanting to talk at once.

"Have you heard of this astounding thing, sir?" exclaimed one. "It is actually proposed to keep the body of the Rajah of

Jazelpur for days, until we reach Calcutta, so that he may be sent up-country!"

"It is disgraceful!" declared a second.

"I protest against it," declared a third; "and if you do not interfere, I shall lodge a complaint with the company!"

"Of course you won't allow it, captain?" put in another. "In this tropical climate—this hot weather—it would be a serious menace to all of us, a danger to health. The corpse must be buried at sea."

"Or at least embalmed, captain."

"I quite understand your feelings in this matter, gentlemen," replied Captain Binney, when he could get a chance to speak, "and I am anxious to meet your wishes; but you must remember that the deceased Hindu was of high rank, and that he has been travelling on this vessel as the guest of the British Government. However, it is certain that——"

He paused, and a breathless hush fell on all, for Mervanji Singh, unperceived until now, was standing close by.

"What foolish talk is this?" he cried loudly and fiercely. "What have the sahibs to do with his Illustrious Highness? You shall not put my master under the waves! His bones shall lie at Jazelpur, in the grave of his ancestors!"

With that, rattling his tulwar in its sheath, the Hindu strode away and vanished. Captain Binney shrugged his shoulders, looked troubled and perplexed.

"I will do my duty, gentlemen," he vowed. "I will act in your interests, and you may be assured that the body of the rajah will either be buried at sea or that it will be embalmed."

"He must be dropped overboard," several voices declared.

A buzz of conversation rose from the passengers, and a moment later Dr. Lambrick stepped up to the captain.

"I am a medical man, sir," he said in a low tone, "and I may be of assistance to you in this matter. I should like to have a few words with you."

This little incident was missed by Sexton Blake, who had just then gone below. He hurried through the saloon, overtook Mervanji Singh, and touched him on the shoulder.

"What does the sahib wish?" demanded the dewan, turning with a start.

"Do you not know me?" asked the detective, as he removed his false beard for an instant. "Look at my face. Am I not the Maker of Magic, who rescued your master in London?"

"It is true!" Mervanji Singh exclaimed in astonishment. "You are indeed the Wise One. But alas! you are too late! You can do nothing, for our beloved master has breathed his last."

"I am deeply distressed by the sad news," said Sexton Blake. "Will you let me gaze upon his Highness?"

"It is impossible!" was the curt reply.

"But I am a friend, and you can trust me. You know that. Moreover, I will use my influence with the captain, and urge him to take the body to Calcutta."

"Our master shall be buried at Jazelpur, and nowhere else!" swore the dewan. "But come, sahib," he added. "It shall be as you wish. We have nothing to conceal from the Maker of Magic."

Consent had been won, and more easily than the detective had expected, which damped his faint hopes. The two went softly down the alley in which were the Royal apartments, and half a dozen armed retainers, who were posted there on guard, stared at them in silent surprise. They passed into the rajah's state-room, and as the door was closed behind them, Sikander Jung, who was here alone, whipped out his tulwar.

"Yet another sahib?" he said angrily. "How is this?"

"I have brought the Maker of Magic, who is still our friend," replied Mervanji Singh.

"He comes too late."

"So I have told him," said the dewan.

Sikander Jung nodded and frowned. Sexton Blake looked about the room, wondering what the result of his visit would be, and then, very quietly and reverently, with bared head, he stepped over to the berth. Here, uncovered, lay his Highness Kumar Beg. Cotton-wool had been stuffed into his nostrils, and he was cold and rigid to the touch. His eyes were shut, and his waxen features wore a peaceful expression. The detective held a small mirror to his lips, but not the faintest film of breath appeared on the glass.

Was the Rajah of Jazelpur really dead? There was no reason to think otherwise, but Sexton Blake was loath to believe.

For a few moments he examined the corpse, and still he was not convinced.

"Is the sahib satisfied?" inquired Mervanji Singh.

"Life has fled from his Highness," said the detective. "His spirit seems to have departed. But is he dead to you, his faithful servants?"

The Hindus looked at each other. There was a moment of tense silence, followed by a noise out in the passage. Angry, protesting voices were heard, and then there was a rap at the door.

"A curse on these sahibs!" muttered Mervanji Singh.

"Hush! Let nobody know that I am here!" whispered the detective. And with that he slipped under a curtain that hung close to the foot of the berth.

The door had now opened, and Captain Binney entered the state-room with Dr. Lambrick. The chief steward and a couple of officers followed them, and in the doorway loomed the fierce, threatening faces of the retainers.

"Begone, sahibs!" bade Sikander Jung.

"Have you no respect for the dead?" cried Mervanji Singh.

"I am here for your own good," replied the captain, who was pale and agitated. "I want to meet your wishes, but I have the passengers to consider, and they insist that your master should be buried at sea, which is the usual custom, or else that he must be——"

"The bones of the Illustrious One shall lie at Jazelpur!" vowed the dewan, rattling his sword.

Captain Binney mopped his perspiring brow. He had an unpleasant duty to perform, and he felt that for the present he had better not mention the alternative course—the embalming process—which he judged would be equally repugnant to the Hindus.

"Wait!" he said. "Be patient, and hear me. I have brought with me a sahib doctor, one of great skill, who has offered his services. Let him make an examination, therefore, and if his report is favourable the body of his Highness shall be taken to Calcutta."

Sexton Blake, listening attentively and peering through a tiny hole in the curtain, was pondering a dark suspicion that gripped him with a stronger hold each instant.

"I must be vigilant," he told himself. "If this fellow is the

Russian, and if he suspects what I know to be the truth, I can guess why he is here."

It seemed at first that Captain Binney's proposal would be rejected. There was hesitation and muttering, while the retainers conferred among themselves.

"The doctor sahib may do as he likes, for it can make no difference to us," Mervanji Singh finally said. "By the beard of Mahadera we swear, one and all, that his Highness shall not be buried at sea."

The captain nodded to Dr. Lambrick, who stepped forward. Slowly and carefully he set about his task, touching the rigid form, gazing at it closely, and holding the mirror to the waxen lips. Then he laid bare the rajah's breast, and as he placed his hand on the cold flesh directly over the heart, only one person—the hidden watcher—saw the gleam of a steel instrument that was protruding from his sleeve.

There was the sound of a gasping breath, and with that, as the curtain was thrust aside, Sexton Blake sprang out and seized Dr. Lambrick by both arms.

"Just in time!" he cried. "Just in time to prevent a foul murder! Serge Zouroff, you are my prisoner!"

And, as he spoke, releasing one hand, he tore the false beard and moustache from the Russian's face, and snatched the wig off his head.

The Eighth Chapter.
Caught at Last—The End of Zouroff—
Sikander Jung's Magic.

It was as if a bomb had exploded in the state-room, so staggering was the surprise. As Serge Zouroff recoiled, with a choking imprecation, something dropped from his grasp. White as chalk, he threw a despairing look towards the doorway, and then began to fight in the wild hope of escaping. All joined in the struggle—captain, officers, and Hindus—but twice he shook them off, with the strength of a tiger. Now he was down, now on his feet, and as he continued to fight against overwhelming odds he saw that the game was up, realised that he must suffer the penalty of his crimes. With a last effort he wrenched one hand free, thrust it into his pocket, and raised it quickly to his mouth.

"Stop him!" cried the detective, who had been hurled back by a heavy blow. "Stop him!"

But it was too late. The guilty man swayed, trying to clutch at his heart, and then, with a gasping scream of agony, with foam oozing to his lips, he fell prone with a crash. He writhed for an instant, and lay quite still.

"By heavens, he is dead!" Captain Binney exclaimed, in horror. "He has taken poison!"

"Yes, he has killed himself," declared Sexton Blake, as he picked up something from the floor. "He was afraid of his punishment. Look!" he added, holding out a thin instrument of steel like a fine dagger, that was three or four inches in length. "This was hidden up the assassin's sleeve, and he meant to drive it deep through the heart of the rajah, entirely under the flesh, trusting that it would not be discovered. I was just in time."

"The dog deserved his fate," said Mervanji Singh. "Maker of Magic, we thank you."

"There can be no doubt that he is the right man, I suppose?" asked Mr. Perks.

"Not the slightest," replied the detective. "This is the Russian spy, Serge Zouroff. He is one of the two scoundrels who made various attempts on the life of the rajah."

"It is a mystery to me—I don't understand it!" cried the captain. "Why, by all that's amazing, should the fellow have tried to drive a needle into the heart of a dead man?"

"For an answer to that question," said Sexton Blake, "I must refer you to the servants of his Highness. I hope, under the circumstances, that they will now consent to explain the mystery."

"Does the Maker of Magic think it wise that we should do so?" asked Mervanji Singh.

"It will be both wise and safe," declared the detective. "Heera Beg is a prisoner, with irons on his wrists, and the Russian is dead. There is nothing to fear. Let the rajah come back to life. Bid him rise up and speak to me."

"What tomfoolery is this?" muttered Captain Binney. "I never heard of such nonsense!"

"Let us first behold Heera Beg, that we may believe," said the dewan.

"Wait, and you shall see," replied the detective.

He hurried away, and when he returned five minutes later, followed by the bloodhound, Tinker was with him, and the two were holding between them the manacled form of Heera Beg. He was recognised by the Hindus, who glared at him in fury and triumph, and could hardly be restrained from slaying him on the spot.

"The Maker of Magic has not deceived us, Sikander Jung," said the dewan. "Let his wish be obeyed."

Sikander Jung stepped with alacrity to the bedside, and his first act was to remove the plugs of cotton-wool from the nostrils of the corpse. Then, amid breathless silence, he touched the rajah's forehead, breathed in his face, and poured a few drops of a colourless fluid between his lips. He stood aside and made several passes over the body.

"What rot!" murmured Mr. Perks.

But he did not think so an instant later. His Highness Kumar Beg had perceptibly stirred. His fingers twitched, his legs moved, and with a sigh he slowly opened his eyes.

"Behold," said Mervanji Singh, "the mystery is revealed to you. The life of the Illustrious One having been often attempted, and the sahib protector having deserted us, we were in such terror of the assassins that we gladly listened to the proposal of Sikander Jung, who is very learned and skilled in the ancient and magic arts of India. Therefore, by his own consent, our beloved master was put into a sleep that none can tell from death. He might have been buried in the ground, and yet he would have lived until the spell was broken."

"Well, by all that's wonderful!" gasped Captain Binney. "Did you know this, Mr. Blake?"

"Yes, I guessed it," was the reply.

The Rajah of Jazelpur was now sitting up in bed. He yawned, stretched his arms, as if waking from slumber, and looked consciously at those around him.

"What means this?" he demanded. "Why have you brought me back to life when I am still on the big ship?"

"Your Highness is no longer in peril," replied Mervanji Singh. "Here lies the Russian dog, dead by his own hand, and yonder stands your wicked brother, Heera Beg."

"It is well," the rajah said drowsily. "Let food be brought, slaves. I would eat and drink."

With the capture of Heera Beg and the death of Serge Zouroff, the danger was indeed at an end, as far as the detective was concerned. He and Tinker would have taken up their manual employment again, but Captain Binney would not permit them to do so, and during the rest of the voyage they, and Pedro as well, were honoured and popular guests, with the run of the vessel and the best of everything at their disposal.

When the *Darjeeling* reached Calcutta, where the military escort was waiting, the rajah obstinately refused to part with those to whom he owed so much, and he had his way. The detective and his companions travelled up to Jazelpur with the escort, and they spent a wonderful week in Kumar Beg's palace—a week that was like a magnificent dream. At least, to Sexton Blake and Tinker; though Pedro seemed to enjoy it just as much. Then, gifts of gold and jewels having been pressed upon them, a special train whirled them down to the coast, and they sailed for England, to receive the thanks of the Foreign Office—and more substantial reward as well—for their services to the Empire.

As for Heera Beg, that cunning rogue was tried for his sins and sent to the penal colony on the Andaman Islands; and as long as he remains there—which will be to the end of his life, if he doesn't escape—peace and loyalty will rule in the State of Jazelpur.

MARTIN HEWITT

Arthur Morrison was writing about mean streets when Raymond Chandler was barely out of rompers. Commencing in 1891, he wrote a series of stories dealing with life, and death, in the slums of London. "Naturalistic themes and treatment had occurred previously in English literature," E. F. Bleiler has written, "but Morrison portrayed depths of brutality and squalor that had never before been described." These stories were brought together in 1894 as Tales of Mean Streets, *a book that has remained in print, in various editions, ever since. When presented with the opportunity to create a new detective, though, Morrison shied away from the mean streets he knew first hand, thereby passing up the chance to found the hard-boiled school some thirty years before* Black Mask. *He chose instead to stick close to the pattern set forth by Doyle. His Martin Hewitt, who first appeared in* The Strand *in 1894 only months after Doyle had "killed" Sherlock Holmes, is comfortably middle class and operates in a safer, more sedate world than that of the slums. "Hewitt is obviously based on Sherlock Holmes via the identity of opposites," Bleiler points out. "Whereas Holmes is tall and gaunt, Hewitt is of medium stature and plump; whereas Holmes is egotistical and arrogant, Hewitt is pleasant and unctuously affable; whereas Holmes scorns Scotland Yard, Hewitt is grateful for cooperation."*

Morrison produced enough Hewitt stories, for all of which he was well paid, to make up four collections. Although he was apparently not extremely fond of his private detective, he nonetheless turned out many first rate potboilers about him. And Hewitt is usually ranked very near Holmes in any list of the best fictional detectives of the Victorian era. The stories are narrated by Brett, a young journalist who occupies bachelor chambers on an upper floor of the ancient building near the Strand in which Hewitt has offices.

The Stanway Cameo Mystery
by Arthur Morrison

It is now a fair number of years back since the loss of the famous Stanway Cameo made its sensation, and the only person who had the least interest in keeping the real facts of the case secret has now been dead for some time, leaving neither relatives nor other representatives. Therefore no harm will be done in making the inner history of the case public; on the contrary, it will afford an opportunity of vindicating the professional reputation of Hewitt, who is supposed to have completely failed to make anything of the mystery surrounding the case. At the present time, connoisseurs in ancient objects of art are often heard regretfully to wonder whether the wonderful cameo—so suddenly discovered and so quickly stolen—will ever again be visible to the public eye. Now this question need be asked no longer.

The cameo, as may be remembered from the many descriptions published at the time, was said to be absolutely the finest extant. It was a sardonyx of three strata—one of those rare sardonyx cameos in which it has been possible for the artist to avail himself of three different colours of superimposed stone—the lowest for the ground and the two others for the middle and high relief of the design. In size it was, for a cameo, immense, measuring seven and a half inches by nearly six. In subject it was similar to the renowned Gonzaga Cameo—now the property of the Czar of Russia—a male and a female head with Imperial insignia; but in this case supposed to represent Tiberius Claudius and Messalina. Experts considered it probably to be the work of Athenion, a famous gem-cutter of the first Christian century, whose most notable other work now extant is a smaller cameo, with a mythological subject, preserved in the Vatican.

The Stanway Cameo had been discovered in an obscure Italian village by one of those travelling agents who scour all Europe for valuable antiquities and objects of art. This man had hurried immediately to London with his prize and sold it to Mr. Claridge, of St. James's Street, eminent as a dealer in such objects. Mr. Claridge, recognising the importance and value of the article, lost no opportunity of making its existence known, and very soon the Claudius Cameo, as it was at first usually called, was as famous as any in the world. Many experts in ancient art examined it, and several large bids were made for its purchase. In the end it was bought by the Marquis of Stanway for £5,000 for the purpose of presentation to the British Museum. The Marquis kept the cameo at his town house for a few days, showing it to his friends, and then returned it to Mr. Claridge to be finally and carefully cleaned before passing into the national collection. Two nights after, Mr. Claridge's premises were broken into and the cameo stolen.

Such, in outline, was the generally known history of the Stanway Cameo. The circumstances of the burglary in detail were these: Mr. Claridge had himself been the last to leave the premises at about eight in the evening, at dusk, and had locked the small side door as usual. His assistant, Mr. Cutler, had left an hour and a half earlier. When Mr. Claridge left everything was in order, and the policeman on fixed point duty just opposite, who bade Mr. Claridge good evening as he left, saw nothing suspicious during the rest of his term of duty, nor did his successors at the point throughout the night.

In the morning, however, Mr. Cutler, the assistant, who arrived first, soon after nine o'clock, at once perceived that something unlooked-for had happened. The door, of which he had a key, was still fastened, and had not been touched; but in the room behind the shop Mr. Claridge's private desk had been broken open, and the contents turned out in confusion. The door leading on to the staircase had also been forced. Proceeding up the stairs, Mr. Cutler found another door open, leading from the top landing to a small room—this door had been opened by the simple expedient of unscrewing and taking off the lock, which had been on the inside. In the ceiling of this room was a trap-door, and this was six or eight inches open, the edge resting on the half-wrenched-off bolt, which had been torn away when the trap was levered open from the outside.

Plainly, then, this was the path of the thief or thieves. Entrance had been made through the trap-door, two more doors had been opened, and then the desk had been ransacked. Mr. Cutler afterwards explained that at this time he had no precise idea what had been stolen, and did not know where the cameo had been left on the previous evening. Mr. Claridge had himself undertaken the cleaning and had been engaged on it, the assistant said, when he left.

There was no doubt, however, after Mr. Claridge's arrival at ten o'clock: The cameo was gone. Mr. Claridge, utterly confounded at his loss, explained incoherently, and with curses on his own carelessness, that he had locked the previous article in his desk on relinquishing work on it the previous evening, feeling rather tired and not taking the trouble to carry it as far as the safe in another part of the house.

The police were sent for at once, of course, and every investigation made, Mr. Claridge offering a reward of £ 500 for the recovery of the cameo. The affair was scribbled of at large in the earliest editions of the evening papers, and by noon all the world was aware of the extraordinary theft of the Stanway Cameo, and many people were discussing the probabilities of the case, with very indistinct ideas of what a sardonyx cameo precisely was.

It was in the afternoon of this day that Lord Stanway called on Martin Hewitt. The Marquis was a tall, upstanding man of spare figure and active habits, well known as a member of learned societies and a great patron of art. He hurried into Hewitt's private room as soon as his name had been announced, and, as soon as Hewitt had given him a chair, plunged into business.

"Probably you already guess my business with you, Mr. Hewitt—you have seen the early evening papers? Just so; then I needn't tell you again what you already know. My cameo is gone, and I badly want it back. Of course, the police are hard at work at Claridge's, but I'm not quite satisfied. I have been there myself for two or three hours, and can't see that they know any more about it than I do myself. Then, of course, the police, naturally and properly enough from their point of view, look first to find the criminal—regarding the recovery of the property almost as a secondary consideration. Now, from *my* point of view, the chief consideration is the property. Of course I want the thief caught, if possible, and properly punished; but still more, I want the cameo."

"Certainly it is a considerable loss. Five thousand pounds——"

"Ah, but don't misunderstand me. It isn't the monetary value of the thing that I regret. As a matter of fact, I am indemnified for that already. Claridge has behaved most honourably—more than honourably. Indeed, the first intimation I had of the loss was a cheque from him for £5,000, with a letter assuring me that the restoration to me of the amount I had paid was the least he could do to repair the result of what he called his unpardonable carelessness. Legally, I'm not sure that I could demand anything of him, unless I could prove very flagrant neglect indeed to guard against theft."

"Then I take it, Lord Stanway," Hewitt observed, "that you much prefer the cameo to the money?"

"Certainly. Else I should never have been willing to pay the money for the cameo. It was an enormous price—perhaps much above the market value, even for such a valuable thing; but I was particularly anxious that it should not go out of the country. Our public collections here are not so fortunate as they should be in the possession of the very finest examples of that class of work. In short, I had determined on the cameo, and, fortunately, happen to be able to carry out determinations of that sort without regarding an extra thousand pounds or so as an obstacle. So that, you see, what I want is not the value, but the thing itself. Indeed, I don't think I can possibly keep the money Claridge has sent me—the affair is more his misfortune than his fault. But I shall say nothing about returning it for a little while: it may possibly have the effect of sharpening everybody in the search."

"Just so. Do I understand that you would like me to look into the case independently, on your behalf?"

"Exactly. I want you, if you can, to approach the matter entirely from *my* point of view—your sole object being to find the cameo. Of course, if you happen on the thief as well, so much the better. Perhaps, after all, looking for the one is the same thing as looking for the other?"

"Not always; but usually it is, of course—even if they are not together, they certainly *have* been at one time, and to have one is a very long step toward having the other. Now, to begin with, is anybody suspected?"

"Well, the police are reserved, but I believe the fact is they've nothing to say. Claridge won't admit that he suspects anyone, though he believes that whoever it was must have watched him yesterday evening through the back window of his room, and must have seen him put the cameo away in his desk; because the thief would seem to have gone straight to the place. But I half fancy that, in his inner mind, he is inclined to suspect one of two people. You see, a robbery of this sort is different from others. That cameo would never be stolen, I imagine, with the view of its being sold—it is much too famous a thing; a man might as well walk about offering to sell the Tower of London. There are only a very few people who buy such things, and every one of them knows all about it. No dealer would touch it—he could never even show it, much less sell it, without being called to account. So that it really seems more likely that it has been taken by somebody who wishes to keep it for mere love of the thing—a collector, in fact—who would then have to keep it secretly at home, and never let a soul beside himself see it, living in the consciousness that at his death it must be found and his theft known; unless, indeed, an ordinary vulgar burglar has taken it without knowing its value."

"That isn't likely," Hewitt replied. "An ordinary burglar, ignorant of its value, wouldn't have gone straight to the cameo and have taken it in preference to many other things of more apparent worth, which must be lying near in such a place as Claridge's."

"True—I suppose he wouldn't. Although the police seem to think that the breaking in is clearly the work of a regular criminal—from the jemmy marks, you know, and so on."

"Well, but what of the two people you think Mr. Claridge suspects?"

"Of course, I can't say that he does suspect them—I only fancied from his tone that it might be possible; he himself insists that he can't in justice suspect anybody. One of these men is Hahn, the travelling agent who sold him the cameo. This man's character does not appear to be absolutely irreproachable—no dealer trusts him very far. Of course, Claridge doesn't say what he paid him for the cameo—these dealers are very reticent about their profits, which I believe are as often something like 500 percent as not. But it seems Hahn bargained to have something extra, depending on the amount Claridge could sell the carving for. According to the appointment he should have turned up this morning, but he hasn't been seen, and nobody seems to know exactly where he is."

"Yes; and the other person?"

"Well, I scarcely like mentioning him, because he is certainly a gentleman, and I believe, in the ordinary way, quite incapable of anything in the least degree dishonourable; although, of course, they say a collector has no conscience in the matter of his own particular hobby, and certainly Mr. Woollett is as keen a collector as any man alive. He lives in chambers in the next turning past Claridge's premises—can, in fact, look into Claridge's back windows if he likes. He examined the cameo several times before I bought it, and made several high offers—appeared, in fact, very anxious indeed to get it. After I had bought it, he made, I understand, some rather strong remarks about people like myself 'spoiling the market' by paying extravagant prices, and altogether cut up 'crusty,' as they say, at losing the specimen." Lord Stanway paused for a few seconds, and then went on: "I'm not sure that I ought to mention Mr. Woollett's name for a moment in connection with such a matter—I am personally perfectly certain that he is as incapable of anything like theft as myself. But I am telling you all I know."

"Precisely. I can't know too much in a case like this. It can do no harm if I know all about fifty innocent people, and may save me from the risk of knowing nothing about the thief. Now, let me see: Mr. Woollett's rooms, you say, are near Mr. Claridge's place of business? Is there any means of communication between the roofs?"

"Yes, I am told that it is perfectly possible to get from one place to the other by walking along the leads."

"Very good. Then, unless you can think of any other information that may help me, I think, Lord Stanway, I will go at once and look at the place."

"Do, by all means. I think I'll come back with you. Somehow, I don't like to feel idle in the matter, though I suppose I can't do much. As to more information—I don't think there is any."

"In regard to Mr. Claridge's assistant, now: do you know anything of him?"

"Only that he has always seemed a very civil and decent sort of man. Honest, I should say, or Claridge wouldn't have kept him so many years—there are a good many valuable things about at Claridge's. Besides, the man has keys of the place himself, and even if he were a thief he wouldn't need to go breaking in through the roof."

"So that," said Hewitt, "we have, directly connected with this cameo, besides yourself, these people: Mr. Claridge, the dealer, Mr. Cutler, the assistant in Mr. Claridge's business, Hahn, who sold the article to Claridge, and Mr. Woollett, who made bids for it. These are all?"

"All that I know of. Other gentlemen made bids, I believe, but I don't know them."

"Take these people in their order. Mr. Claridge is out of the question, as a dealer with a reputation to keep up would be, even if he hadn't immediately sent you this £5,000—more than the market value, I understand, of the cameo. The assistant is a reputable man, against whom nothing is known, who would never need to break in, and who must understand his business well enough to know that he could never attempt to sell the missing stone without instant detection. Hahn is a man of shady antecedents, probably clever enough to know as well as anybody how to dispose of such plunder—if it be possible to dispose of it at all; also, Hahn hasn't been to Claridge's to-day, although he had an appointment to take money. Lastly, Mr. Woollett is a gentleman of the most honourable record, but a perfectly rabid collector, who had made every effort to secure the cameo before you bought it; who, moreover, could have seen Mr. Claridge working in his back room, and who has perfectly easy access to Mr. Claridge's roof. If we find it can be none of these, then we must look where circumstances indicate."

There was unwonted excitement at Mr. Claridge's place

when Hewitt and his client arrived. It was a dull old building, and in the windows there was never more show than an odd blue china vase or two, or, mayhap, a few old silver shoe-buckles and a curious small-sword. Nine men out of ten would have passed it without a glance; but the tenth at least would probably know it for a place famous through the world for the number and value of the old and curious objects of art that had passed through it.

On this day two or three loiterers, having heard of the robbery, extracted what gratification they might from staring at nothing between the railings guarding the windows. Within, Mr. Claridge, a brisk, stout, little old man, was talking earnestly to a burly police inspector in uniform, and Mr. Cutler, who had seized the opportunity to attempt amateur detective work on his own account, was grovelling perseveringly about the floor among old porcelain and loose pieces of armour in the futile hope of finding any clue that the thieves might have considerately dropped.

Mr. Claridge came forward eagerly.

"The leather case has been found, I am pleased to be able to tell you, Lord Stanway, since you left."

"Empty, of course?"

"Unfortunately, yes. It had evidently been thrown away by the thief behind a chimney-stack a roof or two away, where the police have found it. But it is a clue, of course."

"Ah, then this gentleman will give me his opinion of it," Lord Stanway said, turning to Hewitt. "This, Mr. Claridge, is Mr. Martin Hewitt, who has been kind enough to come with me here at a moment's notice. With the police on the one hand, and Mr. Hewitt on the other, we shall certainly recover that cameo if it is to be recovered, I think."

Mr. Claridge bowed, and beamed on Hewitt through his spectacles. "I'm very glad Mr. Hewitt has come," he said. "Indeed, I had already decided to give the police till this time tomorrow, and then, if they had found nothing, to call in Mr. Hewitt myself."

Hewitt bowed in his turn, and then asked, "Will you let me see the various breakages? I hope they have not been disturbed."

"Nothing whatever has been disturbed. Do exactly as seems best—I need scarcely say that everything here is perfectly at your disposal. You know all the circumstances, of course?"

"In general, yes. I suppose I am right in the belief that you have no resident housekeeper?"

"No," Claridge replied, "I haven't. I had one housekeeper who sometimes pawned my property in the evening, and then another who used to break my most valuable china, till I could never sleep or take a moment's ease at home for fear my stock was being ruined here. So I gave up resident housekeepers. I felt some confidence in doing it, because of the policeman who is always on duty opposite."

"Can I see the broken desk?"

Mr. Claridge led the way into the room behind the shop. The desk was really a sort of work-table, with a lifting top and a lock. The top had been forced roughly open by some instrument which had been pushed in below it and used as a lever, so that the catch of the lock was torn away. Hewitt examined the damaged parts and the marks of the lever, and then looked out at the back window.

"There are several windows about here," he remarked, "from which it might be possible to see into this room. Do you know any of the people who live behind them?"

"Two or three I know," Mr. Claridge answered, "but there are two windows—the pair almost immediately before us—belonging to a room or office which is to let. Any stranger might get in there and watch."

"Do the roofs above any of those windows communicate in any way with yours?"

"None of those directly opposite. Those at the left do—you may walk all the way along the leads."

"And whose windows are they?"

Mr. Claridge hesitated. "Well," he said, "they're Mr. Woollett's—an excellent customer of mine. But he's a gentleman and—well, I really think it's absurd to suspect him."

"In a case like this," Hewitt answered, "one must disregard nothing but the impossible. Somebody—whether Mr. Woollett himself or another person—could possibly have seen into this room from those windows, and equally possibly could have reached this roof from that one. Therefore, we must not forget Mr. Woollett. Have any of your neighbours been burgled during the night? I mean that strangers anxious to get at your trap-door would probably have to begin by getting into some other house close by, so as to reach your roof."

"No," Mr. Claridge replied; "there has been nothing of that sort. It was the first thing the police ascertained."

Hewitt examined the broken door and then made his way up the stairs, with the others. The unscrewed lock of the door of the top back room required little examination. In the room, below the trap-door, was a dusty table on which stood a chair, and at the other side of the table sat Detective-Inspector Plummer, whom Hewitt knew very well, and who bade him "good day" and then went on with his docket.

"This chair and table were found as they are now, I take it?" Hewitt asked.

"Yes," said Mr. Claridge; "the thieves, I should think, dropped in through the trap-door, after breaking it open, and had to place this chair where it is to be able to climb back."

Hewitt scrambled up through the trap-way and examined it from the top. The door was hung on long external barn-door hinges, and had been forced open in a similar manner to that practised on the desk. A jemmy had been pushed between the frame and the door near the bolt, and the door had been prised open, the bolt being torn away from the screws in the operation.

Presently, Inspector Plummer, having finished his docket, climbed up to the roof after Hewitt, and the two together went to the spot, close under a chimney-stack on the next roof but one, where the case had been found. Plummer produced the case, which he had in his coat-tail pocket, for Hewitt's inspection.

"I don't see anything particular about it; do you?" he said. "It shows us the way they went, though, being found just here."

"Well, yes," Hewitt said; "if we kept on in this direction we should be going towards Mr. Woollett's house, and *his* trap-door, shouldn't we?"

The inspector pursed his lips, smiled, and shrugged his shoulders. "Of course, we haven't waited till now to find that out," he said.

"No, of course. And, as you say, I don't think there is much to be learned from this leather case. It is almost new, and there isn't a mark on it." And Hewitt handed it back to the inspector.

"Well," said Plummer, as he returned the case to his pocket, "what's your opinion?"

"It's rather an awkward case."

"Yes, it is. Between ourselves, I don't mind telling you, I'm having a sharp lookout kept over there"—Plummer jerked his head in the direction of Mr. Woollett's chambers—"because the robbery's an unusual one. There's only two possible motives—the sale of the cameo or the keeping of it. The sale's out of the question, as you know—the thing's only saleable to those who would collar the thief at once, and who wouldn't have the thing in their places now for anything. So that it must be taken to keep—and that's a thing nobody but the maddest of collectors would do—just such persons as——" and the inspector nodded again towards Mr. Woollett's quarters. "Take that with the other circumstances," he added, "and I think you'll agree it's worth while looking a little farther that way. Of course, some of the work—taking off the lock and so on—looks rather like a regular burglar, but it's just possible that anyone badly wanting the cameo would hire a man who was up to the work."

"Yes, it's possible."

"Do you know anything of Hahn, the agent?" Plummer asked, a moment later.

"No, I don't. Have you found him yet?"

"I haven't yet, but I'm after him. I've found he was at Charing Cross a day or two ago, booking a ticket for the Continent. That and his failing to turn up to-day seem to make it worth while not to miss *him* if we can help it. He isn't the sort of man that lets a chance of drawing a bit of money go for nothing."

They returned to the room. "Well," said Lord Stanway, "what's the result of the consultation? We've been waiting here very patiently while you two clever men have been discussing the matter on the roof."

On the wall just beneath the trap-door a very dusty old tall hat hung on a peg. This Hewitt took down and examined very closely, smearing his fingers with the dust from the inside lining. "Is this one of your valuable and crusted old antiques?" he asked, with a smile, of Mr. Claridge.

"That's only an old hat that I used to keep here for use in bad weather," Mr. Claridge said, with some surprise at the question. "I haven't touched it for a year or more."

"Oh, then it couldn't have been left here by your last night's visitor," Hewitt replied, carelessly replacing it on the hook. "You left here at eight last night, I think?"

"Eight exactly—or within a minute or two."

"Just so. I think I'll look at the room on the opposite side of the landing, if you'll let me."

"Certainly, if you'd like to," Claridge replied; "but they haven't been there—it is exactly as it was left. Only a lumber-room, you see," he concluded, flinging the door open.

A number of partly broken-up packing-cases littered about this room, with much other rubbish. Hewitt took the lid of one of the newest-looking packing-cases, and glanced at the address label. Then he turned to a rusty old iron box that stood against a wall. "I should like to see behind this," he said, tugging at it with his hands. "It is heavy and dirty. Is there a small crowbar about the house, or some similar lever?"

Mr. Claridge shook his head. "Haven't such a thing in the place," he said.

"Never mind," Hewitt replied, "another time will do to shift that old box, and perhaps after all there's little reason for moving it. I will just walk round to the police-station, I think, and speak to the constables who were on duty opposite during the night. I think, Lord Stanway, I have seen all that is necessary here."

"I suppose," asked Mr. Claridge, "it is too soon yet to ask if you have formed any theory in the matter?"

"Well—yes, it is," Hewitt answered. "But perhaps I may be able to surprise you in an hour or two; but that I don't promise. By-the-bye," he added, suddenly, "I suppose you're sure the trap-door was bolted last night?"

"Certainly," Mr. Claridge answered, smiling. "Else how could the bolt have been broken? As a matter of fact, I believe the trap hasn't been opened for months. Mr. Cutler, do you remember when the trap-door was last opened?"

Mr. Cutler shook his head. "Certainly not for six months," he said.

"Ah, very well—it's not very important," Hewitt replied.

As they reached the front shop, a fiery faced old gentleman bounced in at the street door, stumbling over an umbrella that stood in a dark corner, and kicking it three yards away.

"What the deuce do you mean," he roared at Mr. Claridge, "by sending these police people smelling about my rooms and asking questions of my servants? What do you mean, sir, by treating me as a thief? Can't a gentleman come into this place to look at an article without being suspected of stealing it, when it disappears through your wretched carelessness? I'll ask my solicitor, sir, if there isn't a remedy for this sort of thing. And if I catch another of your spy fellows on my staircase, or crawling about my roof, I'll—I'll shoot him!"

"Really, Mr. Woollett," began Mr. Claridge, somewhat abashed, but the angry old man would hear nothing.

"Don't talk to me, sir—you shall talk to my solicitor. And am I to understand, my lord"—turning to Lord Stanway—"that these things are being done with your approval?"

"Whatever is being done," Lord Stanway answered, "is being done by the police on their own responsibility, and entirely without prompting, I believe, by Mr. Claridge—certainly without a suggestion of any sort from myself. I think that the personal opinion of Mr. Claridge—certainly my own—is that anything like a suspicion of your position in this wretched matter is ridiculous. And if you will only consider the matter calmly——"

"Consider it calmly? Imagine yourself considering such a thing calmly, Lord Stanway. I *won't* consider it calmly. I'll—I'll—I won't have it. And if I find another man on my roof, I'll pitch him off." And Mr. Woollett bounced into the street again.

"Mr. Woollett is annoyed," Hewitt observed, with a smile. "I'm afraid Plummer has a clumsy assistant somewhere."

Mr. Claridge said nothing, but looked rather glum. For Mr. Woollett was a most excellent customer.

Lord Stanway and Hewitt walked slowly down the street, Hewitt staring at the pavement in profound thought. Once or twice Lord Stanway glanced at his face, but refrained from disturbing him. Presently, however, he observed, "You seem at least, Mr. Hewitt, to have noticed something that has set you thinking. Does it look like a clue?"

Hewitt came out of his cogitation at once. "A clue?" he

said; "the case bristles with clues. The extraordinary thing to me is that Plummer, usually a smart man, doesn't seem to have seen one of them. He must be out of sorts, I'm afraid. But the case is decidedly a very remarkable one."

"Remarkable, in what particular way?"

"In regard to motive. Now it would seem, as Plummer was saying to me just now on the roof, that there were only two possible motives for such a robbery. Either the man who took all this trouble and risk to break into Claridge's place must have desired to sell the cameo at a good price, or he must have desired to keep it for himself, being a lover of such things. But neither of these has been the actual motive."

"Perhaps he thinks he can extort a good sum from me by way of ransom?"

"No, it isn't that. Nor is it jealousy, nor spite, nor anything of that kind. I know the motive, I *think*—but I wish we could get hold of Hahn. I will shut myself up alone and turn it over in my mind for half an hour presently."

"Meanwhile, what I want to know is, apart from all your professional subtleties—which I confess I can't understand—can you get back the cameo?"

"That," said Hewitt, stopping at the corner of the street, "I am rather afraid I cannot—nor anybody else. But I am pretty sure I know the thief."

"Then surely that will lead you to the cameo?"

"It *may*, of course; but then it is just possible that by this evening you may not want to have it back after all."

Lord Stanway stared in amazement.

"Not want to have it back!" he exclaimed. "Why, of course, I shall want to have it back. I don't understand you in the least; you talk in conundrums. Who is the thief you speak of?"

"I think, Lord Stanway," Hewitt said, "that perhaps I had better not say until I have quite finished my inquiries, in case of mistakes. The case is quite an extraordinary one, and of quite a different character from what one would at first naturally imagine, and I must be very careful to guard against the possibility of error. I have very little fear of a mistake, however, and I hope I may wait on you in a few hours at Piccadilly with news. I have only to see the police-men."

"Certainly, come whenever you please. But why see the policemen? They have already most positively stated that they saw nothing whatever suspicious in the house or near it."

"I shall not ask them anything at all about the house," Hewitt responded. "I shall just have a little chat with them—about the weather." And with a smiling bow, he turned away, while Lord Stanway stood and gazed after him, with an expression that implied a suspicion that his special detective was making a fool of him.

In rather more than an hour Hewitt was back in Mr. Claridge's shop. "Mr. Claridge," he said, "I think I must ask you one or two questions in private. May I see you in your own room?"

They went there at once, and Hewitt, pulling a chair before the window, sat down with his back to the light. The dealer shut the door, and sat opposite him, with the light full in his face.

"Mr. Claridge," Hewitt proceeded, slowly, *"when did you first find that Lord Stanway's cameo was a forgery?"*

Claridge literally bounced in his chair. His face paled, but he managed to stammer, sharply, "What—what—what d'you mean? Forgery? Do you mean to say I sell forgeries? Forgery? It wasn't a forgery!"

"Then," continued Hewitt, in the same deliberate tone, watching the other's face the while, "if it wasn't a forgery, *why did you destroy it and burst your trap-door and desk to imitate a burglary?"*

The sweat stood thick on the dealer's face, and he gasped. But he struggled hard to keep his faculties together, and ejaculated, hoarsely: "Destroy it? What—what—I didn't—didn't destroy it!"

"Threw it into the river, then—don't prevaricate about details."

"No—no—it's a lie. Who says that? Go away. You're insulting me!" Claridge almost screamed.

"Come, come, Mr. Claridge," Hewitt said, more placably, for he had gained his point; "don't distress yourself, and don't attempt to deceive me—you can't, I assure you. I know everything you did before you left here last night—everything."

Claridge's face worked painfully. Once or twice he appeared to be on the point of returning an indignant reply, but hesitated, and finally broke down altogether.

"Don't expose me, Mr. Hewitt," he pleaded; "I beg you won't expose me. I haven't harmed a soul but myself. I've paid Lord Stanway every penny back, and I never knew the thing was a forgery till I began to clean it. I'm an old man, Mr. Hewitt, and my professional reputation has been spotless till now. I beg you won't expose me."

Hewitt's voice softened. "Don't make an unnecessary trouble of it," he said. "I see a decanter on your sideboard—let me give you a little brandy and water. Come, there's nothing criminal, I believe, in a man's breaking open his own desk, or his own trap-door, for that matter. Of course, I'm acting for Lord Stanway in this affair, and I must, in duty, report to him without reserve. But Lord Stanway is a gentleman, and I'll undertake he'll do nothing inconsiderate of your feelings, if you're disposed to be frank. Let us talk the affair over—tell me about it."

"It was that swindler Hahn who deceived me in the beginning," Claridge said. "I have never made a mistake with a cameo before, and I never thought so close an imitation was possible. I examined it most carefully, and was perfectly satisfied, and many experts examined it afterwards, and were all equally deceived. I felt as sure as I possibly could feel that I had bought one of the finest, if not actually the finest cameo known to exist. It was not until after it had come back from Lord Stanway's, and I was cleaning it, the evening before last, that in course of my work it became apparent that the thing was nothing but a consummately clever forgery. It was made of three layers of moulded glass, nothing more or less. But the glass was treated in a way I had never before known of, and the surface had been cunningly worked on till it defied any ordinary examination. Some of the glass imitation cameos made in the latter part of the last century, I may tell you, are regarded as marvellous pieces of work, and, indeed, command very fair prices, but this was something quite beyond any of those.

"I was amazed and horrified. I put the thing away and went home. All that night I lay awake in a state of distraction, quite unable to decide what to do. To let the cameo go out of my possession was impossible. Sooner or later the forgery would be discovered, and my reputation—the highest in these matters in this country, I may safely claim, and the growth of nearly fifty years of honest application and good judgment—this reputation would be gone for ever. But without considering this, there was the fact that I had taken £5,-000 of Lord Stanway's money for a mere piece of glass, and that money I must, in mere common honesty as well as for my own sake, return. But how? The name of the Stanway Cameo had become a household word, and to confess that the whole thing was a sham would ruin my reputation and destroy all confidence—past, present, and future—in me and in my transactions. Either way spelled ruin. Even if I confided in Lord Stanway privately, returned his money and destroyed the cameo, what then? The sudden disappearance of an article so famous would excite remark at once. It had been presented to the British Museum, and if it never appeared in that collection, and no news were to be got of it, people would guess at the truth at once. To make it known that I myself had been deceived would have availed nothing. It is my business *not* to be deceived; and to have it known that my most expensive specimens might be forgeries would equally mean ruin, whether I sold them cunningly as a rogue or ignorantly as a fool. Indeed, my pride, my reputation as a connoisseur is a thing near to my heart, and it would be an unspeakable humiliation to me to have it known that I had been imposed on by such a forgery. What could I do? Every expedient seemed useless, but one—the one I adopted. It was not straightforward, I admit; but, oh! Mr. Hewitt, consider the temptation—and remember that it couldn't do a soul any harm. No matter who might be suspected, I know there could not possibly be evidence to make them suffer. All the next day—yesterday—I was anxiously worrying out the thing in my mind and carefully devising the—the trick, I'm afraid you'll call it—that you by some extraordinary means have seen through. It seemed the only thing—what else was there? More I needn't tell you—you know it. I have only now to beg that you will use your best influence with Lord Stanway to save me from public derision and exposure. I will do anything—pay anything—anything but exposure, at my age, and with my position."

"Well, you see," Hewitt replied, thoughtfully, "I've no

doubt Lord Stanway will show you every consideration, and certainly I will do what I can to save you, in the circumstances; though you must remember that you *have* done some harm—you have caused suspicions to rest on at least one honest man. But as to reputation—I've a professional reputation of my own. If I help to conceal your professional failure, I shall appear to have failed in *my* part of the business."

"But the cases are different, Mr. Hewitt—consider. You are not expected—it would be impossible—to succeed invariably; and there are only two or three who know you have looked into the case. Then your other conspicuous successes———"

"Well, well—we shall see. One thing I don't know, though—whether you climbed out of a window to break open the trap-door, or whether you got up through the trap-door itself and pulled the bolt with a string through the jamb, so as to bolt it after you."

"There was no available window—I used the string, as you say. My poor little cunning must seem very transparent to you, I fear. I spent hours of thought over the question of the trap-door—how to break it open so as to leave a genuine appearance, and especially how to bolt it inside after I had reached the roof. I thought I had succeeded beyond the possibility of suspicion; how you penetrated the device surpasses my comprehension. How, to begin with, could you possibly know that the cameo was a forgery? Did you ever see it?"

"Never. And if I had seen it, I fear I should never have been able to express an opinion on it; I'm not a connoisseur. As a matter of fact, I *didn't* know that the thing was a forgery in the first place; what I knew in the first place was that it was *you* who had broken into the house. It was from that that I arrived at the conclusion—after a certain amount of thought—that the cameo must have been forged. Gain was out of the question—you, beyond all men, could never sell the Stanway Cameo again, and, besides, you had paid back Lord Stanway's money. I knew enough of your reputation to know that you would never incur the scandal of a great theft at your place for the sake of getting the cameo for yourself, when you might have kept it in the beginning, with no trouble and mystery. Consequently, I had to look for another motive, and at first another motive seemed an impossibility. Why should you wish to take all this trouble to lose £5,000? You had nothing to gain; perhaps you had something to save—your professional reputation, for instance. Looking at it so, it was plain that you were *suppressing* the cameo—burking it; since, once taken as you had taken it, it could never come to light again. That suggested the solution of the mystery at once—you had discovered, after the sale, that the cameo was not genuine."

"Yes, yes—I see; but you say you began with the knowledge that I broke into the place myself. How did you know that? I cannot imagine a trace——"

"My dear sir, you left traces everywhere. In the first place, it struck me as curious, before I came here, that you had sent off that cheque for £5,000 to Lord Stanway an hour or so after the robbery was discovered—it looked so much as though you were sure of the cameo never coming back, and were in a hurry to avert suspicion. Of course, I understood that, so far as I then knew the case, you were the most unlikely person in the world, and that your eagerness to repay Lord Stanway might be the most creditable thing possible. But the point was worth remembering, and I remembered it.

"When I came here I saw suspicious indications in many directions, but the conclusive piece of evidence was that old hat hanging below the trap-door."

"But I never touched it, I assure you, Mr. Hewitt, I never touched the hat—haven't touched it for months——"

"Of course. If you *had* touched it, I might never have got the clue. But we'll deal with the hat presently; that wasn't what struck me at first. The trap-door first took my attention. Consider, now: here was a trap-door, most insecurely hung on *external* hinges; the burglar had a screw-driver, for he took off the door-lock below with it. Why, then, didn't he take this trap off by the hinges, instead of making a noise and taking longer time and trouble to burst the bolt from its fastenings? And why, if he were a stranger, was he able to plant his jemmy from the outside just exactly opposite the interior bolt? There was only one mark on the frame, and that precisely in the proper place.

"After that, I saw the leather case. It had not been thrown away, or some corner would have shown signs of the fall. It had been put down carefully where it was found. These things, however, were of small importance compared with the hat. The hat, as you know, was exceedingly thick with dust—the accumulation of months. But, on the top side, presented toward the trap-door, were a score or so of *rain-drop marks*. That was all. They were new marks, for there was no dust over them; they had merely had time to dry and cake the dust they had fallen on. *Now, there had been no rain since a sharp shower just after seven o'clock last night.* At that time you, by your own statement, were in the place. You left at eight, and the rain was all over at ten minutes or a quarter-past seven. The trap-door, you also told me, had not been opened for months. The thing was plain. You, or somebody who was here when you were, had opened that trap-door during, or just before, that shower. I said little then, but went, as soon as I had left, to the police-station. There I made perfectly certain that there had been no rain during the night by questioning the policemen who were on duty outside all the time. There had been none. I knew everything.

"The only other evidence there was pointed with all the rest. There were no rain-marks on the leather case; it had been put on the roof as an after-thought when there was no rain. A very poor after-thought, let me tell you, for no thief would throw away a useful case that concealed his booty and protected it from breakage, and throw it away just so as to leave a clue to what direction he had gone in. I also saw, in the lumber-room, a number of packing-cases—one with a label dated two days back—which had been opened with an iron lever; and yet, when I made an excuse to ask for it, you said there was no such thing in the place. Inference: you didn't want me to compare it with the marks on the desks and doors. That is all, I think."

Mr. Claridge looked dolorously down at the floor. "I'm afraid," he said, "that I took an unsuitable *rôle* when I undertook to rely on my wits to deceive men like you. I thought there wasn't a single vulnerable spot in my defence, but you walk calmly through it at the first attempt. Why did I never think of those raindrops?"

"Come," said Hewitt, with a smile, "that sounds unrepentant. I am going, now, to Lord Stanway's. If I were you, I think I should apologize to Mr. Woollett in some way."

Lord Stanway, who, in the hour or two of reflection left

him after parting with Hewitt, had come to the belief that he
had employed a man whose mind was not always in order,
received Hewitt's story with natural astonishment. For some
time he was in doubt as to whether he would be doing right
in acquiescing in anything but a straightforward public statement of the facts connected with the disappearance of the
cameo, but in the end was persuaded to let the affair drop, on
receiving an assurance from Mr. Woollett that he unre-
servedly accepted the apology offered him by Mr. Claridge.

As for the latter, he was at least sufficiently punished in
loss of money and personal humiliation for his escapade. But
the bitterest and last blow he sustained when the unblushing
Hahn walked smilingly into his office two days later to demand the extra payment agreed on in consideration of the
sale. He had been called suddenly away, he explained, on the
day he should have come, and hoped his missing the appointment had occasioned no inconvenience. As to the robbery of
the cameo, of course he was very sorry, but "pishness was
pishness," and he would be glad of a cheque for the sum
agreed on. And the unhappy Claridge was obliged to pay it,
knowing that the man had swindled him, but unable to open
his mouth to say so.

The reward remained on offer for a long time—indeed, it
was never publicly withdrawn, I believe, even at the time of
Claridge's death. And several intelligent newspapers enlarged
upon the fact that an ordinary burglar had completely baffled
and defeated the boasted acumen of Mr. Martin Hewitt, the
well-known private detective.

COLONEL CLAY

That standard library reference volume, British Authors of the Ninteenth Century *devotes over a page of fine print to the many works and short life of Grant Allen (1848–1899), but there is no mention of Colonel Clay nor of the book,* An African Millionaire, *that collected together the twelve episodes making up his illustrious and larcenous career. That wouldn't have ruffled Allen, since he considered himself a fallen author of scientific works, one for whom fiction of any kind represented the "downward path." Like Conan Doyle, his friend and neighbor in his last years, Grant Allen misjudged what constituted his best work. He is remembered today almost solely for his detective stories, and especially for those about the audacious Colonel Clay. In the years since* British Authors *first appeared in 1936, a growing number of critics and readers have been discovering Allen's crime stories. Ellery Queen was one of the early champions, singling out the colonel as "the first great rogue of mystery fiction, preceding Raffles by two years." The initial two exploits of Clay were included in Hugh Greene's* Cosmopolitan Crimes *in 1971 and, in 1980, Dover reprinted* An African Millionaire.

Grant Allen was a transplanted Canadian. He had taught at a short-lived college for black students in Jamaica before settling in England, his health none too good, and concentrating on earning his living as a writer. When he discovered that his first attempts at fiction sold where his last several dozen scientific articles hadn't, he increased, reluctantly, his production of fiction. With him it was always a business, a way of earning money. Allen wrote all types of novels and short sto-

117

ries, turning out mysteries, science fiction, and more serious stuff he felt carried a social message.

In 1896, he began a series of stories for The Strand, the same magazine that had run the first Sherlock Holmes and Martin Hewitt short stories. There were twelve episodes grouped under the umbrella title of An African Millionaire and dealing with the dozen incredible schemes of the gifted Colonel Clay to fleece, steal, and otherwise coax various sorts of worldly goods away from the fabulously wealthy Sir Charles Vandrift, the recurrent mark who gives his name to the series. A master of disguise, a genius at strategy, and an expert in psychology, the colonel is able to outwit his chosen victim over and over, basing his cons on the ancient theory, more crudely put by W. C. Fields, that you can't cheat an honest man. Each of the stories is narrated by Seymour Wentworth, brother-in-law and secretary to the South African millionaire. He, too, is always hoodwinked by Colonel Clay. In this set of stories, Grant Allen achieved just the right mixture of social satire and detective plotting. Our episode comes midway in the series, at a point where Sir Charles and Wentworth are quite wary, and it also gives an interesting picture of the life of a private detective of the period.

The Episode of the Arrest of the Colonel
by Grant Allen

How much precisely Charles dropped over the slump in Cloetedorps I never quite knew. But the incident left him dejected, limp, and dispirited.

"Hang it all, Sey," he said to me in the smoking-room, a few evenings later. "This Colonel Clay is enough to vex the patience of Job—and Job had large losses, too, if I recollect aright, from the Chaldeans and other big operators of the period."

"Three thousand camels," I murmured, recalling my dear

mother's lessons; "all at one fell swoop; not to mention five hundred yoke of oxen, carried off by the Sabeans, then a leading firm of speculative cattle-dealers!"

"Ah, well," Charles meditated aloud, shaking the ash from his cheroot into a Japanese tray—fine antique bronze-work. "There were big transactions in live-stock even then! Still, Job or no Job, the man is too much for me."

"The difficulty is," I assented, "you never know where to have him."

"Yes," Charles mused; "if he were always the same, like Horniman's tea or a good brand of whisky, it would be easier, of course; you'd stand some chance of spotting him. But when a man turns up smiling every time in a different disguise, which fits him like a skin, and always apparently with the best credentials, why, hang it all, Sey, there's no wrestling with him anyhow."

"Who could have come to us, for example, better vouched," I acquiesced, "than the Honourable David?"

"Exactly so," Charles murmured. "I invited him myself, for my own advantage. And he arrived with all the prestige of the Glen-Ellachie connection."

"Or the Professor?" I went on. "Introduced to us by the leading mineralogist of England."

I had touched a sore point. Charles winced and remained silent.

"Then, women again," he resumed, after a painful pause. "I must meet in society many charming women. I can't everywhere and always be on my guard against every dear soul of them. Yet the moment I relax my attention for one day— or even when I don't relax it—I am bamboozled and led a dance by that arch Mme. Picardet, or that transparently simple little minx, Mrs. Granton. She's the cleverest girl I ever met in my life, that hussy, whatever we're to call her. She's a different person each time; and each time, hang it all, I lose my heart afresh to that different person."

I glanced round to make sure Amelia was well out of earshot.

"No, Sey," my respected connection went on, after another long pause, sipping his coffee pensively, "I feel I must be aided in this superhuman task by a professional unraveller of cunning disguises. I shall go to Marvillier's to-morrow—fortunate man, Marvillier—and ask him to supply me with a really good 'tec, who will stop in the house and keep an eye upon every living soul that comes near me. He shall scan each nose, each eye, each wig, each whisker. He shall be my watchful half, my unsleeping self; it shall be his business to suspect all living men, all breathing women. The Archbishop of Canterbury shall not escape for a moment his watchful regard; he will take care that royal princesses don't collar the spoons or walk off with the jewel-cases. He must see possible Colonel Clays in the guard of every train and the parson of every parish; he must detect the off-chance of a Mme. Picardet in every young girl that takes tea with Amelia, every fat old lady that comes to call upon Isabel. Yes, I have made my mind up. I shall go to-morrow and secure such a man at once at Marvillier's."

"If you please, Sir Charles," Césarine interposed, pushing her head through the portière, "her ladyship says, will you and Mr. Wentworth remember that she goes out with you both this evening to Lady Carisbrooke's?"

"Bless my soul," Charles cried, "so she does! And it's now past ten! The carriage will be at the door for us in another five minutes!"

Next morning, accordingly, Charles drove round to Marvillier's. The famous detective listened to his story with glistening eyes; then he rubbed his hands and purred. "Colonel Clay!" he said; "Colonel Clay! That's a very tough customer! The police of Europe are on the look-out for Colonel Clay. He is wanted in London, in Paris, in Berlin. It is *le Colonel Caoutchouc* here, *le Colonel Caoutchouc* there; till one begins to ask, at last *is* there *any* Colonel Caoutchouc, or is it a convenient class name invented by the Force to cover a gang of undiscovered sharpers? However, Sir Charles, we will do our best. I will set on the track without delay the best and cleverest detective in England."

"The very man I want," Charles said. "What name, Marvillier?"

The principal smiled. "Whatever name you like," he said. "He isn't particular. Medhurst he's called at home. *We* call him Joe. I'll send him round to your house this afternoon for certain."

"Oh no," Charles said promptly, "you won't; or Colonel

Clay himself will come instead of him. I've been sold too often. No casual strangers! I'll wait here and see him."

"But he isn't in," Marvillier objected.

Charles was firm as a rock. "Then send and fetch him."

In half an hour, sure enough, the detective arrived. He was an odd-looking small man, with hair cut short and standing straight up all over his head, like a Parisian waiter. He had quick, sharp eyes, very much like a ferret's; his nose was depressed, his lips thin and bloodless. A scar marked his left cheek—made by a sword-cut, he said, when engaged one day in arresting a desperate French smuggler, disguised as an officer of Chasseurs d'Afrique. His mien was resolute. Altogether, a quainter or 'cuter little man it has never yet been my lot to set eyes on. He walked in with a brisk step, eyed Charles up and down, and then, without much formality, asked for what he was wanted.

"This is Sir Charles Vandrift, the great diamond king," Marvillier said, introducing us.

"So I see," the man answered.

"Then you know me?" Charles asked.

"I wouldn't be worth much," the detective replied, "if I didn't know everybody. And *you're* easy enough to know; why, every boy in the street knows you."

"Plain spoken!" Charles remarked.

"As you like it, sir," the man answered in a respectful tone. "I endeavour to suit my dress and behaviour on every occasion to the taste of my employers."

"Your name?" Charles asked, smiling.

"Joseph Medhurst, at your service. What sort of work? Stolen diamonds? Illicit diamond-buying?"

"No," Charles answered, fixing him with his eye. "Quite another kind of job. You've heard of Colonel Clay?"

Medhurst nodded. "Why, certainly," he said; and, for the first time, I detected a lingering trace of American accent. "It's my business to know about him."

"Well, I want you to catch him," Charles went on.

Medhurst drew a long breath. "Isn't that rather a large order?" he murmured, surprised.

Charles explained to him exactly the sort of services he required. Medhurst promised to comply. "If the man comes near you, I'll spot him," he said, after a moment's pause. "I can promise you that much. I'll pierce any disguise. I should know in a minute whether he's got up or not. I'm death on wigs, false moustaches, artificial complexions. I'll engage to bring the rogue to book if I see him. You may set your mind at rest, that, while *I'm* about you, Colonel Clay can do nothing without my instantly spotting him."

"He'll do it," Marvillier put in. "He'll do it, if he says it. He's my very best hand. Never knew any man like him for unravelling and unmasking the cleverest disguises."

"Then he'll suit me," Charles answered, "for *I* never knew any man like Colonel Clay for assuming and maintaining them."

It was arranged accordingly that Medhurst should take up his residence in the house for the present, and should be described to the servants as assistant secretary. He came that very day, with a marvellously small portmanteau. But from the moment he arrived, we noticed that Césarine took a violent dislike to him.

Medhurst was a most efficient detective. Charles and I told him all we knew about the various shapes in which Colonel Clay had "materialised," and he gave us in turn many valuable criticisms and suggestions. Why, when we began to suspect the Honourable David Granton, had we not, as if by accident, tried to knock his red wig off? Why, when the Reverend Richard Peploe Brabazon first discussed the question of the paste diamonds, had we not looked to see if any of Amelia's unique gems were missing? Why, when Professor Schleiermacher made his bow to assembled science at Lancaster Gate, had we not strictly inquired how far he was personally known beforehand to Sir Adolphus Cordery and the other mineralogists? He supplied us also with several good hints about false hair and make-up; such as that Schleiermacher was probably much shorter than he looked, but by imitating a stoop with padding at his back he had produced the illusion of a tall bent man, though in reality no bigger than the little curate or the Graf von Lebenstein. High heels did the rest; while the scientific keenness we noted in his face was doubtless brought about by a trifle of wax at the end of the nose, giving a peculiar tilt that is extremely effective. In short, I must frankly admit, Medhurst made us feel ashamed of ourselves. Sharp as Charles is, we realised at once he was nowhere in observation beside the trained and experienced senses of this professional detective.

The worst of it all was, while Medhurst was with us, by some curious fatality, Colonel Clay stopped away from us. Now and again, to be sure, we ran up against somebody whom Medhurst suspected; but after a short investigation (conducted, I may say, with admirable cleverness), the spy always showed us the doubtful person was really some innocent and well-known character, whose antecedents and surroundings he elucidated most wonderfully. He was a perfect marvel, too, in his faculty of suspicion. He suspected everybody. If an old friend dropped in to talk business with Charles, we found out afterwards that Medhurst had lain concealed all the time behind the curtain, and had taken short-hand notes of the whole conversation, as well as snapshot photographs of the supposed sharper, by means of a kodak. If a fat old lady came to call upon Amelia, Medhurst was sure to be lurking under the ottoman in the drawing-room, and carefully observing, with all his eyes, whether or not she was really Mme. Picardet, padded. When Lady Tresco brought her four plain daughters to an "At Home" one night, Medhurst, in evening dress, disguised as a waiter, followed them each round the room with obtrusive ices, to satisfy himself just how much of their complexion was real, and how much was patent rouge and Bloom of Ninon. He doubted whether Simpson, Sir Charles's valet, was not Colonel Clay in plain clothes; and he had half an idea that Césarine herself was our saucy White Heather in an alternative avatar. We pointed out to him in vain that Simpson had often been present in the very same room with David Granton, and that Césarine had dressed Mrs. Brabazon's hair at Lucerne: this partially satisfied him, but only partially. He remarked that Simpson might double both parts with somebody else unknown; and that as for Césarine, she might well have a twin sister who took her place when she was Mme. Picardet.

Still, in spite of all his care—or because of all his care—Colonel Clay stopped away for whole weeks together. An explanation occurred to us. Was it possible he knew we were guarded and watched? Was he afraid of measuring swords with this trained detective?

If so, how had he found it out? I had an inkling, myself—but, under all the circumstances, I did not mention it to
Charles. It was clear that Césarine intensely disliked this new
addition to the Vandrift household. She would not stop in the
room where the detective was, or show him common politeness. She spoke of him always as "that odious man, Medhurst." Could she have guessed, what none of the other
servants knew, that the man was a spy in search of the
Colonel? I was inclined to believe it. And then it dawned
upon me that Césarine had known all about the diamonds
and their story; that it was Césarine who took us to see
Schloss Lebenstein; that it was Césarine who posted the letter
to Lord Craig-Ellachie! If Césarine was in league with Colonel
Clay, as I was half inclined to surmise, what more natural
than her obvious dislike to the detective who was there to
catch her principal? What more simple for her than to warn
her fellow-conspirator of the danger that awaited him if he
approached this man Medhurst?

However, I was too much frightened by the episode of the
cheque to say anything of my nascent suspicions to Charles. I
waited rather to see how events would shape themselves.

After a while Medhurst's vigilance grew positively annoying. More than once he came to Charles with reports and
short-hand notes distinctly distasteful to my excellent brother-
in-law. "The fellow is getting to know too much about us,"
Charles said to me one day. "Why, Sey, he spies out everything. Would you believe it, when I had that confidential interview with Brookfield the other day, about the new issue of
Golcondas, the man was under the easy-chair, though I
searched the room beforehand to make sure he wasn't there;
and he came to me afterwards with full notes of the conversation, to assure me he thought Brookfield—whom I've
known for ten years—was too tall by half an inch to be one
of Colonel Clay's impersonations."

"Oh, but, Sir Charles," Medhurst cried, emerging suddenly
from the bookcase, "you must never look upon *any one* as
above suspicion merely because you've known him for ten
years or thereabouts. Colonel Clay may have approached you
at various times under many disguises. He may have built up
this thing gradually. Besides, as to my knowing too much,
why, of course, a detective always learns many things about

his employer's family which he is not supposed to know; but professional honour and professional etiquette, as with doctors and lawyers, compel him to lock them up as absolute secrets in his own bosom. You need never be afraid I will divulge one jot of them. If I did, my occupation would be gone, and my reputation shattered."

Charles looked at him, appalled. "Do you dare to say," he burst out, "you've been listening to my talk with my brother-in-law and secretary?"

"Why, of course," Medhurst answered. "It's my business to listen, and to suspect everybody. If you push me to say so, how do I know Colonel Clay is not—Mr. Wentworth?"

Charles withered him with a look. "In future, Medhurst," he said, "you must never conceal yourself in a room where I am without my leave and knowledge."

Medhurst bowed politely. "Oh, as you will, Sir Charles," he answered; "that's *quite* at your own wish. Though how can I act as an efficient detective, any way, if you insist upon tying my hands like that, beforehand?"

Again I detected a faint American flavour.

After that rebuff, however, Medhurst seemed put upon his mettle. He redoubled his vigilance in every direction. "It's not my fault," he said plaintively, one day, "if my reputation's so good that, while I'm near you, this rogue won't approach you. If I can't *catch* him, at least I keep him away from coming near you!"

A few days later, however, he brought Charles some photographs. These he produced with evident pride. The first he showed us was a vignette of a little parson. "Who's that, then?" he inquired, much pleased.

We gazed at it, open-eyed. One word rose to our lips simultaneously: "Brabazon!"

"And how's this for high?" he asked again, producing another—the photograph of a gay young dog in a Tyrolese costume.

We murmured, "Von Lebenstein!"

"*And* this?" he continued, showing us the portrait of a lady with a most fetching squint.

We answered with one voice, "Little Mrs. Granton!"

Medhurst was naturally proud of this excellent exploit. He replaced them in his pocket-book with an air of just triumph.

"How did you get them?" Charles asked.

Medhurst's look was mysterious. "Sir Charles," he answered, drawing himself up, "I must ask you to trust me a while in this matter. Remember, there are people whom you decline to suspect. *I* have learned that it is always those very people who are most dangerous to capitalists. If I were to give you the names, now, you would refuse to believe me. Therefore, I hold them over discreetly for the moment. One thing, however, I say. I *know* to a certainty where Colonel Clay is at this present speaking. But I will lay my plans deep, and I hope before long to secure him. You shall be present when I do so; and I shall make him confess his personality openly. More than that you cannot reasonably ask. I shall leave it to *you*, then, whether or not you wish to arrest him."

Charles was considerably puzzled, not to say piqued, by this curious reticence; he begged hard for names; but Medhurst was adamant. "No, no," he replied; "we detectives have our own just pride in our profession. If I told you now, you would probably spoil all by some premature action. You are too open and impulsive! I will mention this alone: Colonel Clay will be shortly in Paris, and before long will begin from that city a fresh attempt at defrauding you, which he is now hatching. Mark my words, and see whether or not I have been kept well informed of the fellow's movements!"

He was perfectly correct. Two days later, as it turned out, Charles received a "confidential" letter from Paris, purporting to come from the head of a second-rate financial house with which he had had dealings over the Craig-Ellachie Amalgamation—by this time, I ought to have said, an accomplished union. It was a letter of small importance in itself—a mere matter of detail; but it paved the way, so Medhurst thought, to some later development of more serious character. Here once more the man's singular foresight was justified. For, in another week, we received a second communication, containing other proposals of a delicate financial character, which would have involved the transference of some two thousand pounds to the head of the Parisian firm at an address given. Both these letters Medhurst cleverly compared with those written to Charles before, in the names of Colonel Clay and of Graf von Lebenstein. At first sight, it is true, the differences between the two seemed quite enormous: the Paris and was broad and black, large and bold; while the earlier manuscript was small, neat, thin, and gentlemanly. Still, when Medhurst pointed out to us certain persistent twists in the formation of his capitals, and certain curious peculiarities in the relative length of his *t*'s, his *l*'s, his *b*'s, and his *h*'s, we could see for ourselves he was right; both were the work of one hand, writing in the one case with a sharp-pointed nib, very small, and in the other with a quill, very large and freely.

This discovery was *most* important. We stood now within measurable distance of catching Colonel Clay, and bringing forgery and fraud home to him without hope of evasion.

To make all sure, however, Medhurst communicated with the Paris police, and showed us their answers. Meanwhile, Charles continued to write to the head of the firm, who had given a private address in the Rue Jean Jacques, alleging, I must say, a most clever reason why the negotiations at this stage should be confidentially conducted. But one never expected from Colonel Clay anything less than consummate cleverness. In the end, it was arranged that we three were to go over to Paris together, that Medhurst was to undertake, under the guise of being Sir Charles, to pay the two thousand pounds to the pretended financier, and that Charles and I, waiting with the police outside the door, should, at a given signal, rush in with our forces and secure the criminal.

We went over accordingly, and spent the night at the Grand, as is Charles's custom. The Bristol, which I prefer, he finds too quiet. Early next morning we took a *fiacre* and drove to the Rue Jean Jacques. Medhurst had arranged everything in advance with the Paris police, three of whom, in plain clothes, were waiting at the foot of the staircase to assist us. Charles had further provided himself with two thousand pounds, in notes of the Bank of France, in order that the payment might be duly made, and no doubt arise as to the crime having been perpetrated as well as meditated—in the former case, the penalty would be fifteen years; in the latter, three only. He was in very high spirits. The fact that we had tracked the rascal to earth at last, and were within an hour of apprehending him, was in itself enough to raise his courage greatly. We found, as we expected, that the number given in the Rue Jean Jacques was that of an hotel, not a private residence. Medhurst went in first, and inquired of the landlord whether our man was at home, at the same time informing him of the nature of our errand, and giving him to understand that if we effected the capture by his friendly aid, Sir Charles would see that the expenses incurred on the swindler's bill were met in full, as the price of his assistance. The landlord bowed; he expressed his deep regret, as M. le Colonel—so we heard him call him—was a most amiable person, much liked by the household; but justice, of course, must have its way; and, with a regretful sigh, he undertook to assist us.

The police remained below, but Charles and Medhurst were each provided with a pair of handcuffs. Remembering the Polperro case, however, we determined to use them with the greatest caution. We would only put them on in case of violent resistance. We crept up to the door where the miscreant was housed. Charles handed the notes in an open envelope to Medhurst, who seized them hastily and held them in his hands in readiness for action. We had a sign concerted. Whenever he sneezed—which he could do in the most natural manner—we were to open the door, rush in, and secure the criminal!

He was gone for some minutes. Charles and I waited outside in breathless expectation. Then Medhurst sneezed. We flung the door open at once, and burst in upon the creature.

Medhurst rose as we did so. He pointed with his finger. "*This* is Colonel Clay!" he said; "keep him well in charge while I go down to the door for the police to arrest him!"

A gentlemanly man, about middle height, with a grizzled beard and a well-assumed military aspect, rose at the same moment. The envelope in which Charles had placed the notes lay on the table before him. He clutched it nervously. "I am at a loss, gentlemen," he said, in an excited voice, "to account for this interruption." He spoke with a tremor, yet with all the politeness to which we were accustomed in the little curate and the Honourable David.

"No nonsense!" Charles exclaimed, in his authoritative way. "We know who you are. We have found you out this time. You are Colonel Clay. If you attempt to resist—take care—I will handcuff you!"

The military gentleman gave a start. "Yes, I *am* Colonel Clay," he answered. "On what charge do you arrest me?"

Charles was bursting with wrath. The fellow's coolness seemed never to desert him. "You *are* Colonel Clay!" he muttered. "You have the unspeakable effrontery to stand there and admit it?"

"Certainly," the Colonel answered, growing hot in turn. "I have done nothing to be ashamed of. What do you mean by this conduct? How dare you talk of arresting me?"

Charles laid his hand on the man's shoulder. "Come, come, my friend," he said. "That sort of bluff won't go down with us. You know very well on what charge I arrest you; and here are the police to give effect to it."

He called out "Entrez!" The police entered the room. Charles explained as well as he could in most doubtful Parisian what they were next to do. The Colonel drew himself up in an indignant attitude. He turned and addressed them in excellent French.

"I am an officer in the service of her Britannic Majesty," he said. "On what ground do you venture to interfere with me, messieurs?"

The chief policeman explained. The Colonel turned to Charles. "*Your* name, sir?" he inquired.

"You know it very well," Charles answered. "I am Sir Charles Vandrift; and, in spite of your clever disguise, I can instantly recognise you. I know your eyes and ears. I can see the same man who cheated me at Nice, and who insulted me on the island."

"*You* Sir Charles Vandrift!" the rogue cried. "No, no, sir, you are a madman!" He looked round at the police. "Take care what you do!" he cried. "This is a raving maniac. I had business just now with Sir Charles Vandrift, who quitted the room as these gentlemen entered. This person is mad, and you, monsieur, I doubt not," bowing to me, "you are, of course, his keeper."

"Do not let him deceive you," I cried to the police, beginning to fear that with his usual incredible cleverness the fellow would even now manage to slip through our fingers. "Arrest him, as you are told. *We* will take the responsibility." Though I trembled when I thought of that cheque he held of mine.

The chief of our three policemen came forward and laid his hand on the culprit's shoulder. "I advise you, M. le Colonel," he said, in an official voice, "to come with us quietly for the present. Before the *juge d'instruction* we can enter at length into all these questions."

The Colonel, very indignant still—and acting the part marvellously—yielded and went along with them.

"Where's Medhurst?" Charles inquired, glancing round as we reached the door. "I wish he had stopped with us."

"You are looking for monsieur your friend?" the landlord inquired, with a side bow to the Colonel. "He has gone away in a *fiacre*. He asked me to give this note to you."

He handed us a twisted note. Charles opened and read it. "Invaluable man!" he cried. "Just hear what he says, Sey: 'Having secured Colonel Clay, I am off now again on the track of Mme. Picardet. She was lodging in the same house. She has just driven away; I know to what place; and I am after her to arrest her. In blind haste, Medhurst.' That's smartness, *if* you like. Though poor little woman, I think he might have left her."

"Does a Mme. Picardet stop here?" I inquired of the landlord, thinking it possible she might have assumed again the same old alias.

He nodded assent. "*Oui, oui, oui,*" he answered. "She has just driven off, and monsieur your friend has gone posting after her."

"Splendid man!" Charles cried. "Marvillier was quite right. He is the prince of detectives!"

We hailed a couple of *fiacres,* and drove off, in two detachments, to the *juge d'instruction.* There Colonel Clay continued to brazen it out, and asserted that he was an officer in the Indian Army, home on six months' leave, and spending some weeks in Paris. He even declared he was known at the Embassy, where he had a cousin an *attaché;* and he asked that this gentleman should be sent for at once from our Ambassador's to identify him. The *juge d'instruction* insisted that this must be done; and Charles waited in very bad humour for the foolish formality. It really seemed as if, after all, when we had actually caught and arrested our man, he was going by some cunning device to escape us.

After a delay of more than an hour, during which Colonel

Clay fretted and fumed quite as much as we did, the *attaché* arrived. To our horror and astonishment, he proceeded to salute the prisoner most affectionately.

"Halloa, Algy!" he cried, grasping his hand; "what's up? What do these ruffians want with you?"

It began to dawn upon us, then, what Medhurst had meant by "suspecting everybody": the real Colonel Clay was no common adventurer, but a gentleman of birth and high connections!

The Colonel glared at us. "This fellow declares he's Sir Charles Vandrift," he said sulkily. "Though, in fact, there are two of them. And he accuses me of forgery, fraud, and theft, Bertie."

The *attaché* stared hard at us. "This *is* Sir Charles Vandrift," he replied, after a moment. "I remember hearing him make a speech once at a City dinner. And what charge have you to prefer, Sir Charles, against my cousin?"

"Your cousin?" Charles cried. "This is Colonel Clay, the notorious sharper!"

The *attaché* smiled a gentlemanly and superior smile. "This is Colonel Clay," he answered, "of the Bengal Staff Corps."

It began to strike us there was something wrong somewhere.

"But he has cheated me, all the same," Charles said—"at Nice two years ago, and many times since; and this very day he has tricked me out of two thousand pounds in French bank-notes, which he has now about him!"

The Colonel was speechless. But the *attaché* laughed. "What he has done to-day I don't know," he said; "but if it's as apocryphal as what you say he did two years ago, you've a thundering bad case, sir; for he was then in India, and I was out there, visiting him."

"Where are the two thousand pounds?" Charles cried. "Why, you've got them in your hand! You're holding the envelope!"

The Colonel produced it. "This envelope," he said, "was left with me by the man with short stiff hair, who came just before you, and who announced himself as Sir Charles Vandrift. He said he was interested in tea in Assam, and wanted me to join the board of directors of some bogus company.

These are his papers, I believe," and he handed them to his cousin.

"Well, I'm glad the notes are safe, anyhow," Charles murmured, in a tone of relief, beginning to smell a rat. "Will you kindly return them to me?"

The *attaché* turned out the contents of the envelope. They proved to be prospectuses of bubble companies of the moment, of no importance.

"Medhurst must have put them there," I cried, "and decamped with the cash."

Charles gave a groan of horror. "And Medhurst is Colonel Clay!" he exclaimed, clapping his hand to his forehead.

"I beg your pardon, sir," the Colonel interposed. "I have but one personality, and no aliases."

It took quite half an hour to explain this imbroglio. But as soon as all was explained, in French and English, to the satisfaction of ourselves and the *juge d'instruction*, the real Colonel shook hands with us in a most forgiving way, and informed us that he had more than once wondered, when he gave his name at shops in Paris, why it was often received with such grave suspicion. We instructed the police that the true culprit was Medhurst, whom they had seen with their own eyes, and whom we urged them to pursue with all expedition. Meanwhile, Charles and I, accompanied by the Colonel and the *attaché*—"to see the fun out," as they said—called at the Bank of France for the purpose of stopping the notes immediately. It was too late, however. They had been presented at once, and cashed in gold, by a pleasant little lady in an American costume, who was afterwards identified by the hotel-keeper (from our description) as his lodger, Mme. Picardet. It was clear she had taken rooms in the same hotel, to be near the Indian Colonel; and it was *she* who had received and sent the letters. As for our foe, he had vanished into space, as always.

Two days later we received the usual insulting communication on a sheet of Charles's own dainty note. Last time he wrote it was on Craig-Ellachie paper: this time, like the wanton lapwing, he had got himself another crest.

Most Perspicacious of Millionaires!—Said I not well, as Medhurst, that you must distrust everybody? And the one man you never dreamt of distrusting was—Medhurst. Yet see how truthful I was! I told you I knew where Colonel Clay was living—and I *did* know, exactly. I promised to take you to Colonel Clay's rooms, and to get him arrested for you—and I kept my promise. I even exceeded your expectations; for I gave you *two* Colonel Clays instead of one—and you took the wrong man—that is to say, the real one. This was a neat little trick; but it cost me some trouble.

First, I found out there *was* a real Colonel Clay, in the Indian Army. I also found out he chanced to be coming home on leave this season. I might have made more out of him, no doubt; but I disliked annoying him, and preferred to give myself the fun of this peculiar mystification. I therefore waited for him to reach Paris, where the police arrangements suited me better than in London. While I was looking about, and delaying operations for his return, I happened to hear you wanted a detective. So I offered myself as out of work to my old employer, Marvillier, from whom I have had many good jobs in the past; and there you get, in short, the kernel of the Colonel.

Naturally, after this, I can never go back as a detective to Marvillier's. But, on the large scale on which I have learned to work since I first had the pleasure of making your delightful acquaintance, this matters little. To say the truth, I begin to feel detective work a cut or two below me. I am now a gentleman of means and leisure. Besides, the extra knowledge of your movements which I have acquired in your house has helped still further to give me various holds upon you. So the fluke will be true to his own pet lamb. To vary the metaphor, you are not fully shorn yet.

Remember me most kindly to your charming family, give Wentworth my love, and tell Mlle. Césarine I owe her a grudge which I shall never forget. She clearly suspected me. You are much too rich, dear Charles; I relieve your plethora. I bleed you financially. Therefore I consider myself—Your sincerest friend,

Clay-Brabazon-Medhurst,
Fellow of the Royal College of Surgeons.

Charles was threatened with apoplexy. This blow was severe. "Whom can I trust," he asked, plaintively, "when the detectives themselves, whom I employ to guard me, turn out to be swindlers? Don't you remember that line in the Latin

grammar—something about, 'Who shall watch the watchers?'
I think it used to run, '*Quis custodes custodiet ipsos?*' "

But I felt this episode had at least disproved my suspicions
of poor Césarine.

EUGENE VALMONT

Robert Barr, was a friend of Arthur Conan Doyle. He did not, however, take the detective story quite as seriously as did his colleague, which is why it was Barr and not Doyle who created Eugène Valmont, "the first important humorous detective in English literature." Barr also perpetrated one of the pioneer Sherlock Holmes parodies, The Great Pegram Mystery, *in the pages of his magazine,* The Idler, *in 1892. A Scot who grew up in Canada and later worked on an American newspaper, Barr set up shop in England in the early 1880s. He was a model of what a professional writer should be, capable of turning out articles, short stories, and novels in assorted categories. He wrote mystery, science fiction, historical fiction. His* A Rock in the Baltic, *published in 1906, is an early example of the novel of international intrigue and his* From Whose Bourne *is a detective novel in which the central characters comes back as a ghost to help solve his own murder. Barr was also a friend of the ill-fated Stephen Crane, and completed his novel* The O'Ruddy *after Crane's death.*

Valmont is a vain, elegant Frenchman. Having left his position as a detective for the French government under a cloud, he set up practice in London as a private detective. All of his cases are to be found in the relatively rare volume The Triumphs of Eugène Valmont, *published in 1906. He almost always shows up in anthologies in his most famous exploit, "The Absent-Minded Coterie." Some historians feel Valmont may have provided Agatha Christie part of the in-*

135

spiration for Poirot. Our story, only reprinted once before in this country, originally appeared in Pearson's *magazine in 1904.*

The Clue of the Silver Spoons
by Robert Barr

When the card was brought in to me, I looked upon it with some misgiving, for I scented a commercial transaction; and although such cases are lucrative enough, nevertheless I, Eugène Valmont, formerly high in the service of the French Government, do not care to be connected with them. They usually pertain to sordid business affairs that present little that is of interest to a man who, in his time, has dealt with subtle questions of diplomacy upon which the welfare of nations sometimes turned.

The name of Bentham Gibbes is familiar to everyone, connected as it is with the much-advertised pickles, whose glaring announcements in crude crimson and green strike the eye everywhere in England, and shock the artistic taste wherever seen. Me, I have never tasted them, and shall not, so long as a French restaurant remains open in London; but I doubt not they are as pronounced to the palate as their advertisement is distressing to the eye.

If, then, this gross pickle manufacturer expected me to track down those who were infringing upon the recipes for making his so-called sauces, chutneys, and the like, he would find himself mistaken, for I was now in a position to pick and choose my cases, and a case of pickles did not allure me. "Beware of imitations," said the advertisement, "none genuine without a facsimile of the signature of Bentham Gibbes." Ah, well, not for me were either the pickles or the tracking of imitators. A forged cheque: yes, if you like, but the forged signature of Mr. Gibbes on a pickle bottle was not for me. Nevertheless, I said to Armand:

"Show the gentleman in," and he did so.

To my astonishment there entered a young man, quite correctly dressed in dark frock coat, faultless waistcoat and trousers, that proclaimed the Bond Street tailor. When he spoke, his voice and language were those of a gentleman.

"Monsieur Valmont?" he inquired.

"At your service," I replied, bowing and waving my hand as Armand placed a chair for him and withdrew.

"I am a barrister, with chambers in the Temple," began Mr. Gibbes, "and for some days a matter has been troubling me about which I have now come to seek your advice, your name having been suggested by a friend in whom I confided."

"Am I acquainted with him?" I asked.

"I think not," replied Mr. Gibbes; "he also is a barrister with chambers in the same building as my own. Lionel Dacre is his name."

"I never heard of him."

"Very likely not. Nevertheless, he recommended you as a man who could keep his own counsel; and if you take up this case I desire the utmost secrecy preserved, whatever may be the outcome."

I bowed, but made no protestation. Secrecy is a matter of course with me.

The Englishman paused for a few moments, as if he expected fervent assurances; then he went on with no trace of disappointment on his countenance at not receiving them.

"On the night of the twenty-third I gave a little dinner to six friends of mine in my own rooms. I may say that so far as I am aware they are all gentlemen of unimpeachable character. On the night of the dinner I was detained later than expected at a reception, and in driving to the Temple was still further delayed by a block of traffic in Piccadilly, so that when I arrived at my chambers there was barely time for me to dress and receive my guests. My man Johnson had everything laid out ready for me in my dressing-room, and as I passed through to it, I hurriedly flung off the coat I was wearing and carelessly left it over the back of a chair in the dining-room, where neither Johnson nor myself noticed it until my attention was called to it after the dinner was over, and everyone was rather jolly with wine.

"This coat had an inside pocket. Usually any frock coat I wear at an afternoon reception has not an inside pocket, but I had been rather on the rush all day. My father is a manufacturer, whose name may be familiar to you, and I am on the directors' board of his company. On this occasion I had to take a cab from the city to the reception I spoke of, and had not time to go and change at my rooms. The reception was a somewhat Bohemian affair, extremely interesting, of course, but not too particular as to costume, so I went as I was. In this inside pocket rested a thin package, composed of two pieces of pasteboard, and between them five twenty-pound Bank of England notes, folded lengthways and held in place between the pasteboards by an elastic rubber band.

"I had thrown the coat over the chair in such a way that the inside pocket was exposed, and the ends of the notes plainly recognisable. Over the coffee and cigars one of my guests laughingly called attention to what he termed my vulgar display of wealth, and Johnson, in some confusion at having neglected to put away the coat, now picked it up and took it to the reception room, where the wraps of my guests lay about promiscuously. He should, of course, have placed it in my wardrobe, but he said afterwards he thought it belonged to the guest who had spoken. You see, he was in my dressing-room when I threw my coat on the chair in making my way thither, and, of course, he had not noticed the coat in the hurry of arriving guests, otherwise he would have put it where it belonged. After everybody had gone, Johnson came to me and said the coat was there, but the package was missing, nor has any trace of it been found since that night."

"The dinner was fetched in from outside, I suppose?"

"Yes."

"How many waiters served it?"

"Two. They are men who have often been in my employ before; but, apart from that, they had left my chambers before the incident of the coat happened."

"Neither of them went into the reception room, I take it?"

"No. I am certain that not even suspicion can attach to either of the waiters."

"Your man Johnson—"

"Has been with me for years. He could easily have stolen much more than the hundred pounds if he had wished to do so, but I have never known him to take a penny that did not belong to him."

"Will you favour me with the names of your guests, Mr. Gibbes?"

"Viscount Stern sat at my right hand, and at my left Lord Templemore; Sir John Sanclere next to him, and Angus McKeller next to Sanclere. After Viscount Stern was Lionel Dacre, and at his right was Vincent Innis."

On a sheet of paper I had written the names of the guests, and noted their places at the table.

"Which guest drew your attention to the money?"

"Lionel Dacre."

"Is there a window looking out from the reception room?"

"Two of them."

"Were they fastened on the night of the dinner party?"

"I could not be sure; Johnson would know, very likely. You are hinting at the possibility of a thief coming in through a reception room window while we were somewhat noisy over our wine. I think such a solution highly improbable. My rooms are on the third floor, and a thief would scarcely venture to make an entrance when he could not but know there was a company being entertained. Besides this, the coat was there but an hour or so, and it seems to me whoever stole those notes knew where they were."

"That sounds reasonable," I had to admit. "Have you spoken to anyone of your loss?"

"To no one but Dacre, who recommended me to see you. Oh, yes, and to Johnson, of course."

I could not help noting that this was the fourth or fifth time Dacre's name had come up during our conversation.

"Why to Dacre?" I asked.

"Oh, well, you see, he occupies chambers in the same building, on the ground floor. He is a very good fellow, and we are by way of being firm friends. Then it was he who had called attention to the money, so I thought he should know the sequel."

"How did he take your news?"

"Now that you call attention to the fact, he seemed slightly troubled. I should like to say, however, that you must not be misled by that. Lionel Dacre could no more steal than he could lie."

"Did he seem surprised when you mentioned the theft?"

Bentham Gibbes paused a moment before replying, knitting his brows in thought.

"No," he said at last; "and, come to think of it, it almost appears as if he had been expecting my announcement."

"Doesn't that strike you as rather strange, Mr. Gibbes?"

"Really, my mind is in such a whirl, I don't know what to think. But it's perfectly absurd to suspect Dacre. If you knew the man you would understand what I mean. He comes of an excellent family, and he is—oh! he is Lionel Dacre, and when you have said that, you have made any suspicion absurd."

"I suppose you had the rooms thoroughly searched. The packet didn't drop out and remain unnoticed on some corner?"

"No; Johnson and myself examined every inch of the premises."

"Have you the numbers of the notes?"

"Yes; I got them from the bank next morning. Payment was stopped, and so far not one of the five has been presented. Of course, one or more may have been cashed at some shop, but none have been offered to any of the banks."

"A twenty-pound note is not accepted without scrutiny, so the chances are the thief may have some difficulty in disposing of them."

"As I told you, I don't mind the loss of the money at all. It is the uncertainty, the uneasiness, caused by the incident which troubles me. You will comprehend this when I say that if you are good enough to interest yourself in this case, I shall be disappointed if your fee does not exceed the amount I have lost."

Mr. Gibbes rose as he said this, and I accompanied him to the door, assuring him that I should do my best to solve the mystery. Whether he sprang from pickles or not, I realised he was a polished and generous gentleman, who estimated the services of a professional expert like myself at their true value.

I shall not give the details of my researches during the following few days, because the trend of them must be gone over in the remarkable interview I had somewhat later, and there is little use in repeating myself. Suffice it to say, then, that an examination of the rooms and a close cross-questioning of Johnson satisfied me that he and the two waiters were innocent. I was also convinced that no thief made his way through the window, and I came to the conclusion that the notes were stolen by one of the guests.

Further investigation convinced me that the thief was no other than Lionel Dacre, the only one of the six in pressing need of money at that time.

I had Dacre shadowed, and during one of his absences made the acquaintance of his man Hopper, a surly, impolite brute who accepted my golden sovereign quickly enough, but gave me little in exchange for it. But while I conversed with him, there arrived in the passage where we were talking together, a large case of champagne, bearing one of the best-known names in the trade, and branded as being of the vintage of '78. Now, I know that the product of Camelot Frères is not bought as cheaply as British beer, and I also had learned that two short weeks before Mr. Lionel Dacre was at his wits' end for money. Yet he was still the same briefless barrister he had ever been.

On the morning after my unsatisfactory conversation with his man Hopper, I was astonished to receive the following note, written on a dainty correspondence card:—

> 3 and 4 Vellum Buildings,
> Inner Temple, E.C.
>
> Mr. Lionel Dacre presents his compliments to Monsieur Eugène Valmont, and would be obliged if Monsieur Valmont could make it convenient to call upon him in his chambers tomorrow morning at eleven.

Had the man become aware that he was being shadowed, or did the surly servant inform him of the inquiries made? I was soon to know. I called punctually at eleven next morning, and was received with charming urbanity by Mr. Dacre himself. The taciturn Hopper had evidently been sent away for the occasion.

"My dear Monsieur Valmont, I am delighted to meet you," said the young man with more effusiveness than I had ever noticed in an Englishman before, although his very next words supplied an explanation that did not occur to me until afterwards as somewhat far-fetched. "I believe we are by way of being countrymen, and, therefore, although the hour is early, I hope you will allow me to offer you some of that bottled sunshine of the year '78, from la belle France, to whose prosperity and honour we shall drink together. For such a toast any hour is propitious," and to my amazement he brought forth from the case I had seen arrive two days before a bottle of that superb vintage.

"Now," said I to myself, "it is going to be difficult to keep a clear head if the aroma of that nectar rises to the brain. But, tempting as is the cup, I shall drink sparingly, and hope he may not be so judicious."

Sensitive, I already experienced the charm of his personality, and well understood the friendship Mr. Bentham Gibbes felt for him. But I saw the trap spread before me. He expected, under the influence of champagne and courtesy, to extract a promise from me which I must find myself unable to give.

"Sir, you interest me by claiming kinship with France. I had understood that you belonged to one of the oldest families of England."

"Ah, England!" he cried, with an expressive gesture of outspreading hands truly Parisian in its significance. "The trunk belongs to England, of course, but the root—ah! the root, Monsieur Valmont, penetrated the soil from which this vine of the gods has been drawn."

Then, filling my glass and his own, he cried.

"To France, which my family left in the year 1066!"

I could not help laughing at his fervent ejaculation.

"1066! Ah, that is a long time ago, Mr. Dacre."

"In years, perhaps; in feelings but a day. My forefathers came over to steal, and, Lord! how well they accomplished it! They stole the whole country—something like a theft, say I—under that Prince of robbers well named the Conqueror. In our secret hearts we all admire a great thief, and if not a great one, then an expert one, who covers his tracks so perfectly that the hounds of justice are baffled in attempting to follow them. Now, even you, Monsieur Valmont—I can see you are the most generous of men, with a lively sympathy found to perfection only in France—even you must suffer a pang of regret when you lay a thief by the heels who has done his task deftly."

"I fear, Mr. Dacre, you credit me with a magnanimity to

which I dare not lay claim. The criminal is a danger to society."

"True, true; you are in the right, Monsieur Valmont. Still, admit there are cases that would touch you tenderly. For example, a man, ordinarily honest; a great need; a sudden opportunity. He takes that of which another has abundance, and he, nothing. What then, Monsieur Valmont? Is the man to be sent to perdition for a momentary weakness?"

His words astonished me. Was I on the verge of hearing a confession? It almost amounted to that already.

"Mr. Dacre," I said, "I cannot enter into the subtleties you pursue. My duty is to find the criminal."

"You are in the right, Monsieur Valmont, and I am enchanted to find so sensible a head on French shoulders. Although you are a more recent arrival, if I may say so, than myself, you nevertheless already give utterance to sentiments which do honour to England. It is your duty to hunt down the criminal. Very well. In that I think I can aid you, so have taken the liberty of requesting your attendance here this morning. Let me fill your glass again, Monsieur Valmont."

"No more, I beg of you, Mr. Dacre."

"What, do you think the receiver is as bad as the thief?"

I was so taken aback at his remark that I suppose my face showed the amazement within me. But the young man merely laughed with apparently free-hearted enjoyment, poured more wine in his own glass, and tossed it off. Not knowing what to say, I changed the trend of conversation.

"Mr. Gibbes said you had been kind enough to recommend me to his attention. May I ask how you came to hear of me?"

"Ah, who has not heard of the renowned Monsieur Valmont?" and as he said this, for the first time there began to grow a suspicion in my mind that he was chaffing me, as it is called in England, a procedure which I cannot endure. Indeed, if this young man practised it in my own country he would find himself with a duel on his hands before he had gone far. However, the next instant his voice resumed its original fascination, and I listened to it as to some delicious melody.

"I have only to mention my cousin, Lady Gladys Dacre, and you will at once understand why I recommended you to my friend. The case of Lady Gladys, you will remember, required a delicate touch which is not always to be had in this land of England, except when those who possess the gift do us the honour to sojourn with us."

I noticed that my glass was again filled, and as I bowed my acknowledgements of his compliment, I indulged in another sip of the delicious wine; and then I sighed, for I began to realise it was going to be difficult for me, in spite of my disclaimer, to tell this man's friend he had stolen the money.

All this time he had been sitting on the edge of the table, while I occupied a chair at its end. He sat there in careless fashion, swinging a foot to and fro. Now he sprang to the floor and drew up a chair, placing on the table a blank sheet of paper. Then he took from the mantelshelf a packet of letters, and I was astonished to see they were held together by two bits of cardboard and a rubber band similar to the combination that had held the folded banknotes. With great nonchalance he slipped off the rubber band, threw it and the pieces of cardboard on the table before me, leaving the documents loose to his hand.

"Now, Monsieur Valmont," he cried jauntily, "you have been occupied for several days on this case—the case of my dear friend, Bentham Gibbes, who is one of the best fellows in the world."

"He said the same of you, Mr. Dacre."

"I am gratified to hear it. Would you mind letting me know to what point your researches have led you?"

"They have led me to a direction rather than to a point."

"Ah! In the direction of a man, of course?"

"Certainly."

"Who is he?"

"Will you pardon me if I decline to answer you at the present moment?"

"That means you are not sure."

"It may mean, Mr. Dacre, that I am employed by Mr. Gibbes, and do not feel at liberty to disclose to another the results of my quest without his permission."

"But Mr. Bentham Gibbes and I are entirely at one in this matter. Perhaps you are aware that I am the only person with whom he discussed the case besides yourself."

"That is undoubtedly true, Mr. Dacre; still, you see the difficulty of my position."

"Yes, I do, and so shall not press you further. But I have also been interesting myself, in a purely amateurish way, of course. You would, perhaps, have no disinclination to learn whether my deductions agree with yours."

"Not in the least. I should be very glad to know the conclusion at which you have arrived. May I ask if you suspect anyone in particular?"

"Yes, I do."

"Will you name him?"

"No, I shall copy the admirable reticence you yourself have shown. And now let us attack this mystery in a sane and businesslike manner. You have already examined the room. Well, here is a rough sketch of it. There is the table; in this corner the chair on which the coat was flung. Here sat Gibbes at the head of the table. Those on the left-hand side had their backs to the chair. I, being in the centre to the right, saw the chair, the coat, and the notes, and called attention to them. Now our first duty is to find a motive. If it were a murder, our motive might be hatred, revenge, robbery, what you like. As it is simply the stealing of money, the man must have been either a born thief, or else some hitherto innocent person pressed to the crime by great necessity. Do you agree with me, Monsieur Valmont?"

"Perfectly. You follow exactly the line of my own reasoning."

"Very well. It is unlikely that a born thief was one of Mr. Gibbes' guests. Therefore we are reduced to look for a man under the spur of necessity—a man who has no money of his own, but who must raise a certain amount, let us say by a certain date, if we can find such a man in that company. Do you not agree with me that he is likely to be the thief?"

"Yes, I do."

"Then let us start our process of elimination. Out goes Viscount Stern, a man with twenty thousand acres of land, and nobody quite knows what income. I mark off the name of Lord Templemere, one of His Majesty's judges, entirely above suspicion. Next Sir John Sanclare; he also is rich, but Vincent Innis is still richer, so the pencil obliterates his name. Now we have Angus McKeller, an author of some note, as you are well aware, deriving a good income from his books, and a better one from his plays; a canny Scot, so we may rub his name from our paper and our memory. How do my erasures correspond with yours, Monsieur Valmont?"

"They correspond exactly, Mr. Dacre."

"I am flattered to hear it. There remains one name untouched; Mr. Lionel Dacre, the descendant, as we have said, of robbers."

"I have not said so, Mr. Dacre."

"Ah, my dear Valmont, the politeness of your country asserts itself. Let us not be deluded, but follow our inquiry wherever it leads. I suspect Lionel Dacre. What do you know of his circumstances before the dinner of the twenty-third?"

As I made no reply, he looked up at me with his frank boyish face illumined with a winning smile.

"You know nothing of his circumstances?" he asked.

"It grieves me to state that I do. Mr. Lionel Dacre was penniless on the night of the dinner on the twenty-third."

"Oh, don't exaggerate, Monsieur Valmont," cried Dacre, with a laugh, "he had one sixpence, two pennies, and a halfpenny. How did you know he was penniless?"

"I knew he ordered a case of champagne from the London representative of Camelot Frères, and was refused unless he paid the money down."

"Quite right; and then when you were talking to Hopper you saw that case of champagne delivered. Excellent, excellent, Monsieur Valmont. But will a man steal, think you, to supply himself with even so delicious a wine as this we have been tasting—and, by the way, forgive my neglect. Allow me to fill your glass, Monsieur Valmont."

"Not another drop, if you will excuse me, Mr. Dacre."

"Ah, yes, champagne should not be mixed with evidence. When we have finished, perhaps. What further proof have you?"

"I have proof that Mr. Dacre was threatened with bankruptcy, if on the twenty-fourth he did not pay a bill of seventy-eight pounds that had long been outstanding. I have proof that this was paid, not on the twenty-fourth, but on the twenty-sixth. Mr. Dacre had gone to the solicitor and assured him he would have the money on that date, whereupon he was given two days' grace."

"Ah, well, he was entitled to three, you know, in law. Yes, there, Monsieur Valmont, you touch the fatal point. The threat of bankruptcy will drive a man in Dacre's position to almost any crime. Bankruptcy to a barrister spells ruin. It means a career blighted; it means a life buried with little chance of resurrection. I see you grasp the supreme importance of that bit of evidence. The case of champagne is as nothing compared with it; and this reminds me that in the crisis I shall take another sip, with your permission. Sure you won't join me?"

"Not at this juncture, Mr. Dacre."

"I envy your moderation. Here's to the success of our search, Monsieur Valmont."

I felt sorry for the gay young fellow as with smiling face he drank the champagne.

"Now, monsieur," he went on, "I am amazed to learn how much you have found out. Really, I think tradespeople, solicitors, and all such should keep better guard on their tongues than they do. Nevertheless, these documents I have at my elbow, and which I expected would surprise you, are merely the letters and receipts. Here is the letter from the solicitor threatening me with bankruptcy; here is his receipt dated the twenty-sixth; here is the refusal of the wine merchant, and here is his receipt for the money. Here are smaller bills liquidated. With my pencil we will add them up. Seventy-eight pounds bulks large. We add the smaller items, and it totals ninety-three pounds, seven shillings, and fourpence. Let us now examine my purse. Here is a five-pound note; there is a minted sovereign. Here is twelve and sixpence in silver; here is twopence in coppers. Now the purse is empty. Let us add this to the amount on the paper. Do my eyes deceive me, or is the total exactly a hundred pounds? There is the stolen money accounted for."

"Pardon me, Mr. Dacre," I said, "but there is still a sovereign on the mantelpiece."

Dacre threw back his head, and laughed with greater heartiness than I had yet known him to indulge in during our short acquaintance.

"By Jove!" he cried, "you've got me there. I'd forgotten entirely about that pound on the mantelpiece, which belongs to you."

"To me? Impossible!"

"It does, and cannot interfere in the least with our hundred pound calculation. That is the sovereign you gave to my man, Hopper, who, believing me hard pressed, took it that I might have the enjoyment of it. Hopper belongs to our family, or the family belongs to him, I am never sure which. You must have missed in him the deferential bearing of a man-servant in Paris, yet he is true gold, like the sovereign you bestowed upon him, and he bestowed upon me. Now here, monsieur, is the evidence of the theft, together with the rubber band and two pieces of cardboard. Ask my friend Gibbes to examine them minutely. They are all at your disposition, monsieur, and you will learn how much easier it is to deal with the master than with the servant when you wish information. All the gold you possess would not have wrung these incriminating documents from old Hopper. I had to send him away to-day to the West End, fearing that in his brutal British way he might have assaulted you if he got an inkling of your mission."

"Mr. Dacre," said I slowly, "you have thoroughly convinced me——"

"I thought I would," he interrupted with a laugh.

"——that you did not take the money."

"Oh, this is a change of wind, surely. Many a man has been hanged through a chain of circumstantial evidence much weaker than this which I have exhibited to you. Don't you see the subtlety of my action? Ninety-nine persons in a hundred would say, 'No man could be such a fool as to put Valmont on his track, and then place in Valmont's hands such striking evidence.' But there comes in my craftiness. Of course the rock you run up against will be Gibbes' incredulity. The first question he will ask you may be this: 'Why did not Dacre come and borrow the money from me?' Now there you have a certain weakness in your chain of evidence. I know perfectly well that Gibbes would lend me the money, and he knew perfectly well that if I were pressed to the wall I should ask him."

"Mr. Dacre," said I, "you have been playing with me. I should resent that with most men, but whether it is your own genial manner, or the effect of this excellent champagne, or both together, I forgive you. But I am convinced of another thing. You know who took the money."

"I don't know, but I suspect."

"Will you tell me whom you suspect?"

"That would not be fair, but I shall now take the liberty of filling your glass with champagne."

"I am your guest, Mr. Dacre."

"Admirably answered, monsieur," he replied, pouring out the wine; "and now I shall give you the clue. Find out all about the story of the silver spoons."

"The story of the silver spoons? What silver spoons?"

"Ah, that is the point. You step out of the Temple into Fleet Street, seize by the shoulder the first man you meet, and ask him to tell you about the silver spoons. There are but two men and two spoons concerned. When you learn who those two men are, you will know that one of them did not take the money, and I give you my assurance that the other did."

"You speak in mystery, Mr. Dacre."

"But certainly, for I am speaking to Monsieur Eugène Valmont."

"I echo your words, sir. Admirably answered. You put me on my mettle, and I flatter myself that I see your kindly drift. You wish me to solve the mystery of this stolen money. Sir, you do me honour, and I drink to your health."

"To yours, monsieur," said Lionel Dacre, "and here is a further piece of information which my friend Gibbes would never have given you. When he told me the money was gone, I cried in the anguish of impending bankruptcy: 'I wish to goodness I had it!' Whereupon he immediately compelled me to accept his cheque for a hundred pounds, of which, as I have shown you, alas! only six pounds twelve and eightpence remains."

On leaving Mr. Dacre I took a hansom to a *café* in Regent Street, which is a passable imitation of similar places of refreshment in Paris. There, calling for a cup of black coffee, I sat down to think. The clue of the silver spoons! He had laughingly suggested that I should take by the shoulders the first man I met, and ask him what the story of the silver spoons was. This course naturally struck me as absurd. Nevertheless, it contained a hint. I must ask somebody, and that the right person, to tell me the tale of the silver spoons.

Under the influence of the black coffee, I reasoned it out in this way. On the night of the twenty-third some one of the six guests there present stole a hundred pounds, but Dacre had said that one of the actors in the silver spoon episode was the actual thief. That person, then, must have been one of Mr. Gibbes' guests at the dinner of the twenty-third. Probably two of the guests were the participators in the silver spoon comedy, but be that as it may, it followed that one at least of the men around Mr. Gibbes' table knew the episode of the silver spoons.

Perhaps Bentham Gibbes himself was cognisant of it. It followed, therefore, that the easiest plan was to question each of the men who partook of that dinner. Yet if only one knew about the spoons, that one must also have some idea that these spoons formed the clue which attached him to the crime of the twenty-third, in which case he was little likely to divulge what he knew, and that to an entire stranger. Of course I might go to Dacre himself and demand the story of the silver spoons, but this would be a confession of failure on my part, and I rather dreaded Lionel Dacre's hearty laughter when I admitted that the mystery was too much for me. Besides this, I was very well aware of the young man's kindly intentions towards me. He wished me to unravel the coil myself, and so I determined not to go to him except as a last resource.

I resolved to begin with Mr. Gibbes, and, finishing my coffee, got again into a hansom and drove back to the Temple. I found Mr. Gibbes in his room, and after greeting me, his first inquiry was about the case.

"How are you getting on?" he asked.

"I think I am getting on fairly well," I replied, "and expect to finish in a day or two, if you will kindly tell me the story of the silver spoons."

"The silver spoons?" he echoed, quite evidently not understanding me.

"There happened an incident in which two men were engaged, and this incident related to a pair of silver spoons. I want to get the particulars of that."

"I haven't the slightest idea what you are talking about," replied Gibbes, thoroughly bewildered. "You will have to be more definite, I fear, if you are to get any help from me."

"I cannot be more definite, because I have already told you all I know."

"What bearing has all this on our own case?"

"I was informed that if I got hold of the clue of the silver spoons I should be in a fair way of settling our case."

"Who told you that?"

"Mr. Lionel Dacre."

"Oh, does Dacre refer to his own conjuring?"

"I don't know, I'm sure. What was his conjuring?"

"A very clever trick he did one night at dinner here about two months ago."

"Had it anything to do with silver spoons?"

"Well, it was silver spoons or silver forks, or something of that kind. I had entirely forgotten the incident. So far as I recollect at the moment, there was a sleight-of-hand man of great expertness in one of the music-halls, and the talk turned upon him. Then Dacre said the tricks he did were easy, and holding up a spoon or a fork, I don't remember which, he asserted his ability to make it disappear before our eyes, to be found afterwards in the clothing of someone there present. Several offered to make him a bet that he could do nothing of the kind, but he said he would bet with no one but Innis, who sat opposite him. Innis, with some reluctance, accepted the bet, and then Dacre, with a great show of the usual conjurer's gesticulations, spread forth his empty hands, and said we should find the spoon in Innis' pocket, and there, sure enough, it was. It was a clever trick, but we were never able to get him to repeat it."

"Thank you very much, Mr. Gibbes; I think I see daylight now."

"If you do, you are cleverer than I, by a long chalk," cried Bentham Gibbes, as I took my departure.

I went directly downstairs, and knocked at Mr. Dacre's door once more. He opened the door himself, his man not yet having returned.

"Ah, monsieur," he cried; "back already? You didn't mean to tell me you have so soon got to the bottom of the silver spoon entanglement?"

"I think I have, Mr. Dacre. You were sitting at dinner opposite Mr. Vincent Innis. You saw him conceal a silver spoon in his pocket. You probably waited for some time to understand what he meant by this, and as he did not return the spoon to its place, you proposed a conjuring trick, made the bet with him, and thus the spoon was returned to the table."

"Excellent, excellent, monsieur! That is very nearly what occurred, except that I acted at once. I had had experiences with Mr. Vincent Innis before. Never did he come to these rooms without my missing some little trinket after he was gone. I am not a man of many possessions, while Mr. Innis is a very rich person, and so, if anything is taken, I have little difficulty in coming to a knowledge of my loss. Of course, I never mentioned these disappearances to him. They were all trivial, as I have said, and, so far as the silver spoon was concerned, it was of no great value either. But I thought the bet and the recovery of the spoon would teach him a lesson; it apparently has not done so. On the night of the twenty-third he sat at my right hand, as you will see by consulting your diagram of the table and the guests. I asked him a question twice to which he did not reply, and, looking at him, I was startled by the expression in his eyes. They were fixed on a distant corner of the room, and following his gaze I saw what he was looking at with such hypnotising concentration.

"So absorbed was he in contemplation of the packet there so plainly exposed, that he seemed to be entirely oblivious of what was going on around him. I roused him from his trance by jocularly calling Gibbes' attention to the display of money. I expected in this way to save Innis from committing the act which he seemingly did commit. Imagine, then, the dilemma in which I was placed when Gibbes confided to me the morning after what had occurred the night before.

"I was positive that Innis had taken the money, yet I possessed no proof of it. I could not tell Gibbes, and I dare not speak to Innis. Of course, monsieur, you do not need to be told that Innis is not a thief in the ordinary sense of the word. He has no need to steal, and yet apparently cannot help doing so. I am sure that no attempt has been made to pass those notes. They are doubtless in his house at Kensington at this present moment. He is, in fact, a kleptomaniac, or a maniac of some sort. And now, Monsieur Valmont, was my hint regarding the silver spoons of any value to you?"

"Of the most infinite value, Mr. Dacre."

"Then let me make another suggestion. I leave it entirely

to your bravery; a bravery which I confess I do not myself possess. Will you take a hansom, drive to Mr. Innis' house in the Cromwell Road, confront him quietly, and ask for the return of the packet? I am anxious to know what will happen. If he hands it to you, as I expect he will, then you must tell Mr. Gibbes the whole story."

"Mr. Dacre, your suggestion shall be immediately acted upon, and I thank you for your compliment to my courage."

I found that Mr. Innis inhabited a very grand house. After a time he entered the study on the ground floor, to which I had been conducted. He held my card in his hand, and was looking at it with some surprise.

"I think I have not the pleasure of knowing you, Mr. Valmont," he said, courteously enough.

"No. I have called on a matter of business. I was once investigator for the French Government, and now am doing private detective work here in London."

"Ah! And how is that supposed to interest me? I have nothing that I wish investigated. I did not send for you, did I?"

"No, Mr. Innis; I merely took the liberty of calling to ask you to let me have the package you took out of Mr. Bentham Gibbes' frock coat pocket on the night of the twenty-third."

"He wishes it returned, does he?"

"Yes."

Mr. Innis calmly went to a desk, which he unlocked and opened, displaying a veritable museum of trinkets of one sort and another. Pulling out a small drawer, he took from it the packet containing the five twenty-pound notes. Apparently it had never been undone. With a smile he handed it to me.

"You will make my apologies to Mr. Gibbes for not returning it before. Tell him I have been unusually busy of late."

"I shall not fail to do so," said I, with a bow.

"Thanks so much. Good morning, Monsieur Valmont."

"Good morning, Mr. Innis."

And so I returned the packet to Mr. Bentham Gibbes, who pulled the notes from between their pasteboard protection, and begged me to accept them.

DR. THORNDYKE

Dr. John Thorndyke, of 5A King's Bench Walk, Inner Temple, London, has been called the world's foremost scientific detective. When he made his debut in 1907, in the novel The Red Thumb Mark, he was still something of a fantasy character, since in real life few detectives, private or police, were as devoted to the painstaking investigation of crime as was Dr. Thorndyke. Like Holmes, Thorndyke was the creation of a doctor whose literary ambitions eventually got the better of him. R. Austin Freeman (1862–1943) was in his middle forties when he first wrote of Dr. Thorndyke. He was a member of the Royal College of Surgeons, had served as a colonial physician on the African Gold Coast, and, back again in England, had been associated with the medical staff of Holloway Prison. Freeman's career as a medical practitioner was not marked by conspicuous success, mainly because he had contracted black water fever in Africa and returned to England a semi-invalid.

His early successes as a writer were in collaboration with a fellow doctor, John Pitcairn. Under the pen name Clifford Ashdown they produced a series of short stories devoted to the exploits of a gentleman crook named Romney Pringle. These stories—there were twelve in all in Cassell's magazine in the early 1900s—are in the same vein as Grant Allen's tales of Colonel Clay. More serious, and moving toward Thorndyke, was a series of six that ran under the title From a Surgeon's Diary.

Freeman eventually began to sell fiction on his own and in the Christmas 1908 issue of Pearson's the first Thorndyke short story appeared. A few years later Freeman decided to

*experiment with what he called the inverted detective story,
to see if he could write, "a detective story in which, from the
outset, the reader was taken entirely into the author's confidence, was made an actual witness of the crime, and furnished with every fact that could possibly be used in its detection. Would there be any story left to tell when the reader
had all the facts and knew the identity of the criminal? I
believed that there would." Freeman proved his point in
eight of his forty short stories and also in some of his novels,
most notably in* Mr. Pottermack's Oversight. *The format is
still with us, even showing up on television in such recent hit
shows as Levinson and Link's* Columbo.

*This story was the fourth Freeman did in the inverted
style. As was most often the case, Dr. Thorndyke's part of
the tale is narrated by his friend and associate Christopher
Jervis, M.D.*

A Case of Premeditation
by R. Austin Freeman

I. The Elimination of Mr. Pratt

The wine merchant who should supply a consignment of
petit vin to a customer who had ordered, and paid for, a vintage wine, would render himself subject to unambiguous comment. Nay! more; he would be liable to certain legal
penalties. And yet his conduct would be morally indistin-
guishable from that of the railway company which, having
accepted a first-class fare, inflicts upon the passenger that
kind of company which he has paid to avoid. But the cor-
porate conscience, as Herbert Spencer was wont to explain, is
an altogether inferior product to that of the individual.

Such were the reflections of Mr. Rufus Pembury when, as
the train was about to move out of Maidstone (West) station, a coarse and burly man (clearly a denizen of the third-
class) was ushered into his compartment by the guard. He
had paid the higher fare, not for cushioned seats, but for se-

clusion or, at least, select companionship. The man's entry had deprived him of both, and he resented it.

But if the presence of this stranger involved a breach of contract, his conduct was a positive affront—an indignity; for, no sooner had the train started than, he fixed upon Mr. Pembury a gaze of impertinent intensity, and continued thereafter to regard him with a stare as steady and unwinking as that of a Polynesian idol.

It was offensive to a degree, and highly disconcerting withal. Mr. Pembury fidgeted in his seat with increasing discomfort and rising temper. He looked into his pocketbook, read one or two letters and sorted a collection of visiting-cards. He even thought of opening his umbrella. Finally, his patience exhausted and his wrath mounting to boiling-point, he turned to the stranger with frosty remonstrance.

"I imagine, sir, that you will have no difficulty in recognising me, should we ever meet again—which God forbid."

"I should recognise you among ten thousand," was the reply, so unexpected as to leave Mr. Pembury speechless. "You see," the stranger continued impressively, "I've got the gift of faces. I never forget."

"That must be a great consolation," said Pembury.

"It's very useful to me," said the stranger, "at least, it used to be, when I was a warder at Portland—you remember me, I dare say: my name is Pratt. I was assistant-warder in your time. God-forsaken hole, Portland, and mighty glad I was when they used to send me up to town on reckernising duty. Holloway was the house of detention then, you remember; that was before they moved to Brixton."

Pratt paused in his reminiscences, and Pembury, pale and gasping with astonishment, pulled himself together.

"I think," said he, "you must be mistaking me for someone else."

"I don't," replied Pratt. "You're Francis Dobbs, that's who you are. Slipped away from Portland one evening about twelve years ago. Clothes washed up on the Bill next day. No trace of fugitive. As neat a mizzle as ever I heard of. But there are a couple of photographs and a set of finger-prints at the Habitual Criminals Register. P'raps you'd like to come and see 'em?"

"Why should I go to the Habitual Criminals Register?" Pembury demanded faintly.

"Ah! Exactly. Why should you? When you are a man of means, and a little judiciously invested capital would render it unnecessary?"

Pembury looked out of the window, and for a minute or more preserved a stony silence. At length he turned suddenly to Pratt. "How much?" he asked.

"I shouldn't think a couple of hundred a year would hurt you," was the calm reply.

Pembury reflected a while. "What makes you think I am a man of means?" he asked presently.

Pratt smiled grimly. "Bless you, Mr. Pembury," said he, "I know all about you. Why, for the last six months I have been living within half-a-mile of your house."

"The devil you have!"

"Yes. When I retired from the service, General O'Gorman engaged me as a sort of steward or caretaker of his little place in Baysford—he's very seldom there himself—and the very day after I came down, I met you and spotted you, but, naturally, I kept out of sight myself. Thought I'd find out whether you were good for anything before I spoke, so I've been keeping my ears open and I find you are good for a couple of hundred."

There was an interval of silence, and then the ex-warder resumed—

"That's what comes of having a memory of faces. Now there's Jack Ellis, on the other hand; he must have had you under his nose for a couple of years, and yet he's never twigged—he never will either," added Pratt, already regretting the confidence into which his vanity had led him.

"Who is Jack Ellis?" Pembury demanded sharply.

"Why, he's a sort of supernumary at the Baysford Police Station; does odd jobs; rural detective, helps in the office and that sort of thing. He was in the Civil Guard at Portland, in your time, but he got his left forefinger chopped off, so they pensioned him, and, as he was a Baysford man, he got this billet. But he'll never reckernise you, don't you fear."

"Unless you direct his attention to me," suggested Pembury.

"There's no fear of that," laughed Pratt. "You can trust me

to sit quiet on my own nest-egg. Besides, we're not very friendly. He came nosing around our place after the parlour-maid—him a married man, mark you! But I soon boosted him out, I can tell you; and Jack Ellis don't like me now."

"I see," said Pembury reflectively; then, after a pause, he asked: "Who is this General O'Gorman? I seem to know the name."

"I expect you do," said Pratt. "He was governor of Dartmoor when I was there—that was my last billet—and, let me tell you, if he'd been at Portland in your time, you'd never have got away."

"How is that?"

"Why, you see, the general is a great man on bloodhounds. He kept a pack at Dartmoor and, you bet, those lags knew it. There were no attempted escapes in those days. They wouldn't have had a chance."

"He has the pack still, hasn't he?" asked Pembury.

"Rather. Spends any amount of time on training 'em, too. He's always hoping there'll be a burglary or a murder in the neighbourhood so as he can try 'em, but he's never got a chance yet. P'raps the crooks have heard about 'em. But, to come back to our little arrangement: what do you say to a couple of hundred, paid quarterly, if you like?"

"I can't settle the matter off-hand," said Pembury. "You must give me time to think it over."

"Very well," said Pratt. "I shall be back at Baysford to-morrow evening. That will give you a clear day to think it over. Shall I look in at your place to-morrow night?"

"No," replied Pembury; "you'd better not be seen at my house, nor I at yours. If I meet you at some quiet spot, where we shan't be seen, we can settle our business without anyone knowing that we have met. It won't take long, and we can't be too careful."

"That's true," agreed Pratt. "Well, I'll tell you what. There's an avenue leading up to our house; you know it, I expect. There's no lodge, and the gates are always ajar, except-ing at night. Now I shall be down by the six-thirty at Baysford. Our place is a quarter of an hour from the station. Say you meet me in the avenue at a quarter to seven. How will that do?"

"That will suit me," said Pembury; "that is, if you are sure the bloodhounds won't be straying about the grounds."

"Lord bless you, no!" laughed Pratt. "D'you suppose the general lets his precious hounds stray about for any casual crook to feed with poisoned sausage? No, they're locked up safe in the kennels at the back of the house. Hallo! This'll be Swanley, I expect. I'll change into a smoker here and leave you time to turn the matter over in your mind. So long. To-morrow evening in the avenue at a quarter to seven. And, I say, Mr. Pembury, you might as well bring the first in-stallment with you—fifty, in small notes or gold."

"Very well," said Mr. Pembury. He spoke coldly enough, but there was a flush on his cheeks and an angry light in his eyes, which, perhaps, the ex-warder noticed; for when he had stepped out and shut the door, he thrust his head in at the window and said threateningly—

"One more word, Mr. Pembury-Dobbs: no hanky-panky, you know. I'm an old hand and pretty fly, I am. So don't you try any chickery-pokery on me. That's all." He withdrew his head and disappeared, leaving Pembury to his reflections.

The nature of those reflections, if some telepathist—trans-ferring his attention for the moment from hidden court-cards or missing thimbles to more practical matters—could have conveyed them into the mind of Mr. Pratt, would have caused that quondam official some surprise and, perhaps, a little disquiet. For long experience of the criminal, as he ap-pears when in durance, had produced some rather misleading ideas as to his behaviour when at large. In fact, the ex-warder had considerably underestimated the ex-convict.

Rufus Pembury, to give him his real name—for Dobbs was literally a *nom de guerre*—was a man of strong character and intelligence. So much so that, having tried the criminal career and found it not worth pursuing, he had definitely abandoned it. When the cattle-boat that picked him up off Portland Bill had landed him at an American port, he brought his entire ability and energy to bear on legitimate commercial pursuits, and with such success that, at the end of ten years, he was able to return to England with a moderate competence. Then he had taken a modest house near the little town of Baysford, where he had lived quietly on his savings for the last two years, holding aloof without much difficulty from the rather exclusive local society; and here he might have lived out the rest of his life in peace but for the unlucky chance that brought the man Pratt into the neighbourhood. With the arrival of Pratt his security was utterly destroyed.

There is something eminently unsatisfactory about a blackmailer. No arrangement with him has any permanent validity. No undertaking that he gives is binding. The thing which he has sold remains in his possession to sell over again. He pockets the price of emancipation, but retains the key of the fetters. In short, the blackmailer is a totally impossible person.

Such were the considerations that had passed through the mind of Rufus Pembury, even while Pratt was making his proposals; and those proposals he had never for an instant entertained. The ex-warder's advice to him to "turn the matter over in his mind" was unnecessary. For his mind was already made up. His decision was arrived at in the very moment when Pratt had disclosed his identity. The conclusion was self-evident. Before Pratt appeared he was living in peace and security. While Pratt remained, his liberty was precarious from moment to moment. If Pratt should disappear, his peace and security would return. Therefore Pratt must be eliminated.

It was a logical consequence.

The profound meditations, therefore, in which Pembury remained immersed for the remainder of the journey had nothing whatever to do with the quarterly allowance; they were concerned exclusively with the elimination of ex-warder Pratt.

Now Rufus Pembury was not a ferocious man. He was not even cruel. But he was gifted with a certain magnanimous cynicism which ignored the trivialities of sentiment and regarded only the main issues. If a wasp hummed over his teacup, he would crush that wasp; but not with his bare hand. The wasp carried the means of aggression. That was the wasp's look-out, *His* concern was to avoid being stung.

So it was with Pratt. The man had elected, for his own profit, to threaten Pembury's liberty. Very well. He had done it at his own risk. That risk was no concern of Pembury's. *His* concern was his own safety.

When Pembury alighted at Charing Cross, he directed his steps (after having watched Pratt's departure from the station) to Buckingham Street, Strand, where he entered a quiet private hotel. He was apparently expected, for the manageress greeted him by his name as she handed him his key.

"Are you staying in town, Mr. Pembury?" she asked.

"No," was the reply. "I go back to-morrow morning, but I may be coming up again shortly. By the way, you used to have an encyclopædia in one of the rooms. Could I see it for a moment?"

"It is in the drawing-room," said the manageress. "Shall I show you?—but you know the way, don't you?"

Certainly Mr. Pembury knew the way. It was on the first floor; a pleasant old-world room looking on the quiet old street, and on a shelf, amidst a collection of novels, stood the sedate volumes of *Chambers's Encyclopædia*.

That a gentleman from the country should desire to look up the subject of "hounds" would not, to a casual observer, have seemed unnatural. But when from hounds the student proceeded to the article on blood, and thence to one devoted to perfumes, the observer might reasonably have felt some surprise; and this surprise might have been augmented if he had followed Mr. Pembury's subsequent proceedings, and especially if he had considered them as the actions of a man whose immediate aim was the removal of a superfluous unit of the population.

Having deposited his bag and umbrella in his room, Pembury set forth from the hotel as one with a definite purpose; and his footsteps led, in the first place, to an umbrella shop in the Strand, where he selected a thick rattan cane. There was nothing remarkable in this, perhaps; but the cane was of an uncomely thickness and the salesman protested. "I like a thick cane," said Pembury.

"Yes, sir; but for a gentleman of your height" (Pembury was a small, slightly-built man) "I would venture to suggest——"

"I like a thick cane," repeated Pembury. "Cut it down to the proper length and don't rivet the ferrule on. I'll cement it on when I get home."

His next investment would have seemed more to the purpose, though suggestive of unexpected crudity of method. It was a large Norwegian knife. But not content with this he went on forthwith to a second cutler's and purchased a second knife, the exact duplicate of the first. Now, for what purpose could he want two identically similar knives? And why not have bought them both at the same shop? It was highly mysterious.

Shopping appeared to be a positive mania with Rufus Pembury. In the course of the next half-hour he acquired a cheap hand-bag, an artist's black-japanned brush-case, a three-cornered file, a stick of elastic glue and a pair of iron crucible-tongs. Still insatiable, he repaired to an old-fashioned chemist's shop in a by-street, where he further enriched himself with a packet of absorbent cotton-wool and an ounce of permanganate of potash; and, as the chemist wrapped up these articles, with the occult and necromantic air peculiar to chemists, Pembury watched him impassively.

"I suppose you don't keep musk?" he asked carelessly.

The chemist paused in the act of heating a stick of sealing-wax, and appeared as if about to mutter an incantation. But he merely replied: "No, sir. Not the solid musk; it's so very costly. But I have the essence."

"That isn't as strong as the pure stuff, I suppose?"

"No," replied the chemist, with a cryptic smile, "not *so* strong, but strong enough. These animal perfumes are so very penetrating, you know; and so lasting. Why, I venture to say that if you were to sprinkle a table-spoonful of the essence in the middle of St. Paul's, the place would smell of it six months hence."

"You don't say so!" said Pembury. "Well, that ought to be enough for anybody. I'll take a small quantity, please, and, for goodness' sake, see that there isn't any on the outside of the bottle. The stuff isn't for myself, and I don't want to go about smelling like a civet cat."

"Naturally you don't, sir," agreed the chemist. He then produced an ounce bottle, a small glass funnel and a stoppered bottle labelled "Ess. Moschi," with which he proceeded to perform a few trifling feats of legerdemain.

"There, sir," said he, when he had finished the performance, "there is not a drop on the outside of the bottle, and, if I fit it with a rubber cork, you will be quite secure."

Pembury's dislike of musk appeared to be excessive, for, when the chemist had retired into a secret cubicle as if to hold converse with some familiar spirit (but actually to change half-a-crown), he took the brush-case from his bag, pulled off its lid, and then, with the crucible-tongs, daintily lifted the bottle off the counter, slid it softly into the brush case, and, replacing the lid, returned the case and tongs to the bag. The other two packets he took from the counter and dropped into his pocket, and when the presiding wizard, having miraculously transformed a single half-crown into four pennies, handed him the product, he left the shop and walked thoughtfully back towards the Strand. Suddenly a new idea seemed to strike him. He halted, considered for a few moments and then strode away northward to make the oddest of all his purchases.

The transaction took place in a shop in the Seven Dials, whose strange stock-in-trade ranged the whole zoological gamut, from water-snails to Angora cats. Pembury looked at a cage of guinea-pigs in the window and entered the shop.

"Do you happen to have a dead guinea-pig?" he asked.

"No; mine are all alive," replied the man, adding, with a sinister grin: "but they're not immortal, you know."

Pembury looked at the man distastefully. There is an appreciable difference between a guinea-pig and a blackmailer. "Any small mammal would do," he said.

"There's a dead rat in that cage, if he's any good," said the man. "Died this morning, so he's quite fresh."

"I'll take the rat," said Pembury; "he'll do quite well."

The little corpse was accordingly made into a parcel and deposited in the bag, and Pembury, having tendered a complimentary fee, made his way back to the hotel.

After a modest lunch he went forth and spent the remainder of the day transacting the business which had originally brought him to town. He dined at a restaurant and did not return to his hotel until ten o'clock, when he took his key, and tucking under his arm a parcel that he had brought in with him, retired for the night. But before undressing—and after locking his door—he did a very strange and unaccountable thing. Having pulled off the loose ferrule from his newly-purchased cane, he bored a hole in the bottom of it with the spike end of the file. Then, using the latter as a broach, he enlarged the hole until only a narrow rim of the bottom was left. He next rolled up a small ball of cotton-wool and pushed it into the ferrule; and, having smeared the end of the cane with elastic glue, he replaced the ferrule, warming it over the gas to make the glue stick.

When he had finished with the cane, he turned his attention to one of the Norwegian knives. First, he carefully removed with the file most of the bright, yellow varnish from the wooden case or handle.

Then he opened the knife, and, cutting the string of the parcel that he had brought in, took from it the dead rat which he had bought at the zoologist's. Laying the animal on a sheet of paper, he cut off its head, and, holding it up by the tail, allowed the blood that oozed from the neck to drop on the knife, spreading it over both sides of the blade and handle with his finger.

Then he laid the knife on the paper and softly opened the window. From the darkness below came the voice of a cat, apparently perfecting itself in the execution of chromatic scales; and in that direction Pembury flung the body and head of the rat, and closed the window. Finally, having washed his hands and stuffed the paper from the parcel into the fireplace, he went to bed.

But his proceedings in the morning were equally mysterious. Having breakfasted betimes, he returned to his bedroom and locked himself in. Then he tied his new cane, handle downwards, to the leg of the dressing-table. Next, with the crucible-tongs, he drew the little bottle of muck from the brush-case, and, having assured himself, by sniffing at it, that the exterior was really free from odour, he withdrew the rubber cork. Then, slowly and with infinite care, he poured a few drops—perhaps half-a-teaspoonful—of the essence on the cotton-wool that bulged through the hole in the ferrule, watching the absorbent material narrowly as it soaked up the liquid. When it was saturated he proceeded to treat the knife in the same fashion, letting fall a drop of the essence on the wooden handle—which soaked it up readily. This done, he slid up the window and looked out. Immediately below was a tiny yard in which grew, or rather survived, a couple of faded laurel bushes. The body of the rat was nowhere to be seen; it had apparently been spirited away in the night. Holding out the bottle, which he still held, he dropped it into the bushes, flinging the rubber cork after it.

His next proceeding was to take a tube of vaseline from

his dressing-bag and squeeze a small quantity on to his fingers. With this he thoroughly smeared the shoulder of the brush-case and the inside of the lid, so as to ensure an airtight joint. Having wiped his fingers, he picked the knife up with the crucible-tongs, and, dropping it into the brush-case, immediately pushed on the lid. Then he heated the tips of the tongs in the gas flame, to destroy the scent, packed the tongs and brush-case in the bag, untied the cane—carefully avoiding contact with the ferrule—and, taking up the two bags, went out, holding the cane by its middle.

There was no difficulty in finding an empty compartment, for first-class passengers were few at that time in the morning. Pembury waited on the platform until the guard's whistle sounded, when he stepped into the compartment, shut the door and laid the cane on the seat with its ferrule projecting out of the off-side window, in which position it remained until the train drew up in Baysford station.

Pembury left his dressing-bag at the cloakroom, and, still grasping the cane by its middle, he sallied forth. The town of Baysford lay some half-a-mile to the east of the station; his own house was a mile along the road to the west; and halfway between his house and the station was the residence of General O'Gorman. He knew the place well. Originally a farmhouse, it stood on the edge of a great expanse of flat meadows and communicated with the road by an avenue, nearly three hundred yards long, of ancient trees. The avenue was shut off from the road by a pair of iron gates, but these were merely ornamental, for the place was unenclosed and accessible from the surrounding meadows—indeed, an indistinct footpath crossed the meadows and intersected the avenue about half-way up.

On this occasion Pembury, whose objective was the avenue, elected to approach it by the latter route; and at each stile or fence that he surmounted, he paused to survey the country. Presently the avenue arose before him, lying athwart the narrow track, and, as he entered it between two of the trees, he halted and looked about him.

He stood listening for a while. Beyond the faint rustle of leaves no sound was to be heard. Evidently there was no one about, and, as Pratt was at large, it was probable that the general was absent.

And now Pembury began to examine the adjacent trees with more than a casual interest. The two between which he had entered were respectively an elm and a great pollard oak, the latter being an immense tree whose huge, warty bole divided about seven feet from the ground into tree limbs, each as large as a fair-sized tree, of which the largest swept outward in a great curve half-way across the avenue. On this patriarch Pembury bestowed especial attention, walking completely round it and finally laying down his bag and cane (the latter resting on the bag with the ferrule off the ground) that he might climb up, by the aid of the warty outgrowths, to examine the crown; and he had just stepped up into the space between the three limbs, when the creaking of the iron gates was followed by a quick step in the avenue. Hastily he let himself down from the tree, and, gathering up his possessions, stood close behind the great bole.

"Just as well not to be seen," was his reflection, as he hugged the tree closely and waited, peering cautiously round the trunk. Soon a streak of moving shadow heralded the stranger's approach, and he moved round to keep the trunk between himself and the intruder. On the footsteps came, until the stranger was abreast of the tree; and when he had passed Pembury peeped round at the retreating figure. It was only the postman but then the man knew him, and he was glad he had kept out of sight.

Apparently the oak did not meet his requirements, for he stepped out and looked up and down the avenue. Then, beyond the elm, he caught sight of an ancient pollard hornbeam—a strange, fantastic tree whose trunk widened out trumpet-like above into a broad crown, from the edge of which multitudinous branches uprose like the limbs of some weird hamadryad.

That tree he approved at a glance, but he lingered behind the oak until the postman, returning with brisk step and cheerful whistle, passed down the avenue and left him once more in solitude. Then he moved on with a resolute air to the hornbeam.

The crown of the trunk was barely six feet from the ground. He could reach it easily, as he found on trying. Standing the cane against the tree—ferrule downwards, this time—he took the brush-case from the bag, pulled off the lid, and, with the crucible-tongs, lifted out the knife and laid it on the crown of the tree, just out of sight, leaving the tongs—also invisible—still grasping the knife. He was about to replace the brush-case in the bag, when he appeared to alter his mind. Sniffing at it, and finding it reeking with the sickly perfume, he pushed the lid on again and threw the case up into the tree, where he heard it roll down into the central hollow of the crown. Then he closed the bag, and, taking the cane by its handle, moved slowly away in the direction whence he had come, passing out of the avenue between the elm and the oak.

His mode of progress was certainly peculiar. He walked with excessive slowness, trailing the cane along the ground, and every few paces he would stop and press the ferrule firmly against the earth, so that, to any one who should have observed him, he would have appeared to be wrapped in an absorbing reverie.

Thus he moved on across the fields, not, however, returning to the high road, but crossing another stretch of fields until he emerged into a narrow lane that led out into the High Street. Immediately opposite to the lane was the police station, distinguished from the adjacent cottages only by its lamp, its open door and the notices pasted up outside. Straight across the road Pembury walked, still trailing the cane, and halted at the station door to read the notices, resting his cane on the doorstep as he did so. Through the open doorway he could see a man writing at a desk. The man's back was towards him, but, presently, a movement brought his left hand into view, and Pembury noted that the forefinger was missing. This, then, was Jack Ellis, late of the Civil Guard at Portland.

Even while he was looking the man turned his head, and Pembury recognised him at once. He had frequently met him on the road between Baysford and the adjoining village of Thorpe, and always at the same time. Apparently Ellis paid a daily visit to Thorpe—perhaps to receive a report from the rural constable—and he started between three and four and returned between seven and a quarter past.

Pembury looked at his watch. It was a quarter past three. He moved away thoughtfully (holding his cane, now, by the

middle), and began to walk slowly in the direction of Thorpe
—westward.

For a while he was deeply meditative, and his face wore a
puzzled frown. Then, suddenly, his face cleared and he strode
forward at a brisker pace. Presently he passed through a gap
in the hedge, and, walking in a field parallel with the road,
took out his purse—a small pigskin pouch. Having frugally
emptied it of its contents, excepting a few shillings, he thrust
the ferrule of his cane into the small compartment ordinarily
reserved for gold or notes.

And thus he continued to walk on slowly, carrying the
cane by the middle and the purse jammed on the end.

At length he reached a sharp double curve in the road
whence he could see back for a considerable distance; and
here, opposite a small opening, he sat down to wait. The
hedge screened him effectually from the gaze of passers-by—
though these were few enough—without interfering with his
view.

A quarter of an hour passed. He began to be uneasy. Had
he been mistaken? Were Ellis's visits only occasional instead
of daily, as he had thought? That would be tiresome though
not actually disastrous. But at this point in his reflections a
figure came into view, advancing along the road with a
steady swing. He recognised the figure. It was Ellis.

But there was another figure advancing from the opposite
direction: a labourer, apparently. He prepared to shift his
ground, but another glance showed him that the labourer
would pass first. He waited. The labourer came on and, at
length, passed the opening, and, as he did so, Ellis disappeared for a moment in a bend of the road. Instantly Pembury passed his cane through the opening in the hedge, shook
off the purse and pushed it into the middle of the footway.
Then he crept forward, behind the hedge, towards the approaching official, and again sat down to wait. On came the
steady tramp of the unconscious Ellis, and, as it passed, Pembury drew aside an obstructing branch and peered out at the
retreating figure. The question now was, would Ellis see the
purse? It was not a very conspicuous object.

The footsteps stopped abruptly. Looking out, Pembury saw
the police official stoop, pick up the purse, examine its contents and finally stow it in his trousers pocket. Pembury

heaved a sigh of relief; and, as the dwindling figure passed out of sight round a curve in the road, he rose, stretched himself and strode away briskly.

Near the gap was a group of ricks, and, as he passed them, a fresh idea suggested itself. Looking round quickly, he passed to the farther side of one and, thrusting his cane deeply into it, pushed it home with a piece of stick that he picked up near the rick, until the handle was lost among the straw. The bag was now all that was left, and it was empty—for his other purchases were in the dressing-bag, which, by the way, he must fetch from the station. He opened it and smelt the interior, but, though he could detect no odour, he resolved to be rid of it if possible.

As he emerged from the gap a wagon jogged slowly past. It was piled high with sacks, and the tail-board was down. Stepping into the road, he quickly overtook the wagon, and, having glanced round, laid the bag lightly on the tail-board. Then he set off for the station.

On arriving home he went straight up to his bedroom, and, ringing for his housekeeper, ordered a substantial meal. Then he took off all his clothes and deposited them, even to his shirt, socks and necktie, in a trunk, wherein his summer clothing was stored with a plentiful sprinkling of naphthol to preserve it from the moth. Taking the packet of permanganate of potash from his dressing-bag, he passed into the adjoining bathroom, and, tipping the crystals into the bath, turned on the water. Soon the bath was filled with a pink solution of the salt, and into this he plunged, immersing his entire body and thoroughly soaking his hair. Then he emptied the bath and rinsed himself in clear water, and, having dried himself, returned to the bedroom and dressed himself in fresh clothing. Finally he took a hearty meal, and then lay down on the sofa to rest until it should be time to start for the rendezvous.

Half-past six found him lurking in the shadow by the station-approach, within sight of the solitary lamp. He heard the train come in, saw the stream of passengers emerge, and noted one figure detach itself from the throng and turn on to the Thorpe road. It was Pratt, as the lamplight showed him; Pratt, striding forward to the meeting-place with an air of jaunty satisfaction and an uncommonly creaky pair of boots.

Pembury followed him at a safe distance, and rather by sound than sight, until he was well past the stile at the entrance to the footpath. Evidently he was going on to the gates. Then Pembury vaulted over the stile and strode away swiftly across the dark meadows.

When he plunged into the deep gloom of the avenue, his first act was to grope his way to the hornbeam and slip his hand up on the crown and satisfy himself that the tongs were as he had left them. Reassured by the touch of his fingers on the iron loops, he turned and walked slowly down the avenue. The duplicate knife—ready opened—was in his left inside breast-pocket, and he fingered its handle as he walked.

Presently the iron gate squeaked mournfully, and then the rhythmical creak of a pair of boots was audible, coming up the avenue. Pembury walked forward slowly until a darker smear emerged from the surrounding gloom, when he called out—

"Is that you, Pratt?"

"That's me," was the cheerful, if ungrammatical response, and, as he drew nearer, the ex-warder asked: "Have you brought the rhino, old man?"

The insolent familiarity of the man's tone was agreeable to Pembury: it strengthened his nerve and hardened his heart. "Of course," he replied; "but we must have a definite understanding, you know."

"Look here," said Pratt, "I've got no time for jaw. The general will be here presently; he's riding over from Bingfield with a friend. You hand over the dibs and we'll talk some other time."

"That is all very well," said Pembury, "but you must understand——" He paused abruptly and stood still. They were now close to the hornbeam, and, as he stood, he stared up into the dark mass of foliage.

"What's the matter?" demanded Pratt. "What are you staring at?" He, too, had halted and stood gazing intently into the darkness.

Then, in an instant, Pembury whipped out the knife and drove it, with all his strength, into the broad back of the ex-warder, below the left shoulder-blade.

With a hideous yell Pratt turned and grappled with his assailant. A powerful man and a competent wrestler, too, he was far more than a match for Pembury unarmed, and, in a moment, he had him by the throat. But Pembury clung to him tightly, and, as they trampled to and fro round and round, he stabbed again and again with the viciousness of a scorpion, while Pratt's cries grew more gurgling and husky. Then they fell heavily to the ground, Pembury underneath. But the struggle was over. With a last bubbling groan, Pratt relaxed his hold and in a moment grew limp and inert. Pembury pushed him off and rose, trembling and breathing heavily.

But he wasted no time. There had been more noise than he had bargained for. Quickly stepping up to the hornbeam, he reached up for the tongs. His fingers slid into the looped handles; the tongs grasped the knife, and he lifted it out from its hiding-place and carried it to where the corpse lay, depositing it in the ground a few feet from the body. Then he went back to the tree and carefully pushed the tongs over into the hollow of the crown.

At this moment a woman's voice sounded shrilly from the top of the avenue.

"Is that you, Mr. Pratt?" it called.

Pembury started and then stepped back quickly, on tiptoe, to the body. For there was the duplicate knife. He must take that away at all costs.

The corpse was lying on its back. The knife was underneath it, driven in to the very haft. He had to use both hands to lift the body, and even then he had some difficulty in disengaging the weapon. And, meanwhile, the voice, repeating its question, drew nearer.

At length he succeeded in drawing out the knife and thrust it into his breast-pocket. The corpse fell back, and he stood up gasping.

"Mr. Pratt! Are you there?" The nearness of the voice startled Pembury, and, turning sharply, he saw a light twinkling between the trees. And then the gates creaked loudly and he heard the crunch of a horse's hoofs on the gravel.

He stood for an instant bewildered—utterly taken by surprise. He had not reckoned on a horse. His intended flight across the meadows towards Thorpe was now impracticable. If he were overtaken he was lost, for he knew there was blood on his clothes and his hands were wet and slippery—to say nothing of the knife in his pocket.

But his confusion lasted only for an instant. He remembered the oak tree; and, turning out of the avenue, he ran to it, and, touching it as little as he could with his bloody hands, climbed quickly up into the crown. The great horizontal limb was nearly three feet in diameter, and, as he lay out on it, gathering his coat closely round him, he was quite invisible from below.

He had hardly settled himself when the light which he had seen came into full view, revealing a woman advancing with a stable lantern in her hand. And, almost at the same moment, a streak of brighter light burst from the opposite direction. The horseman was accompanied by a man on a bicycle.

The two men came on apace, and the horseman, sighting the woman, called out: "Anything the matter, Mrs. Parton?" But, at that moment, the light of the bicycle lamp fell full on the prostrate corpse. The two men uttered a simultaneous cry of horror; the woman shrieked aloud: and then the horseman sprang from the saddle and ran forward to the body.

"Why," he exclaimed, stooping over it, "it's Pratt"; and, as the cyclist came up and the glare of his lamp shone on a great pool of blood, he added: "There's been foul play here, Hanford."

Hanford flashed his lamp around the body, lighting up the ground for several yards.

"What is that behind you, O'Gorman?" he said suddenly; "isn't it a knife?" He was moving quickly towards it when O'Gorman held up his hand.

"Don't touch it!" he exclaimed. "We'll put the hounds on it. They'll soon track the scoundrel, whoever he is. By God! Hanford, this fellow has fairly delivered himself into our hands." He stood for a few moments looking down at the knife with something uncommonly like exultation, and then turning quickly to his friend, said: "Look here, Hanford; you ride off to the police station as hard as you can pelt. It is only three-quarters of a mile; you'll do it in five minutes. Send or bring an officer and I'll scour the meadows meanwhile. If I haven't got the scoundrel when you come back, we'll put the hounds on to this knife and run the beggar down."

"Right," replied Hanford, and without another word he wheeled his machine about, mounted and rode away into the darkness.

"Mrs. Parton," said O'Gorman, "watch that knife. See that nobody touches it while I go and examine the meadows."

"Is Mr. Pratt dead, sir?" whimpered Mrs. Parton.

"Gad! I hadn't thought of that," said the general. "You'd better have a look at him; but mind! nobody is to touch that knife or they will confuse the scent."

He scrambled into the saddle and galloped away across the meadows in the direction of Thorpe; and, as Pembury listened to the diminuendo of the horse's hoofs, he was glad that he had not attempted to escape; for that was the direction in which he had meant to go, and he would surely have been overtaken.

As soon as the general was gone, Mrs. Parton, with many a terror-stricken glance over her shoulder, approached the corpse and held the lantern close to the dead face. Suddenly she stood up, trembling violently, for footsteps were audible coming down the avenue. A familiar voice reassured her.

"Is anything wrong, Mrs. Parton?" The question proceeded from one of the maids who had come in search of the elder woman, escorted by a young man, and the pair now came out into the circle of light.

"Good God!" ejaculated the man. "Who's that?"

"It's Mr. Pratt," replied Mrs. Parton. "He's been murdered."

The girl screamed, and then the two domestics approached on tiptoe, staring at the corpse with the fascination of horror.

"Don't touch that knife," said Mrs. Parton, for the man was about to pick it up. "The general's going to put the bloodhounds on to it."

"Is the general here, then?" asked the man; and, as he spoke, the drumming of hoofs, growing momentarily louder, answered him from the meadow.

O'Gorman reined in his horse as he perceived the group of servants gathered about the corpse. "Is he dead, Mrs. Parton?" he asked.

"I am afraid so, sir," was the reply.

"Ha! Somebody ought to go for the doctor; but not you,

Bailey. I want you to get the hounds ready and wait with them at the top of the avenue until I call you."

He was off again into the Baysford meadows, and Bailey hurried away, leaving the two women staring at the body and talking in whispers.

Pembury's position was cramped and uncomfortable. He dared not move, hardly dared to breathe, for the women below him were not a dozen yards away; and it was with mingled feelings of relief and apprehension that he presently saw from his elevated station a group of lights approaching rapidly along the road from Baysford. Presently they were hidden by the trees, and then, after a brief interval, the whirr of wheels sounded on the drive and streaks of light on the tree-trunks announced the new arrivals. There were three bicycles, ridden respectively by Mr. Hanford, a police inspector and a sergeant; and, as they drew up, the general came thundering back into the avenue.

"Is Ellis with you?" he asked, as he pulled up.

"No, sir," was the reply. "He hadn't come in from Thorpe when we left. He's rather late to-night."

"Have you sent for a doctor?"

"Yes, sir, I've sent for Dr. Hills," said the inspector, resting his bicycle against the oak. Pembury could smell the reek of the lamp as he crouched. "Is Pratt dead?"

"Seems to be," replied O'Gorman, "but we'd better leave that to the doctor. There's the murderer's knife. Nobody has touched it. I'm going to fetch the bloodhounds now."

"Ah! that's the thing," said the inspector. "The man can't be far away." He rubbed his hands with a satisfied air as O'Gorman cantered away up the avenue.

In less than a minute there came out from the darkness the deep baying of a hound followed by quick footsteps on the gravel. Then into the circle of light emerged three sinister shapes, loose-limbed and gaunt, and two men advancing at a shambling trot.

"Here, inspector," shouted the general, "you take one; I can't hold 'em both."

The inspector ran forward and seized one of the leashes, and the general led his hound up to the knife, as it lay on the ground. Pembury, peering cautiously round the bough, watched the great brute with almost impersonal curiosity;

noted its high poll, its wrinkled forehead and melancholy face as it stooped to snuff suspiciously at the prostrate knife.

For some moments the hound stood motionless, sniffing at the knife; then it turned away and walked to and fro with its muzzle to the ground. Suddenly it lifted its head, bayed loudly, lowered its muzzle and started forward between the oak and the elm, dragging the general after it at a run.

The inspector next brought his hound to the knife, and was soon bounding away to the tug of the leash in the general's wake.

"They don't make no mistakes, they don't," said Bailey, addressing the gratified sergeant, as he brought forward the third hound; "you'll see——" But his remark was cut short by a violent jerk of the leash, and the next moment he was flying after the others, followed by Mr. Hanford.

The sergeant daintily picked the knife up by its ring, wrapped it in his handkerchief and bestowed it in his pocket. Then he ran off after the hounds.

Pembury smiled grimly. His scheme was working out admirably in spite of the unforeseen difficulties. If those confounded women would only go away, he could come down and take himself off while the course was clear. He listened to the baying of the hounds, gradually growing fainter in the increasing distance, and cursed the dilatoriness of the doctor. Confound the fellow! Didn't he realise that this was a case of life or death? These infernal doctors had no sense of responsibility.

Suddenly his ear caught the tinkle of a bicycle bell; a fresh light appeared coming up the avenue and then a bicycle swept up swiftly to the scene of the tragedy, and a small elderly man jumped down by the side of the body. Giving his machine to Mrs. Parton, he stooped over the dead man, felt the wrist, pushed back an eyelid, held a match to the eye and then rose. "This is a shocking affair, Mrs. Parton," said he. "The poor fellow is quite dead. You had better help me to carry him to the house. If you two take the feet I will take the shoulders."

Pembury watched them raise the body and stagger away with it up the avenue. He heard their shuffling steps die away and the door of the house shut. And still he listened. From far away in the meadows came, at intervals, the baying of the hounds. Other sound there was none. Presently the doctor would come back for his bicycle, but, for the moment, the coast was clear. Pembury rose stiffly. His hands had stuck to the tree where they had pressed against it, and they were still sticky and damp. Quickly he let himself down to the ground, listened again for a moment, and then, making a small circuit to avoid the lamplight, softly crossed the avenue and stole away across the Thorpe meadows.

The night was intensely dark, and not a soul was stirring in the meadows. He strode forward quickly, peering into the darkness and stopping now and again to listen; but no sound came to his ears, save the now faint baying of the distant hounds. Not far from his house, he remembered, was a deep ditch spanned by a wooden bridge, and towards this he now made his way; for he knew that his appearance was such as to convict him at a glance. Arrived at the ditch, he stooped to wash his hands and wrists; and, as he bent forward, the knife fell from his breast-pocket into the shallow water at the margin. He groped for it, and, having found it, drove it deep into the mud as far out as he could reach. Then he wiped his hands on some water-weed, crossed the bridge and started homewards.

He approached his house from the rear, satisfied himself that his housekeeper was in the kitchen, and, letting himself in very quietly with his key, went quickly up to his bedroom. Here he washed thoroughly—in the bath, so that he could get rid of the discoloured water—changed his clothes and packed those that he took off in a portmanteau.

By the time he had done this the gong sounded for supper. As he took his seat at the table, spruce and fresh in appearance, quietly cheerful in manner, he addressed his housekeeper. "I wasn't able to finish my business in London," he said. "I shall have to go up again to-morrow."

"Shall you come home the same day?" asked the housekeeper.

"Perhaps," was the reply, "and perhaps not. It will depend on circumstances."

He did not say what the circumstances might be, nor did the housekeeper ask. Mr. Pembury was not addicted to confidences. He was an eminently discreet man: and discreet men say little.

II. Rival Sleuth-hounds
(Related by Christopher Jervis, M.D.)

The half-hour that follows breakfast, when the fire has, so to speak, got into its stride, and the morning pipe throws up its clouds of incense, is, perhaps, the most agreeable in the whole day. Especially so when a sombre sky, brooding over the town, hints at streets pervaded by the chilly morning air, and hoots from protesting tugs upon the river tell of lingering mists, the legacy of the lately-vanished night.

The autumn morning was raw: the fire burned jovially. I thrust my slippered feet towards the blaze and meditated, on nothing in particular, with cat-like enjoyment. Presently a disapproving grunt from Thorndyke attracted my attention, and I looked round lazily. He was extracting, with a pair of office shears, the readable portions of the morning paper, and had paused with a small cutting between his finger and thumb.

"Bloodhounds again," said he. "We shall be hearing presently of the revival of the ordeal by fire."

"And a deuced comfortable ordeal, too, on a morning like this," I said, stroking my legs ecstatically. "What is the case?"

He was about to reply when a sharp rat-tat from the brass knocker announced a disturber of our peace. Thorndyke stepped over to the door and admitted a police inspector in uniform, and I stood up, and, presenting my dorsal aspect to the fire, prepared to combine bodily comfort with attention to business.

"I believe I am speaking to Dr. Thorndyke," said the officer, and, as Thorndyke nodded, he went on. "My name, sir, is Fox, Inspector Fox of the Baysford Police. Perhaps you've seen the morning paper?"

Thorndyke held up the cutting, and, placing a chair by the fire, asked the inspector if he had breakfasted.

"Thank you, sir, I have," replied Inspector Fox. "I came up to town by the late train last night so as to be here early, and stayed at an hotel. You see, from the paper, that we have had to arrest one of our own men. That's rather awkward, you know, sir."

"Very," agreed Thorndyke.

"Yes; it's bad for the force and bad for the public too. But

we had to do it. There was no way out that we could see.
Still, we should like the accused to have every chance, both
for our sake and his own, so the chief constable thought he'd
like to have your opinion on the case, and he thought that,
perhaps, you might be willing to act for the defence."

"Let us have the particulars," said Thorndyke, taking a
writing-pad from a drawer and dropping into his arm-chair.
"Begin at the beginning," he added, "and tell us all you
know."

"Well," said the inspector, after a preliminary cough, "to
begin with the murdered man: his name is Pratt. He was a
retired prison warder, and was employed as steward by General O'Gorman, who is a retired prison governor—you may
have heard of him in connection with his pack of bloodhounds. Well, Pratt came down from London yesterday evening by a train arriving at Baysford at six-thirty. He was seen
by the guard, the ticket collector and the outside porter. The
porter saw him leave the station at six-thirty-seven. General
O'Gorman's house is about half-a-mile from the station. At
five minutes to seven the general and a gentleman named
Hanford and the general's housekeeper, a Mrs. Parton, found
Pratt lying dead in the avenue that leads up to the house. He
had apparently been stabbed, for there was a lot of blood
about, and a knife—a Norwegian knife—was lying on the
ground near the body. Mrs. Parton had thought she heard
someone in the avenue calling out for help, and, as Pratt was
just due, she came out with a lantern. She met the general
and Mr. Hanford, and all three seem to have caught sight of
the body at the same moment. Mr. Hanford cycled down to
us, at once, with the news; we sent for a doctor, and I went
back with Mr. Hanford and took a sergeant with me. We arrived at twelve minutes past seven, and then the general, who
had galloped his horse over the meadows each side of the
avenue without having seen anybody, fetched out his bloodhounds and led them up to the knife. All three hounds took
up the scent at once—I held the leash of one of them—and
they took us across the meadows without a pause or a falter,
over stiles and fences, along a lane, out into the town, and
then, one after the other, they crossed the road in a bee-line
to the police station, bolted in at the door, which stood open,
and made straight for the desk, where a supernumerary of-

ficer, named Ellis, was writing. They made a rare to-do, struggling to get at him, and it was as much as we could manage to hold them back. As for Ellis, he turned as pale as a ghost."

"Was anyone else in the room?" asked Thorndyke.

"Oh, yes. There were two constables and a messenger. We led the hounds up to them, but the brutes wouldn't take any notice of them. They wanted Ellis."

"And what did you do?"

"Why, we arrested Ellis, of course. Couldn't do anything else—especially with the general there."

"What had the general to do with it?" asked Thorndyke.

"He's a J.P. and a late governor of Dartmoor, and it was his hounds that had run the man down. But we must have arrested Ellis in any case."

"Is there anything against the accused man?"

"Yes, there is. He and Pratt were on distinctly unfriendly terms. They were old comrades, for Ellis was in the Civil Guard at Portland when Pratt was warder there—he was pensioned off from the service because he got his left forefinger chopped off—but lately they had had some unpleasantness about a woman, a parlourmaid of the general's. It seems that Ellis, who is a married man, paid the girl too much attention—or Pratt thought he did—and Pratt warned Ellis off the premises. Since then they had not been on speaking terms."

"And what sort of a man is Ellis?"

"A remarkably decent fellow he always seemed; quiet, steady, good-natured; I should have said he wouldn't have hurt a fly. We all liked him—better than we liked Pratt, in fact; for poor Pratt was what you'd call an old soldier—sly, you know, sir—and a bit of a sneak."

"You searched and examined Ellis, of course?"

"Yes. There was nothing suspicious about him except that he had two purses. But he says he picked up one of them—a small, pigskin pouch—on the footpath of the Thorpe road yesterday afternoon; and there's no reason to disbelieve him. At any rate, the purse was not Pratt's."

Thorndyke made a note on his pad, and then asked: "There were no blood-stains or marks on his clothing?"

"No. His clothing was not marked or disarranged in any way."

"Any cuts, scratches or bruises on his person?"

"None whatever," replied the inspector.

"At what time did you arrest Ellis?"

"Half-past seven exactly."

"Have you ascertained what his movements were? Had he been near the scene of the murder?"

"Yes; he had been to Thorpe and would pass the gates of the avenue on his way back. And he was later than usual in returning, though not later than he has often been before."

"And now, as to the murdered man: has the body been examined?"

"Yes; I had Dr. Hills's report before I left. There were no less than seven deep knife-wounds, all on the left side of the back. There was a great deal of blood on the ground, and Dr. Hills thinks Pratt must have bled to death in a minute or two."

"Do the wounds correspond with the knife that was found?"

"I asked the doctor that, and he said 'Yes,' though he wasn't going to swear to any particular knife. However, that point isn't of much importance. The knife was covered with blood, and it was found close to the body."

"What has been done with it, by the way?" asked Thorndyke.

"The sergeant who was with me picked it up and rolled it in his handkerchief to carry in his pocket. I took it from him, just as it was, and locked it in a dispatch-box, handkerchief and all."

"Has the knife been recognised as Ellis's property?"

"No, sir, it has not."

"Were there any recognisable footprints or marks of a struggle?" Thorndyke asked.

The inspector grinned sheepishly. "I haven't examined the spot, of course, sir," said he, "but, after the general's horse and the bloodhounds and the general on foot and me and the gardener and the sergeant and Mr. Hanford had been over it twice, going and returning, why, you see, sir——"

"Exactly, exactly," said Thorndyke. "Well, inspector, I

shall be pleased to act for the defence; it seems to me that the case against Ellis is in some respects rather inconclusive."

The inspector was frankly amazed. "It certainly hadn't struck me in that light, sir," he said.

"No? Well, that is my view; and I think the best plan will be for me to come down with you and investigate matters on the spot."

The inspector assented cheerfully, and, when we had provided him with a newspaper, we withdrew to the laboratory to consult time-tables and prepare for the expedition.

"You are coming, I suppose, Jervis?" said Thorndyke.

"If I shall be of any use," I replied.

"Of course you will," said he. "Two heads are better than one, and, by the look of things, I should say that ours will be the only ones with any sense in them. We will take the research case, of course, and we may as well have a camera with us. I see there is a train from Charing Cross in twenty minutes."

For the first half-hour of the journey Thorndyke sat in his corner, alternately conning over his notes and gazing with thoughtful eyes out of the window. I could see that the case pleased him, and was careful not to break in upon his train of thought. Presently, however, he put away his notes and began to fill his pipe with a more companionable air, and then the inspector, who had been wriggling with impatience, opened fire.

"So you think, sir, that you see a way out for Ellis?"

"I think there is a case for the defence," replied Thorndyke. "In fact, I call the evidence against him rather flimsy."

The inspector gasped. "But the knife, sir? What about the knife?"

"Well," said Thorndyke, "what about the knife? Whose knife was it? You don't know. It was covered with blood. Whose blood? You don't know. Let us assume, for the sake of argument, that it was the murderer's knife. Then the blood on it was Pratt's blood. But if it was Pratt's blood, when the hounds had smelt it they should have led you to Pratt's body, for blood gives a very strong scent. But they did not. They ignored the body. The inference seems to be that the blood on the knife was not Pratt's blood."

The inspector took off his cap and gently scratched the

back of his head. "You're perfectly right, sir," he said. "I'd never thought of that. None of us had."

"Then," pursued Thorndyke, "let us assume that the knife was Pratt's. If so, it would seem to have been used in self-defence. But this was a Norwegian knife, a clumsy tool—not a weapon at all—which takes an appreciable time to open and requires the use of two free hands. Now, had Pratt both hands free? Certainly not after the attack had commenced. There were seven wounds, all on the left side of the back; which indicates that he held the murderer locked in his arms and that the murderer's arms were around him. Also, incidentally, that the murderer is right-handed. But, still, let us assume that the knife was Pratt's. Then the blood on it was that of the murderer. Then the murderer must have been wounded. But Ellis was not wounded. Then Ellis is not the murderer. The knife doesn't help us at all."

The inspector puffed out his cheeks and blew softly. "This is getting out of my depth," he said. "Still, sir, you can't get over the bloodhounds. They tell us distinctly that the knife is Ellis's knife and I don't see any answer to that."

"There is no answer because there has been no statement. The bloodhounds have told you nothing. You have drawn certain inferences from their actions, but those inferences may be totally wrong and they are certainly not evidence."

"You don't seem to have much opinion of bloodhounds," the inspector remarked.

"As agents for the detection of crime," replied Thorndyke, "I regard them as useless. You cannot put a bloodhound in the witness-box. You can get no intelligible statement from it. If it possesses any knowledge, it has no means of communicating it. The fact is," he continued, "that the entire system of using bloodhounds for criminal detection is based on a fallacy. In the American plantations these animals were used with great success for tracking runaway slaves. But the slave was a known individual. All that was required was to ascertain his whereabouts. That is not the problem that is presented in the detection of a crime. The detection is not concerned in establishing the whereabouts of a known individual, but in discovering the identity of an unknown individual. And for this purpose bloodhounds are useless. They may discover such identity, but they cannot communicate their knowledge. If the criminal is unknown they cannot identify him: if he is known, the police have no need of the blood-hound.

"To return to our present case," Thorndyke resumed after a pause; "we have employed certain agents—the hounds—with whom we are not *en rapport*, as the spiritualists would say; and we have no 'medium.' The hound possesses a special sense—the olfactory—which in man is quite rudimentary. He thinks, so to speak, in terms of smell, and his thoughts are untranslatable to beings in whom the sense of smell is unde-veloped. We have presented to the hound a knife, and he dis-covers in it certain odorous properties; he discovers similar or related odorous properties in a tract of land and a human in-dividual—Ellis. We cannot verify his discoveries or ascertain their nature. What remains? All that we can say is that there appears to exist some odorous relation between the knife and the man Ellis. But until we can ascertain the nature of that relation, we cannot estimate its evidential value or bearing. All the other 'evidence' is the product of your imagination and that of the general. There is, at present, no case against Ellis."

"He must have been pretty close to the place when the murder happened," said the inspector.

"So, probably, were many other people," answered Thorn-dyke; "but had he time to wash and change? Because he would have needed it."

"I suppose he would," the inspector agreed dubiously.

"Undoubtedly. There were seven wounds which would have taken some time to inflict. Now we can't suppose that Pratt stood passively while the other man stabbed him—indeed, as I have said, the position of the wounds shows that he did not. There was a struggle. The two men were locked together. One of the murderer's hands was against Pratt's back; probably both hands were, one clasping and the other stabbing. There must have been blood on one hand and prob-ably on both. But you say there was no blood on Ellis, and there doesn't seem to have been time or opportunity for him to wash."

"Well, it's a mysterious affair," said the inspector; "but I don't see how you are going to get over the bloodhounds."

Thorndyke shrugged his shoulders impatiently. "The bloodhounds are an obsession," he said. "The whole problem really centres around the knife. The questions are, Whose knife was it? and what was the connection between it and Ellis? There is a problem, Jervis," he continued, turning to me, "that I submit for your consideration. Some of the possible solutions are exceedingly curious."

As we set out from Baysford station, Thorndyke looked at his watch and noted the time. "You will take us the way that Pratt went," he said.

"As to that," said the inspector, "he may have gone by the road or by the footpath; but there's very little difference in the distance."

Turning away from Baysford, we walked along the road westward, towards the village of Thorpe, and presently passed on our right a stile at the entrance to a footpath.

"The path," said the inspector, "crosses the avenue about half-way up. But we'd better keep to the road." A quarter of a mile farther on we came to a pair of rusty iron gates, one of which stood open, and, entering, we found ourselves in a broad drive bordered by two rows of trees, between the trunks of which a long stretch of pasture meadows could be seen on either hand. It was a fine avenue, and, late in the year as it was, the yellowing foliage clustered thickly overhead.

When we had walked about a hundred and fifty yards from the gates, the inspector halted.

"This is the place," he said; and Thorndyke again noted the time.

"Nine minutes exactly," said he. "Then Pratt arrived here about fourteen minutes to seven, and his body was found at five minutes to seven—nine minutes after his arrival. The murderer couldn't have been far away then."

"No, it was a pretty fresh scent," replied the inspector. "You'd like to see the body first, I think you said, sir?"

"Yes; and the knife, if you please."

"I shall have to send down to the station for that. It's locked up in the office."

He entered the house, and, having dispatched a messenger to the police station, came out and conducted us to the outbuilding where the corpse had been deposited. Thorndyke made a rapid examination of the wounds and the holes in the clothing, neither of which presented anything particularly suggestive. The weapon used had evidently been a thick-backed, single-edged knife similar to the one described, and the discoloration around the wounds indicated that the weapon had a definite shoulder like that of a Norwegian knife, and that it had been driven in with savage violence.

"Do you find anything that throws any light on the case?" the inspector asked, when the examination was concluded.

"That is impossible to say until we have seen the knife," replied Thorndyke; "but while we are waiting for it, we may as well go and look at the scene of the tragedy. These are Pratt's boots, I think?" He lifted a pair of stout laced boots from the table and turned them up to inspect the soles.

"Yes, those are his boots," replied Fox, "and pretty easy they'd have been to track, if the case had been the other way about. Those Blakey's protectors are as good as a trademark."

"We'll take them, at any rate," said Thorndyke; and, the inspector having taken the boots from him, we went out and retraced our steps down the avenue.

The place where the murder had occurred was easily identified by a large dark stain on the gravel at one side of the drive, half-way between two trees, an ancient pollard hornbeam and an elm. Next to the elm was a pollard oak with a squat, warty bole about seven feet high, and three enormous limbs, of which one slanted half-way across the avenue; and between these two trees the ground was covered with the tracks of men and hounds superimposed upon the hoof-prints of a horse.

"Where was the knife found?" Thorndyke asked.

The inspector indicated a spot near the middle of the drive, almost opposite the hornbeam and Thorndyke, picking up a large stone, laid it on the spot. Then he surveyed the scene thoughtfully, looking up and down the drive and at the trees that bordered it, and, finally, walked slowly to the space between the elm and the oak, scanning the ground as he went. "There is no dearth of footprints," he remarked grimly, as he looked down at the trampled earth.

"No, but the question is, whose are they?" said the inspector.

"Yes, that is the question," agreed Thorndyke; "and we will begin the solution by identifying those of Pratt."

"I don't see how that will help us," said the inspector. "We know he was here."

Thorndyke looked at him in surprise, and I must confess that the foolish remark astonished me too, accustomed as I was to the quick-witted officers from Scotland Yard.

"The hue-and-cry procession," remarked Thorndyke, "seems to have passed out between the elm and the oak; elsewhere the ground seems pretty clear." He walked round the elm, still looking earnestly at the ground, and presently continued: "Now here, in the soft earth bordering the turf, are the prints of a pair of smallish feet wearing pointed boots; a rather short man, evidently, by the size of foot and length of stride, and he doesn't seem to have belonged to the procession. But I don't see any of Pratt's; he doesn't seem to have come off the hard gravel." He continued to walk slowly towards the hornbeam with his eyes fixed on the ground. Suddenly he halted and stooped with an eager look at the earth; and, as Fox and I approached, he stood up and pointed. "Pratt's footprints—faint and fragmentary, but unmistakable. And now, inspector, you see their importance. They furnish the time factor in respect of the other footprints. Look at this one and then look at that." He pointed from one to another of the faint impressions of the dead man's foot.

"You mean that there are signs of a struggle?" said Fox.

"I mean more than that," replied Thorndyke. "Here is one of Pratt's footprints treading into the print of a small, pointed foot; and there at the edge of the gravel is another of Pratt's nearly obliterated by the tread of a pointed foot. Obviously the first pointed footprint was made before Pratt's, and the second one after his; and the necessary inference is that the owner of the pointed foot was here at the same time as Pratt."

"Then he must have been the murderer!" exclaimed Fox.

"Presumably," answered Thorndyke; "but let us see whither he went. You notice, in the first place, that the man stood close to this tree"—he indicated the hornbeam—"and that he went towards the elm. Let us follow him. He passes the elm, you see, and you will observe that these tracks form a regular series leading from the hornbeam and not mixed up with the marks of the struggle. They were, therefore, probably made after the murder had been perpetrated. You will also notice that they pass along the backs of the trees—outside the avenue, that is; what does that suggest to you?"

"It suggests to me," I said, when the inspector had shaken his head hopelessly, "that there was possibly someone in the avenue when the man was stealing off."

"Precisely," said Thorndyke. "The body was found not more than nine minutes after Pratt arrived here. But the murder must have taken some time. Then the housekeeper thought she heard someone calling and came out with a lantern, and, at the same time, the general and Mr. Hanford came up the drive. The suggestion is that the man sneaked along outside the trees to avoid being seen. However, let us follow the tracks. They pass the elm and they pass on behind the next tree; but wait! There is something odd here." He passed behind the great pollard oak and looked down at the soft earth by its roots. "Here is a pair of impressions much deeper than the rest, and they are not a part of the track since their toes point towards the tree. What do you make of that?" Without waiting for an answer he began closely to scan the bole of the tree and especially a large, warty protuberance about three feet from the ground. On the bark above this was a vertical mark, as if something had scraped down the tree, and from the wart itself a dead twig had been newly broken off and lay upon the ground. Pointing to these marks Thorndyke set his foot on the protuberance, and, springing up, brought his eye above the level of the crown, whence the great boughs branched off.

"Ah!" he exclaimed. "Here is something much more definite." With the aid of another projection, he scrambled up into the crown of the tree, and, having glanced quickly round, beckoned to us. I stepped up on the projecting lump and, as my eyes rose above the crown, I perceived the brown, shiny impression of a hand on the edge. Climbing into the crown, I was quickly followed by the inspector, and we both stood up by Thorndyke between the three boughs. From where we stood we looked on the upper side of the great limb that swept out across the avenue; and there on its lichen-covered surface, we saw the imprints in reddish-brown of a pair of open hands.

"You notice," said Thorndyke, leaning out upon the bough, "that he is a short man; I cannot conveniently place my hands so low. You also note that he has both forefingers intact, and so is certainly not Ellis."

"If you mean to say, sir, that these marks were made by the murderer," said Fox, "I say it's impossible. Why, that would mean that he was here looking down at us when we were searching for him with the hounds. The presence of the hounds proves that this man could not have been the murderer."

"On the contrary," said Thorndyke, "the presence of this man with bloody hands confirms the other evidence, which all indicates that the hounds were never on the murderer's trail at all. Come now, inspector, I put it to you: Here is a murdered man; the murderer has almost certainly blood upon his hands; and here is a man with bloody hands, lurking in a tree within a few feet of the corpse and within a few minutes of its discovery (as is shown by the footprints); what are the reasonable probabilities?"

"But you are forgetting the bloodhounds, sir, and the murderer's knife," urged the inspector.

"Tut, tut, man!" exclaimed Thorndyke; "those bloodhounds are a positive obsession. But I see a sergeant coming up the drive, with the knife, I hope. Perhaps that will solve the riddle for us."

The sergeant, who carried a small dispatch-box, halted opposite the tree in some surprise while we descended, when he came forward with a military salute and handed the box to the inspector, who forthwith unlocked it, and, opening the lid, displayed an object wrapped in a pocket-handkerchief.

"There is the knife, sir," said he, "just as I received it. The handkerchief is the sergeant's."

Thorndyke unrolled the handkerchief and took from it a large-sized Norwegian knife, which he looked at critically and then handed to me. While I was inspecting the blade, he shook out the handkerchief and, having looked it over on both sides, turned to the sergeant.

"At what time did you pick up this knife?" he asked.

"About seven-fifteen, sir; directly after the hounds had started. I was careful to pick it up by the ring, and I wrapped it in the handkerchief at once."

"Seven-fifteen," said Thorndyke. "Less than half-an-hour after the murder. That is very singular. Do you observe the state of this handkerchief? There is not a mark on it. Not a trace of any bloodstain; which proves that when the knife was picked up, the blood on it was already dry. But things dry slowly, if they dry at all, in the saturated air of an autumn evening. The appearances seem to suggest that the blood on the knife was dry when it was thrown down. By the way, sergeant, what do you scent your handkerchief with?"

"Scent, sir!" exclaimed the astonished officer in indignant accents; "me scent my handkerchief! No, sir, certainly not. Never used scent in my life, sir."

Thorndyke held out the handkerchief, and the sergeant sniffed at it incredulously. "It certainly does seem to smell of scent," he admitted, "but it must be the knife." The same idea having occurred to me, I applied the handle of the knife to my nose and instantly detected the sickly-sweet odour of musk.

"The question is," said the inspector, when the two articles had been tested by us all, "was it the knife that scented the handkerchief or the handkerchief that scented the knife?"

"You heard what the sergeant said," replied Thorndyke. "There was no scent on the handkerchief when the knife was wrapped in it. Do you know, inspector, this scent seems to me to offer a very curious suggestion. Consider the facts of the case: the distinct trail leading straight to Ellis, who is, nevertheless, found to be without a scratch or a spot of blood; the inconsistencies in the case that I pointed out in the train, and now this knife, apparently dropped with dried blood on it and scented with musk. To me it suggests a carefully-planned, coolly-premeditated crime. The murderer knew about the general's bloodhounds and made use of them as a blind. He planted this knife, smeared with blood and tainted with musk, to furnish a scent. No doubt some object, also scented with musk, would be drawn over the ground to give the trail. It is only a suggestion, of course, but it is worth considering."

"But, sir," the inspector objected eagerly, "if the murderer had handled the knife, it would have scented him too."

"Exactly; so, as we are assuming that the man is not a fool, we may assume that he did not handle it. He will have left it here in readiness, hidden in some place whence he could knock it down, say, with a stick, without touching it."

"Perhaps in this very tree, sir," suggested the sergeant, pointing to the oak.

"No," said Thorndyke, "he would hardly have hidden in the tree where the knife had been. The hounds might have scented the place instead of following the trail at once. The most likely hiding-place for the knife is the one nearest the spot where it was found." He walked over to the stone that marked the spot, and, looking round, continued: "You see, that hornbeam is much the nearest, and its flat crown would be very convenient for the purpose—easily reached even by a short man, as he appears to be. Let us see if there are any traces of it. Perhaps you will give me a 'back up,' sergeant, as we haven't a ladder."

The sergeant assented with a faint grin, and, stooping beside the tree in an attitude suggesting the game of leap-frog, placed his hands firmly on his knees. Grasping a stout branch, Thorndyke swung himself up on the sergeant's broad back, whence he looked down into the crown of the tree. Then, parting the branches, he stepped on to the ledge and disappeared into the central hollow.

When he reappeared he held in his hands two very singular objects: a pair of iron crucible-tongs and an artist's brush-case of black-japanned tin. The former article he handed down to me, but the brush-case he held carefully by its wire handle as he dropped to the ground.

"The significance of these things is, I think, obvious," he said. "The tongs were used to handle the knife with and the case to carry it in, so that it should not scent his clothes or bag. It was very carefully planned."

"If that is so," said the inspector, "the inside of the case ought to smell of musk."

"No doubt," said Thorndyke; "but before we open it, there is a rather important matter to be attended to. Will you give me the Vitogen powder, Jervis?"

I opened the canvas-covered "research case" and took from it an object like a diminutive pepper-caster—an iodoform dredger in fact—and handed it to him. Grasping the brush-case by its wire handle, he sprinkled the pale yellow powder from the dredger freely all round the pull-off lid, tapping the top with his knuckles to make the fine particles spread. Then he blew off the superfluous powder, and the two police officers gave a simultaneous gasp of joy; for now, on the black background, there stood out plainly a number of fingerprints, so clear and distinct that the ridge-pattern could be made out with perfect ease.

"These will probably be his right hand," said Thorndyke. "Now for the left." He treated the body of the case in the same way, and, when he had blown off the powder, the entire surface was spotted with yellow, oval impressions. "Now, Jervis," said he, "if you will put on a glove and pull off the lid, we can test the inside."

There was no difficulty in getting the lid off, for the shoulder of the case had been smeared with vaseline—apparently to produce an airtight joint—and, as it separated with a hollow sound, a faint, musky odour exhaled from its interior.

"The remainder of the inquiry," said Thorndyke, when I had pushed the lid on again, "will be best conducted at the police station, where, also, we can photograph these fingerprints."

"The shortest way will be across the meadows," said Fox; "the way the hounds went."

By this route we accordingly travelled, Thorndyke carrying the brush-case tenderly by its handle.

"I don't quite see where Ellis comes in in this job," said the inspector, as we walked along, "if the fellow had a grudge against Pratt. They weren't chums."

"I think I do," said Thorndyke. "You say that both men were prison officers at Portland at the same time. Now doesn't it seem likely that this is the work of some old convict who had been identified—and perhaps blackmailed—by Pratt, and possibly by Ellis too? That is where the value of the finger-prints comes in. If he is an old 'lag,' his prints will be at Scotland Yard. Otherwise they are not of much value as a clue."

"That's true, sir," said the inspector. "I suppose you want to see Ellis."

"I want to see that purse that you spoke of, first," replied Thorndyke. "That is probably the other end of the clue."

As soon as we arrived at the station, the inspector unlocked a safe and brought out a parcel. "These are Ellis's things," said he, as he unfastened it, "and that is the purse."

He handed Thorndyke a small pigskin pouch, which my

colleague opened, and, having smelt the inside, passed to me. The odour of musk was plainly perceptible, especially in the small compartment at the back.

"It has probably tainted the other contents of the parcel," said Thorndyke, sniffing at each article in turn, "but my sense of smell is not keen enough to detect any scent. They all seem odourless to me, whereas the purse smells quite distinctly. Shall we have Ellis in now?"

The sergeant took a key from a locked drawer and departed for the cells, whence he presently reappeared accompanied by the prisoner—a stout, burly man, in the last stage of dejection.

"Come, cheer up, Ellis," said the inspector. "Here's Dr. Thorndyke come down to help us and he wants to ask you one or two questions."

Ellis looked piteously at Thorndyke, and exclaimed:

"I know nothing whatever about this affair, sir, I swear to God I don't."

"I never supposed you did," said Thorndyke. "But there are one or two things that I want you to tell me. To begin with, that purse: where did you find it?"

"On the Thorpe road, sir. It was lying in the middle of the footway."

"Had anyone else passed the spot lately? Did you meet or pass anyone?"

"Yes, sir, I met a labourer about a minute before I saw the purse. I can't imagine why he didn't see it."

"Probably because it wasn't there," said Thorndyke. "Is there a hedge there?"

"Yes, sir; a hedge on a low bank."

"Ha! Well, now, tell me: is there anyone about here whom you knew when you and Pratt were together at Portland? Any old lag—to put it bluntly—whom you and Pratt have been putting the screw on?"

"No, sir, I swear there isn't. But I wouldn't answer for Pratt. He had a rare memory for faces."

Thorndyke reflected. "Were there any escapes from Portland in your time?" he asked.

"Only one—a man named Dobbs. He made off to the sea in a sudden fog and he was supposed to be drowned. His clothes washed up on the Bill, but not his body. At any rate, he was never heard of again."

"Thank you, Ellis. Do you mind my taking your finger-prints?"

"Certainly not, sir," was the almost eager reply; and the office inking-pad being requisitioned, a rough set of finger-prints was produced; and when Thorndyke had compared them with those on the brush-case and found no resemblance, Ellis returned to his cell in quite buoyant spirits.

Having made several photographs of the strange finger-prints, we returned to town that evening, taking the negatives with us; and while we waited for our train, Thorndyke gave a few parting injunctions to the inspector. "Remember," he said, "that the man must have washed his hands before he could appear in public. Search the banks of every pond, ditch and stream in the neighbourhood for footprints like those in the avenue; and, if you find any, search the bottom of the water thoroughly, for he is quite likely to have dropped the knife into the mud."

The photographs, which we handed in at Scotland Yard that same night, enabled the experts to identify the finger-prints as those of Francis Dobbs, an escaped convict. The two photographs—profile and full-face—which were attached to his record, were sent down to Baysford with a description of the man, and were, in due course, identified with a some-what mysterious individual, who passed by the name of Rufus Pembury and who had lived in the neighbourhood as a private gentleman for some two years. But Rufus Pembury was not to be found either at his genteel house or elsewhere. All that was known was, that on the day after the murder, he had converted his entire "personalty" into "bearer securities," and then vanished from mortal ken. Nor has he ever been heard of to this day.

"And, between ourselves," said Thorndyke, when we were discussing the case some time after, "he deserved to escape. It was clearly a case of blackmail, and to kill a blackmailer—when you have no other defence against him—is hardly murder. As to Ellis, he could never have been convicted, and Dobbs or Pembury must have known it. But he would have been committed to the Assizes, and that would have given time for all traces to disappear. No, Dobbs was a man of courage, ingenuity and resource; and, above all, he knocked the bottom out of the great bloodhound superstition."

FATHER BROWN

Father Brown's first name might be Paul and it might not. **In**
The Sign of the Broken Sword *we are told it is, but in* The
Eye of Apollo *he is introduced to us as the Reverend J.
Brown. In none of the forty-nine other Father Brown stories
does the plump, self-effacing priest have a first name at all.
Although the tales tell us something about what Father Brown
looks like and a good deal about how he goes about solving a
mystery, they tell us nothing at all about his private life and
background. As Kenneth Macgowan points out in* Sleuths,
*"Father Brown is the deepest mystery in the detective stories
of G. K. Chesterton. He has no past; his birth, his priestly
education, his present church are all puzzles no reader can
solve." The good father, whatever his background and first
name may be, made his debut early in the second decade of
this century and appeared between hard covers for the first
time in the 1911 collection* The Innocence of Father Brown.
*Our story is from that initial collection and is one of the
classic cautionary tales about not overlooking the obvious.
No less than Dr. Watson himself refers to this particular story
in the 1944 Sherlock Holmes film* The Scarlet Claw.

*Born in London in 1874, Gilbert Keith Chesterton became
a prime example of that now nearly vanished breed, the professional man of letters. He wrote poems, novels, essays, short
stories, and reviews. In his fiction he often followed in the
footsteps of Robert Louis Stevenson (the Stevenson, that is, of*
The New Arabian Nights *and* The Wrong Box), *finding adventure, mystery and fantasy in the streets and byways of the*

*city. A fat, rumbling man in his mature years, Chesterton
served as the inspiration for Dr. Fell, whom we'll meet later
in this book.*

The Invisible Man
by G. K. Chesterton

In the cool blue twilight of two steep streets in Camden
Town, the shop at the corner, a confectioner's, glowed like
the butt of a cigar. One should rather say, perhaps, like the
butt of a firework, for the light was of many colours and
some complexity, broken up by many mirrors and dancing on
many gilt and gaily-coloured cakes and sweetmeats. Against
this one fiery glass were glued the noses of many gutter-
snipes, for the chocolates were all wrapped in those red and
gold and green metallic colours which are almost better than
chocolate itself; and the huge white wedding-cake in the window was somehow at once remote and satisfying, just as if
the whole North Pole were good to eat. Such rainbow provo-
cations could naturally collect the youth of the neighbourhood up to the ages of ten or twelve. But this corner was
also attractive to youth at a later stage; and a young man,
not less than twenty-four, was staring into the same shop window. To him, also, the shop was of fiery charm, but this at-
traction was not wholly to be explained by chocolates; which,
however, he was far from despising.

He was a tall, burly, red-haired young man, with a resolute
face but a listless manner. He carried under his arm a flat,
grey portfolio of black-and-white sketches, which he had sold
with more or less success to publishers ever since his uncle
(who was an admiral) had disinherited him for Socialism,
because of a lecture which he had delivered against that
economic theory. His name was John Turnbull Angus.

Entering at last, he walked through the confectioner's shop
to the back room, which was a sort of pastry-cook restaurant,
merely raising his hat to the young lady who was serving
there. She was a dark, elegant, alert girl in black, with a high

colour and very quick, dark eyes; and after the ordinary interval she followed him into the inner room to take his order.

His order was evidently a usual one. "I want, please," he said with precision, "one halfpenny bun and a small cup of black coffee." An instant before the girl could turn away he added, "Also, I want you to marry me."

The young lady of the shop stiffened suddenly and said, "Those are jokes I don't allow."

The red-haired young man lifted grey eyes of an unexpected gravity.

"Really and truly," he said, "it's as serious—as serious as the half-penny bun. It is expensive, like the bun; one pays for it. It is indigestible, like the bun. It hurts."

The dark young lady had never taken her dark eyes off him, but seemed to be studying him with almost tragic exactitude. At the end of her scrutiny she had something like the shadow of a smile, and she sat down in a chair.

"Don't you think," observed Angus, absently, "that it's rather cruel to eat these halfpenny buns? They might grow up into penny buns. I shall give up these brutal sports when we are married."

The dark young lady rose from her chair and walked to the window, evidently in a state of strong but not unsympathetic cogitation. When at last she swung round again with an air of resolution she was bewildered to observe that the young man was carefully laying out on the table various objects from the shop window. They included a pyramid of highly coloured sweets, several plates of sandwiches, and the two decanters containing that mysterious port and sherry which are peculiar to pastry-cooks. In the middle of this neat arrangement he had carefully let down the enormous load of white sugared cake which had been the huge ornament of the window.

"What on earth are you doing?" she asked.

"Duty, my dear Laura," he began.

"Oh, for the Lord's sake, stop a minute," she cried, "and don't talk to me in that way. I mean, what is all that?"

"A ceremonial meal, Miss Hope."

"And what is *that*?" she asked impatiently, pointing to the mountain of sugar.

"The wedding-cake, Mrs. Angus," he said.

The girl marched to that article, removed it with some clatter, and put it back in the shop window; she then returned, and, putting her elegant elbows on the table, regarded the young man not unfavourably but with considerable exasperation,

"You don't give me any time to think," she said.

"I'm not such a fool," he answered; "that's my Christian humility."

She was still looking at him; but she had grown considerably graver behind the smile.

"Mr. Angus," she said steadily, "before there is a minute more of this nonsense I must tell you something about myself as shortly as I can."

"Delighted," replied Angus gravely. "You might tell me something about myself, too, while you are about it."

"Oh, do hold your tongue and listen," she said. "It's nothing that I'm ashamed of, and it isn't even anything that I'm specially sorry about. But what would you say if there were something that is no business of mine and yet is my nightmare?"

"In that case," said the man seriously, "I should suggest that you bring back the cake."

"Well, you must listen to the story first," said Laura, persistently. "To begin with, I must tell you that my father owned the inn called the 'Red Fish' at Ludbury, and I used to serve people in the bar."

"I have often wondered," he said, "why there was a kind of a Christian air about this one confectioner's shop."

"Ludbury is a sleepy, grassy little hole in the Eastern Counties, and the only kind of people who ever came to the 'Red Fish' were occasional commercial travellers, and for the rest, the most awful people you can see, only you've never seen them. I mean little, loungy men, who had just enough to live on and had nothing to do but lean about in bar-rooms and bet on horses, in bad clothes that were just too good for them. Even these wretched young rotters were not very common at our house; but there were two of them that were a lot too common—common in every sort of way. They both lived on money of their own, and were wearisomely idle and over-dressed. But yet I was a bit sorry for them, because I half believe they slunk into our little empty bar because each of them had a slight deformity; the sort of thing that some yokels laugh at. It wasn't exactly a deformity either; it was more an oddity. One of them was a surprisingly small man, something like a dwarf, or at least like a jockey. He was not at all jockeyish to look at, though; he had a round black head and a well-trimmed black beard, bright eyes like a bird's; he jingled money in his pockets; he jangled a great gold watch chain; and he never turned up except dressed just too much like a gentleman to be one. He was no fool though, though a futile idler; he was curiously clever at all kinds of things that couldn't be the slightest use; a sort of impromptu conjuring; making fifteen matches set fire to each other like a regular firework; or cutting a banana or some such thing into a dancing doll. His name was Isidore Smythe; and I can see him still, with his little dark face, just coming up to the counter, making a jumping kangaroo out of five cigars.

"The other fellow was more silent and more ordinary; but somehow he alarmed me much more than poor little Smythe. He was very tall and slight, and light-haired; his nose had a high bridge, and he might almost have been handsome in a spectral sort of way; but he had one of the most appalling squints I have ever seen or heard of. When he looked straight at you, you didn't know where you were yourself, let alone what he was looking at. I fancy this sort of disfigurement embittered the poor chap a little; for while Smythe was ready to show off his monkey tricks anywhere, James Welkin (that was the squinting man's name) never did anything except soak in our bar parlour, and go for great walks by himself in the flat, grey country all round. All the same, I think Smythe, too, was a little sensitive about being so small, though he carried it off more smartly. And so it was that I was really puzzled, as well as startled, and very sorry, when they both offered to marry me in the same week.

"Well, I did what I've since thought was perhaps a silly thing. But, after all, these freaks were my friends in a way; and I had a horror of their thinking I refused them for the real reason, which was that they were so impossibly ugly. So I made up some gas of another sort, about never meaning to marry anyone who hadn't carved his way in the world. I said it was a point of principle with me not to live on money that was just inherited like theirs. Two days after I had talked in this well-meaning sort of way, the whole trouble began. The first thing I heard was that both of them had gone off to seek their fortunes, as if they were in some silly fairy tale.

"Well, I've never seen either of them from that day to this. But I've had two letters from the little man called Smythe, and really they were rather exciting."

"Ever heard of the other man?" asked Angus.

"No, he never wrote," said the girl, after an instant's hesitation. "Smythe's first letter was simply to say that he had started out walking with Welkin to London; but Welkin was such a good walker that the little man dropped out of it, and took a rest by the roadside. He happened to be picked up by some travelling show, and, partly because he was nearly a dwarf, and partly because he was really a clever little wretch, he got on quite well in the show business, and was soon sent up to the Aquarium, to do some tricks that I forget. That was his first letter. His second was much more of a startler, and I only got it last week."

The man called Angus emptied his coffee-cup and regarded her with mild and patient eyes. Her own mouth took a slight twist of laughter as she resumed, "I suppose you've seen on the hoardings all about this 'Smythe's Silent Service'? Or you must be the only person that hasn't. Oh, I don't know much about it, it's some clockwork invention for doing all the housework by machinery. You know the sort of thing: 'Press a Button—A Butler who Never Drinks.' 'Turn a Handle—Ten Housemaids who Never Flirt.' You must have seen the advertisements. Well, whatever these machines are, they are making pots of money; and they are making it all for that little imp whom I knew down in Ludbury. I can't help feeling pleased the poor little chap has fallen on his feet; but the plain fact is, I'm in terror of his turning up any minute and telling me he's carved his way in the world—as he certainly has."

"And the other man?" repeated Angus with a sort of obstinate quietude.

Laura Hope got to her feet suddenly. "My friend," she said, "I think you are a witch. Yes, you are quite right. I have not seen a line of the other man's writing; and I have no more notion than the dead of what or where he is. But it is of him that I am frightened. It is he who is all about my path. It is he who has half driven me mad. Indeed, I think he has driven me mad; for I have felt him where he could not have been, and I have heard his voice when he could not have spoken."

"Well, my dear," said the young man, cheerfully, "if he were Satan himself, he is done for now you have told somebody. One goes mad all alone, old girl. But when was it you fancied you felt and heard our squinting friend?"

"I heard James Welkin laugh as plainly as I hear you speak," said the girl, steadily. "There was nobody there, for I stood just outside the shop at the corner, and could see down both streets at once. I had forgotten how he laughed, though his laugh was as odd as his squint. I had not thought of him for nearly a year. But it's a solemn truth that a few seconds later the first letter came from his rival."

"Did you ever make the spectre speak or squeak, or anything?" asked Angus, with some interest.

Laura suddenly shuddered, and then said, with an unshaken voice, "Yes. Just when I had finished reading the second letter from Isidore Smythe announcing his success, just then, I heard Welkin say, 'He shan't have you, though.' It was quite plain, as if he were in the room. It is awful, I think I must be mad."

"If you really were mad," said the young man, "you would think you must be sane. But certainly there seems to me to be something a little rum about this unseen gentleman. Two heads are better than one—I spare you allusions to any other organs—and really, if you would allow me, as a sturdy, practical man, to bring back the wedding-cake out of the window——"

Even as he spoke, there was a sort of steely shriek in the street outside, and a small motor, driven at devilish speed, shot up to the door of the shop and stuck there. In the same flash of time a small man in a shiny top hat stood stamping in the outer room.

Angus, who had hitherto maintained hilarious ease from motives of mental hygiene, revealed the strain of his soul by striding abruptly out of the inner room and confronting the new-comer. A glance at him was quite sufficient to confirm the savage guesswork of a man in love. This very dapper but dwarfish figure, with the spike of black beard carried insolently forward, the clever unrestful eyes, the neat but very nervous fingers, could be none other than the man just described to him: Isidore Smythe, who made dolls out of banana skins and match-boxes; Isidore Smythe, who made millions out of undrinking butlers and unflirting housemaids of metal. For a moment the two men, instinctively understanding each other's air of possession, looked at each other with that curious cold generosity which is the soul of rivalry.

Mr. Smythe, however, made no allusion to the ultimate ground of their antagonism, but said simply and explosively, "Has Miss Hope seen that thing on the window?"

"On the window?" repeated the staring Angus.

"There's no time to explain other things," said the small millionaire shortly. "There's some tomfoolery going on here that has to be investigated."

He pointed his polished walking-stick at the window, recently depleted by the bridal preparations of Mr. Angus; and that gentleman was astonished to see along the front of the glass a long strip of paper pasted, which had certainly not been on the window when he looked through it some time before. Following the energetic Smythe outside into the street, he found that some yard and a half of stamp paper had been carefully gummed along the glass outside, and on this was written in straggly characters, "If you marry Smythe, he will die."

"Laura," said Angus, putting his big red head into the shop, "you're not mad."

"It's the writing of that fellow Welkin," said Smythe gruffly. "I haven't seen him for years, but he's always bothering me. Five times in the last fortnight he's had threatening letters left at my flat, and I can't even find out who leaves them, let alone if it is Welkin himself. The porter of the flats swears that no suspicious characters have been seen, and here he has pasted up a sort of dado on a public shop window, while the people in the shop——"

"Quite so," said Angus modestly, "while the people in the shop were having tea. Well, sir, I can assure you I appreciate your common sense in dealing so directly with the matter. We can talk about other things afterwards. The fellow cannot be very far off yet, for I swear there was no paper there when I went last to the window, ten or fifteen minutes ago. On the other hand, he's too far off to be chased, as we don't even know the direction. If you'll take my advice, Mr. Smythe, you'll put this at once in the hands of some energetic inquiry man, private rather than public. I know an extremely clever fellow, who has set up in business five minutes from here in your car. His name's Flambeau, and though his youth was a bit stormy, he's a strictly honest man now, and his brains are worth money. He lives in Lucknow Mansions, Hampstead."

"That is odd," said the little man, arching his black eyebrows. "I live, myself, in Himylaya Mansions, round the corner. Perhaps you might care to come with me; I can go to my rooms and sort out these queer Welkin documents, while you run round and get your friend the detective."

"You are very good," said Angus politely. "Well, the sooner we act the better."

Both men, with a queer kind of impromptu fairness, took the same sort of formal farewell of the lady, and both jumped into the brisk little car. As Smythe took the handles and they turned the great corner of the street, Angus was amused to see a gigantesque poster of "Smythe's Silent Service," with a picture of a huge headless iron doll, carrying a saucepan with the legend, "A Cook who is Never Cross."

"I use them in my own flat," said the little black-bearded man, laughing, "partly for advertisements, and partly for real convenience. Honestly, and all above board, those big clockwork dolls of mine do bring your coals or claret or a timetable quicker than any live servants I've ever known, if you know which knob to press. But I'll never deny, between ourselves, that such servants have their disadvantages, too."

"Indeed?" said Angus; "is there something they can't do?"

"Yes," replied Smythe coolly; "they can't tell me who left those threatening letters at my flat."

The man's motor was small and swift like himself; in fact, like his domestic service, it was of his own invention. If he was an advertising quack, he was one who believed in his own wares. The sense of something tiny and flying was accentuated as they swept up long white curves of road in the dead but open daylight of evening. Soon the white curves came sharper and dizzier; they were upon ascending spirals, as they say in the modern religions. For, indeed, they were cresting a corner of London which is almost as precipitous as

Edinburgh, if not quite so picturesque. Terrace rose above terrace, and the special tower of flats they sought, rose above them all to almost Egyptian height, gilt by the level sunset. The change, as they turned the corner and entered the crescent known as Himylaya Mansions, was as abrupt as the opening of a window; for they found that pile of flats sitting above London as above a green sea of slate. Opposite to the mansions, on the other side of the gravel crescent, was a bushy enclosure more like a steep hedge or dyke than a garden, and some way below that ran a strip of artificial water, a sort of canal, like the moat of that embowered fortress. As the car swept round the crescent it passed, at one corner, the stray stall of a man selling chestnuts; and right away at the other end of the curve, Angus could see a dim blue policeman walking slowly. These were the only human shapes in that high suburban solitude; but he had an irrational sense that they expressed the speechless poetry of London. He felt as if they were figures in a story.

The little car shot up to the right house like a bullet, and shot out its owner like a bomb shell. He was immediately inquiring of a tall commissionaire in shining braid, and a short porter in shirt sleves, whether anybody or anything had been seeking his apartments. He was assured that nobody and nothing had passed these officials since his last inquiries; whereupon he and the slightly bewildered Angus were shot up in the lift like a rocket, till they reached the top floor.

"Just come in for a minute," said the breathless Smythe. "I want to show you those Welkin letters. Then you might run round the corner and fetch your friend." He pressed a button concealed in the wall, and the door opened of itself.

It opened on a long, commodious ante-room, of which the only arresting features, ordinarily speaking, were the rows of tall half-human mechanical figures that stood up on both sides like tailors' dummies. Like tailors' dummies they were headless; and like tailors' dummies they had a handsome unnecessary humpiness in the shoulders, and a pigeon-breasted protuberance of chest; but barring this, they were not much more like a human figure than any automatic machine at a station that is about the human height. They had two great hooks like arms, for carrying trays; and they were painted pea-green, or vermilion, or black for convenience of distinction; in every other way they were only automatic machines and nobody would have looked twice at them. On this occasion, at least, nobody did. For between the two rows of these domestic dummies lay something more interesting than most of the mechanics of the world. It was a white, tattered scrap of paper scrawled with red ink; and the agile inventor had snatched it up almost as soon as the door flew open. He handed it to Angus without a word. The red ink on it actually was not dry, and the message ran, "If you have been to see her today, I shall kill you."

There was a short silence, and then Isidore Smythe said quietly, "Would you like a little whiskey? I rather feel as if I should."

"Thank you; I should like a little Flambeau," said Angus, gloomily. "This business seems to me to be getting rather grave. I'm going round at once to fetch him."

"Right you are," said the other, with admirable cheerfulness. "Bring him round here as quick as you can."

But as Angus closed the front door behind him he saw Smythe push back a button, and one of the clockwork images glided from its place and slid along a groove in the floor carrying a tray with syphon and decanter. There did seem something a trifle weird about leaving the little man alone among those dead servants, who were coming to life as the door closed.

Six steps down from Smythe's landing the man in shirt sleeves was doing something with a pail. Angus stopped to extract a promise, fortified with a prospective bribe, that he would remain in that place until the return with the detective, and would keep count of any kind of stranger coming up those stairs. Dashing down to the front hall he then laid similar charges of vigilance on the commissionaire at the front door, from whom he learned the simplifying circumstances that there was no back door. Not content with this, he captured the floating policeman and induced him to stand opposite the entrance and watch it; and finally paused an instant for a pennyworth of chestnuts, and an inquiry as to the probable length of the merchant's stay in the neighbourhood.

The chestnut seller, turning up the collar of his coat, told him he should probably be moving shortly, as he thought it was going to snow. Indeed, the evening was growing grey and bitter, but Angus, with all his eloquence, proceeded to nail the chestnut man to his post.

"Keep yourself warm on your own chestnuts," he said earnestly. "Eat up your whole stock; I'll make it worth your while. I'll give you a sovereign if you'll wait here till I come back, and then tell me whether any man, woman, or child has gone into that house where the commissionaire is standing."

He then walked away smartly, with a last look at the besieged tower.

"I've made a ring round that room, anyhow," he said. "They can't all four of them be Mr. Welkin's accomplices."

Lucknow Mansions were, so to speak, on a lower platform of that hill of houses, of which Himylaya Mansions might be called the peak. Mr. Flambeau's semi-official flat was on the ground floor, and presented in every way a marked contrast to the American machinery and cold hotel-like luxury of the flat of the Silent Service. Flambeau, who was a friend of Angus, received him in a rococo artistic den behind his office, of which the ornaments were sabres, harquebuses, Eastern curiosities, flasks of Italian wine, savage cooking-pots, a plumy Persian cat, and a small dusty-looking Roman Catholic priest, who looked particularly out of place.

"This is my friend Father Brown," said Flambeau. "I've often wanted you to meet him. Splendid weather, this; a little cold for Southerners like me."

"Yes, I think it will keep clear," said Angus, sitting down on a violet-striped Eastern ottoman.

"No," said the priest quietly, "it has begun to snow."

And, indeed, as he spoke, the first few flakes, foreseen by the man of chestnuts, began to drift across the darkening windowpane.

"Well," said Angus heavily. "I'm afraid I've come on business, and rather jumpy business at that. The fact is, Flambeau, within a stone's throw of your house is a fellow who badly wants your help; he's perpetually being haunted and threatened by an invisible enemy—a scoundrel whom nobody has even seen." As Angus proceeded to tell the whole tale of Smythe and Welkin, beginning with Laura's story, and going on with his own, the supernatural laugh at the corner of two empty streets, the strange distinct words spoken in an

empty room, Flambeau grew more and more vividly concerned, and the little priest seemed to be left out of it, like a
piece of furniture. When it came to the scribbled stamp paper
pasted on the window, Flambeau rose, seeming to fill the
room with his huge shoulders.

"If you don't mind," he said, "I think you had better tell
me the rest on the nearest road to this man's house. It strikes
me, somehow, that there is no time to be lost."

"Delighted," said Angus, rising also, "though he's safe
enough for the present, for I've set four men to watch the
only hole to his burrow."

They turned out into the street, the small priest trundling
after them with the docility of a small dog. He merely said,
in a cheerful way, like one making conversation, "How quick
the snow gets thick on the ground."

As they threaded the steep side streets already powdered
with silver, Angus finished his story; and by the time they
reached the crescent with the towering flats, he had leisure to
turn his attention to the four sentinels. The chestnut seller,
both before and after receiving a sovereign, swore stubbornly
that he had watched the door and seen no visitor enter. The
policeman was even more emphatic. He said he had had experience of crooks of all kinds; in top hats and in rags; he
wasn't so green as to expect suspicious characters to look suspicious; he looked out for anybody, and, so help him, there
had been nobody. And when all three men gathered round
the gilded commissionaire, who still stood smiling astride of
the porch, the verdict was more final still.

"I've got a right to ask any man, duke or dustman, what
he wants in these flats," said the genial and gold-laced giant,
"and I'll swear there's been nobody to ask since this gentleman went away."

The unimportant Father Brown, who stood back, looking
modestly at the pavement, here ventured to say meekly, "Has
nobody been up and down stairs, then, since the snow began
to fall? It began while we were all round at Flambeau's."

"Nobody's been in here, sir, you can take it from me," said
the official, with beaming authority.

"Then I wonder what that is?" said the priest, and stared at
the ground blankly like a fish.

The others all looked down also; and Flambeau used a

fierce exclamation and a French gesture. For it was unquestionably true that down the middle of the entrance guarded by the man in gold lace, actually between the arrogant, stretched legs of that colossus, ran a stringy pattern of grey footprints stamped upon the white snow.

"God!" cried Angus involuntarily, "the Invisible Man!"

Without another word he turned and dashed up the stairs, with Flambeau following; but Father Brown still stood looking about him in the snow-clad street as if he had lost interest in his query.

Flambeau was plainly in a mood to break down the door with his big shoulders; but the Scotchman, with more reason, if less intuition, fumbled about on the frame of the door till he found the invisible button; and the door swung slowly open.

It showed substantially the same serried interior; the hall had grown darker, though it was still struck here and there with the last crimson shafts of sunset, and one or two of the headless machines had been moved from their places for this or that purpose, and stood here and there about the twilit place. The green and red of their coats were all darkened in the dusk; and their likeness to human shapes slightly increased by their very shapelessness. But in the middle of them all, exactly where the paper with the red ink had lain, there lay something that looked like red ink spilt out of its bottle. But it was not red ink.

With a French combination of reason and violence Flambeau simply said "Murder!" and, plunging into the flat, had explored every corner and cupboard of it in five minutes. But if he expected to find a corpse he found none. Isidore Smythe was not in the place, either dead or alive. After the most tearing search the two men met each other in the outer hall, with streaming faces and staring eyes. "My friend," said Flambeau, talking French in his excitement, "not only is your murderer invisible, but he makes invisible also the murdered man."

Angus looked round at the dim room full of dummies, and in some Celtic corner of his Scotch soul a shudder started. One of the life-size dolls stood immediately overshadowing the blood stain, summoned, perhaps, by the slain man an instant before he fell. One of the high-shouldered hooks that served the thing for arms, was a little lifted, and Angus had suddenly the horrid fancy that poor Smythe's own iron child had struck him down. Matter had rebelled, and these machines had killed their master. But even so, what had they done with him?

"Eaten him?" said the nightmare at his ear; and he sickened for an instant at the idea of rent, human remains absorbed and crushed into all that acephalous clockwork.

He recovered his mental health by an emphatic effort, and said to Flambeau, "Well, there it is. The poor fellow has evaporated like a cloud and left a red streak on the floor. The tale does not belong to this world."

"There is only one thing to be done," said Flambeau, "whether it belongs to this world or the other. I must go down and talk to my friend."

They descended, passing the man with the pail, who again asserverated that he had let no intruder pass, down to the commissionaire and the hovering chestnut man, who rigidly reasserted their own watchfulness. But when Angus looked round for his fourth confirmation he could not see it, and called out with some nervousness, "Where is the policeman?"

"I beg your pardon," said Father Brown; "that is my fault. I just sent him down the road to investigate something—that I just thought worth investigating."

"Well, we want him back pretty soon," said Angus abruptly, "for the wretched man upstairs has not only been murdered, but wiped out."

"How?" asked the priest.

"Father," said Flambeau, after a pause, "upon my soul I believe it is more in your department than mine. No friend or foe has entered the house, but Smythe is gone, as if stolen by the fairies. If that is not supernatural, I——"

As he spoke they were all checked by an unusual sight; the big blue policeman came round the corner of the crescent, running. He came straight up to Brown.

"You're right, sir," he panted, "they've just found poor Mr. Smythe's body in the canal down below."

Angus put his hand wildly to his head. "Did he run down and drown himself?" he asked.

"He never came down, I'll swear," said the constable, "and

he wasn't drowned either, for he died of a great stab over the heart."

"And yet you saw no one enter?" said Flambeau in a grave voice.

"Let us walk down the road a little," said the priest.

As they reached the other end of the crescent he observed abruptly, "Stupid of me! I forgot to ask the policeman something. I wonder if they found a light brown sack."

"Why a light brown sack?" asked Angus, astonished.

"Because if it was any other coloured sack, the case must begin over again," said Father Brown; "but if it was a light brown sack, why, the case is finished."

"I am pleased to hear it," said Angus with hearty irony. "It hasn't begun, so far as I am concerned."

"You must tell us all about it," said Flambeau with a strange heavy simplicity, like a child.

Unconsciously they were walking with quickening steps down the long sweep of road on the other side of the high crescent, Father Brown leading briskly, though in silence. At last he said with an almost touching vagueness, "Well, I'm afraid you'll think it so prosy. We always begin at the abstract end of things, and you can't begin this story anywhere else.

"Have you ever noticed this—that people never answer what you say? They answer what you mean—or what they think you mean. Suppose one lady says to another in a country house, 'Is anybody staying with you?' the lady doesn't answer 'Yes; the butler, the three footmen, the parlourmaid, and so on,' though the parlourmaid may be in the room, or the butler behind her chair. She says 'There is *nobody* staying with us,' meaning nobody of the sort you mean. But suppose a doctor inquiring into an epidemic asks, 'Who is staying in the house?' then the lady will remember the butler, the parlourmaid, and the rest. All language is used like that; you never get a question answered literally, even when you get it answered truly. When those four quite honest men said that no man had gone into the Mansions, they did not really mean that *no man* had gone into them. They meant no man whom they could suspect of being your man. A man did go into the house, and did come out of it, but they never noticed him."

"An invisible man?" inquired Angus, raising his red eyebrows.

"A mentally invisible man," said Father Brown.

A minute or two after he resumed in the same unassuming voice, like a man thinking his way. "Of course you can't think of such a man, until you do think of him. That's where his cleverness comes in. But I came to think of him through two or three little things in the tale Mr. Angus told us. First, there was the fact that this Welkin went for long walks. And then there was the vast lot of stamp paper on the window. And then, most of all, there were the two things the young lady said—things that couldn't be true. Don't get annoyed," he added hastily, noting a sudden movement of the Scotchman's head; "she thought they were true. A person *can't* be quite alone in a street a second before she receives a letter. She can't be quite alone in a street when she starts reading a letter just received. There must be somebody pretty near her; he must be mentally invisible."

"Why must there be somebody near her?" asked Angus.

"Because," said Father Brown, "barring carrier-pigeons, somebody must have brought her the letter."

"Do you really mean to say," asked Flambeau, with energy, "that Welkin carried his rival's letters to his lady?"

"Yes," said the priest. "Welkin carried his rival's letters to his lady. You see, he had to."

"Oh, I can't stand much more of this," exploded Flambeau. "Who is this fellow? What does he look like? What is the usual get-up of a mentally invisible man?"

"He is dressed rather handsomely in red, blue and gold," replied the priest promptly with precision, "and in this striking, and even showy, costume he entered Himylaya Mansions under eight human eyes; he killed Smythe in cold blood, and came down into the street again carrying the dead body in his arms——"

"Reverend sir," cried Angus, standing still, "are you raving mad, or am I?"

"You are not mad," said Brown, "only a little unobservant. You have not noticed such a man as this, for example."

He took three quick strides forward, and put his hand on the shoulder of an ordinary passing postman who had bustled by them unnoticed under the shade of the trees.

"Nobody ever notices postmen somehow," he said thoughtfully; "yet they have passions like other men, and even carry large bags where a small corpse can be stowed quite easily."

The postman, instead of turning naturally, had ducked and tumbled against the garden fence. He was a lean fair-bearded man of very ordinary appearance, but as he turned an alarmed face over his shoulder, all three men were fixed with an almost fiendish squint.

Flambeau went back to his sabres, purple rugs and Persian cat, having many things to attend to. John Turnbull Angus went back to the lady at the shop, with whom that imprudent young man contrives to be extremely comfortable. But Father Brown walked those snow-covered hills under the stars for many hours with a murderer, and what they said to each other will never be known.

MR. FORTUNE

Had Mr. Fortune practiced medicine, or detection, in our country he would have been called Dr. Fortune, since he was a fully credited surgeon. He was also a scientific advisor to Scotland Yard and it is in this capacity that he appears in most of the nine novels and more than eighty short stories devoted to his career. In describing him we can safely say Reggie Fortune was plump and cherubic-looking. But going beyond that can be risky. Many of his other attributes, such as his sometimes languid manner and his clipped speech, laced with upper class slang, are affectations put on to annoy and disarm his unwary opponents. Some critics and historians of the genre have also been fooled by Reggie's tricks and have written him off as a hopeless snob, fit to associate only with the likes of our homegrown silly-ass detective, Philo Vance. Obviously they've missed the point, or, as Mr. Fortune would put it, "Oh, my aunt!"

The first collection of short stories, Call Mr. Fortune, appeared in 1920. Satisfied with the short form, Henry Christopher Bailey (1878–1961) didn't get around to writing a novel about his medical man detective until 1934. As a matter of fact, Bailey was approaching forty before he wrote even a short story about Reggie Fortune. His first book, published in 1901 while he was still an Oxford undergraduate, was a historical romance. Bailey turned out quite a few swashbucklers, both novels and short stories. It was while working as a war correspondent during the First World War for the London Daily Telegram that he first began thinking about detective stories and Mr. Fortune. In the years immediately after that war, his detective became one of the most

213

popular in the world and Bailey found himself listed among England's top mystery writers, along with Agatha Christie and Dorothy L. Sayers.

This story appeared in the 1927 collection Mr. Fortune, Please *and was the one Bailey picked for inclusion in a 1931 British anthology called* My Best Detective Story.

The Violet Farm
by H. C. Bailey

In the consulting-room of Mr. Fortune stands an ancient oak chest on which by the curious may be read the inscription: Y AI IOX IO IO EPIKALL H. This is the explanation of it.

The Chief of the Criminal Investigation Department complained of the world. It was after dinner. It was in fact after one of Mr. Fortune's dinners, the exquisite beauty of which is apt to make men think of the faults in common life. A pensive murmur rose to something sharp. "Do you know my aunt, Reginald?" said Lomas.

Mr. Fortune opened his eyes. "This is so sudden. I thought you were just moaning at large. No. I do not know your aunt. Not as such. But tell me the worst. I feel for you. I have lots of relations myself."

"You know what aunts are?"

"Yes, by letter. They're the only people now alive who write letters. Lots of letters."

"She does," said Lomas with emotion.

"Well, you should answer sometimes. Not often. Every Christmas or so."

"Oh, I've answered her early and often. Now she's coming up to town to see me."

Mr. Fortune sat up. "Lomas!" he said severely. "What have you been doing? What has alarmed aunt? Have you been moving towards matrimony?"

"I wish I had," said Lomas bitterly.

"Oh, my dear fellow! As bad as that?"

"There are times when a wife would be useful."

"Is it possible?"

"One could turn her on to one's female relations."

"What a murderous plan! Tell me all, Lomas."

"My aunt's Lady Sancreed, pillar of the Low Church, you know, lived all her life in the country. She has a ward, parson's daughter, who ran a bit wild, went to Rome and studied painting—that sort of thing. This chit, Vera Daymer, picked up with another minx, Isabel Villaret, in the same line. They came back to England and set up a studio in Chelsea. I went to look at their pictures, the usual stuff, latest fashion—fair work—not worth doing. The first odd thing is they chucked it all up and retired to the backwoods. Well, I don't expect Vera to have a reason for anything she does. She's quite an advanced young woman. But the simple life in the country is not her sort of craze. She's urban, highly urban. She told me they'd found out they would never be more than third class in painting so they decided to wash it out and do something real. And that isn't like her either. It's almost common sense. Well, they went. They went right off the map. Place called Cele in Staneshire. They bought a pre-historic cottage and started a violet farm."

"A what?" said Mr. Fortune.

"Yes, it sounds crazy, doesn't it? A violet farm, Reginald. Growing violets for the London market. It is done, you know."

"Of course it's done. Charmin' trade. But you wouldn't go to Staneshire to grow violets."

"Then it's just where Vera would go. There they are, two high-browed Bohemians growing violets where violets won't grow, living alone in an ancient solitary cottage—if they are alone. That's one of Lady Sancreed's troubles."

"Aunts will be aunts."

"Oh, yes quite. If Vera can look after herself racketing round Europe, she ought to be all right in a country cottage. I mentioned that. But my aunt says they're getting a horrid name in the country. She's been writing to the local archdeacon and the good man's quite shocked at them."

"I never shocked an archdeacon myself," said Mr. Fortune, dreamily. "But I should think it was quite easy."

"Yes, that's what he's for. You can cut out the archdeacon. You can cut out everything separately. But taken altogether it's a queer business. There's Vera. She's been writing that the people are horrid—not the country people, she don't bother about society, she's far too highbrow, but the villagers. They won't do anything for her, they make things as difficult as they can and so on. She's put their backs up, I suppose. She would. You can cut that out too. Vera and Isabel doing the intellectual Bohemian would annoy any decent village. But that's not the end of it. I've had an official inquiry from the Staneshire chief constable. Is anything known about Vera Daymer and Isabel Villaret?"

Mr. Fortune put out the end of his cigar with great care. "Well, well, well," he murmured. "And did you refer him to aunt?"

"I told him who they were and asked what he meant by it. He was very civil. Said it was perfectly satisfactory and regretted troubling me. There had been some rumours in the district as the ladies were strangers. You know what the country is."

"Yes, I think so," said Mr. Fortune dreamily. "And what is aunt's idea?"

"Aunt's idea is that something has to be done about it. I ought to stop this persecution of poor Vera instantly and I ought to get the dreadful girl away from this horrible cottage at once and show her the error of her ways. Aunt must really come and see me and settle something immediately. That's where the canker gnaws."

"My poor Lomas!" Mr. Fortune held out his hand.

"Yes. Why are aunts?" said Lomas sadly. "But it is a crazy business, isn't it?"

"I wonder," Mr. Fortune murmured. He poured himself a glass of Vichy water and tasted it critically. "There are points. I should like to meet Vera."

"Good Gad!" Lomas was much affected. "This is true friendship."

"No, no. Only curiosity. But I think I'll go and have a look at the violet farmers."

Lomas stared at him. "You're a noble fellow, Reginald. My aunt would love you."

"I wonder."

"But you frighten me. Have you got something in your wonderful head?"

"No, no. The open mind. That's what the case wants. You're so prejudiced."

"The case!" Lomas gasped. "It isn't a case. It's clotted nonsense."

"That's why it's interesting," said Mr. Fortune.

On the next afternoon a large car drew up in the village of Cele, which consists of two farms and six cottages in brown stone and thatch and offers no other entertainment to large cars than a beer house and a post office. The chauffeur spoke to his master, got out, opened the car's bonnet and bent over his engine. He emerged with a worried and apologetic face to say that it would be a long job, sir. Some women and children assembled to have a look at it. Out of the rugs in the car rose a pink face, round, sleepy, wrathful, which swore. The owner came heavily to ground. "What is this place, anyway?" he growled. The chauffeur passed the question on to the gazing women. "What? Cele? Cele? Never heard of it. Any inn?" The pink face looked at the beer house with disgust. "No, there wouldn't be. Just the sort of place you would break down. Get busy, damn your eyes." He lounged away.

The chauffeur winked at the women. "Bit of a lad, ain't he?" and began to talk.

Out of sight of the village of Cele, Mr. Fortune sat down with a map. He found thereon a lane beside a brook which became in practice a brook flowing down a lane. Thus he arrived damply at the mellow stone building which is Hill Barn and was then the property of Miss Vera Daymer. It stands alone on a ridge in rolling miles of pasture sheltered by an ancient oak and some younger brethren. It is in the shape of a barn, but has windows cut in it and chimneys built on to it. An old and broken hedge about it was then patched with flimsy fencing of wood and wire. Mr. Fortune, contemplating it with a frown, became aware that somebody was contemplating him: a brown face in a frame of whiskers. "Good day," said Mr. Fortune. The man in whiskers grunted and spat and vanished behind the hedge and was heard digging. "I say, could you tell me where I am?" said Mr. Fortune.

The whiskers again came into sight: dull eyes stared. "Where be going to?" said a slow voice.

"Well, I don't quite know. What is this place?"

"What's brought 'e to here?"

"William! Whoever are you talking to?" a girl cried.

"Dunno who 'e be," said William and again vanished and dug.

To the gate which was a hurdle came what looked like a boy. Its hair was cut short, it wore a tennis shirt and plus fours, its shape was boyish, but it spoke in a girl's voice: "Good Lord, what do you want?"

Mr. Fortune lifted his hat. "I'm so sorry to trouble you, but I'm lost."

"You must be to get here. What did you do it for?"

Mr. Fortune gazed at her. "But I didn't do it," he protested. "My car broke down in some deserted village and my fool of a man said it would be a two hours' job and there was only a pot-house, so I came for a walk and there doesn't seem to be a way to anywhere."

"There isn't."

"Thanks very much." He sighed heavily.

The girl was affected. His round face is absurdly childish. "Well, I dare say it will run to a cup of tea," she said.

"Oh no, really," said Mr. Fortune. "But it would probably save my life."

She opened the gate. "Come on then. You mustn't die here. Our reputation wouldn't stand it."

"Jolly old place to live in," said Mr. Fortune.

"Jolly old ruin. Bell!" she called. "Bell! Where the devil are you?"

The man in whiskers, who had been watching them with a dull cow-like stare, spat and resumed digging.

"Bell!" the girl called fiercely. "Bell, you pig!" There was no answer.

"Lovely garden," Mr. Fortune murmured, thinking that it was the worst garden he had ever seen.

The girl looked at him with suspicion. "We grow for the market," she snapped. "Bell! Bella!"

"Quite," Mr. Fortune murmured. It was indeed planned like a market garden with plants arranged in battalions, violets for the most part, carnations, chrysanthemums, but all puny and sickly, the garden of people who knew nothing about flowers.

What looked like a large boy scout came through the hedge. With relief Mr. Fortune discovered it was not Isabel.

It had a ruddy moustache. Its khaki shorts displayed very masculine legs. It was expansive and cheery. "Hullo, hullo, hullo," it said, "what's the excitement, V.? What ho! Who is the little gentleman?"

"Oh, don't be sprightly. When you've quite finished with Bell you might tell her I'm making tea."

"Snubs to me," he grinned. "My error, so sorry and what not," but she marched past him to the house. Mr. Fortune, following her timidly, saw the delinquent Isabel appear among the chrysanthemums. She also wore knickerbockers and shirt, but she had no resemblance to a boy. There was a murmured conversation.

"I say, Bella, we've been naughty."

"Oh help! But what's up now? Who's her young man?"

"Ask me another. Looks like a curate in disguise. He's come to tea."

"Golly!"

Mr. Fortune contracted a dislike for them. He hurried after Vera. The door opened into a large living-room which was full of chaos. It had several tables covered with a miscellany of eating apparatus, books, tools, papers, a fiddle, clothes, food in the raw. There were two oil-stoves with kettles. Pots and pans were kept in the vast and cold fireplace. An easel with drawing board stood by the window. More drawing things were on a high desk. Halting beside two pails of water, Mr. Fortune tried to see it all. What in the world was that thing in the corner under the shelf of chemists' bottles? A little printing press?

Vera, whirling about the room, tossed a rug over it. "Where has that wretched girl put the matches? Oh, sit down, can't you? This place is a pigsty." She made chaos worse confounded. Mr. Fortune lit an oil-stove for her.

"But it's a noble old place," he said, looking up at the massive black beams which bore the high roof. "What was it?"

"Aha, what was it?" the large youth chuckled in the doorway. "Why, sir, the buzz is it was built by Noah on the model of the ark and never used since."

"Don't be an owl, Charles," said Isabel hastily. "Clear the table. Where's the bread, V.?" Vera raised a flushed face from the oil-stove and asked fiercely if she could do something.

"Bread? Bread?" Charles inquired. "I don't mind telling you, sir, yesterday the bread was found in—well, well, mother wouldn't like it at all. It had been bread anyway. The trouble is you can't get bread canned, but we generally have milk, if they haven't lost the tin opener."

Mr. Fortune withdrew himself from the conversation. The spasmodic movements of Vera suggested an explosive temperature. He wandered into remote corners of the room. They had some rare old things among their rubbish. That chest might be fifteenth-century. There was something of an inscription on it. Much later work though. Queer lettering.

The girls were muttering together, not amiably. He was reminded of the rumbling of angry cats. When he turned they were both flushed and the large Charles, spread in a deckchair staring at his big nailed boots, looked gloomily helpless.

It was in no way a pleasant tea. The fluid which he drank tasted of oil-stove. The bread was ancient and the butter remembered the tin from which it was dug. His hosts were even less agreeable. The exuberance of Charles was blighted. The two girls talked of the faults of the meal and the discomforts of their life, talked at each other acidly. Mr. Fortune was soon asking the way to Cele. As he fled he heard Vera grow shrill and something like weeping from Isabel.

When he came in sight of the village, his chauffeur Sam emerged from the post office hurriedly, wiping his mouth, trying not to look happy and succeeded completely on Mr. Fortune's announcement that he would now drive the dam' thing. They departed from the village of Cele like a projectile. "Get anything?" said Mr. Fortune.

Sam braced himself in his seat. "These village people are all right, sir. What you might call 'omely: very nice and 'omely. But they got a good old down on the young ladies. Fair 'ate 'em."

"Why?"

"I didn't get the 'ang of it all. They're calling 'em Bolsheviks. They believe it too. I don't know why. I couldn't 'ear of anything the young ladies 'ave done except smacking a boy's 'ead what was killing a bird. I seen him. He could do with smacking. But the village people are nervy about it. Seems as if they was afraid. Sounds silly sir, but that was the idea I got. They tell me as no one in Cele won't go near the young ladies' cottage now except the postman—and 'e 'as to. No one won't sell 'em anything, not milk nor nothing."

"Yes. I noticed that," Mr. Fortune sighed. "Anything occur to you, Sam?"

"No, sir, not clearly. Beg pardon, sir, you didn't ought to look at me driving like this. Ah!" The car swung in serpentine curves round cows and a horse rake.

"You've no imagination," said Mr. Fortune sadly.

Sam swallowed once and again.

But they arrived safe at Stanchester and there, Mr. Fortune announced, they would stay if a man could live in the inn. He consumed another tea and considered it possible. He engaged in a hot bath and meditation and emerged to telephone to Lomas.

"There's more in this than meets the eye. You'd better come down." A groan rattled in the telephone. It asked why. "Well, you might appeal to Vera's better nature. I didn't. I was quite bad for her." The telephone, rather shrill, wanted to know what was the matter. "Ask me no more. The moon may draw the sea. But I couldn't. I couldn't draw any of 'em. Not even Charles. And he's resilient, is Charles." The telephone asked who the devil was Charles. "Ah, that's a very difficult part of the problem. Who is Charles and what's he for? Come along. I want you as a witness to character. Before the chief constable. Chief constables don't take to me."

"What have you been up to?" the telephone cried.

"Heaven knows. See you in the morning. Good-bye."

Morning brought the Chief of the Criminal Investigation Department in a petulant mood. It was not dispelled by Mr. Fortune's account of his investigations. "I'm much obliged to you, Reginald," he said bitterly. "I have a little work to do. And you dragged me down here to listen to this! Damme, you've got nothing at all."

"Oh, my Lomas! How can you? And after that tea I suffered for your dear sake! You're very unkind. Aunt wouldn't like it at all. How is aunt, by the way? Oh hush! Control yourself. You've got to call on the chief constable. I telephoned to him you were coming."

"The devil you did! What do you think I'm going to say to him?"

"I haven't the slightest idea," said Mr. Fortune sweetly.

But in the presence of the chief constable, a solid, square-cut man with the stamp of the navy on his manner and speech, Lomas became formally official. They had come down about the case which the chief constable referred to them. There were one or two small points . . .

"The young ladies at Cele?" Captain Camber said sharply. "I'm taking your word for them. Isn't that right, sir?"

"Well, of course, it's all in the family, captain," Mr. Fortune smiled. "Lomas's aunt, you know——"

"Quite, quite," Captain Camber hastily agreed.

"Thanks very much. We'll leave the family out, please," Lomas cried. "You asked who they were and I told you. You didn't say what you had against them."

"Because I hadn't anything like evidence. But there's some queer tales going about."

"Let's hear them, please."

"Very good. We had some forged notes passed here a month ago. We couldn't trace their origin—haven't traced it yet. What we did find was people saying that these strangers out at Cele were up to some queer game: brought a mysterious machine down with them, had chemist's stuff sent from London and so on. I suppose you don't wonder I wanted to know who they were."

Lomas laughed angrily. "No, I don't wonder at anything after that. Very imaginative people you've got down here, captain. What else has Miss Daymer been doing, please?"

Captain Camber shrugged. "Sorry you don't like it. You asked for it. I told you I was satisfied."

"Lomas apologizes," Mr. Fortune smiled. "Family indignation, you know, captain. Very natural and laudable but not relevant. Anything else being said against Miss Daymer?"

"If you put it to me, there is. Quite a lot." Captain Camber frowned at Lomas. "The country people don't like the way the young ladies carried on out there."

"I dare say. Miss Daymer's habits weren't learnt in the country."

"And that don't explain why she comes to live out in the country."

"Good gad, do you expect a young woman to be reasonable nowadays?"

"I don't expect anything of her. She's not my cousin. What they say is that she and her friends are Bolsheviks."

"My dear fellow! That's what everybody says of people they don't like nowadays."

"Yes. Yes." Mr. Fortune's quiet voice purred into this altercation. "But why don't they like her?"

"You'll pardon me," said Captain Camber with decision. "If you gentlemen came to ask me why Mr. Lomas's cousin isn't popular, I'm only saying you surprise me."

"You know, we're missing all the points, Lomas," Mr. Fortune said gently. "I wonder if Captain Camber could put his hand on anybody who started this forged note story."

"No idea, sir. Common gossip. That's all."

"Yes. But somebody thought of it first. Well now, what was this cottage of theirs before they took it?"

"Before? It's been a cottage time out of mind. Ramshackle old place. They bought it for a song from Lord Stanchester's trustees."

"Any competition from other buyers?"

"Good Lord, no," Captain Camber laughed. "It isn't much of a catch, sir."

"Did they turn anybody out?"

"Oh no. It's been empty for years."

Mr. Fortune sighed and stood up. "I'm afraid we've given you a lot of trouble, captain."

"I'm afraid you've drawn a lot of blanks, sir," Captain Camber smiled. "If I can be of any use," his tone declared certainly that he could not, "delighted, delighted, Mr. Lomas. But my idea is you'd better take Miss Daymer back to London."

"My dear fellow, I wish you knew her," said Lomas, and when they were outside condemned the eyes of Captain Camber.

"Quite. Quite," said Mr. Fortune. "Not one of our brighter minds. But there seem to be other people who agree with the captain."

"What do you mean?"

"I haven't decided. But the provisional hypothesis is that somebody here wants to get Miss Daymer out of her cottage."

"That's what you were working at, is it? You didn't make

much out of it. Why should any of these country people want to turn her out? She can't do them any harm. They don't want her cottage. The fellow said it had been derelict for years."

"I know. It's all very curious and disappointing. Why do they want to get rid of Vera? I think we'd better go and ask her."

It took much trouble; it took a good and long lunch to persuade Lomas to this desperate enterprise, but at last he was brought, strong and resolute, if slightly somnolent, to the big car. The lane which leads from the high road to Cele is narrow. The big car slowed, drew in to the bank and stopped to give way to a battered Ford which met it hooting furiously. Mr. Fortune raised himself in his seat. "My only aunt!" he groaned. The Ford rattled by and he stared after it.

"What's the matter with your aunt?" said Lomas sleepily.

"Wake up. That was Vera's friend Isabel and Isabel's friend Charles. With a policeman. He had the air of one who pinches them. And will you tell me what that means?"

"Good gad!" said Lomas and became quite awake. "I should say it means that your provisional hypothesis is cancelled."

"I wonder." Mr. Fortune frowned.

"Yes. I wonder too. I wonder what they've done with Vera?"

"They?" Mr. Fortune stared at him with dull eyes.

"I mean these local police, of course."

"Oh, ah. I was thinking of Isabel and Charles. Who is Charles, anyway? What's his function?"

"Great heavens, how can I tell? Vera used to know half the detrimental highbrows in London. I always thought she'd get into an unholy mess with them some day. She's done it in style."

"My dear old thing!" said Mr. Fortune. "A little above normal, aren't you? A little jumpy. We don't know, you know." He stopped the car. They were on the verge of the village of Cele. It had a certain liveliness: it was being conversational. Half a dozen women and several men were gathered together. But the arrival of strangers produced a staring silence. Mr. Fortune with his most engaging manner wondered if anybody could tell him where Miss Daymer lived. A man slowly directed him and was nudged by a woman and bidden tell the gentleman. "Why, what have you got to tell me?"

"You won't find her, sir, that's a fact. There's been murder done here."

"What, who's murdered?"

"She be. They ha' took her into Stanchester all bloody and dead."

"Why, who did it?"

"Ah, 'tis her own fine friends done it," a woman cried. "That's what comes of their carrying on. They be took away to jail, the pair of them."

"Her friends murdered her? You don't mean that?"

"There's them as saw it. Albert! Tell the gentleman." A lad was thrust forward, shuffling, proud of his importance, frightened. "Tell un what you saw."

" 'Twere the other one with her sweetheart," said Albert. "They was cuddling by the old quarry and she come on them. She did let 'em have it proper, jealous like," he grinned. "The other one give her back as good. Then the man he ups and hits her a clout on the head and down her went into the quarry. So I run home."

"Ah, he's a wild one, him in the short pants. I see his eye," one of the women said. "I always told you, Martha Biggs."

"So you did surely. But I do reckon t'other wench is to blame for all. She's wanton."

They were scattered by the coming of another car. It pulled up short. Captain Camber sprang out and made for Lomas. "I tried to get you in Stanchester. You've heard, have you?"

"They tell me Miss Daymer has been murdered," Lomas said.

"I'm sorry," Captain Camber lowered his voice. "Well, she's not dead. The doctors won't promise anything. But she may pull through. We've had to arrest her friends. There's an eye-witness——"

"Yes, we've met him," said Mr. Fortune. "It's concussion, I suppose. Anything worse?"

"Broken a rib and an arm. She's unconscious. They hope it's only bad concussion. Will you go back and see her? I'm going up to the place where it happened."

"I'd better see the place," Mr. Fortune said. "Lomas, old man, I'll take that first. There's nothing for her yet but quiet."

"Thanks," Lomas nodded. "You're in charge."

"Albert Small," Captain Camber called in a naval voice. "I want you."

The quarry has long been out of action. It looks much like a natural sandstone cliff. Heather and bracken and gorse grow all around. "Now, my lad, where were you when you saw them?" said Captain Camber. Albert, something scared by these great people, pointed to the sandy bank and hedge which divided a turnip field from the waste. "Humph. Rabbiting, eh?" said the captain and Albert grinned uncomfortably. Captain Camber marched to the hedge. "Yes, there's your snares. I thought so."

"They ain't mine, sir," Albert whined. "Take my dying oath, they ain't."

"Cut it out. You were down by the hedge here——"

"I was only picking a few berries."

"And what did you see?"

"I see them up there," Albert pointed up to the edge of the cliff. "Them two. Cuddling. I seen 'em at it before. Then the other one come along. She set about 'em. And the man he give her one on the head and down she goes. And I run away."

Captain Camber looked at Lomas. "That's pretty straight." And Lomas nodded. "We'd better go up there." Mr. Fortune had already gone. They arrived to find him frowning at some marks in the sand. "Nailed boots, eh? That young fellow was wearing nailed boots."

"Yes, I'm afraid so," Mr. Fortune murmured.

"Here's a woman's footprints quite close."

"Yes. Yes." Mr. Fortune glanced at him. "Where's our Albert? Oh, Albert: stand quite still. What were the two doing when you saw them first?"

"Cuddling," Albert grinned.

"Yes, as you were saying. But I mean, were they sitting down?"

Albert considered that. "Sort of setting. More like lying," he pronounced. "You know how 'tis."

"Just here?"

"Hereabouts."

"And you saw nobody else here?"

"Wasn't nobody to see."

"And when the lady was knocked over the edge what did you do?"

"I run home quick. For to get help like. I was afeared, I was."

"Yes, I see." Mr. Fortune turned to Captain Camber. "Now I think Albert can run home again."

"I think so. Run away, my lad. Don't get talking." Albert vanished and the captain approached Lomas with sympathy. "A bad business, sir. You see there's no help for it, we shall have to charge them. We'll go as slow as we can. When the young lady can tell her story, it may look different——"

"If she ever does tell it," Lomas shrugged. "Oh, you must go on with the case of course."

"You don't know the fellow who struck her?"

"Not from Adam. Fortune has seen him. Fortune!"

Mr. Fortune was a little way off. He was on his knees by a clump of gorse and brambles. He was looking at some wet brown stains. He was smelling them. "Did you want me?" He rose. "Has Albert gone?" He made out the lad's retreating figure on the path below. "Oh yes. What did you make of our Albert?"

"He's got it all clear," said Captain Camber.

"Yes. Yes. Quite clear. I thought he was telling the truth in one place. Where he said he hadn't been rabbiting. Not elsewhere."

"Well, I'll be hanged!" said Captain Camber. "That's where I thought he was lying."

"Perhaps you're right. But I shouldn't believe the rest, if I were you. I don't think it happened."

"Damme, sir, we know it happened. The girl was found lying down there senseless. The doctors say she'd been hit on the head."

"Yes, I think so."

"Oh, you do believe that! Well, what's the matter with the boy's story?"

"It's a good story. But it don't fit the facts. He says there were two women here and there's only one woman's footprints. He says a woman and a man were embracin' on the ground and the heather isn't crushed anywhere. He says Miss Daymer was hit in a quarrel and she was hit by a man who came up behind her. Look at the footprints. His toes to her heels. He says Charles hit her. The man who hit her came from behind that gorse. He'd been chewing tobacco and spitting. I don't care for Charles myself. He's too sprightly. But he don't spit!"

"Good gad!" said Lomas. "That lets these two out."

"You mean to say I've got no evidence at all, sir!" cried Captain Camber.

"My dear fellow! Oh, my dear fellow! Lots of evidence," Mr. Fortune murmured. "There's our Albert. Albert was up here."

"Of course he was up here. We brought him."

Mr. Fortune gazed at Captain Camber with patient wonder. "Yes, captain. Quite so. There's his footmarks. He shuffles, doesn't he? But look. There's his footmarks, too, coming by the gorse. We didn't bring him there. He was up there beside the gentleman who wears nailed boots with toe and heel pieces, the gentleman who spits, the gentleman who came behind Vera and knocked her out. Lots of nice evidence. Somebody's been making great use of our Albert."

"The young devil!" said Captain Camber with fury.

"Yes, I think so," Mr. Fortune smiled. "You might look into Albert."

"I'll deal with him. I'll have the truth out of him."

"Oh, no rash haste. Keep quite calm. Give Albert rope. We don't want him. We want the fellow that's behind him."

"The fellow that spits, eh?"

"I wonder." Mr. Fortune looked away at the dim blue of distant hills.

"What do you wonder?"

"The fellow that spits—or the fellow behind that fellow——"

"Well, I'll be hanged!" said Captain Camber. "You're going pretty far."

"You think so? Let's go up to the cottage, anyway." He looked at Lomas. "That's all right, old man?"

"Lord yes, if you like. But what's it all mean, Reginald? What's it for?"

"There you have me," said Mr. Fortune sadly.

"Damme, I'm glad to hear it," Captain Camber gave forth an angry laugh. "It has me beat. Crazy, I call it."

"Yes, it always was," Lomas agreed. "It gets worse as it goes on."

"Oh, no, no. Quite a nice case. Only nobody's worked at it. You people are so flippant."

Captain Camber's feelings were too deep for words. His eyes swelled at Mr. Fortune. He breathed hard. Thus at very high pressure he led the way up that wet and stony lane to the cottage. Suddenly a roar came out of him. He plunged forward shouting.

"Oh Peter!" Mr. Fortune groaned and stood still shaking his head at Lomas. "Well-meaning man. Did it all for the best."

"What's the matter with him?"

"Zeal, all zeal," Mr. Fortune sighed. "He's seen our Albert. He's mentioning it," and the fields resounded Albert's name.

The captain came back puffing and red. "Young devil, he's bolted like a rabbit. He knows he's for it."

"Yes, I fear so," said Mr. Fortune.

"What the deuce is he up to here?"

"Watching what we're doing. But we may as well do it," Mr. Fortune went on quickly.

Even as when he came to the cottage first, a brown face framed in whiskers stared at him over the broken hedge. William was still digging. But he had somebody with him, a small man, neatly bearded, in neat dark clothes who saw Captain Camber's large red face and touched his hat. "Good day, sir. I was just asking for Miss Daymer. There's nobody here but old William. I can't make out what's happened."

"What do you want with Miss Daymer, Tidford?"

"Little matter of an account, sir. Has she had an accident sir?"

"Something like that."

"Dear, dear. Poor lady. Nothing serious, I hope?"

Mr. Fortune coughed. "I hope not," said Captain Camber solemnly and Mr. Fortune sighed. "I'm afraid your little bill will have to wait, Tidford."

"To be sure, sir. To be sure. Of course if I'd known I shouldn't have thought—but I'm in the way, captain. Good day, sir." He turned to a bicycle by the hedge and went jolting off.

William rested on the spade to stare after him. "Been here all day, William?" said Mr. Fortune.

"Ay," William turned over a spadeful of the light brown earth and stopped.

"What do you know about it?"

"Dunno nothing. They all went out in the morning. T'other ones first. Then mistress. T'other ones come back. Then police come and took 'em away. I did hear as mistress were picked up in th' old quarry dead. Dunno if it be true." His dull eyes stared at Mr. Fortune. "Do'e know, sir?"

"Good mistress, was she?"

"Ay, surely. I be fain to know how she be."

Mr. Fortune shook his head. "A bad business," he said.

"Look here, my man," Captain Camber struck in, "do you know if any of the country folk had a quarrel with her?" Here Mr. Fortune groaned and turned away.

"They did have rare quarrels among theirselves," said William. "Since the young man come. What I wants to know is how I be—if she be dead?"

"You carry on, my lad," said Captain Camber. "I'll look after you." William touched his forehead and resumed digging. "Well, Mr. Fortune, what now? Want to go into the house, eh?"

Mr. Fortune was looking at the ground. "Yes. I suppose so," he said slowly: and slowly followed Captain Camber.

The door stood open. "Hullo! Here's a mess," the captain cried. "Somebody's been here before us, sir. The place has been turned upside down."

Mr. Fortune looked round his shoulder. "Well, it's possible. But I doubt it. There was just as much mess yesterday."

"Queer way to live," the captain muttered. "Beg your pardon, Mr. Lomas."

"Don't mind me. If you can think of anything adequate, say it. I can't."

They moved about in the chaos, Lomas looking for letters, the captain looking at everything. After some time he emitted an exclamation. He had discovered the printing press. "Look at this, Mr. Lomas. What were they doing with this, please?"

"Heaven only knows."

"If you don't mind my saying so, it looks as if there might be something in that idea about forged notes being printed here."

"I don't mind your saying so. But it don't make sense," said Lomas.

"Thank you. I dare say I'm as good a judge of that as you, sir."

The voice of Mr. Fortune arose. "Oh don't blether," it said irritably. "They weren't printing notes, of course. Etchings. Woodcuts. You'll find some of the stuff under the dirty plates. They think they're artists, heaven forgive them."

Captain Camber snorted and sought these works of art and surveyed them with disgust while Lomas laughed. He flung them down and marched on Mr. Fortune who was bent over the old oak chest peering at its rough worm-eaten inscription. "What have you got, sir?"

"I haven't the slightest idea," said Mr. Fortune.

"Anything in the old thing?" The captain opened it to behold a tumbled mass of women's clothes. "Humph. Just like 'em. Well, gentlemen, I've got no more time to waste in this mess. My notion is we'd better lock the place up, get back to Stanchester and see if these two people we've arrested have got anything to say for themselves."

Mr. Fortune straightened himself. "I shouldn't wonder if Isabel says quite a lot," he said and lounged out.

But half-way down the garden Captain Camber halted. "Hallo! Where's that fellow William?" He shouted to an empty world.

"I infer he's gone to look for Albert," Mr. Fortune murmured. "I thought he would. You see, you're so frank, captain."

"What do you mean, sir?"

"Well, you tell 'em all what they've got to expect. You told Albert to look out for himself. You told Tidford Miss Daymer wasn't dead. You told William you had a notion some country fellow did the job."

"I told them?" Captain Camber roared.

"Oh Lord, yes. You showed your hand," Lomas assured him.

"What do you mean? What's William got to do with it?"

"Look. There's William's footprints: nails, toe-pieces, heel-pieces. There's where William was spitting."

The captain grew red. "You mean to say you made sure he's the man?"

"Not sure, no. There are probably others in the countryside who chew and spit and wear this kind of boot. But William is indicated."

"Might have warned me, mightn' you?" Captain Camber growled.

"I'm sorry," said Mr. Fortune meekly. "I did what I could. Ask Tidford some time. He noticed it."

Captain Camber glared. "Tidford? What do you mean? What do you keep dragging in Tidford for? What's he got to do with it?"

"I think our Mr. Tidford could tell you why it all happened."

"Tidford? He's a dealer in antiques."

"Yes. I thought he was."

"Oh, did you! And why do you suppose he wanted to kill Miss Daymer?"

"I think he wanted her antiques," said Mr. Fortune.

"Damme, sir, that's not sense. He could have bought the place for a song, lock, stock and barrel, any time before she came. Tidford's not the man to be mixed up in any foul play. He's been in Stanchester all his life, ay, and his father before him. Most respected people."

"You think so? And why did the respectable Tidford hurry up to see William at the cottage as soon as the girl was knocked on the head?"

"I'll be hanged if I know," Captain Camber puffed. "Damme, the more you find, the crazier it looks." He pushed back his hat and wiped a damp head. "Do you think you see your way, sir? I don't."

"But it's quite simple. Do the work that's nearest though it's dull at whiles. On returnin' to civilization send a hefty constable or so to spend the night at the cottage, appoint some unobtrusive fellows to watch Mr. Tidford's business and then have a heart-to-heart talk with Isabel and Charles. Meanwhile your men might look for William and Albert in their wonted haunts. From all which the fundamental facts may emerge. But I don't think so myself."

"Not very hopeful, are you?"

"No. No. Not hopeful. Only patient."

They left Captain Camber in the village barking questions about Albert; they took their own car back to Stanchester. "If Vera can speak that may clear it all up," Lomas said.

"Oh no, no," Mr. Fortune murmured.

"Well, I'd like you to see her, Reginald."

"My dear old thing! Of course I will." Mr. Fortune shut his eyes and lay limp.

He was upstairs in the hospital some time. He came down and smiled at Lomas. "I believe she'll be all right. Bad concussion. Nothing worse. Skull not fractured. No spinal injuries. I shouldn't worry, old thing."

"Still unconscious?"

"Oh yes. Yes. It'll be a long business, poor girl." Mr. Fortune's mind seemed to be withdrawn. He wandered out dreamily.

The car took them to the police station. Captain Camber had been asking for them. Captain Camber was very brisk but a little embarrassed. He had made all his arrangements, he was just going to have these people brought up, he didn't quite know—perhaps Mr. Fortune——

"Oh, Lord no," said Mr. Fortune.

"All right, captain," said Lomas and took charge.

Isabel and Charles were produced, dishevelled, startled, angry. Lomas wished them to understand the position. They were charged on the evidence of a boy, Albert Small, who said he had seen it, with an attack on Miss Daymer. It was right to tell them that investigation did not support the charge. But Miss Daymer had been injured and was still unconscious. Could they throw any light on the matter?

"Isn't she going to die?" Isabel cried.

"We hope not."

"They told us she was dead. How wicked! How perfectly wicked!"

"Rotten," said Charles. "But I say, is she going to be all right, sir?"

"We hope so."

"Well!" Isabel looked at Charles and began to cry. Charles also showed signs of emotion and Captain Camber became very uncomfortable. But Lomas watched them with professional interest and after a minute scrawled on a piece of paper and pushed across to Mr. Fortune this message:

"You win. Nails but no toe-piece or heel-piece." Mr. Fortune contemplated it with pensive lack of interest.

Isabel dried her eyes—quelled her sobs—exploded. It was utterly beastly of them. Of course Charles never did it. Just the very last person. What did they suppose he came to the horrid place for?

Here Charles flushed and muttered something about going easy.

Isabel was not to be checked. She turned fiercely upon Mr. Fortune. "You know perfectly well."

Mr. Fortune's mouth was open a long moment before he could speak. "Me?" he gasped. "Did you mean me?"

"Don't try and play tricks. Do you think I don't remember you? You came spying on us yesterday. You must have seen. (Oh shut up, Charles.) Charles and Vera are as good as engaged."

"I hadn't thought of that," said Mr. Fortune humbly. "My mistake."

"Oh I see now!" she cried. "You have been clever. You thought because he was with me and Vera was horrid to him, it was me he wanted and she was jealous. That was bright! Of course she was being horrid. She's proud, she knows she can't help liking him and she hates it. It's been so jolly for me."

"Yes. All my apologies. But I haven't done anything. I hadn't even an opinion about you. This is all very natural and human and interestin' and I sympathize deeply. But it don't clear things up. Why did Albert tell this tale?"

"Albert is a horror. He's been the plague of our lives." Albert was always lurking, Albert was always playing tricks, Albert was always making mischief. In their troubles with tradesmen, with farmers, in the hostility of the village she saw the hand of Albert. "I don't know why the wretched youth hates us. But there it is. I suppose he's just a natural fiend."

"Yes. And other fiends?" said Mr. Fortune.

"Everybody's been horrid. They've made things just as awkward as they could. But I believe it's really all Albert."

"Yes, yes. Did it ever occur to you that somebody wanted to get you out of that cottage?"

"Whatever for?" said Miss Villaret. "Why should they? Horrid barn of a place. It had been empty for ages when Vera took it. I wish she'd never seen it."

"Nobody ever made you an offer for it?"

"Why? Yes, I believe there was somebody," Vera said. "Some agent wrote to her. She turned him down."

"Of course you don't know who he was? No. You wouldn't. I wonder. Have you ever got rid of any of the old stuff in the place?"

"Oh yes, Vera sold an old oak cupboard thing, all falling to pieces. The man in Stanchester bought it, Tidford, the man we got our furniture from."

"Was there anything in it?"

"Only some books and papers. Awful old stuff. Sermons and things like that."

"I say, you know," Charles broke in. "This is all very well, sir. But I mean to say you're not getting anywhere. I want to know who it was slogged Vera."

"I don't blame you," said Captain Camber. "We are a bit off the line. Now"—a police inspector came in, begged pardon, sir, whispered to him. His large red face split in a smile—"Now I'll just ask you to wait awhile. We'll make you quite comfortable. Bit of dinner, eh? We can manage that." He bustled the two bewildered creatures out and turning, clapped Mr. Fortune on the back. "I've got 'em, my lad. All the three of 'em. My fellows caught Albert and William coming around Tidford's back door. Brought 'em all along." He rubbed his hands and chuckled. "You think we're dull dogs down here. But we don't miss much, eh?"

Lomas laughed.

Mr. Fortune lay back and gazed at him. "Splendid, captain. I don't know how you can do it. All my congratulations. Now you've got everything except evidence."

"Ah, I'll soon have that," said Captain Camber.

His confidence was justified. He knew how to deal with Albert. He scolded, he commanded, and a frightened lout was soon whimpering the truth. Mr. Tidford told Albert as they had to be cleared out of that cottage. Mr. Tidford told Albert all about what he was to do making trouble for them. Gave him five shillings a week for it. But it was William as done it. Albert never touched the lady. He wouldn't have, not for nothing. Mr. Tidford told him what he was to say. But he never did no harm to her, no really he didn't, captain.

The methods of Captain Camber had some success with William, too. William was tougher stuff than the boy. He could not be frightened. His power of holding his tongue endured till his dull mind was convinced that the captain knew enough to bring him in guilty. Then " 'Twas Tidford," he growled. "Tidford would have her put away. I done what he said." And he supplied details.

But with Mr. Tidford, Captain Camber failed completely. Mr. Tidford, neat, composed, master of himself, let the captain talk. He knew nothing, he would explain nothing. If he was to be charged, a smile, a wave of the hand suggested the folly of the charge against so respectable a man, he would know how to defend himself.

"You'll be charged, my man," Captain Camber assured him. "No answer, eh? Well, perhaps you know best." He sent Tidford away and looked at Lomas.

"He was in it all right," Lomas pronounced.

"I should say so! That's a case, eh?"

But Mr. Fortune sat in a dreary heap making letters on a sheet of paper. "Well, Reginald?"

"Oh yes, yes. You've got the men."

"What more do you want?" cried Captain Camber.

Mr. Fortune stared at his inscription. "I want my dinner primarily," he murmured.

"That's up to me," said Captain Camber jovially.

But the admirable mutton and the tolerable port of Captain Camber did not avail to cheer Mr. Fortune. While the captain explained his own genius in handling the affair, while Lomas, loquacious and sprightly, demonstrated the advantages of getting the silly girls out of the business without scandal, he sat in a cloud of smoke and made inarticulate murmurs, till at last "Reginald! We're not interesting you," Lomas reproached him.

"Oh yes. I heard every word. I quite agree. I was just thinking."

"What's your trouble?" Captain Camber smiled and passed the port.

"Reginald!" said Lomas severely. "What have you got up your sleeve?"

"I don't know. I don't know if it's anything." He took out a piece of paper on which was written Y AI IOX IO IO EPIKALL H. "What do you make of that?"

Captain Camber read it out in a jocose manner. "Y, ai! Iox, io, io, epikall. What are you giving us, sir? Where did you get it from?"

"It's carved on that fifteenth-century chest in the cottage. Later work than the chest though. There are other letters, but I couldn't make them out."

"It wouldn't make sense, anyway. Iox, io, io!" The captain laughed. "What about it?"

"Do you read it as cipher, Reginald?" Lomas asked.

"I don't read it at all. I don't know what it is. But it's very interesting."

"I'm no hand at cryptograms, myself," Captain Camber announced. "But what's the good of it, anyway? We've got our case."

"Yes. In a way. We've got the respectable Tidford——"

"By the short hairs," Captain Camber chuckled. "Don't you worry."

"But we haven't got what he was after. Why did he want to get the girls out of the cottage? The provisional hypothesis is there was something in the place he wanted."

"Then why the deuce didn't he get it before they came?"

"Yes, that was a difficulty. But you heard Isabel's story. They sold him an old cupboard full of books and papers. That's where he got the tip. He put on an agent to buy the cottage. They wouldn't deal. Then he put on Albert and Co. to make the place too hot to hold them. That didn't work. So he arranged to have Vera knocked out and the other two accused of the crime. Very neat scheme. If we hadn't blown in, he'd have had the cottage empty for as long as he needed. It's all quite clear except two things. What was it our Tidford wanted so bad? And I'm afraid he won't tell us that. Secondly, where is it? That I fancy he don't know, or William would have got it for him."

"I don't know what there could be," Captain Camber declared. "The place was only a barn in the old days. You can see that. It's been a labourer's cottage the last century. Not much hidden treasure about."

"I wonder," Mr. Fortune murmured. And again contemplated the letters Y AI IOX IO IO EPIKALL H.

"Queer sort of cipher," Lomas frowned. "The repetitions aren't reasonable. Io three times over, Reginald."

"Yes. Very improbable. I wonder."

"What do you want to do?"

"I want to see the books our Tidford found in the old cupboard."

"All right. All right," Captain Camber chuckled. "Dig 'em out to-morrow, sir. Iox, io, io!"

In the morning a search party dealt with Mr. Tidford's shop and his scared assistant. The cupboard from the cottage was discovered, the books which had been in it, a pile of decaying theology. Captain Camber facetiously swore that Mr. Fortune would know a lot when he had worked through that. But Mr. Fortune's researches were not profound. Having discovered that the books had belonged to one Gualt. Hailes S.T.P. he sought the neat private apartments of Mr. Tidford. There by the respectable man's bedside was a fat book bound in rough crumbling calf inscribed on the first page Diurna, Gualt. Hailes. "Yes. I thought our Tidford wouldn't leave it lying about," Mr. Fortune murmured.

"What is it?"

"It's the diary of Walter Hailes, D.D., in the years 1640 onwards." He turned yellow quarto pages full of cramped writing.

"Good gad!" said Lomas. "My poor Reginald. Dr. Hailes was a fluent fellow. Not even English, is it?"

"Some of it's English. Rather ready with his classics though. I wonder." He looked up at Lomas with a slow, benign smile. "Well, well. A little earnest study is indicated."

He tucked the book under his arm and marched off.

Lomas, coming back to the hotel for lunch, found him in the courtyard flirting with the Persian cat of the house, a proud cat. "Is this industry, Reginald?" he said severely. "What of your divine?"

"This is dalliance. Isn't it, Artaxerxes?" He caressed the cat's ear and received a low, plaintive curse. "Here's our naval officer, brisk and breezy. Come on. I've got grayling for lunch."

They sat down to it and Captain Camber also made haste to ask how he had got on with the parson. Mr. Fortune passed him the menu. "I sometimes wonder whether I like grayling as much as I think I do," he explained. "I've never had it often enough to be quite sure." He tasted the Sauternes anxiously and sighed. "Well, well. Life is full of uncertainties. Do you think this is the right wine for grayling?"

"It's good enough for me, sir. Yquem, is it?"

"Oh no, no. La Tour Blanche. But I wonder. Perhaps something drier——"

"You are pensive, Reginald," Lomas smiled. "Did you draw a blank with the divine?"

"I am not pensive," Mr. Fortune was pained. "I like to treat serious things seriously," and did so. It was not till they had passed by way of duckling to peaches that he came back to earth. "You were asking about my parson. Yes. He's a dear old thing. Dr. Walter Hailes came to Hill Barn when the Puritans chucked him out of his living. It used to be the tithe-barn of the abbey at Cele. That was all gone even in his time—destroyed at the Reformation. He's very sad about that. He was a high old churchman as near a Roman Catholic as no matter. The local squire let him stay up there in the barn. Sir Amyas Boileau—old family in what he calls the great house. I don't know where it is."

"Over at Cele Regis, sir. That's gone too. The Boileau family died out long ago."

"Yes. I rather fancy Dr. Hailes saw the last of them."

"All very interesting, Reginald. But it doesn't take us anywhere."

"No, no. But it's suggestive."

"Is it? I don't see Mr. Tidford losing much sleep over this."

"Well, I think he'd found something more. I think this is what started our Tidford on his career of crime. In August, 1644: 'Comes Tho. Hewings with news that the crop eared rogues have sent summons to my lady. So I to the great house to take counsel. God guide all.' The next day Dr. Hailes drops into Latin: '*Hodie reliquias oblitae eheu gloriae ex magna domo in pusillam tabernam lacrimans gaudensque recepi et in secretum condidi. Quo usque Domine?*' He received the relics of a glory—alas! forgotten—from the great house into his puny hut with tears and joy and put them into a secret place. And he says 'How long, oh Lord?' "

"Oh, that's it, it is? The padre had the Boileau family jewels!" Captain Camber cried. "But in 1644! You wouldn't expect to find 'em now."

"Our Tidford expected to find 'em."

"Nothing more in the diary, Reginald?" said Lomas.

"No. Nothing to be sure of. There's some odd prayers in Greek."

"He wouldn't pray about the squire's jewels," Captain Camber objected. "You mean to say Tidford had nothing more to work on than that?"

"Well, I should guess there is a local tradition of stuff from the big house being hidden. He'd know that. And this gave him the clue."

"But he'd have to pull the place to bits."

Again Lomas saw on Mr. Fortune's face a slow benign smile. "I object to the mirth, Reginald," he complained, "you are also being superior. What have you kept from us?"

"I'm not. I wouldn't. There's only this." On the menu card he wrote again the letters Y AI IOX IO IO EPIKALL H.

"That cipher, eh?" Captain Camber growled.

"No. I don't think it's cipher. Come along. We'll go out to Hill Barn and try."

They arrived at that lonely cottage and the large constable in charge opened the door. But Mr. Fortune did not go in. He wandered here and there on the outskirts of the garden. "It's only a chance, you know. But that is rather a fine tree." He stopped beneath the ancient oak. "He was here in 1644 and quite a big fellow then. Can the constabulary dig, captain?"

The constable was anxious to do so and the brown earth flew. The spade struck splinters of old wood. There came out an iron-bound box, its hinges rusting asunder. Mr. Fortune knelt over it and drew out a shapeless mass wrapped in leather. From that emerged to the sunlight two strange things that glittered and flashed: tarnished gold, blue and white enamel wrought about cylinders of rock crystal and set above with gems.

"What in the world are they?" cried Captain Camber. "Don't look like anything."

"No. They're not common. They are reliquaries. Things made to contain holy relics. Quite old." Mr. Fortune was handling them delicately. "Look. You can make it out. *LIGNUM CRUCIS*. The wood of the Cross. That's what Dr. Hailes wanted to save. I suppose they came from the shrine in the old abbey. The Boileau family saved them when that was destroyed. When the Puritan troops came to the Boileaus' house, Dr. Hailes had to hide them. Well, well." He lifted them reverently. "The wood of the Cross. That's what our Tidford put up his murder for. A queer world."

"Well, I suppose they're worth thousands," said Captain Camber.

"Oh yes, yes. Anything you please. That didn't occur to Dr. Walter Hailes."

"And you got at 'em out of that bit of cipher! What is it? Iox, io, io?" Captain Camber gazed at him.

"It wasn't cipher. It was Greek. I ought to have known that at first. My error. I only got at it when I found Dr. Hailes was so fond of the classics. He wanted to leave some record and he thought, bless him, only the right sort of man would understand it if he put it in Greek. You see? Y is U, of course, and X is CH and P is R and H is E. Then some of the lost letters came in easy and I saw it must be Homer and turned it up at the grammar school. Here you are." He filled in the gaps. "HUP AIGIOCHOIO DIOS PERIKALLEI PHEGO. Under the beautiful oak of ægis-bearing Zeus. Quite simple."

A solemn silence reigned. Lomas first recovered consciousness. "Quite," he gasped. "Oh, quite. I feel that. But I'm afraid Mr. Tidford will be annoyed about it."

HERCULE POIROT

Hercule Poirot is almost certainly the only fictional detective to have his obituary printed on the front page of the New York Times. That was in 1975, when the publication of Curtain, the novel in which Poirot dies, was announced. By that time the dapper and self-satisfied little Belgian investigator, despite a name that is a challenge to pronounce, was among the best known detective characters in the world, right up there with Sherlock Holmes, Charlie Chan, Sam Spade, Ellery Queen, and Dick Tracy. He was introduced in 1920 in Agatha Christie's first novel, The Mysterious Affair at Styles, *and went on to star in nearly three dozen novels and several short story collections. The Poirot stories appeared in every sort of magazine in this country, from slicks like* Collier's *to pulps like* Blue Book. *There have been Poirot movies, most recently with Albert Finney and then Peter Ustinov as the handsomely moustached detective. Charles Laughton played Poirot on Broadway in the early 1930s and Harold Huber played him on radio in the 1940s. Huber, who'd portrayed policemen of various nationalities in the Charlie Chan films, always began the radio show as Poirot saying, "Time and the little grey cells . . . these will always catch the criminal." An apt motto for a detective who consistently proved that patience and brains, plus a strong dash of ego, were what solved mysteries.*

In looking back, from her seventies, Agatha Christie had this to say about how she had conceived the Poirot character:

"Why not make my detective a Belgian? I thought. There were all types of refugees. How about a refugee police officer? A retired police officer. Not too young a one. What a mistake I made there. The result is that my fictional detective must real-

242

ly be well over a hundred by now. . . . I could see him as a tidy little man, always arranging things in pairs, liking things square instead of round. And he would be very brainy. . . . He would have rather a grand name—one of those names that Sherlock Holmes and his family had. . . . How about calling my little man Hercules? He would be a small man—Hercules: a good name. His last name was more difficult. I don't know why I settled on the name Poirot: whether it just came into my head or whether I saw it in some newspaper or written on something—anyway it came. It went well not with Hercules but Hercule—Hercule Poirot. That was all right—settled, thank goodness."

The Disappearance of Mr. Davenheim
by Agatha Christie

Poirot and I were expecting our old friend Inspector Japp of Scotland Yard to tea. We were sitting round the teatable awaiting his arrival. Poirot had just finished carefully straightening the cups and saucers which our landlady was in the habit of throwing, rather than placing, on the table. He had also breathed heavily on the metal teapot, and polished it with a silk handkerchief. The kettle was on the boil, and a small enamel saucepan beside it contained some thick, sweet chocolate which was more to Poirot's palate than what he described as "your English poison."

A sharp "rat-tat" sounded below, and a few minutes afterwards Japp entered briskly.

"Hope I'm not late," he said as he greeted us. "To tell the truth, I was yarning with Miller, the man who's in charge of the Davenheim case."

I pricked up my ears. For the last three days the papers had been full of the strange disappearance of Mr. Davenheim, senior partner of Davenheim and Salmon, the well-known bankers and financiers. On Saturday last he had walked out of his house, and had never been seen since. I looked forward to extracting some interesting details from Japp.

"I should have thought," I remarked, "that it would be almost impossible for anyone to 'disappear' nowadays."

Poirot moved a plate of bread and butter the eighth of an inch, and said sharply:

"Be exact, my friend. What do you mean by 'disappear'? To which class of disappearance are you referring?"

"Are disappearances classified and labeled, then?" I laughed.

Japp smiled also. Poirot frowned at us both.

"But certainly they are! They fall into three categories. First, and most common, the voluntary disappearance. Second, the much abused 'loss of memory' case—rare, but occasionally genuine. Third, murder, and a more or less successful disposal of the body. Do you refer to all three as impossible of execution?"

"Very nearly so, I should think. You might lose your own memory, but some one would be sure to recognize you—especially in the case of a well-known man like Davenheim. Then 'bodies' can't be made to vanish into thin air. Sooner or later they turn up, concealed in lonely places, or in trunks. Murder will out. In the same way, the absconding clerk, or the domestic defaulter, is bound to be run down in these days of wireless telegraphy. He can be headed off from foreign countries; ports and railway stations are watched; and, as for concealment in this country, his features and appearance will be known to everyone who reads a daily newspaper. He's up against civilization."

"*Mon ami*," said Poirot, "you make one error. You do not allow for the fact that a man who had decided to make away with another man—or with himself in a figurative sense— might be that rare machine, a man of method. He might bring intelligence, talent, a careful calculation of detail to the task; and then I do not see why he should not be successful in baffling the police force."

"But not *you*, I suppose?" said Japp good-humoredly, winking at me. "He couldn't baffle *you*, eh, Monsieur Poirot?"

Poirot endeavored, with a marked lack of success, to look modest. "Me, also! Why not? It is true that I approach such problems with an exact science, a mathematical precision, which seems, alas, only too rare in the new generation of detectives!"

Japp grinned more widely.

"I don't know," he said. "Miller, the man who's on this case is a smart chap. You may be very sure he won't overlook a footprint, or a cigar-ash, or a crumb even. He's got eyes that see everything."

"So, *mon ami,*" said Poirot, "has the London sparrow. But all the same, I should not ask the little brown bird to solve the problem of Mr. Davenheim."

"Come now, monsieur, you're not going to run down the value of details as clues?"

"By no means. These things are all good in their way. The danger is they may assume undue importance. Most details are insignificant; one or two are vital. It is the brain, the little gray cells" he tapped his forehead—"on which one must rely. The senses mislead. One must seek the truth within—not without."

"You don't mean to say, Monsieur Poirot, that you would undertake to solve a case without moving from your chair, do you?"

"That is exactly what I do mean—granted the facts were placed before me. I regard myself as a consulting specialist."

Japp slapped his knee. "Hanged if I don't take you at your word. Bet you a fiver that you can't lay your hand—or rather tell me where to lay my hand—on Mr. Davenheim, dead or alive, before a week is out."

Poirot considered. *"Eh bien, mon ami,* I accept. *Le sport,* it is the passion of you English. Now—the facts."

"On Saturday last, as is his usual custom, Mr. Davenheim took the 12:40 train from Victoria to Chingside, where his palatial country place, The Cedars, is situated. After lunch, he strolled round the grounds, and gave various directions to the gardeners. Everybody agrees that his manner was absolutely normal and as usual. After tea he put his head into his wife's boudoir, saying that he was going to stroll down to the village and post some letters. He added that he was expecting a Mr. Lowen, on business. If Lowen should come before he himself returned, he was to be shown into the study and asked to wait. Mr. Davenheim then left the house by the front door, passed leisurely down the drive, and out at the gate, and—was never seen again. From that hour, he vanished completely."

"Pretty—very pretty—altogether a charming little problem," murmured Poirot. "Proceed, my good friend."

"About a quarter of an hour later a tall, dark man with a thick black mustache rang the front-door bell, and explained that he had an appointment with Mr. Davenheim. He gave the name of Lowen, and in accordance with the banker's instructions was shown into the study. Nearly an hour passed. Mr. Davenheim did not return. Finally Mr. Lowen rang the bell, and explained that he was unable to wait any longer, as he must catch his train back to town. Mrs. Davenheim apologized for her husband's absence, which seemed unaccountable, as she knew him to have been expecting the visitor. Mr. Lowen reiterated his regrets and took his departure.

"Well, as everyone knows, Mr. Davenheim did *not* return. Early on Sunday morning the police were communicated with, but could make neither head nor tail of the matter. Mr. Davenheim seemed literally to have vanished into thin air. He had not been to the post office; nor had he been seen passing through the village. At the station they were positive he had not departed by any train. His own motor had not left the garage. If he had hired a car to meet him in some lonely spot, it seems almost certain that by this time, in view of the large reward offered for information, the driver of it would have come forward to tell what he knew. True, there was a small race-meeting at Entfield, five miles away, and if he had walked to that station he might have passed unnoticed in the crowd. But since then his photograph and a full description of him have been circulated in every newspaper, and nobody has been able to give any news of him. We have, of course, received many letters from all over England, but each clue, so far, has ended in disappointment.

"On Monday morning a further sensational discovery came to light. Behind a *portière* in Mr. Davenheim's study stands a safe, and that safe had been broken into and rifled. The windows were fastened securely on the inside, which seems to put an ordinary burglary out of court, unless, of course, an accomplice within the house fastened them again afterwards. On the other hand, Sunday having intervened, and the household being in a state of chaos, it is likely that the burglary was committed on the Saturday, and remained undetected until Monday."

"*Précisément*," said Poirot dryly. "Well, is he arrested, *ce pauvre M. Lowen?*"

Japp grinned. "Not yet. But he's under pretty close supervision."

Poirot nodded. "What was taken from the safe? Have you any idea?"

"We've been going into that with the junior partner of the firm and Mrs. Davenheim. Apparently there was a considerable amount in bearer bonds, and a very large sum in notes, owing to some large transaction having been just carried through. There was also a small fortune in jewelry. All Mrs. Davenheim's jewels were kept in the safe. The purchasing of them had become a passion with her husband of late years, and hardly a month passed that he did not make her a present of some rare and costly gem."

"Altogether a good haul," said Poirot thoughtfully. "Now, what about Lowen? Is it known what his business was with Davenheim that evening?"

"Well, the two men were apparently not on very good terms. Lowen is a speculator in quite a small way. Nevertheless, he has been able once or twice to score a *coup* off Davenheim in the market, though it seems, they seldom or never actually met. It was a matter concerning some South American shares which led the banker to make his appointment."

"Had Davenheim interests in South America, then?"

"I believe so. Mrs. Davenheim happened to mention that he spent all last autumn in Buenos Ayres."

"Any trouble in his home life? Were the husband and wife on good terms?"

"I should say his domestic life was quite peaceful and uneventful. Mrs. Davenheim is a pleasant, rather unintelligent woman. Quite a nonentity, I think."

"Then we must not look for the solution of the mystery there. Had he any enemies?"

"He had plenty of financial rivals, and no doubt there are many people whom he has got the better of who bear him no particular good will. But there was no one likely to make away with him—and, if they had, where is the body?"

"Exactly. As Hastings says, bodies have a habit of coming to light with fatal persistency."

"By the way, one of the gardeners says he saw a figure going round to the side of the house toward the rose-garden. The long French window of the study opens on the rose-garden, and Mr. Davenheim frequently entered and left the house that way. But the man was a good way off, at work on some cucumber frames, and cannot even say whether it was the figure of his master or not. Also, he cannot fix the time with any accuracy. It must have been before six, as the gardeners cease work at that time."

"And Mr. Davenheim left the house?"

"About half-past five or thereabouts."

"What lies beyond the rose-garden?"

"A lake."

"With a boathouse?"

"Yes, a couple of punts are kept there. I suppose you're thinking of suicide, Monsieur Poirot? Well, I don't mind telling you that Miller's going down to-morrow expressly to see that piece of water dragged. That's the kind of man he is!"

Poirot smiled faintly, and turned to me. "Hastings, I pray you, hand me that copy of the *Daily Megaphone*. If I remember rightly, there is an unusually clear photograph there of the missing man."

I rose, and found the sheet required. Poirot studied the features attentively.

"H'm!" he murmured. "Wears his hair rather long and wavy, full mustache and pointed beard, bushy eyebrows. Eyes dark?"

"Yes."

"Hair and beard turning gray?"

The detective nodded. "Well, Monsieur Poirot, what have you got to say to it all? Clear as daylight, eh?"

"On the contrary, most obscure."

The Scotland Yard man looked pleased.

"Which gives me great hopes of solving it," finished Poirot placidly.

"Eh?"

"I find it a good sign when a case is obscure. If a thing is clear as daylight—*eh bien*, mistrust it! Someone has made it so."

Japp shook his head almost pityingly. "Well, each to their ancy. But it's not a bad thing to see your way clear ahead."

"I do not see," murmured Poirot. "I shut my eyes—and hink."

Japp sighed. "Well, you've got a clear week to think in."

"And you will bring me any fresh developments that arise—the result of the labors of the hard-working and lynx-eyed Inspector Miller, for instance?"

"Certainly. That's in the bargain."

"Seems a shame, doesn't it?" said Japp to me as I accompanied him to the door. "Like robbing a child!"

I could not help agreeing with a smile. I was still smiling as I re-entered the room.

"*Eh bien!*" said Poirot immediately. "You make fun of Papa Poirot, is it not so?" He shook his finger at me. "You do not trust his gray cells? Ah, do not be confused! Let us discuss this little problem—incomplete as yet, I admit, but already showing one or two points of interest."

"The lake!" I said significantly.

"And even more than the lake, the boathouse!"

I looked sidewise at Poirot. He was smiling in his most inscrutable fashion. I felt that, for the moment, it would be quite useless to question him further.

We heard nothing of Japp until the following evening, when he walked in about nine o'clock. I saw at once by his expression that he was bursting with news of some kind.

"*Eh bien*, my friend," remarked Poirot. "All goes well? But do not tell me that you have discovered the body of Mr. Davenheim in your lake, because I shall not believe you."

"We haven't found the body, but we did find his *clothes*—the identical clothes he was wearing that day. What do you say to that?"

"Any other clothes missing from the house?"

"No, his valet is quite positive on that point. The rest of his wardrobe is intact. There's more. We've arrested Lowen. One of the maids, whose business it is to fasten the bedroom windows, declares that she saw Lowen coming *towards* the study through the rose-garden about a quarter past six. That would be about ten minutes before he left the house."

"What does he himself say to that?"

"Denied first of all that he had ever left the study. But the maid was positive, and he pretended afterwards that he had forgotten just stepping out of the window to examine an unusual species of rose. Rather a weak story! And there's fresh evidence against him come to light. Mr. Davenheim always wore a thick gold ring set with a solitaire diamond on the little finger of his right hand. Well, that ring was pawned in London on Saturday night by a man called Billy Kellett! He's already known to the police—did three months last autumn for lifting an old gentleman's watch. It seems he tried to pawn the ring at no less than five different places, succeeded at the last one, got gloriously drunk on the proceeds, assaulted a policeman, and was run in in consequence. I went to Bow Street with Miller and saw him. He's sober enough now, and I don't mind admitting we pretty well frightened the life out of him, hinting he might be charged with murder. This is his yarn, and a very queer one it is.

"He was at Entfield races on Saturday, though I dare say scarfpins was his line of business, rather than betting. Anyway, he had a bad day, and was down on his luck. He was tramping along the road to Chingside, and sat down in a ditch to rest just before he got into the village. A few minutes later he noticed a man coming along the road to the village, 'dark-complexioned gent, with a big mustache, one of them city toffs,' is his description of the man.

"Kellett was half concealed from the road by a heap of stones. Just before he got abreast of him, the man looked quickly up and down the road, and seeing it apparently deserted he took a small object from his pocket and threw it over the hedge. Then he went on towards the station. Now, the object he had thrown over the hedge had fallen with a slight 'chink' which aroused the curiosity of the human derelict in the ditch. He investigated and, after a short search, discovered the ring! That is Kellett's story. It's only fair to say that Lowen denies it utterly, and of course the word of a man like Kellett can't be relied upon in the slightest. It's within the bounds of possibility that he met Davenheim in the lane and robbed and murdered him."

Poirot shook his head.

"Very improbable, *mon ami*. He had no means of disposing of the body. It would have been found by now. Secondly, the open way in which he pawned the ring makes it unlikely that he did murder to get it. Thirdly, your sneak-thief is rarely a murderer. Fourthly, as he has been in prison since Saturday, it would be too much of a coincidence that he is able to give so accurate a description of Lowen."

Japp nodded. "I don't say you're not right. But all the same, you won't get a jury to take much note of a jailbird's evidence. What seems odd to me is that Lowen couldn't find a cleverer way of disposing of the ring."

Poirot shrugged his shoulders. "Well, after all, if it were found in the neighborhood, it might be argued that Davenheim himself had dropped it."

"But why remove it from the body at all?" I cried.

"There might be a reason for that," said Japp. "Do you know that just beyond the lake, a little gate leads out on to the hill, and not three minutes' walk brings you to—what do you think?—a *lime kiln.*"

"Good heavens!" I cried. "You mean that the lime which destroyed the body would be powerless to affect the metal of the ring?"

"Exactly."

"It seems to me," I said, "that that explains everything. What a horrible crime!"

By common consent we both turned and looked at Poirot. He seemed lost in reflection, his brow knitted, as though with some supreme mental effort. I felt that at last his keen intellect was asserting itself. What would his first words be? We were not long left in doubt. With a sigh, the tension of his attitude relaxed, and turning to Japp, he asked:

"Have you any idea, my friend, whether Mr. and Mrs. Davenheim occupied the same bedroom?"

The question seemed so ludicrously inappropriate that for a moment we both stared in silence. Then Japp burst into a laugh. "Good Lord, Monsieur Poirot, I thought you were coming out with something startling. As to your question, I'm sure I don't know."

"You could find out?" asked Poirot with curious persistence.

"Oh, certainly—if you *really* want to know."

"*Merci, mon ami.* I should be obliged if you would make a point of it."

Japp stared at him a few minutes longer, but Poirot

seemed to have forgotten us both. The detective shook his head sadly at me, and murmuring, "Poor old fellow! War's been too much for him!" gently withdrew from the room.

As Poirot still seemed sunk in a daydream, I took a sheet of paper, and amused myself by scribbling notes upon it. My friend's voice aroused me. He had come out of his reverie, and was looking brisk and alert.

"Que faites vous là, mon ami?"

"I was jotting down what occurred to me as the main points of interest in this affair."

"You become methodical—at last!" said Poirot approvingly.

I concealed my pleasure. "Shall I read them to you?"

"By all means."

I cleared my throat.

" 'One: All the evidence points to Lowen having been the man who forced the safe.

" 'Two: He had a grudge against Davenheim.

" 'Three: He lied in his first statement that he had never left the study.

" 'Four: If you accept Billy Kellett's story as true, Lowen is unmistakably implicated.' "

I paused. "Well?" I asked, for I felt that I had put my finger on all the vital facts.

Poirot looked at me pityingly, shaking his head very gently. *"Mon pauvre ami!* But it is that you have not the gift! The important detail, you appreciate him never! Also, your reasoning is false."

"How?"

"Let me take your four points.

"One: Mr. Lowen could not possibly know that he would have the chance to open the safe. He came for a business interview. He could not know beforehand that Mr. Davenheim would be absent posting a letter, and that he would consequently be alone in the study!"

"He might have seized his opportunity," I suggested.

"And the tools? City gentlemen do not carry round housebreaker's tools on the off chance! And one could not cut into that safe with a penknife, *bien entendu!"*

"Well, what about Number Two?"

"You say Lowen had a grudge against Mr. Davenheim.

What you mean is that he had once or twice got the better of him. And presumably those transactions were entered into with the view of benefiting himself. In any case you do not as a rule bear a grudge against a man you have got the better of—it is more likely to be the other way about. Whatever grudge there might have been would have been on Mr. Davenheim's side."

"Well, you can't deny that he lied about never having left the study?"

"No. But he may have been frightened. Remember, the missing man's clothes had just been discovered in the lake. Of course, as usual, he would have done better to speak the truth."

"And the fourth point?"

"I grant you that. If Kellett's story is true, Lowen is undeniably implicated. That is what makes the affair so very interesting."

"Then I did appreciate *one* vital fact?"

"Perhaps—but you have entirely overlooked the two most important points, the ones which undoubtedly hold the clue to the whole matter."

"And pray, what are they?"

"One, the passion which has grown upon Mr. Davenheim in the last few years for buying jewelry. Two, his trip to Buenos Ayres last autumn."

"Poirot, you are joking!"

"I am most serious. Ah, sacred thunder, but I hope Japp will not forget my little commission."

But the detective, entering into the spirit of the joke, had remembered it so well that a telegram was handed to Poirot about eleven o'clock the next day. At his request I opened it and read it out:

" 'Husband and wife have occupied separate rooms since last winter.' "

"Aha!" cried Poirot. "And now we are in mid-June! All is solved!"

I stared at him.

"You have no moneys in the bank of Davenheim and Salmon, *mon ami?*"

"No," I said, wondering. "Why?"

"Because I should advise you to withdraw it—before it is too late."

"Why, what do you expect?"

"I expect a big smash in a few days—perhaps sooner. Which reminds me, we will return the compliment of a *dépêche* to Japp. A pencil, I pray you, and a form. *Voilà!* 'Advise you to withdraw any money deposited with firm in question.' That will intrigue him, the good Japp! His eyes will open wide—wide! He will not comprehend in the slightest—until to-morrow, or the next day!"

I remained skeptical, but the morrow forced me to render tribute to my friend's remarkable powers. In every paper was a huge headline telling of the sensational failure of the Davenheim bank. The disappearance of the famous financier took on a totally different aspect in the light of the revelation of the financial affairs of bank.

Before we were half-way through breakfast, the door flew open and Japp rushed in. In his left hand was a paper; in his right was Poirot's telegram, which he banged down on the table in front of my friend.

"How did you know, Monsieur Poirot? How the blazes could you know?"

Poirot smiled placidly at him. "Ah, *mon ami,* after your wire, it was a certainty! From the commencement, see you, it struck me that the safe burglary was somewhat remarkable. Jewels, ready money, bearer bonds—all so conveniently arranged for—whom? Well, the good Monsieur Davenheim was of those who 'look after Number One' as your saying goes! It seemed almost certain that it was arranged for—himself! Then his passion of late years for buying jewelry! How simple! The funds he embezzled, he converted into jewels, very likely replacing them in turn with paste duplicates, and so he put away in a safe place, under another name, a considerable fortune to be enjoyed all in good time when everyone has been thrown off the track. His arrangements completed, he makes an appointment with Mr. Lowen (who has been imprudent enough in the past to cross the great man once or twice), drills a hole in the safe, leaves orders that the guest is to be shown into the study, and walks out of the house—where?" Poirot stopped, and stretched out his hand for another boiled egg. He frowned. "It is really insupportable," he murmured, "that every hen lays an egg of a different size! What symmetry can there be on the breakfsat table? At least they should sort them in dozens at the shop!"

"Never mind the eggs," said Japp impatiently. "Let 'em lay 'em square if they like. Tell us where our customer went to when he left The Cedars—that is, if you know!"

"Eh bien, he went to his hiding-place. Ah, this Monsieur Davenheim, there may be some malformation in his gray cells, but they are of the first quality!"

"Do you know where he is hiding?"

"Certainly! It is most ingenious."

"For Lord's sake, tell us, then!"

Poirot gently collected every fragment of shell from his plate, placed them in the egg-cup, and reversed the empty egg-shell on top of them. This little operation concluded, he smiled at the neat effect, and then beamed affectionately on us both.

"Come, my friends, you are men of intelligence. Ask yourselves the question which I asked myself. 'If I were this man, where should *I* hide?' Hastings, what do you say?"

"Well," I said, "I'm rather inclined to think I'd not do a bolt at all. I'd stay in London—in the heart of things, travel by tubes and buses; ten to one I'd never be recognized. There's safety in a crowd."

Poirot turned inquiringly to Japp.

"I don't agree. Get clear away at once—that's the only chance. I would have had plenty of time to prepare things beforehand. I'd have a yacht waiting, with steam up, and I'd be off to one of the most out-of-the-way corners of the world before the hue and cry began!"

We both looked at Poirot. "What do *you* say, monsieur?"

For a moment he remained silent. Then a very curious smile flitted across his face.

"My friends, if *I* were hiding from the police, do you know *where* I should hide? *In a prison!*"

"What?"

"You are seeking Monsieur Davenheim in order to put him

in prison, so you never dream of looking to see if he may not be already there!"

"What do you mean?"

"You tell me Madame Davenheim is not a very intelligent woman. Nevertheless I think that if you took her to Bow Street and confronted her with the man Billy Kellett, she would recognize him! In spite of the fact that he has shaved his beard and mustache and those bushy eyebrows, and has cropped his hair close. A woman nearly always knows her husband, though the rest of the world may be deceived!"

"Billy Kellett? But he's known to the police!"

"Did I not tell you Davenheim was a clever man? He prepared his alibi long beforehand. He was not in Buenos Ayres last autumn—he was creating the character of Billy Kellett, 'doing three months,' so that the police should have no suspicions when the time came. He was playing, remember, for a large fortune, as well as liberty. It was worth while doing the thing thoroughly. Only——"

"Yes?"

"*Eh bien,* afterwards he had to wear a false beard and wig, had to *make up as himself* again, and to sleep with a false beard is not easy—it invites detection! He cannot risk continuing to share the chamber of madame his wife. You found out for me that for the last six months, or ever since his supposed return from Buenos Ayres, he and Mrs. Davenheim occupied separate rooms. Then I was sure! Everything fitted in. The gardener who fancied he saw his master going round to the side of the house was quite right. He went to the boat-house, donned his 'tramp' clothes, which you may be sure had been safely hidden from the eyes of his valet, dropped the others in the lake, and proceeded to carry out his plan by pawning the ring in an obvious manner, and then assaulting a policeman, getting himself safely into the haven of Bow Street, where nobody would ever dream of looking for him!"

"It's impossible," murmured Japp.

"Ask Madame," said my friend, smiling.

The next day a registered letter lay beside Poirot's plate. He opened it, and a five-pound note fluttered out. My friend's brow puckered.

"*Ah, sacré!* But what shall I do with it? I have much remorse! *Ce pauvre Japp!* Ah, an idea! We will have a little dinner, we three! That consoles me. It was really too easy. I am ashamed. I, who would not rob a child—*mille tonnerres! Mon ami*, what have you, that you laugh so heartily?"

LORD PETER WIMSEY

Lord Peter Wimsey is the undisputed champ of silly-ass detectives. He is much given to top hats, monocles, and dropping his G's. That his affectations mask a shrewd mind and a kind heart is the opinion shared by an ever-growing band of Dorothy L. Sayers enthusiasts. Furthermore, Wimsey is, to female readers, "sexless and sexy at the same time, underpoweringly sensuous, supremely attractive to women in ways that are inexplicable to other men." So believes mystery scholar Michele Slung, who also extols Lord Peter's "effortless expertise and nonchalance and very high style." Julian Symons, on the other hand, finds him no more than "a caricature of an English aristocrat conceived with an immensely snobbish loving seriousness." Myself, I've always enjoyed Wimsey's exploits, possibly because I grew up reading P. G. Wodehouse.

Thirty year of age when the first Lord Peter novel, Whose Body?, *was published in 1923, Dorothy Sayers saw the mystery novel as a means to earn a reasonable living. Something of a child prodigy, and an honor student at Oxford, she had first tried advertising copywriting as a way of living by her wits. When she gave up the mystery field entirely in the 1940s, she announced, "I wrote the Peter Wimsey books when I was young and had no money. I made some money, and then I stopped writing novels and began to write what I had always wanted to write." Sayers devoted the last years of her life to translating Dante's Divine Comedy, under contract to Penguin books.*

The story you're about to read makes use of a plot that was to delight mad doctors in B-movies, pulps, and comics for many a year.

The Abominable History of the Man
with Copper Fingers
by Dorothy L. Sayers

The Egotists' Club is one of the most genial places in London.
It is a place to which you may go when you want to tell that
odd dream you had last night, or to announce what a good
dentist you have discovered. You can write letters there if
you like, and have the temperament of a Jane Austen, for
there is no silence room, and it would be a breach of club
manners to appear busy or absorbed when another member
addresses you. You must not mention golf or fish, however,
and, if the Hon. Freddy Arbuthnot's motion is carried at the
next committee meeting (and opinion so far appears very favourable), you will not be allowed to mention wireless either.
As Lord Peter Wimsey said when the matter was mooted the
other day in the smoking-room, those are things you can talk
about anywhere. Otherwise the club is not specially exclusive.
Nobody is ineligible *per se,* except strong, silent men. Nomi-
nees are, however, required to pass certain tests, whose nature
is sufficiently indicated by the fact that a certain distinguished
explorer came to grief through accepting, and smoking, a
powerful Trichinopoly cigar as an accompaniment to a '63
port. On the other hand, dear old Sir Roger Bunt (the coster
millionaire who won the £20,000 ballot offered by the *Sunday Shriek,* and used it to found his immense catering
business in the Midlands) was highly commended and unani-
mously elected after declaring frankly that beer and a pipe
were all he really cared for in that way. As Lord Peter said
again: "Nobody minds coarseness but one must draw the line
at cruelty."

On this particular evening, Masterman (the cubist poet)
had brought a guest with him, a man named Varden. Varden
had started life as a professional athlete, but a strained heart
had obliged him to cut short a brilliant career, and turn his
handsome face and remarkably beautiful body to account in

the service of the cinema screen. He had come to London from Los Angeles to stimulate publicity for his great new film, *Marathon*, and turned out to be quite a pleasant, unspoiled person—greatly to the relief of the club, since Masterman's guests were apt to be something of a toss-up.

There were only eight men, including Varden, in the brown room that evening. This, with its panelled walls, shaded lamps, and heavy blue curtains, was perhaps the cosiest and pleasantest of the small smoking-rooms, of which the club possessed half a dozen or so. The conversation had begun quite casually by Armstrong's relating a curious little incident which he had witnessed that afternoon at the Temple Station, and Bayes had gone on to say that that was nothing to the really very odd thing which had happened to him, personally, in a thick fog one night in the Euston Road.

Masterman said that the more secluded London squares teemed with subjects for a writer, and instanced his own singular encounter with a weeping woman and a dead monkey, and then Judson took up the tale and narrated how, in a lonely suburb, late at night, he had come upon the dead body of a woman stretched on the pavement with a knife in her side and a policeman standing motionless near by. He had asked if he could do anything, but the policeman had only said, "I wouldn't interfere if I was you, sir; she deserved what she got." Judson said he had not been able to get the incident out of his mind, and then Pettifer told them of a queer case in his own medical practice, when a totally unknown man had led him to a house in Bloomsbury where there was a woman suffering from strychnine poisoning. This man had helped him in the most intelligent manner all night, and, when the patient was out of danger, had walked straight out of the house and never reappeared; the odd thing being that, when he (Pettifer) questioned the woman, she answered in great surprise that she had never seen the man in her life and had taken him to be Pettifer's assistant.

"That reminds me," said Varden, "of something still stranger that happened to me once in New York—I've never been able to make out whether it was a madman or a practical joke, or whether I really had a very narrow shave."

This sounded promising, and the guest was urged to go on with his story.

"Well, it really started ages ago," said the actor, "seven years it must have been—just before America came into the war. I was twenty-five at the time, and had been in the film business a little over two years. There was a man called Eric P. Loder, pretty well known in New York at that period, who would have been a very fine sculptor if he hadn't had more money than was good for him, or so I understood from the people who go in for that kind of thing. He used to exhibit a good deal and had a lot of one-man shows of his stuff to which the highbrow people went—he did a good many bronzes, I believe. Perhaps you know about him, Masterman?"

"I've never seen any of his things," said the poet, "but I remember some photographs in *The Art of Tomorrow*. Clever, but rather overripe. Didn't he go in for a lot of that chryselephantine stuff? Just to show he could afford to pay for the materials, I suppose."

"Yes, that sounds very like him."

"Of course—and he did a very slick and very ugly realistic group called Lucina, and had the impudence to have it cast in solid gold and stood in his front hall."

"Oh, that thing! Yes—simply beastly I thought it, but then I never could see anything artistic in the idea. Realism, I suppose you'd call it. I like a picture or a statue to make you feel good, or what's it there for? Still, there was something very attractive about Loder."

"How did you come across him?"

"Oh, yes. Well, he saw me in that little picture of mine, *Apollo Comes to New York*—perhaps you remember it. It was my first star part. About a statue that's brought to life—one of the old gods, you know—and how he gets on in a modern city. Dear old Reubenssohn produced it. Now, there was a man who could put a thing through with consummate artistry. You couldn't find an atom of offence from beginning to end, it was all so tasteful, though in the first part one didn't have anything to wear except a sort of scarf—taken from the classical statue, you know."

"The Belvedere?"

"I dare say. Well, Loder wrote to me, and said as a sculptor he was interested in me, because I was a good shape and so on, and would I come and pay him a visit in New York when I was free. So I found out about Loder, and decided it would be good publicity, and when my contract was up, and I had a bit of time to fill in, I went up east and called on him. He was very decent to me, and asked me to stay a few weeks with him while I was looking around.

"He had a magnificent great house about five miles out of the city, crammed full of pictures and antiques and so on. He was somewhere between thirty-five and forty, I should think, dark and smooth, and very quick and lively in his movements. He talked very well; seemed to have been everywhere and have seen everything and not to have any too good an opinion of anybody. You could sit and listen to him for hours; he'd got anecdotes about everybody, from the Pope to old Phineas E. Groot of the Chicago Ring. The only kind of story I didn't care about hearing from him was the improper sort. Not that I don't enjoy an after-dinner story—no, sir, I wouldn't like you to think I was a prig—but he'd tell it with his eye upon you as if he suspected you of having something to do with it. I've known women do that, and I've seen men do it to women and seen the women squirm, but he was the only man that's ever given *me* that feeling. Still, apart from that, Loder was the most fascinating fellow I've ever known. And, as I say, his house surely was beautiful, and he kept a first-class table.

"He liked to have everything of the best. There was his mistress, Maria Morano. I don't think I've ever seen anything to touch her, and when you work for the screen you're apt to have a pretty exacting standard of female beauty. She was one of those big, slow, beautifully moving creatures, very placid, with a slow, wide smile. We don't grow them in the States. She'd come from the South—had been a cabaret dancer he said, and she didn't contradict him. He was very proud of her, and she seemed to be devoted to him in her own fashion. He'd show her off in the studio with nothing on but a fig-leaf or so—stand her up beside one of the figures he was always doing of her, and compare them point by point. There was literally only one half inch of her, it seemed, that wasn't absolutely perfect from the sculptor's point of view— the second toe of her left foot was shorter than the big toe. He used to correct it, of course, in the statues. She'd listen to it all with a good-natured smile, sort of vaguely flattered, you know. Though I think the poor girl sometimes got tired of being gloated over that way. She'd sometimes hunt me out and confide to me that what she had always hoped for was to run a restaurant of her own, with a cabaret show and a great many cooks with white aprons, and lots of polished electric cookers. "And then I would marry," she'd say, "and have four sons and one daughter," and she told me all the names she had chosen for the family. I thought it was rather pathetic. Loder came in at the end of one of these conversations. He had a sort of a grin on, so I dare say he'd overheard. I don't suppose he attached much importance to it, which shows that he never really understood the girl. I don't think he ever imagined any woman would chuck up the sort of life he'd accustomed her to, and if he was a bit possessive in his manner, at least he never gave her a rival. For his talk and his ugly statues, she'd got him, and she knew it.

"I stayed there getting on for a month altogether, having a thundering good time. On two occasions Loder had an art spasm, and shut himself up in his studio to work and wouldn't let anybody in for several days on end. He was rather given to that sort of stunt, and when it was over we would have a party, and all Loder's friends and hangers-on would come to have a look at the work of art. He was doing a figure of some nymph or goddess, I fancy, to be cast in silver, and Maria used to go along and sit for him. Apart from those times, he went about everywhere, and we saw all there was to be seen.

"I was fairly annoyed, I admit, when it came to an end. War was declared, and I'd made up my mind to join up when that happened. My heart put me out of the running for trench service, but I counted on getting some sort of a job, with perseverance, so I packed up and went off.

"I wouldn't have believed Loder would have been so genuinely sorry to say good-bye to me. He said over and over again that we'd meet again soon. However, I did get a job with the hospital people, and was sent over to Europe, and it wasn't till 1920 that I saw Loder again.

"He'd written to me before, but I'd had two big pictures to make in '19, and it couldn't be done. However, in '20 I found myself back in New York, doing publicity for *The Passion Streak*, and got a note from Loder begging me to stay with him, and saying he wanted me to sit for him. Well, that was advertisement that he'd pay for himself, you know, so I agreed. I had accepted an engagement to go out with Mysto-films Ltd in *Jake of Dead Man's Bush*—the dwarfmen picture, you know, taken on the spot among the Australian bushmen. I wired them that I would join them at Sydney the third week in April, and took my bags out to Loder's.

"Loder greeted me very cordially, though I thought he looked older than when I last saw him. He had certainly grown more nervous in his manner. He was—how shall I describe it?—more *intense*—more real, in a way. He brought out his pet cynicisms as if he thoroughly meant them, and more and more with that air of getting at you personally. I used to think his disbelief in everything was a kind of artistic pose, but I began to feel I had done him an injustice. He was really unhappy, I could see that quite well, and soon I discovered the reason. As we were driving out in the car I asked after Maria.

" 'She has left me,' he said.

"Well, now, you know, that really surprised me. Honestly, I hadn't thought the girl had that much initiative. 'Why,' I said, 'has she gone and set up in that restaurant of her own she wanted so much?'

" 'Oh! she talked to you about restaurants, did she?' said Loder. 'I suppose you are one of the men that women tell things to. No. She made a fool of herself. She's gone.'

"I didn't quite know what to say. He was so obviously hurt in his vanity, you know, as well as in his feelings. I muttered the usual things, and added that it must be a great loss to his work as well as in other ways. He said it was.

"I asked him when it had happened and whether he'd finished the nymph he was working on before I left. He said, 'Oh, yes, he'd finished that and done another—something pretty original, which I should like.'

"Well, we got to the house and dined, and Loder told me he was going to Europe shortly, a few days after I left myself, in fact. The nymph stood in the dining-room, in a special niche let into the wall. It really was a beautiful thing, not so showy as most of Loder's work, and a wonderful likeness of Maria. Loder put me opposite it, so that I could see it during dinner, and, really, I could hardly take my eyes off it. He seemed very proud of it, and kept on telling me over and over again how glad he was that I liked it. It struck me that he was falling into a trick of repeating himself.

"We went into the smoking-room after dinner. He'd had it rearranged, and the first thing that caught one's eye was a big settee drawn before the fire. It stood about a couple of feet from the ground, and consisted of a base made like a Roman couch, with cushions and a highish back, all made of oak with a silver inlay, and on top of this, forming the actual seat one sat on, if you follow me, there was a great silver figure of a nude woman, fully life-size, lying with her head back and her arms extended along the sides of the couch. A few big loose cushions made it possible to use the thing as an actual settee, though I must say it never was really comfortable to sit on respectably. As a stage prop. for registering dissipation it would have been excellent, but to see Loder sprawling over it by his own fireside gave me a kind of shock. He seemed very much attached to it, though.

" 'I told you,' he said, 'that it was something original.'

"Then I looked more closely at it, and saw that the figure actually was Maria's, though the face was rather sketchily done, if you understand what I mean. I suppose he thought a bolder treatment more suited to a piece of furniture.

"But I did begin to think Loder a trifle degenerate when I saw that couch. And in the fortnight that followed I grew more and more uncomfortable with him. That personal manner of his grew more marked every day, and sometimes, while I was giving him sittings, he would sit there and tell one of the most beastly things, with his eyes fixed on one in the nastiest way, just to see how one would take it. Upon my word, though he certainly did me uncommonly well, I began to feel I'd be more at ease among the bushmen.

"Well, now I come to the odd thing."

Everybody sat up and listened a little more eagerly.

"It was the evening before I had to leave New York," went on Varden. "I was sitting——"

Here somebody opened the door of the brown room, to be greeted by a warning sign from Bayes. The intruder sank obscurely into a large chair and mixed himself a whisky with extreme care not to disturb the speaker.

"I was sitting in the smoking-room," continued Varden,

"waiting for Loder to come in. I had the house to myself, for Loder had given the servants leave to go to some show or lecture or other, and he himself was getting his things together for his European trip and had had to keep an appointment with his man of business. I must have been very nearly asleep, because it was dusk when I came to with a start and saw a young man quite close to me.

"He wasn't at all like a housebreaker, and still less like a ghost. He was, I might almost say, exceptionally ordinary-looking. He was dressed in a grey English suit, with a fawn overcoat on his arm, and his soft hat and stick in his hand. He had sleek, pale hair, and one of those rather stupid faces, with a long nose and a monocle. I stared at him, for I knew the front door was locked, but before I could get my wits together he spoke. He had a curious, hesitating, husky voice and a strong English accent. He said, surprisingly:

" 'Are you Mr Varden?'

" 'You have the advantage of me,' I said.

"He said, 'Please excuse my butting in; I know it looks like bad manners, but you'd better clear out of this place very quickly, don't you know.'

" 'What the hell do you mean?' I said.

"He said, 'I don't mean it in any impertinent way, but you must realize that Loder's never forgiven you, and I'm afraid he means to make you into a hatstand or an electric-light fitting, or something of that sort.'

"My God! I can tell you I felt queer. It was such a quiet voice, and his manners were perfect, and yet the words were quite meaningless! I remembered that madmen are supposed to be extra strong, and edged towards the bell—and then it came over me with rather a chill that I was alone in the house.

" 'How did you get in here?' I asked, putting a bold face on it.

" 'I'm afraid I picked the lock,' he said, as casually as though he were apologizing for not having a card about him. 'I couldn't be sure Loder hadn't come back. But I do really think you had better get out as quickly as possible.'

" 'See here,' I said, 'who are you and what the hell are you driving at? What do you mean about Loder never forgiving me? Forgiving me what?'

" 'Why,' he said, 'about—you *will* pardon me prancing in on your private affairs, won't you—about Maria Morano.'

" '*What* about her: in the devil's name?' I cried. 'What do you know about her, anyway? She went off while I was at the war. What's it to do with me?'

" 'Oh!' said the very odd young man, 'I beg your pardon. Perhaps I have been relying too much on Loder's judgement. Damned foolish; but the possibility of his being mistaken did not occur to me. He fancies you were Maria Morano's lover when you were here last time.'

" 'Maria's lover?' I said. 'Preposterous! She went off with her man, whoever he was. He must know she didn't go with me.'

" 'Maria never left the house,' said the young man, 'and if you don't get out of it this moment, I won't answer for *your* ever leaving, either.'

" 'In God's name,' I cried, exasperated, 'what do you mean?'

"The man turned and threw the blue cushions off the foot of the silver couch.

" 'Have you ever examined the toes of this?' he asked.

" 'Not particularly,' I said, more and more astonished. 'Why should I?'

" 'Did you ever know Loder make any figure of her but this with that short toe on the left foot?' he went on.

"Well, I did take a look at it then, and saw it was as he said—the left foot had a short second toe.

" 'So it is,' I said, 'but, after all, why not?'

" 'Why not, indeed?' said the young man. 'Wouldn't you like to see why, of all the figures Loder made of Maria Morano, this is the only one that has the feet of the living woman?'

"He picked up the poker.

" 'Look!' he said.

"With a lot more strength than I should have expected from him, he brought the head of the poker down with a heavy crack on the silver couch. It struck one of the arms of the figure neatly at the elbow-joint, smashing a jagged hole in the silver. He wrenched at the arm and brought it away. It was hollow, and, as I am alive, I tell you there was a long, dry arm-bone inside it!"

Varden paused, and put away a good mouthful of whisky.

"Well?" cried several breathless voices.

"Well," said Varden, "I'm not ashamed to say I went out of that house like an old buck-rabbit that hears the man with the gun. There was a car standing just outside, the driver opened the door. I tumbled in, and then it came over me that the whole thing might be a trap, and I tumbled out again and ran till I reached the trolley-cars. But I found my bags at the station next day, duly registered for Vancouver.

"When I pulled myself together I did rather wonder what Loder was thinking about my disappearance, but I could no more have gone back into that horrible house than I could have taken poison. I left for Vancouver next morning, and from that day to this I never saw either of those men again. I've still not the faintest idea who the fair man was, or what became of him, but I heard in a roundabout way that Loder was dead—in some kind of an accident, I fancy."

There was a pause. Then:

"It's a damned good story, Mr Varden," said Armstrong—he was a dabbler in various kinds of handiwork, and was, indeed, chiefly responsible for Mr Arbuthnot's motion to ban wireless—"but are you suggesting there was a complete skeleton inside that silver casting? Do you mean Loder put it into the core of the mould when the casting was done? It would be awfully difficult and dangerous—the slightest accident would have put him at the mercy of his workmen. And that statue must have been considerably over life-size to allow of the skeleton being well covered."

"Mr Varden has unintentionally misled you, Armstrong," said a quiet, husky voice suddenly from the shadow behind Varden's chair. "The figure was not silver, but electro-plated on a copper base deposited direct on the body. The lady was Sheffield-plated, in fact. I fancy the soft parts of her must have been digested away with pepsin, or some preparation of the kind, after the process was complete, but I can't be positive about that."

"Hullo, Wimsey," said Armstrong, "was that you came in just now? And why this confident pronouncement?"

The effect of Wimsey's voice on Varden had been extraordinary. He had leapt to his feet, and turned the lamp so as to light up Wimsey's face.

"Good evening, Mr Varden," said Lord Peter. "I'm delighted to meet you again and to apologize for my unceremonious behaviour on the occasion of our last encounter."

Varden took the proffered hand, but was speechless.

"D'you mean to say, you mad mystery-monger, that *you* were Varden's Great Unknown?" demanded Bayes. "Ah, well," he added rudely, "we might have guessed it from his vivid description."

"Well, since you're here," said Smith-Hartington, the *Morning Yell* man, "I think you ought to come across with the rest of the story."

"Was it just a joke?" asked Judson.

"Of course not," interrupted Pettifer, before Lord Peter had time to reply. "Why should it be? Wimsey's seen enough queer things not to have to waste his time inventing them."

"That's true enough," said Bayes. "Comes of having deductive powers and all that sort of thing, and always sticking one's nose into things that are better not investigated."

"That's all very well, Bayes," said his lordship, "but if I hadn't just mentioned the matter to Mr Varden that evening, where would he be?"

"Ah, where? That's exactly what we want to know," demanded Smith-Hartington. "Come on, Wimsey, no shirking; we must have the tale."

"And the whole tale," added Pettifer.

"And nothing but the tale," said Armstrong, dexterously whisking away the whisky-bottle and the cigars from under Lord Peter's nose. "Get on with it, old son. Not a smoke do you smoke and not a sup do you sip till Burd Ellen is set free."

"Brute!" said his lordship plaintively. "As a matter of fact," he went on, with a change of tone, "it's not really a story I want to get about. It might land me in a very unpleasant sort of position—manslaughter probably, and murder possibly."

"Gosh!" said Bayes.

"That's all right," said Armstrong, "nobody's going to talk. We can't afford to lose you from the club, you know. Smith-Hartington will have to control his passion for copy, that's all."

Pledges of discretion having been given all round, Lord Peter settled himself back and began his tale.

"The curious case of Eric P. Loder affords one more instance of the strange manner in which some power beyond our puny human wills arranges the affairs of men. Call it Providence—call it Destiny——"

"We'll call it off," said Bayes; "you can leave out that part."

Lord Peter groaned and began again.

"Well, the first thing that made me feel a bit inquisitive about Loder was a casual remark by a man at the Emigration Office in New York, where I happened to go about that silly affair of Mrs Bilt's. He said, 'What on earth is Eric Loder going to do in Australia? I should have thought Europe was more in his line.'

" 'Australia?' I said, 'you're wandering, dear old thing. He told me the other day he was off to Italy in three weeks' time.'

" 'Italy, nothing,' he said, 'he was all over our place today, asking about how you got to Sydney and what were the necessary formalities, and so on.'

" 'Oh,' I said, 'I suppose he's going by the Pacific route, and calling at Sydney on his way.' But I wondered why he hadn't said so when I'd met him the day before. He had distinctly talked about sailing for Europe and doing Paris before he went on to Rome.

"I felt so darned inquisitive that I went and called on Loder two nights later.

"He seemed quite pleased to see me, and was full of his forthcoming trip. I asked him again about his route, and he told me quite distinctly he was going via Paris.

"Well, that was that, and it wasn't really any of my business, and we chatted about other things. He told me that Mr Varden was coming to stay with him before he went, and that he hoped to get him to pose for a figure before he left. He said he'd never seen a man so perfectly formed. 'I meant to get him to do it before,' he said, 'but war broke out, and he went and joined the army before I had time to start.'

"He was lolling on that beastly couch of his at the time, and, happening to look round at him, I caught such a nasty sort of glitter in his eyes that it gave me quite a turn. He was stroking the figure over the neck and grinning at it.

" 'None of your efforts in Sheffield-plate, I hope,' said I.

" 'Well,' he said, 'I thought of making a kind of companion to this, *The Sleeping Athlete*, you know, or something of that sort.'

" 'You'd much better cast it,' I said. 'Why did you put the stuff on so thick? It destroys the fine detail.'

"That annoyed him. He never liked to hear any objection made to that work of art.

" 'This was experimental,' he said. 'I mean the next to be a real masterpiece. You'll see.'

"We'd got to about that point when the butler came in to ask should he make up a bed for me, as it was such a bad night. We hadn't noticed the weather particularly, though it had looked a bit threatening when I started from New York. However, we now looked out, and saw that it was coming down in sheets and torrents. It wouldn't have mattered, only that I'd only brought a little open racing car and no overcoat, and certainly the prospect of five miles in that downpour wasn't altogether attractive. Loder urged me to stay, and I said I would.

"I was feeling a bit fagged, so I went to bed right off. Loder said he wanted to do a bit of work in the studio first, and I saw him depart along the corridor.

"You won't allow me to mention Providence, so I'll only say it was a very remarkable thing that I should have woken up at two in the morning to find myself lying in a pool of water. The man had stuck a hot-water bottle into the bed, because it hadn't been used just lately, and the beastly thing had gone and unstoppered itself. I lay awake for ten minutes in the deeps of damp misery before I had sufficient strength of mind to investigate. Then I found it was hopeless—sheets, blankets, mattress, all soaked. I looked at the armchair, and then I had a brilliant idea. I remembered there was a lovely great divan in the studio, with a big skin rug and a pile of cushions. Why not finish the night there? I took the little electric torch which always goes about with me, and started off.

"The studio was empty, so I supposed Loder had finished and trotted off to roost. The divan was there, all right, with a screen drawn partly across it, so I rolled myself up under the rug and prepared to snooze off.

"I was just getting beautifully sleepy again when I heard footsteps, not in the passage, but apparently on the other side of the room. I was surprised, because I didn't know there was any way out in that direction. I lay low, and presently I saw a streak of light appear from the cupboard where Loder kept his tools and things. The streak widened, and Loder emerged, carrying an electric torch. He closed the cupboard door very gently after him, and padded across the studio. He stopped before the easel and uncovered it; I could see him through a crack in the screen. He stood for some minutes gazing at a sketch on the easel, and then gave one of the nastiest gurgly laughs I've ever had the pleasure of hearing. If I'd ever seriously thought of announcing my unauthorized presence, I abandoned all idea of it then. Presently he covered the easel again, and went out by the door at which I had come in.

"I waited till I was sure he had gone, and then got up— uncommonly quietly, I may say. I tiptoed over to the easel to see what the fascinating work of art was. I saw at once it was the design for the figure of *The Sleeping Athlete,* and as I looked at it I felt a sort of horrid conviction stealing over me. It was an idea which seemed to begin in my stomach, and work its way up to the roots of my hair.

"My family say I'm too inquisitive. I can only say that wild horses wouldn't have kept me from investigating that cupboard. With the feeling that something absolutely vile might hop out at me—I was a bit wrought up, and it was a rotten time of night—I put a heroic hand on the door knob.

"To my astonishment, the thing wasn't even locked. It opened at once, to show a range of perfectly innocent and orderly shelves, which couldn't possibly have held Loder.

"My blood was up, you know, by this time, so I hunted round for the spring-lock which I knew must exist, and found it without much difficulty. The back of the cupboard swung noiselessly inwards, and I found myself at the top of a narrow flight of stairs.

"I had the sense to stop and see that the door could be opened from the inside before I went any farther, and I also selected a good stout pestle which I found on the shelves as a weapon in case of accident. Then I closed the door and tripped with elf-like lightness down that jolly old staircase.

"There was another door at the bottom, but it didn't take me long to fathom the secret of that. Feeling frightfully excited, I threw it boldly open, with the pestle ready for action.

"However, the room seemed to be empty. My torch caught the gleam of something liquid, and then I found the wall-switch.

"I saw a biggish square room, fitted up as a workshop. On the right-hand wall was a big switchboard, with a bench beneath it. From the middle of the ceiling hung a great flood-light, illuminating a glass vat, fully seven feet long by about three wide. I turned on the floodlight, and looked down into the vat. It was filled with a dark brown liquid which I recognized as the usual compound of cyanide and copper-sulphate which they use for copper-plating.

"The rods hung over it with their hooks all empty, but there was a packing-case half-opened at one side of the room, and, pulling the covering aside, I could see rows of copper anodes—enough of them to put a plating over a quarter of an inch thick on a life-size figure. There was a smaller case, still nailed up, which from its weight and appearance I guessed to contain the silver for the rest of the process. There was something else I was looking for, and I soon found it—a considerable quantity of prepared graphite and a big jar of varnish.

"Of course, there was no evidence, really, of anything being on the cross. There was no reason why Loder shouldn't make a plaster cast and Sheffield-plate it if he had a fancy for that kind of thing. But then I found something that couldn't have come there legitimately.

"On the bench was an oval slab of copper about an inch and a half long—Loder's night's work, I guessed. It was an electrotype of the American Consular seal, the thing they stamp on your passport photograph to keep you from hiking it off and substituting the picture of your friend Mr. Jiggs, who would like to get out of the country because he is so popular with Scotland Yard.

"I sat down on Loder's stool, and worked out that pretty little plot in all its details. I could see it all turned on three things. First of all, I must find out if Varden was proposing to make tracks shortly for Australia, because, if he wasn't, it threw all my beautiful theories out. And, secondly, it would help matters greatly if he happened to have dark hair like Loder's, as he has, you see—near enough, anyway, to fit the description on a passport. I'd only seen him in that Apollo Belvedere thing, with a fair wig on. But I knew if I hung about I should see him presently when he came to stay with Loder. And, thirdly, of course, I had to discover if Loder was likely to have any grounds for a grudge against Varden.

"Well, I figured out I'd stayed down in that room about as long as was healthy. Loder might come back at any moment, and I didn't forget that a vatful of copper sulphate and cyanide of potassium would be a highly handy means of getting rid of a too-inquisitive guest. And I can't say I had any great fancy for figuring as part of Loder's domestic furniture. I've always hated things made in the shape of things—volumes of Dickens that turn out to be a biscuit-tin, and dodges like that; and, though I take no overwhelming interest in my own funeral, I should like it to be in good taste. I went so far as to wipe away any finger-marks I might have left behind me, and then I went back to the studio and rearranged that divan. I didn't feel Loder would care to think I'd been down there.

"There was just one other thing I felt inquisitive about. I tiptoed back through the hall and into the smoking-room. The silver couch glimmered in the light of the torch. I felt I disliked it fifty times more than ever before. However, I pulled myself together and took a careful look at the feet of the figure. I'd heard all about that second toe of Maria Morano's.

"I passed the rest of the night in the armchair after all.

"What with Mrs Bilt's job and one thing and another, and the inquiries I had to make, I had to put off my interference in Loder's little game till rather late. I found out that Varden had been staying with Loder a few months before the beautiful Maria Morano had vanished. I'm afraid I was rather stupid about that, Mr Varden. I thought perhaps there *had* been something."

"Don't apologize," said Varden, with a little laugh. "Cinema actors are notoriously immoral."

"Why rub it in?" said Wimsey, a trifle hurt. "I apologize. Anyway, it came to the same thing as far as Loder was concerned. Then there was one bit of evidence I had to get to be absolutely certain. Electro-plating—especially such a ticklish job as the one I had in mind—wasn't a job that could be finished in a night; on the other hand, it seemed necessary that Mr Varden should be seen alive in New York up to the day he was scheduled to depart. It was also clear that Loder meant to be able to prove that a Mr Varden had left New York all right, according to plan, and had actually arrived in Sydney. Accordingly, a false Mr Varden was to depart with Varden's papers and Varden's passport, furnished with a new photograph duly stamped with the Consular stamp, and to disappear quietly at Sydney and be retransformed into Mr Eric Loder, travelling with a perfectly regular passport of his own. Well, then, in that case, obviously a cablegram would have to be sent off to Mystofilms Ltd, warning them to expect Varden by a later boat than he had arranged. I handed over this part of the job to my man, Bunter, who is uncommonly capable. The devoted fellow shadowed Loder faithfully for getting on for three weeks, and at length, the very day before Mr Varden was due to depart, the cablegram was sent from an office in Broadway, where by a happy providence (once more) they supply extremely hard pencils."

"By Jove!" cried Varden, "I remember now being told something about a cablegram when I got out, but I never connected it with Loder. I thought it was just some stupidity of the Western Electric people."

"Quite so. Well, as soon as I'd got that, I popped along to Loder's with a picklock in one pocket and an automatic in the other. The good Bunter went with me, and, if I didn't return by a certain time, had orders to telephone for the police. So you see everything was pretty well covered. Bunter was the chauffeur who was waiting for you, Mr Varden, but you turned suspicious—I don't blame you altogether—so all we could do was to forward your luggage along to the train.

"On the way out we met the Loder servants *en route* for New York in a car, which showed us that we were on the right track, and also that I was going to have a fairly simple job of it.

"You've heard all about my interview with Mr Varden. I really don't think I could improve upon his account. When I'd seen him and his traps safely off the premises, I made for the studio. It was empty, so I opened the secret door, and, as I expected, saw a line of light under the workshop door at the far end of the passage."

"So Loder was there all the time?"

"Of course he was. I took my little pop-gun tight in my fist and opened the door very gently. Loder was standing between the tank and the switchboard, very busy indeed—so busy he didn't hear me come in. His hands were black with graphite: a big heap of which was spread on a sheet on the floor, and he was engaged with a long, springy coil of copper wire, running to the output of the transformer. The big packing-case had been opened, and all the hooks were occupied.

"'Loder!' I said.

"He turned on me with a face like nothing human. 'Wimsey!' he shouted, 'what the hell are you doing here?'

"'I have come,' I said, 'to tell you that I know how the apple gets into the dumpling.' And I showed him the automatic.

"He gave a great yell and dashed at the switchboard, turning out the light, so that I could not see to aim. I heard him leap at me—and then there came in the darkness a crash and a splash—and a shriek such as I never heard—not in five years of war—and never want to hear again.

"I groped forward for the switchboard. Of course, I turned on everything before I could lay my hand on the light, but I got it at last—a great white glare from the floodlight over the vat.

"He lay there, still twitching faintly. Cyanide, you see, is about the swiftest and painfullest thing out. Before I could move to do anything, I knew he was dead—poisoned and drowned and dead. The coil of wire that had tripped him had gone into the vat with him. Without thinking, I touched it and got a shock that pretty well staggered me. Then I realized that I must have turned on the current when I was hunting for the light. I looked into the vat again. As he fell, his dying hands had clutched at the wire. The coils were tight round his fingers, and the current was methodically depositing a film of copper all over his hands, which were blackened with the graphite.

"I had just sense enough to realize that Loder was dead, and that it might be a nasty sort of look-out for me if the

hing came out, for I'd certainly gone along to threaten him
vith a pistol.

"I searched about till I found some solder and an iron.
hen I went upstairs and called in Bunter, who had done his
en miles in record time. He went into the smoking-room and
oldered the arm of that cursed figure into place again, as
vell as we could, and then we took everything back into the
vorkshop. We cleaned off every finger-print and removed ev-
ry trace of our presence. We left the light and the switch-
oard as they were, and returned to New York by an
xtremely round-about route. The only thing we brought
way with us was the facsimile of the Consular seal, and that
ve threw into the river.

"Loder was found by the butler next morning. We read in
he papers how he had fallen into the vat when engaged on
ome experiments in electro-plating. The ghastly fact was
:ommented upon that the dead man's hands were thickly
:oppered over. They couldn't get it off without irreverent vio-
ence, so he was buried like that.

"That's all. Please, Armstrong, may I have my whisky-
und-soda now?"

"What happened to the couch?" inquired Smith-Hartington
oresently.

"I bought it at the sale of Loder's things," said Wimsey,
"and got hold of a dear old Catholic priest I knew, to whom
I told the whole story under strict vow of secrecy. He was a
very sensible and feeling old bird; so one moonlight night
Bunter and I carried the thing out in the car to his own little
church, some miles out of the city, and gave it Christian
ourial in a corner of the graveyard. It seemed the best thing
o do."

MR. CAMPION

When *Albert Campion began his career in 1929, in the novel* The Crime at Black Dudley, *he appeared to be just one more young upper-class amateur detective. Lean, fair-haired, gawky and bespectacled, he had a piping voice and was given to behaving like an idiot, a lunatic, and a "silly ass." There were, though, hints that a clever young man lurked behind the twit facade. There were also hints that Campion was a member of a very prestigious British family, possibly linked to the royal family itself. As the Thirties progressed, Campion became more sober in his behavior and, in the words of the* Encyclopedia of Mystery & Detection, *exuded "an aura of confidence that causes people in trouble to turn to him." The truth about his family ties was never revealed.*

Margery Allingham came from a literary family and began writing while still a child. Her first book, an adventure novel about pirates and smugglers, was published when she was nineteen. Her first Campion mystery came out when she was in her middle twenties. An energetic, humorous woman, she married Youngman Carter, an artist and editor, in 1927. He aided her in the plotting of many of the novels and when she died in 1966, he wrote two more Campion novels before his own death. H. R. F. Keating has said of Margery Allingham that she possessed a strong female intelligence that "enabled her to say much that is penetrating and wise about men and women, perhaps especially women."

The Magic Hat
by Margery Allingham

Mr. Campion received the hat as a sentimental tribute. Mrs. Wynyard pressed it into his hand at her farewell party at the Braganza on the night before she sailed home to New York.

"I want you to have it," she said, her curly white head held on one side and her plump hand resting lightly on the sleeve of his tail coat. "It's exclusive. I got it from old Wolfgarten in one of those cute little streets off Bond Street, and he gave me his solemn word by everything he feels to be holy that it's quite u-nique. There's not another one in the world, and I want you to keep it to remind you of me and Mr. Honeyball and the grand times we've had this trip."

Hubert Wynyard, who was so good-humored that he let his wife call him anything, even "Mr. Honeyball," winked at Campion across his glass.

"So you know," he said. "Don't worry about a speech of thanks. Time's short. Where's that confounded wine waiter?"

So Campion pocketed the hat, which was less than half an inch high and made of onyx, with a cunningly carved agate where the opening for the head should have been, and thought no more about it.

He found it again next time he put on full war paint, which was for the first night of Lorimer's *Carry Over* at the Sovereign Theatre. The occasion was so smart that he was beginning to feel that "sticky" might be the term for it when the curtain descended on the second act and someone touched him on the shoulder. It turned out to be Peter Herrick, looking a trifle pink and disconcerted, which was unusual in one normally so very elegantly at ease.

"I say, old man, I need a spot of support," he muttered. "Can you come?"

There was a note of genuine supplication in the plea, and Campion excused himself from his party and joined him.

"What's up? Going to start a fight?"

His whisper was respectfully amused as they pressed their way through the noisy, perfumed crowd in the corridor.

"I hope not. As a matter of fact that's what I'm trying to avoid. It's social support I need."

Peter had edged into a convenient corner between a gilt settee and an enormous basket of hydrangeas. He was a trifle red about the ears and his vivid blue eyes, which lent his young face most of its charm, were laughing but embarrassed.

"I suddenly caught sight of you," he said, "and I realized you were probably the one man in the world of whom one could ask such a damn silly thing and not get cut for the rest of one's life. Come and back me up like a good bloke. You couldn't look like a duke or something, could you?"

"I don't see why not." Mr. Campion's lean face took on an even more vacant expression. "What's the idea? Whom do I impress?"

"You'll see." Peter was grim. "I'm suspect, old boy. I'm not the thing. Not—er—quite *it*, don't you know. I think someone's spread it around that my old man's a bobby."

Campion's eyebrows appeared above his horn-rimmed spectacles and he began to laugh. Major Herrick was well known to him as one of the Assistant Commissioners and one of the more poker-backed of his acquaintances, while Peter's worst enemy, if he had one, which seemed unlikely, could scarcely accuse him of being unpresentable. The whole situation seemed to Campion to have the elements of humor and he said so, delicately.

"But also very charming," he added cheerfully. "All olde worlde and young-man-what-are-your-intentions. Must you bother about the woman? There *is* a woman, I take it?"

Peter shot a revealing glance at him.

"Ah," he said, "but you wait until you see her. I met her on a boat and then I lost her. Now I've found her again at last, and there's this insane old father and the incredible tick of a fellow they're touting around with them. Come on, old boy, do your stuff. I'm out of my depth altogether. Prudence is embarrassed, and the other two have to be seen to be believed."

A trifle under two minutes later Campion was inclined to agree with half the final statement. Old Mr. Thomas K.

Burns was not unbelievable, Norman Whitman was. As for Prudence Burns, he took one look at her slender redheaded loveliness and was prepared to sympathize with any enthusiasm which Peter might evince. The girl was a raving beauty of the modern type. She sat on her gold chair in Box B and smiled up at him with humor and intelligence as well as embarrassment in her brown eyes.

Her escorts were far less pleasant to meet. Old Mr. Burns was a plain man in every sense of the word who had made an enormous amount of money in South Africa. He was in the midst of recounting these two obvious facts to Campion immediately after their introduction when a warning frown from the third member of his party silenced him as though a hand had been placed over his mouth, leaving him deflated. He turned helplessly, an appealing flicker in his small grey eyes.

"This 'ere—I should say, this gentleman is Mr. Norman Whitman," he said, and paused for the name to take effect.

Entirely because he felt it was expected of him, Campion looked interested, while Norman Whitman favored him with a supercilious stare. Campion was puzzled. He saw a plumpish, consequential little person with sleek hair and a pale face in which the eyeglass was a definite mistake. He was well dressed, not to say natty, and from the toes of his shoes to the highlight on his prominent white forehead he was polished until he shone. His voice, which was high, was so carefully modulated as to sound affected, and altogether he exuded an atmosphere of conceit and self-importance which was quite insufferable.

"I have not had the pleasure of meeting you before," he said, making the announcement sound like an accusation. "Not very good acting, is it? I'm afraid poor Emily is a sad disappointment."

Campion had thought that Dame Emily Storm's performance was well up to its usual standard of polished perfection, and said so.

"She always says she's very nervous on first nights," he added.

"Oh, do you know her?" There was real excitement and hero-worship in Prudence Burns's inquiry, and a quality of youthful *naïveté* in her eagerness which made Campion like her.

"My dear child, not the *stage!*" Norman Whitman shook an admonishing finger at the girl and she stared at him blankly, as did they all save old Mr. Burns, who said somewhat hurriedly, "I should think not. Not likely," and assumed a virtuous expression which was patently false and ill suited to his round, red face.

The incredible Norman leaned over the side of the box.

"Isn't that the Countess?" he exclaimed suddenly. "Is it? Why, of course. Yes, it is. You must all excuse me a moment. I really must go and say 'Hello.' "

He bustled off and Mr. Burns moved into his place and looked down at the frothing pool of clothes and their owners in the stalls below. There was something almost pathetic in his interest, a quality of small-boyishness which Campion found disarming. Peter was less sympathetic. He looked scandalized and crossed over to the girl at once. It seemed only charitable to give him a moment or so, and Campion gallantly concentrated on the father.

Mr. Burns glanced up at him and looked away again.

"He's not there yet," he said and hesitated, adding abruptly because of his embarrassment, "Do you see her?"

"Who?"

"The Countess," said Mr. Burns, lowering his voice to a respectful whisper.

Campion became a little embarrassed also. His fingers deep in his pockets found the onyx hat, and he began to play with it, taking it out and letting it roll idly in his hand. He was standing up in the box, a little behind the old man, who seemed in danger of falling out altogether in his eagerness.

"There he is." Mr. Burns's voice rose in his excitement. "That's her, is it? You don't recognize her, do you?"

"No, I'm afraid I don't," said Campion helplessly as he glanced at the large lady in the crimson cloak who had paused to speak to Norman Whitman in the crowd below. Mr. Burns nodded gloomily as though he had feared as much, and Campion was aware that both he and Peter had lost caste. Having stared his fill, the old man straightened himself and stepped back.

"Better not let him catch us," he remarked, and coughed

explosively but a trifle too late to cover the ill-advised statement. For the first time he was able to give Campion his attention.

"You're in business, I suppose?" he inquired, regarding him
morosely.

The tall thin man in the horn-rimmed spectacles grinned
unhappily. The *bourgeois gentilhomme* is an age-old character who moves some people to laughter, but others are apt to
find his wistful gaucherie a little dispiriting, and Campion
was of the latter category. He was so anxious not to hurt in
any way that he hesitated over his answer.

"Not exactly," he said, casually, and flicked the little hat
into the air, catching it again and rolling it over between his
fingers. The gesture was so idle that he was scarcely aware
that he had made it, so that Mr. Burns's reaction came as a
complete surprise to him.

All he saw at first was that the old man's eyes were positively bulging and that there were pale patches in the mottled
crimson of his cheeks. The next moment Prudence's father's
entire attitude toward his new acquaintance underwent a
complete change. His depression vanished and he became
more than merely friendly. Within two minutes he had offered Campion a cigar, told him his hotel, begged him to visit
him, and imparted a tip for the Stock Exchange which his
somewhat startled visitor happened to know was a good one.
Even the young people, who were engrossed in themselves,
were aware of the change of front. Indeed, Campion felt that
the entire theatre must notice it. Old Mr. Burns was not
subtle.

In the midst of his expansiveness he glanced at Peter and,
returning to Campion, jerked his head at the young man.

"Known him long?" he inquired with husky confiding.

"A great many years," Campion assured him.

"Oh, he's all right then, is he?" The red face was very serious.

"He's one of my best friends." Campion had no intention
of sounding severe, but the question was bewildering and in
spite of himself the words came coldly.

Mr. Burns took a rebuke. "That's all right then," he said,
sighing. "To tell you the honest truth, I'm not exactly in my
place yet. A bit out of touch."

He glanced up shyly to see how this confidence had been received and, noting that Campion remained affable if, blank, added in a conspiratorial whisper: "You've no idea what a weight off my mind that is."

Campion began to feel that the weight on his own mind was considerable, and he was on the point of launching out into a minor campaign of discreet inquiry when the curtain bell rang and he was forced to rejoin his own party. Mr. Burns let him go with great reluctance but consoled himself a little when Peter accepted his invitation to remain.

Campion hurried down the corridor in a state of complete mystification. He was used to being a success but not a riot, and the single startled glance which Peter had turned upon him at parting made him laugh whenever he thought of it, but he was thankful he had not been pressed for an explanation.

On the stairs he passed Norman Whitman. The little man was bustling back to his seat and puffing consequentially as he hurried. He glanced at Campion and nodded to him.

"She spared me a word, the dear thing," he said, as if the intelligence was good news of the highest importance, and trotted on out of sight. Campion glanced after him and somewhere in the far depths of his memory something stirred, only to be lost again immediately.

These are few things more irritating than an elusive impression that one has seen someone or something before, and as he went on down the staircase and re-entered the now darkened auditorium Campion walked slowly, his forehead wrinkled. Somewhere, sometime had he seen that plump little figure waddling along; but where and when escaped him utterly. It was most tantalizing.

He did not see Peter again that evening, but the following morning the boy telephoned.

"I say," the young voice sounded enthusiastic over the wire, "that was pretty sensational, wasn't it? How did you do it?"

"Did it last?" Campion inquired cautiously.

"Rather! We're all going off to the races this morning. I'm more than grateful to you. I knew you were remarkable in many ways but I wasn't prepared for a miracle. I'm still bewildered. Do you realize that I'd had the cold shoulder with

icicles on it until you arrived? But now I'm the old man's
white-headed boy. What did you say?"

With pardonable weakness, Campion was loath to cast
down his laurels.

"Nothing much," he said truthfully. "I talked through my
hat a bit, you know."

"I have no doubt you did, old boy," Peter agreed laughing,
"but what did you actually say? Hang it all, you've altered
the man's entire attitude."

"I scarcely spoke," said Campion, regretting that this exactitude was hardly convincing. "How about the 'gentleman
friend'? Did you cut much ice with him?"

"No." Peter's tone carried unutterable contempt. "I'm
afraid I scarcely noticed the little twirp. I say, you might let
me know how to work the oracle."

Since he had no idea at all and could therefore hardly be
helpful, Campion thought it best to change the subject.

"A very pretty girl," he ventured.

Peter rose to the bait like a salmon to a fly.

"Amazing," he said warmly. "I don't mind telling you I'm
not coherent on the subject."

It was nearly ten minutes later when Campion was at last
allowed to hang up the receiver and he re-settled himself,
grinning. Peter had underestimated himself.

Thinking over the entire incident, Campion was inclined to
wash his hands of the whole affair, putting it down as one of
those odd things that do sometimes occur. There are degrees
of oddness, however, and the next time the onyx hat came
under his serious consideration it was in circumstances which
could hardly be disregarded.

The following Wednesday was the seventeenth and on the
seventeenth of September, whenever he was in London, Campion took his Aunt Eva to dinner after the Dahlia Show. This
was one of those family fixtures which begin as a graceful
gesture in commemoration of past favors in the way of
timely financial assistance in mid-term, and may very well
end as awful responsibilities; but Aunt Eva might easily have
been worse. She was a spry little old lady in brown velvet
and bangles, and her mind was almost entirely devoted to
horticulture, whereas, of course, it might easily have been Pe-
kinese or other people's love affairs.

It was a time-honored arrangement between them that she should choose the restaurant and, because of her preference for flower names, they sometimes dined well and sometimes appallingly, which was why Campion was not particularly astonished when he arrived at her hotel to find her all set, in garnets and gold galloon, to visit the Gillyflower.

"I warn you it may be expensive," she said, settling herself in the taxi, "but I remembered poor Marchant left you all that money in the spring, so I dare say you can afford it. Don't hesitate to mention it, my dear boy, if you'd rather not."

"Darling, I can't think of a place in which I should enjoy seeing you more," he assured her, and spoke with a certain amount of truth, for the Gillyflower was an exotic bloom and he was interested to see what she would make of it.

He had visited the place once himself about three months before, just after it opened, and had found it flashy, exorbitant and badly staffed, but there had been an air of ultra-smart sophistication about it which he thought might possibly strike a new note after the homely sobriety of the Manor House dining room.

They found the place noisy but not crowded. It did not yet exude the cold depression of failure, but neither was there the cheerful blare of assured success. Aunt Eva was able to choose a table with an excellent view of the floral display round the band platform, although it only gave her an oblique angle on the cabaret. All the same the meal was not one of their triumphs. The staff still left much to be desired and the food, although quite extraordinarily pretentious, was certainly not cooked by a master.

The quality of the service began to irritate Campion about halfway through the meal. A dirty plate, a forgotten order, a leaking ice-pail, two delays, and impossibly cold coffee reduced him by slow stages to a state of politely repressed irritation, and he was relieved that Aunt Eva was too happily engrossed in her subject for the evening, which appeared to be the merits of ground bones as a fertilizer, to notice the many defects in the meal.

However, what with one thing and another it was a trying experience for Campion, and while he was waiting patiently for the second brew of coffee and the wine waiter his fingers encountered the onyx hat and he took it out and began to play with it, rolling it over and over upon the table cloth.

The first thing that happened was that the waiter spilt the coffee. Campion drew back wearily and looked up to receive his second surprise. He was prepared for some sort of apology but not for abnegation. The unfortunate man was green. He grovelled. He all but wept, and from that moment the Gillyflower appeared to belong to Mr. Campion.

The change was astounding. The head waiter appeared at his elbow in solicitous friendliness, myrmidons arrived on all sides showering little attentions like so many sallow amorelli, Aunt Eva received a bouquet of Lady Forteviot roses, and Campion was tempted with a Napoleon *fine* from a bottle which certainly looked as though it had seen Paris, if not the siege. There was no doubt at all about their sudden rise to importance as guests of the Gillyflower and Campion's eyes grew thoughtful behind his spectacles as he turned the charm over and over.

"That's a nice little hat," remarked Aunt Eva, smiling over her roses.

"Isn't it?" said Campion. "A smart little hat, not to say clever."

Just how clever it was, however, lay as yet unrevealed. That surprise came later when the lady went off to collect her old-fashioned sables and Campion glanced down at a bill for three pounds, seventeen shillings and one penny. On his nod of acceptance the waiter took the bill away. There was no charge, of course, he said, and seemed hurt that the guest should suggest it. "But naturally," no charge at all.

Campion gaped at the man, who smiled at him with bland satisfaction and expressed the pious hope that he had enjoyed the meal. Campion was taking out his notecase in stolid defiance when the *maître d'hôtel*, round as a football and sleek as a seal, appeared to corroborate the first man's story.

"No charge, sir," he said. "No, no, no charge. If only you had telephoned we should have been so happy to reserve you a better table."

Campion looked down at the onyx hat which sat, prim and shining, on the edge of an ashtray. The man followed his glance and beamed.

"You are satisfied?" he inquired.

Campion flicked the trinket with his forefinger and a memory bringing enlightenment in its train blazed up suddenly in his mind.

"That pays the waiter, does it?" he said.

And then they both laughed; but Campion laughed all the way home.

It was over a fortnight later when he received a visit from Peter Herrick. That young man was in an indignant mood.

"I say, I was glad you 'phoned," he said, coming into the study in the Piccadilly flat like a small electric storm. "I was just making up my mind to come down on you for another spot of help when you rang. Your success with old man Burns was so sensational that I was going to risk a second appeal. You wouldn't care to be the complete hero and have another go, would you?"

His host, who was mixing the drinks, looked round from the cocktail cabinet and grinned.

"My influence wore off, did it?" he said. "I wondered if it might."

Peter sat down. "It weakened," he admitted. "It's that unspeakable little toot Whitman, you know. He's got an idiotic line in pseudo smart-set talk that gets the old boy all of a flutter. When we're alone he's perfectly happy, apart from the fact that he wants to talk about you still, which is curious—forgive me, but you know what I mean."

He broke off to laugh at himself.

"I'm an ass," he said. "The whole truth of the matter—and you may be astounded to hear it, for I'm completely bewildered by it myself—the truth is that I'm nuts about Prudence, Campion, absolutely nuts. I want her to marry me, and she's dead keen on the idea, which is another staggering piece of luck, and, logically speaking, everything ought to be pretty good. However, the old boy is completely taken in by Whitman. Whitman sells him the most fantastic hints on etiquette and he falls for it every time."

Campion looked sympathetic.

"Old Burns has an idea that Whitman is some sort of social capture, I take it?" he ventured.

"That's it, I'm afraid." Peter was embarrassed. "It's ludicrous, of course, and very uncomfortable, especially as the old lad himself is quite all right, really. Apart from this fan-

tastic snob complex he's a darned interesting, shrewd old
chap. Whitman is simply taking advantage of his pet
weakness. Prudence says her old man has always had a touch
of it, but it's got worse since he retired and settled down to
enjoy his cash. Still, for Prudence's sake I'd put up with
Whitman if it wasn't for this last piece of cheek. He's had the
impudence to suggest that he might marry her himself."

"Has he, by George?" said Campion. "That's sailing near
the wind, isn't it?"

"I thought so." Peter spoke with feeling. "Unfortunately
the old man is half sold on the idea. He's anxious for
Prudence to be happy, of course, for he's dead set on doing
his duty and that sort of thing, but you can see that the idea
of the socialite son-in-law is going over big. What is so infuri-
ating is that he's being taken in. Whitman is about as bogus
as they go. He's quite sincere, I expect, but look at him!
What is he? A wretched little tufthunter with no more brains
than that soda-water syphon. Wasn't that your impression?"

"Since you press me, no," said Mr. Campion judicially.
"No, old boy, I'm sorry, but it wasn't. I think you underesti-
mate him. However, that's beside the point. What do I do
now? Have you anything in mind?"

"Well——" Peter was evidently leading up to a delicate
subject with some trepidation. "I may as well make a clean
breast of it. Old Burns wants to take Prudence, Whitman and
myself out to a meal tonight to 'talk things over.' It went
through my mind that if I had the infernal cheek to ask you
to join the party you might be able to do your celebrated
heart-softening act once again. The old boy will be tickled to
death, of course. He's worried my life out to get hold of you
again. But I do see that it's a ghastly imposition from your
point of view." He paused unhappily. "It's the limit," he said.
"The ultimate outside edge. But she's grown so darned important to me that I'm forgetting the ordinary decencies."

"My dear chap, not at all. I think it might be an extremely
jolly gathering." Campion sounded positively enthusiastic.
"There's only one thing, though," he hurried on, while his visitor eyed him in astonishment, "you don't think you could fix
it so that we went either to the Gillyflower or the Maison
Grecque?"

The other man sat up, his eyes wide with suspicion. "Why on earth do you suggest that?"

Campion evaded his glance.

"They're the only two places in London at which one can eat, aren't they?" he murmured idiotically.

"Look here, Campion, what do you know about all this business?" Peter was scrambling out of his chair. "You might have been imitating Whitman, except that he's got an extra half-dozen perfectly appalling places of the same type on his list."

"Half a dozen others, has he?" Campion seemed impressed. "What a thorough bird he is."

"Thorough?" said Peter. "I thought he was off his head."

"Oh, dear me, no. He's an intelligent chap. I thought that the first time I saw him. You'll fix it then, will you? Either the Gillyflower or the Maison Grecque."

The younger man stretched out his hand for the telephone.

"I'll get on to the old man this minute before you can change your mind," he announced. "Don't say I didn't warn you it might be a trying party. You're an astonishing chap, aren't you? I didn't know you'd ever seen Whitman before I introduced him. Where do you keep all this information?"

"Under my little hat," said Campion innocently. "All under my remarkable little hat."

The first thirty-five minutes of Mr. Thomas Burns's little dinner party at the Maison Grecque amply justified Peter Herrick's worst fears. The restaurant itself was a trifle more pretentious than the Gillyflower, and on this occasion the service was even more ostentatiously attentive than that which had distinguished the latter half of Aunt Eva's night out. Mr. Burns himself was considerably subdued by the fuss accorded him and frequently fingered his tight evening collar in a wistful fashion which made his desire to take it off as clear as if he had announced it in so many words.

Campion, glancing round the table, decided that Prudence was embarrassed by the avowed object of the gathering, but there was a line of determination in her firm mouth and an expression in her eyes when she glanced at Peter which made him like her.

Mr. Herrick was frankly distrait and unhelpful, while Campion did his gallant best with the conversation.

The only person in the party who seemed both to experience no discomfort himself and to be capable of ignoring it in his fellows was Mr. Norman Whitman. All through the over-elaborate meal he sat bored and superior, smiling superciliously at Campion's conversational efforts and only opening his own mouth to murmur an occasional comment on some celebrity whom he saw, or thought he saw, among the neighboring diners.

Campion, who made a hobby of what he was pleased to call "tick-fancying," could hardly refrain from the open gloat. The man was a collector's piece. His pallid shining forehead could express "refaned distaste" with more downright vulgarity than seemed possible on a single surface and he revealed a line in "host deflation" which had to be heard and seen to be believed.

It soon became clear to everybody that Mr. Burns's hope of a "little friendly chat about love and courtship" was doomed, and the young people were openly relieved. Mr. Burns himself was depressed and Norman remained aloof but condescending.

Towards the end of the meal, however, the host brightened. A childlike gleam of anticipation came into his eyes, and Campion caught him glancing towards him once or twice with disarming eagerness. Moreover, every now and again he felt in his waistcoat pocket and at last, when coffee was served and Peter had carried Prudence off onto the dance floor, he could deny himself no longer but took a small onyx hat out of its hiding place and let it roll over and over in his plump palm.

Norman Whitman frowned at him warningly, but the Burns blood was up and the old man ignored his mentor. He was watching Campion with the same shy delight and triumph which is displayed by the child who suddenly produces a new toy as good as the other boy's.

Campion did not look at Norman Whitman. He stretched out his hand.

"That's very attractive, isn't it?" he said taking up the charm.

The old man laughed. "It's quite genuine," he said. "It's the real McCoy, isn't it?"

Still Campion did not glance at the third man, who was watching the incident with a face as innocent of expression as a ball of wool.

"I think so." Campion spoke softly and frowned. It seemed such a shame.

"I think so, too." The old man chuckled over the words. "Waiter, bring my bill!"

It did not work.

After five minutes of such unbearable embarrassment and chagrin that Campion could have wept for him, Mr. Burns had to face that indubitable fact.

He rolled the hat, he placed it black and shining in the midst of the white table cloth, he waved it frantically beneath the waiter's nose, but the wooden face did not change and the man remained polite but immovable as a rock while the bill stayed folded on the table.

There came a moment—it was nicely timed—when both Mr. Burns and Mr. Campion looked at Norman Whitman. It was a steady inspection which lasted for some little time. The fat man did not change color. His boiled eyes remained blank and his expression reserved. After a while, however, the silence became unendurable and he rose with a conciliatory laugh.

"I'll see the manager for you, Burns," he murmured. "You must forgive these fellows. They have to be very careful."

If the implied insult was unmistakable it was also a master-stroke, and the old man, whose eyes had been slowly narrowing, permitted himself a gleam of hope.

All the same he did not speak. He and Campion sat in silence watching the consequential figure bustling across the room, to disappear finally behind the bank of flowers which masked the exit.

After allowing his host due time for meditation, Campion leaned back in his chair and took out his own onyx hat, which he placed on the table beside the other. They were identical; two little toppers exact in every detail.

"I had mine given me," Campion observed.

Burns raised his eyes from the two trinkets and stared.

"Given you?" he said. "Some gift. I thought I had a fair

enough bank roll, but I couldn't afford to give presents like that."

The lean man in the horn-rimmed spectacles looked apologetic.

"A very charming American and her husband wanted to give me a little keepsake to remind me of their visit here," he said. "They bought this at Wolfgarten's in Cellini Street. He told them it was exclusive and unique, but then he has his own definition of the term. 'Unique' to Wolfgarten means one for London and one for New York. He may have charged them about a fiver. I—er—I thought I'd better tell you."

Mr. Burns was sitting up stiffly, his face blank and his small eyes grown hard. Suddenly he swung round in his chair and gazed at the bank of flowers. Campion put out a gently restraining hand.

"Hold on," he said. "It's entirely up to you. I've taken the liberty of arranging it so that you can have him if you want him. At this moment, I imagine, our Norman is in the manager's office asking why the devil the arrangement which he made here has been ignored. You see, three weeks ago he opened an account of twenty pounds each at quite a number of restaurants on the understanding that anyone who displayed a small onyx top hat, which he showed them, should be taken without question to be his personal representative. It was a curious request, but after all the personal token, the signet ring and so on, has served this sort of purpose from time immemorial, and the restaurants didn't stand to lose anything while each held his twenty pounds."

Mr. Burns swallowed. "Go on," he said.

"Well," Campion was even more diffident, "just now I'm afraid the manager may be explaining to Whitman that the particular twenty pounds which he invested here has been used up. Doubtless he is bringing bills to prove it. I've been eating here and at the Gillyflower until my little hat wouldn't do its trick any more, and I fear I must owe our Norman quite a considerable sum. However, that's beside the point. What is important is that the house detective is sitting in the manager's office. Now the story which he will hear from Mr. Whitman is a perfectly innocent if eccentric one. But should he subsequently get a rather different tale from you—as he certainly has from me—well, it won't be toppers and tails and bogus countesses for our Norman for some time, will it? I'm so sorry to bring it out like this, but it seemed the only satisfactory and safe way if you should decide to prosecute."

The old man sat perfectly still for some moments. He made a stolid, powerful figure, his shoulders bowed and his head, with its thatch of thick grey hair, thrust forward as his eyes dwelt upon the two hats. After a while he glanced up and caught Campion's eye. There was a moment of mutual understanding and then, to the young man's intense relief, they both laughed.

Mr. Burns laughed for rather a long time for one who has been suddenly confronted with unpleasant news, and Campion was growing a trifle apprehensive when the older man pulled himself together and picked up his own hat.

"Five thousand pounds," he said, looking at it. "I thought it was a darned sight too cheap to be sound."

"Too cheap for what?"

"Free food for life at all the best restaurants in London for as many guests up to six as I cared to bring," said the old man calmly. "Wait a minute. I'm not so daft as I look. It was a good story. Norman's a smart fellow. He went to work very carefully. I'd known him about six weeks before he brought me in here one night, and I don't mind admitting that he impressed me with his way of doing things."

He paused and looked at Campion shyly. "I'm not what you might call a social swell," he said. "No, no, don't be nice about it; I'm a fool but not a damned fool. I came over here with plenty of money and plenty of time. I meant to get in with the right lot and learn all the tricks and the refinements that I'd read about, and I got just about what I was asking for. Norman looked all right to me. Obviously I was wrong. Anyway, he taught me one or two useful things about the clothes to wear and so on, and then we came in here and he did his act with his damn-fool hat.

"I was impressed. These stiffs of waiters always get me flustered, and when I saw it all go off so smoothly I was attracted. It seemed to be so easy, so dignified and gentlemanly. No money passing and so on. Well, I asked him about it, and he pretended he didn't want to tell me. But I'm a tenacious sort of chap, and presently out it came. It was a most ingenious spiel. This hat represented the Top Hat Club, he said, a club so exclusive that only the very best people in the land belonged to it . . . royalty and so on. He also explained that, like all these very superior affairs, it was practically secret because the restaurant only entered into the arrangement if they were certain they were getting only the very best people."

He broke off and grinned sheepishly.

"Well, you can guess the rest," he said. "It seemed quite reasonable the way he told it, and the business side of it was sound. If you can buy an annuity for life why shouldn't you buy a meal ticket, providing your honesty is guaranteed and they know you're not the sort of chap to make money on it by hiring it out? Oh, I'm the mug all right, but he had luck. I happened to see your hat, you see. I didn't mention it to him, of course, because he didn't seem to like you and I didn't want him getting jealous."

"He was going to get you elected to this club, I take it?"

"That's about it, son. Five thousand quid entrance fee. It seemed cheap. I'm fifty-six and I may go on eating in restaurants for another twenty years. But what about you? When did you come into this?"

Campion told his story frankly. He felt it was the very least he could do with those bright eyes watching him suspiciously.

"I remember Norman," he said. "He came back to me. It took me a tremendous time, but after my first free meal at the Gillyflower the whole thing suddenly became as clear as mud. I don't want to depress you, but I'm afraid we've stumbled on the great forefather of all confidence tricks. Years and years ago, just after I came down from Cambridge, I went to Canada, and right out in the wilds I came upon a stock company in an awful little one-eyed town. They were real old barnstormers, the last in the world I should think, and they gave a four-hour program, comprising a melodrama, a farce and a variety show all at one sitting. The farce was one of those traditional country tales which are handed down for generations and have no set form. The actors invent the dialogue as they go along. Well, the standard was frightful, of course, but there was one fat young man who played villains who was at least funny. He had a ridiculous walk, for one thing, and when I saw Whitman bolting down the corridor to your box he reminded me of something.

Then of course when I saw the top hat at the dinner table it all came roaring back to me . . . What's the matter?"

Mr. Burns was gazing at him, an incredulous expression growing in his eyes as recollection struggled to life.

"*Touch 'At Pays Waiter!*" he ejaculated, thumping the table with an enormous fist. "Good Lord! My old grandfather told me that story out in South Africa before I was breeched. I remember it! 'Touch 'At Pays Waiter,' the story of the poor silly bumpkin who was persuaded to exchange his cow for a magic hat. Good lord! Before I was breeched!"

Campion hesitated. "What about Norman?" he suggested. "What do you want to do? There may be a certain amount of publicity and——"

He broke off. The old man was not listening. He sat slumped in his chair, his eyes fixed on the far distance. Presently he began to laugh. He laughed so much that the tears ran down his face and he grew purple and breathless.

"Campion," he began weakly, when he had regained comparative coherence, "Campion, do you recall the end of that story?"

His guest frowned. "No," he said at last. "No, I'm sorry, I'm afraid I don't. It's gone completely. What was it?"

Mr. Burns struggled for air.

"The bumpkin didn't pay," he gasped. "The bumpkin ate the meal and didn't part with the cow. That is what I've done! This was the final try-out. I was supposed to part with the cash tonight. I've got the check already made out here in my wallet. I haven't parted and you've eaten his forty quid."

They were still looking at each other when the young people returned. Prudence regarded them with mild astonishment.

"You two seem to be making a lot of noise," she remarked. "What are you talking about?"

Mr. Burns winked at his companion.

"What would you call it? The Hat Trick?" he suggested.

Campion hesitated. "Hardly cricket," he said.

DR. FELL

The heftiest detective in our group, Dr. Gideon Fell, first loomed into view in the 1933 novel Hag's Nook. The good doctor, whose weight never sinks below an impressive 250 pounds, has been described as "bulky and bibulous" and "vast and beaming." A favorite descriptive word of John Dickson Carr's was "piratical." Carr, who admired the work if not the religion and politics of G. K. Chesterton, modeled Fell's character after the creator of Father Brown. He may have been thinking also of Dr. John Fell, the seventeenth-century cleric and scholar who inspired the immortal jingle that begins, "I do not love you, Dr. Fell." Gideon Fell specializes in impossible crimes, especially those that take place in seemingly locked rooms. A vastly eccentric and quirky man, Dr. Fell has an extremely logical mind and is never fooled or flummoxed for long. Over the years, in nearly two dozen novels, Dr. Fell tackled and solved some of the most bizarre and improbable crimes to be found in mystery fiction. Carr almost always lived up to his basic rule about writing. "To me the one unforgivable sin is being dull," he once said.

Carr was an American, born in Pennsylvania in 1906 and the son of a United States congressman. He began traveling in England and Europe when he was in his twenties. And in 1932, after marrying a British girl, he settled in England for a stay of over fifteen years. His other major detective, in novels written under the pen name Carter Dickson, was the equally bulky and quirky Sir Henry Merrivale. John Dickson Carr was also much involved in radio writing. In this country he participated in the early phases of the popular mystery

show Suspense. *He also wrote the lesser known series* Cabin
B-13. *He died in 1977.*

*Of course our story, one of the few shorts Carr wrote
about Dr. Fell, features a locked-room murder.*

The Incautious Burglar
by John Dickson Carr

Two guests, who were not staying the night at Cranleigh
Court, left at shortly past eleven o'clock. Marcus Hunt saw
them to the front door. Then he returned to the dining-room,
where the poker-chips were now stacked into neat piles of
white, red, and blue.

"Another game?" suggested Rolfe.

"No good," said Derek Henderson. His tone, as usual, was
weary. "Not with just the three of us."

Their host stood by the sideboard and watched them. The
long, low house, overlooking the Weald of Kent, was so quiet
that their voices rose with startling loudness. The dining-
room, large and panelled, was softly lighted by electric wall-
candles which brought out the sombre colours of the
paintings. It is not often that anybody sees, in one room of
an otherwise commonplace country house, two Rembrandts
and a Van Dyck. There was a kind of defiance about those
paintings.

To Arthur Rolfe—the art dealer—they represented enough
money to make him shiver. To Derek Henderson—the art
critic—they represented a problem. What they represented to
Marcus Hunt was not apparent.

Hunt stood by the sideboard, his fists on his hips, smiling.
He was a middle-sized, stocky man, with a full face and a
high complexion. Equip him with a tuft of chin-whisker, and
he would have looked like a Dutch burgher for a Dutch
brush. His shirt-front bulged out untidily. He watched with
ironical amusement while Henderson picked up a pack of
cards in long fingers, cut them into two piles, and shuffled

with a sharp flick of each thumb which made the cards melt together like a conjuring trick.

Henderson yawned.

"My boy," said Hunt, "you surprise me."

"That's what I try to do," answered Henderson, still wearily. He looked up. "But why do you say so, particularly?"

Henderson was young, he was long, he was lean, he was immaculate; and he wore a beard. It was a reddish beard, which moved some people to hilarity. But he wore it with an air of complete naturalness.

"I'm surprised," said Hunt, "that you enjoy anything so bourgeois—so plebeian—as poker."

"I enjoy reading people's characters," said Henderson. "Poker's the best way to do it, you know."

Hunt's eyes narrowed. "Oh? Can you read my character, for instance?"

"With pleasure," said Henderson. Absently he dealt himself a poker-hand, face up. It contained a pair of fives, and the last card was the ace of spades. Henderson remained staring at it for a few seconds before he glanced up again.

"And I can tell you," he went on, "that *you* surprise *me*. Do you mind if I'm frank? I had always thought of you as the Colossus of Business; the smasher; the plunger; the fellow who took the long chances. Now, you're not like that at all."

Marcus Hunt laughed. But Henderson was undisturbed.

"You're tricky, but you're cautious. I doubt if you ever took a long chance in your life. Another surprise"—he dealt himself a new hand—"is Mr. Rolfe here. He's the man who, given the proper circumstances, would take the long chances."

Arthur Rolfe considered this. He looked startled, but rather flattered. Though in height and build not unlike Hunt, there was nothing untidy about him. He had a square, dark face, with thin shells of eyeglasses, and a worried forehead.

"I doubt that," he declared, very serious about this. Then he smiled. "A person who took long chances in my business would find himself in the soup." He glanced round the room. "Anyhow, I'd be too cautious to have three pictures, with an aggregate value of thirty thousand pounds, hanging in an unprotected downstairs room with French windows giving on a

terrace." An almost frenzied note came into his voice. "Great
Scot! Suppose a burglar——"

"Damn!" said Henderson unexpectedly.

Even Hunt jumped.

Ever since the poker-party, an uneasy atmosphere had been
growing. Hunt had picked up an apple from a silver fruit-
bowl on the sideboard. He was beginning to pare it with a
fruit-knife, a sharp wafer-thin blade which glittered in the
light of the wall-lamps.

"You nearly made me slice my thumb off," he said, putting
down the knife. "What's the matter with you?"

"It's the ace of spades," said Henderson, still languidly.
"That's the second time it's turned up in five minutes."

Arthur Rolfe chose to be dense. "Well? What about it?"

"I think our young friend is being psychic," said Hunt,
good-humoured again. "Are you reading characters, or only
telling fortunes?"

Henderson hesitated. His eyes moved to Hunt, and then to
the wall over the sideboard where Rembrandt's "Old Woman
with Cap" stared back with the immobility and skin-colouring
of a red Indian. Then Henderson looked towards the French
windows opening on the terrace.

"None of my affair," shrugged Henderson. "It's your house
and your collection and your responsibility. But this fellow
Butler: what do you know about him?"

Marcus Hunt looked boisterously amused.

"Butler? He's a friend of my niece's. Harriet picked him
up in London, and asked me to invite him down here. Nonsense! Butler's all right. What are you thinking, exactly?"

"Listen!" said Rolfe, holding up his hand.

The noise they heard, from the direction of the terrace,
was not repeated. It was not repeated because the person who
had made it, a very bewildered and uneasy young lady, had
run lightly and swiftly to the far end, where she leaned
against the balustrade.

Lewis Butler hesitated before going after her. The moonlight was so clear that one could see the mortar between the
tiles which paved the terrace, and trace the design of the
stone urns along the balustrade. Harriet Davis wore a white

gown with long and filmy skirts, which she lifted clear of the ground as she ran.

Then she beckoned to him.

She was half sitting, half leaning against the rail. Her white arms were spread out, fingers gripping the stone. Dark hair and dark eyes became even more vivid by moonlight. He could see the rapid rise and fall of her breast; he could even trace the shadow of her eyelashes.

"That was a lie, anyhow," she said.

"What was?"

"What my Uncle Marcus said. You heard him." Harriet Davis's fingers tightened still more on the balustrade. But she nodded her head vehemently, with fierce accusation. "About my knowing you. And inviting you here. I never saw you before this week-end. Either Uncle Marcus is going out of his mind, or . . . will you answer me just one question?"

"If I can."

"Very well. Are you by any chance a crook?"

She spoke with as much simplicity and directness as though she had asked him whether he might be a doctor or a lawyer. Lewis Butler was not unwise enough to laugh. She was in that mood where, to any woman, laughter is salt to a raw wound; she would probably have slapped his face.

"To be quite frank about it," he said, "I'm not. Will you tell me why you asked?"

"This house," said Harriet, looking at the moon, "used to be guarded with burglar alarms. If you as much as touched a window, the whole place started clanging like a fire-station. He had all the burglar alarms removed last week. Last week." She took her hands off the balustrade, and pressed them together hard. "The pictures used to be upstairs, in a locked room next to his bedroom. He had them moved downstairs—last week. It's almost as though my uncle *wanted* the house to be burgled."

Butler knew that he must use great care here.

"Perhaps he does." (Here she looked at Butler quickly, but did not comment.) "For instance," he went on idly, "suppose one of his famous Rembrandts turned out to be a fake? It might be a relief not to have to show it to his expert friends."

The girl shook her head.

"No," she said. "They're all genuine. You see, I thought of that too."

Now was the time to hit, and hit hard. To Lewis Butler, in his innocence, there seemed to be no particular problem. He took out his cigarette-case, and turned it over without opening it.

"Look here, Miss Davis, you're not going to like this. But I can tell you of cases in which people were rather anxious to have their property 'stolen.' If a picture is insured for more than its value, and then it is mysteriously 'stolen' one night ——?"

"That might be all very well too," answered Harriet, still calmly. "Except that not one of those pictures has been insured."

The cigarette-case, which was of polished metal, slipped through Butler's fingers and fell with a clatter on the tiles. It spilled cigarettes, just as it spilled and confused his theories. As he bent over to pick it up, he could hear a church clock across the Weald strike the half-hour after eleven.

"You're sure of that?"

"I'm perfectly sure. He hasn't insured any of his pictures for as much as a penny. He says it's a waste of money."

"But——"

"Oh, I know! And I don't know why I'm talking to you like this. You're a stranger, aren't you?" She folded her arms, drawing her shoulders up as though she were cold. Uncertainty, fear, and plain nerves flicked at her eyelids. "But then Uncle Marcus is a stranger too. Do you know what I think? I think he's going mad."

"Hardly as bad as that, is it?"

"Yes, go on," the girl suddenly stormed at him. "*Say* it: go on and say it. That's easy enough. But you don't see him when his eyes seem to get smaller, and all that genial-country-squire look goes out of his face. He's not a fake: he hates fakes, and goes out of his way to expose them. But, if he hasn't gone clear out of his mind, what's he up to? What can he be up to?"

In something over three hours, they found out.

The burglar did not attack until half-past two in the morning. First he smoked several cigarettes in the shrubbery below the rear terrace. When he heard the church clock strike, he waited a few minutes more, and then slipped up the steps to the French windows of the dining-room.

A chilly wind stirred at the turn of the night, in the hour of suicides and bad dreams. It smoothed grass and trees with a faint rustling. When the man glanced over his shoulder, the last of the moonlight distorted his face: it showed less a face than the blob of a black cloth mask, under a greasy cap pulled down over his ears.

He went to work on the middle window, with the contents of a folding tool-kit not so large as a motorist's. He fastened two short strips of adhesive tape to the glass just beside the catch. Then his glass-cutter sliced out a small semi-circle inside the tape.

It was done not without noise: it crunched like a dentist's drill in a tooth, and the man stopped to listen.

There was no answering noise. No dog barked.

With the adhesive tape holding the glass so that it did not fall and smash, he slid his gloved hand through the opening and twisted the catch. The weight of his body deadened the creaking of the window when he pushed inside.

He knew exactly what he wanted. He put the tool-kit into his pocket, and drew out an electric torch. Its beam moved across to the sideboard; it touched gleaming silver, a bowl of fruit, and a wicked little knife thrust into an apple as though into someone's body; finally, it moved up the hag-face of the "Old Woman with Cap."

This was not a large picture, and the burglar lifted it down easily. He pried out glass and frame. Though he tried to roll up the canvas with great care, the brittle paint cracked across in small stars which wounded the hag's face. The burglar was so intent on this that he never noticed the presence of another person in the room.

He was an incautious burglar: he had no sixth sense which smelt murder.

Up on the second floor of the house, Lewis Butler was awakened by a muffled crash like that of metal objects falling.

He had not fallen into more than a half doze all night. He knew with certainty what must be happening, though he had no idea of why, or how, or to whom.

Butler was out of bed, and into his slippers, as soon as he heard the first faint clatter from downstairs. His dressing-gown would, as usual, twist itself up like a rolled umbrella and defy all attempts to find the arm-holes whenever he wanted to hurry. But the little flashlight was ready in the pocket.

That noise seemed to have roused nobody else. With certain possibilities in his mind, he had never in his life moved so fast once he managed to get out of his bedroom. Not using his light, he was down two flights of deep-carpeted stairs without noise. In the lower hall he could feel a draught, which meant that a window or door had been opened somewhere. He made straight for the dining-room.

But he was too late.

Once the pencil-beam of Butler's flashlight had swept round, he switched on a whole blaze of lights. The burglar was still here, right enough. But the burglar was lying very still in front of the sideboard; and, to judge by the amount of blood on his sweater and trousers, he would never move again.

"That's done it," Butler said aloud.

A silver service, including a tea-urn, had been toppled off the sideboard. Where the fruit-bowl had fallen, the dead man lay on his back among a litter of oranges, apples, and a squashed bunch of grapes. The mask still covered the burglar's face; his greasy cap was flattened still further on his ears; his gloved hands were thrown wide.

Fragments of smashed picture-glass lay round him, together with the empty frame, and the "Old Woman with Cap" had been half crumpled up under his body. From the position of the most conspicuous bloodstains, one judged that he had been stabbed through the chest with the stained fruit-knife beside him.

"What is it?" said a voice almost at Butler's ear.

He could not have been more startled if the fruit-knife had pricked his ribs. He had seen nobody turning on lights in the hall, nor had he heard Harriet Davis approach. She was standing just behind him, wrapped in a Japanese kimono, with her dark hair round her shoulders. But, when he explained what had happened, she would not look into the dining-room; she backed away, shaking her head violently, like an urchin ready for flight.

"You had better wake up your uncle," Butler said briskly, with a confidence he did not feel. "And the servants. I must use your telephone." Then he looked her in the eyes. "Yes, you're quite right. I think you've guessed it already. I'm a police-officer."

She nodded.

"Yes. I guessed. Who are you? And is your name really Butler?"

"I'm a sergeant of the Criminal Investigation Department. And my name really is Butler. Your uncle brought me here."

"Why?"

"I don't know. He hasn't got round to telling me."

This girl's intelligence, even when over-shadowed by fear, was direct and disconcerting. "But, if he wouldn't say why he wanted a police-officer, how did they come to send you? He'd have to tell them, wouldn't he?"

Butler ignored it. "I must see your uncle. Will you go upstairs and wake him, please?"

"I can't," said Harriet. "Uncle Marcus isn't in his room."

"Isn't——?"

"No. I knocked at the door on my way down. He's gone."

Butler took the stairs two treads at a time. Harriet had turned on all the lights on her way down, but nothing stirred in the bleak, over-decorated passages.

Marcus Hunt's bedroom was empty. His dinner-jacket had been hung up neatly on the back of a chair, shirt laid across the seat with collar and tie on top of it. Hunt's watch ticked loudly on the dressing-table. His money and keys were there too. But he had not gone to bed, for the bedspread was undisturbed.

The suspicion which came to Lewis Butler, listening to the thin insistent ticking of that watch in the drugged hour before dawn, was so fantastic that he could not credit it.

He started downstairs again, and on the way he met Arthur Rolfe blundering out of another bedroom down the hall. The art dealer's stocky body was wrapped in a flannel dressing-gown. He was not wearing his eyeglasses, which gave his face a bleary and rather caved-in expression. He planted himself in front of Butler, and refused to budge.

"Yes," said Butler. "You don't have to ask. It's a burglar."

"I knew it," said Rolfe calmly. "Did he get anything?"

"No. He was murdered."

For a moment Rolfe said nothing, but his hand crept into the breast of his dressing-gown as though he felt pain there.

"Murdered? You don't mean the *burglar* was murdered?"

"Yes."

"But why? By an accomplice, you mean? Who is the burglar?"

"That," snarled Lewis Butler, "is what I intend to find out."

In the lower hall he found Harriet Davis, who was now standing in the doorway of the dining-room and looking steadily at the body by the sideboard. Though her face hardly moved a muscle, her eyes brimmed over.

"You're going to take off the mask, aren't you?" she asked, without turning round.

Stepping with care to avoid squashed fruit and broken glass, Butler leaned over the dead man. He pushed back the peak of the greasy cap; he lifted the black cloth mask, which was clumsily held by an elastic band; and he found what he expected to find.

The burglar was Marcus Hunt—stabbed through the heart while attempting to rob his own house.

"You see, sir," Butler explained to Dr. Gideon Fell on the following afternoon, "that's the trouble. However you look at it, the case makes no sense."

Again he went over the facts.

"Why should the man burgle his own house and steal his own property? Every one of those paintings is valuable, and not a single one is insured! Consequently, why? Was the man a simple lunatic? What did he think he was doing?"

The village of Sutton Valence, straggling like a grey-white Italian town along the very peak of the Weald, was full of hot sunshine. In the apple orchard behind the white inn of the *Tabard*, Dr. Gideon Fell sat at a garden table among wasps, with a pint tankard at his elbow. Dr. Fell's vast bulk was clad in a white linen suit. His pink face smoked in the heat, and his wary lookout for wasps gave him a regrettably wall-eyed appearance as he pondered.

He said:

"Superintendent Hadley suggested that I might—harrumph—look in here. The local police are in charge, aren't they?"

"Yes. I'm merely standing by."

"Hadley's exact words to me were, 'It's so crazy that nobody but you will understand it.' The man's flattery becomes more nauseating every day." Dr. Fell scowled. "I say. Does anything else strike you as queer about this business?"

"Well, why should a man burgle his own house?"

"No, no, no!" growled Dr. Fell. "Don't be obsessed with that point. Don't become hypnotized by it. For instance"—a wasp hovered near his tankard, and he distended his cheeks and blew it away with one vast puff like Father Neptune—"for instance, the young lady seems to have raised an interesting question. If Marcus Hunt wouldn't say why he wanted a detective in the house, why did the C.I.D. consent to send you?"

Butler shrugged his shoulders.

"Because," he said, "Chief Inspector Ames thought Hunt was up to funny business, and meant to stop it."

"What sort of funny business?"

"A faked burglary to steal his own pictures for the insurance. It looked like the old, old game of appealing to the police to divert suspicion. In other words, sir, exactly what this appeared to be: until I learned (and to-day proved) that not one of those damned pictures has ever been insured for a penny."

Butler hesitated.

"It can't have been a practical joke," he went on. "Look at the elaborateness of it! Hunt put on old clothes from which all tailors' tabs and laundry marks were removed. He put on gloves and a mask. He got hold of a torch and an up-to-date kit of burglar's tools. He went out of the house by the back door; we found it open later. He smoked a few cigarettes in the shrubbery below the terrace; we found his footprints in the soft earth. He cut a pane of glass . . . but I've told you all that."

"And then," mused Dr. Fell, "somebody killed him."

"Yes. The last and worst 'why.' Why should anybody have killed him?"

"H'm. Clues?"

"Negative." Butler took out his notebook. "According to
the police surgeon, he died of a direct heart-wound from a
blade (presumably that fruit-knife) so thin that the wound
was difficult to find. There were a number of his finger-prints,
but nobody else's. We did find one odd thing, though. A
number of pieces in the silver service off the sideboard were
scratched in a queer way. It looked almost as though, instead
of being swept off the sideboard in a struggle, they had been
piled up on top of each other like a tower; and then
pushed——"

Butler paused, for Dr. Fell was shaking his big head back
and forth with an expression of Gargantuan distress.

"Well, well, well," he was saying; "well, well, well. And
you call that negative evidence?"

"Isn't it? It doesn't explain why a man burgles his own
house."

"Look here," said the doctor mildly. "I should like to ask
you just one question. What is the most important point in
this affair? One moment! I did not say the most interesting; I
said the most important. Surely it is the fact that a man has
been murdered?"

"Yes, sir. Naturally."

"I mention the fact"—the doctor was apologetic—"because
it seems in danger of being overlooked. It hardly interests
you. You are concerned only with Hunt's senseless
masquerade. You don't mind a throat being cut; but you
can't stand a leg being pulled. Why not try working at it
from the other side, and asking who killed Hunt?"

Butler was silent for a long time.

"The servants are out of it," he said at length. "They sleep
in another wing on the top floor; and for some reason," he
hesitated, "somebody locked them in last night." His doubts,
even his dreads, were beginning to take form. "There was a
fine blow-up over that when the house was roused. Of course,
the murderer could have been an outsider."

"You know it wasn't," said Dr. Fell. "Would you mind
taking me to Cranleigh Court?"

They came out on the terrace in the hottest part of the afternoon.

Dr. Fell sat down on a wicker settee, with a dispirited Harriet beside him. Derek Henderson, in flannels, perched his long figure on the balustrade. Arthur Rolfe alone wore a dark suit and seemed out of place. For the pale green and brown of the Kentish lands, which rarely acquired harsh colour, now blazed. No air stirred, no leaf moved, in that brilliant thickness of heat; and down in the garden, towards their left, the water of the swimming-pool sparkled with hot, hard light. Butler felt it like a weight on his eyelids.

Derek Henderson's beard was at once languid and yet aggressive.

"It's no good," he said. "Don't keep on asking me why Hunt should have burgled his own house. But I'll give you a tip."

"Which is?" inquired Dr. Fell.

"Whatever the reason was," returned Henderson, sticking out his neck, "it was a good reason. Hunt was much too canny and cautious ever to do anything without a good reason. I told him so last night."

Dr. Fell spoke sharply. "Cautious? Why do you say that?"

"Well, for instance. I take three cards on the draw. Hunt takes one. I bet; he sees me and raises. I cover that, and raise again. Hunt drops out. In other words, it's fairly certain he's filled his hand, but not so certain I'm holding much more than a pair. Yet Hunt drops out. So with my three sevens I bluff him out of his straight. He played a dozen hands last night just like that."

Henderson began to chuckle. Seeing the expression on Harriet's face, he checked himself and became preternaturally solemn.

"But then, of course," Henderson added, "he had a lot on his mind last night."

Nobody could fail to notice the change of tone.

"So? And what did he have on his mind?"

"Exposing somebody he had always trusted," replied Henderson coolly. "That's why I didn't like it when the ace of spades turned up so often."

"You'd better explain that," said Harriet, after a pause. "I don't know what you're hinting at, but you'd better explain that. He told you he intended to expose somebody he had always trusted?"

"No. Like myself, he hinted at it."

It was the stolid Rolfe who stormed into the conversation then. Rolfe had the air of a man determined to hold hard to reason, but finding it difficult.

"Listen to me," snapped Rolfe. "I have heard a great deal, at one time or another, about Mr. Hunt's liking for exposing people. Very well!" He slid one hand into the breast of his coat, in a characteristic gesture. "But where in the name of sanity does that leave us? He wants to expose someone. And, to do that, he puts on outlandish clothes and masquerades as a burglar. Is that sensible? I tell you, the man was mad! There's no other explanation."

"There are five other explanations," said Dr. Fell.

Derek Henderson slowly got up from his seat on the balustrade, but he sat down again at a savage gesture from Rolfe.

Nobody spoke.

"I will not, however," pursued Dr. Fell, "waste your time with four of them. We are concerned with only one explanation: the real one."

"And you know the real one?" asked Henderson sharply.

"I rather think so."

"Since when?"

"Since I had the opportunity of looking at all of you," answered Dr. Fell.

He settled back massively in the wicker settee, so that its frame creaked and cracked like a ship's bulkhead in a heavy sea. His vast chin was outthrust, and he nodded absently as though to emphasize some point that was quite clear in his own mind.

"I've already had a word with the local inspector," he went on suddenly. "He will be here in a few minutes. And, at my suggestion, he will have a request for all of you. I sincerely hope nobody will refuse."

"Request?" said Henderson. "What request?"

"It's a very hot day," said Dr. Fell, blinking towards the swimming-pool. "He's going to suggest that you all go in for a swim."

Harriet uttered a kind of despairing mutter, and turned as though appealing to Lewis Butler.

"That," continued Dr. Fell, "will be the politest way of drawing attention to the murderer. In the meantime, let me call your attention to one point in the evidence which seems to have been generally overlooked. Mr. Henderson, do you know anything about direct heart-wounds, made by a steel blade as thin as a wafer?"

"Like Hunt's wound? No. What about them?"

"There is practically no exterior bleeding," answered Dr. Fell.

"But——!" Harriet was beginning, when Butler stopped her.

"The police surgeon, in fact, called attention to that wound which was so 'difficult to find.' The victim dies almost at once; and the edges of the wound compress. But in that case," argued Dr. Fell, "how did the late Mr. Hunt come to have so much blood on his sweater, and even splashed on his trousers?"

"Well?"

"He didn't," answered Dr. Fell simply. "Mr. Hunt's blood never got on his clothes at all."

"I can't stand this," said Harriet, jumping to her feet. "I—I'm sorry, but have you gone mad yourself? Are you telling us we didn't see him lying by that sideboard, with blood on him?"

"Oh, yes. You saw that."

"Let him go on," said Henderson, who was rather white round the nostrils. "Let him rave."

"It is, I admit, a fine point," said Dr. Fell. "But it answers your question, repeated to the point of nausea, as to why the eminently sensible Mr. Hunt chose to dress up in burglar's clothes and play burglar. The answer is short and simple. He didn't."

"It must be plain to everybody," Dr. Fell went on, opening his eyes wide, "that Mr. Hunt was deliberately setting a trap for someone—the real burglar.

"He believed that a certain person might try to steal one or several of his pictures. He probably knew that this person had tried similar games before, in other country houses: that is, an inside job which was carefully planned to look like an outside job. So he made things easy for this thief, in order to trap him, with a police-officer in the house.

"The burglar, a sad fool, fell for it. This thief, a guest in the house, waited until well past two o'clock in the morning. He then put on his old clothes, mask, gloves, and the rest of it. He let himself out by the back door. He went through all the motions we have erroneously been attributing to Marcus Hunt. Then the trap snapped. Just as he was rolling up the Rembrandt, he heard a noise. He swung his light round. And he saw Marcus Hunt, in pyjamas and dressing-gown, looking at him.

"Yes, there was a fight. Hunt flew at him. The thief snatched up a fruit-knife and fought back. In that struggle, Marcus Hunt forced his opponent's hand back. The fruit-knife gashed the thief's chest, inflicting a superficial but badly bleeding gash. It sent the thief over the edge of insanity. He wrenched Marcus Hunt's wrist half off, caught up the knife, and stabbed Hunt to the heart.

"Then, in a quiet house, with a little beam of light streaming out from the torch on the sideboard, the murderer sees something that will hang him. He sees the blood from his own superficial wound seeping down his clothes.

"How is he to get rid of those clothes? He cannot destroy them, or get them away from the house. Inevitably the house will be searched, and they will be found. Without the blood-stains, they would seem ordinary clothes in his wardrobe. But with the blood-stains——

"There is only one thing he can do."

Harriet Davis was standing behind the wicker settee, shading her eyes against the glare of the sun. Her hand did not tremble when she said:

"He changed clothes with my uncle."

"That's it," growled Dr. Fell. "That's the whole sad story. The murderer dressed the body in his own clothes, making a puncture with the knife in sweater, shirt, and undervest. He then slipped on Mr. Hunt's pyjamas and dressing-gown, which at a pinch he could always claim as his own. Hunt's wound had bled hardly at all. His dressing-gown, I think, had come open in the fight; so that all the thief had to trouble him was a tiny puncture in the jacket of the pyjamas.

"But, once he had done this, he had to hypnotize you all into the belief that there would have been no time for a change of clothes. He had to make it seem that the fight occurred just *then*. He had to rouse the house. So he brought own echoing thunders by pushing over a pile of silver, and lipped upstairs."

Dr. Fell paused.

"The burglar could never have been Marcus Hunt, you now," he added. "We learn that Hunt's fingerprints were all ver the place. Yet the murdered man was wearing gloves."

There was a swishing of feet in the grass below the terrace, nd a tread of heavy boots coming up the terrace steps. The ocal Inspector of police, buttoned up and steaming in his niform, was followed by two constables.

Dr. Fell turned round a face of satisfaction.

"Ah!" he said, breathing deeply. "They've come to see bout that swimming-party, I imagine. It is easy to patch up flesh-wound with lint and cotton, or even a handkerchief. But such a wound will become infernally conspicuous in anyone who is forced to climb into bathing-trunks."

"But it couldn't have been——" cried Harriet. Her eyes moved round. Her fingers tightened on Lewis Butler's arm, an instinctive gesture which he was to remember long afterwards, when he knew her even better.

"Exactly," agreed the doctor, wheezing with pleasure. "It could not have been a long, thin, gangling fellow like Mr. Henderson. It assuredly could not have been a small and slender girl like yourself.

"There is only one person who, as we know, is just about Marcus Hunt's height and build; who could have put his own clothes on Hunt without any suspicion. That is the same person who, though he managed to staunch the wound in his chest, has been constantly running his hand inside the breast of his coat to make certain the bandage is secure. Just as Mr. Rolfe is doing now."

Arthur Rolfe sat very quiet, with his right hand still in the breast of his jacket. His face had grown smeary in the hot sunlight, but the eyes behind those thin shells of glasses remained inscrutable. He spoke only once, through dry lips, after they had cautioned him.

"I should have taken the young pup's warning," he said. "After all, he told me I would take long chances."

THE DEPARTMENT OF DEAD ENDS

Roy Vickers had been writing detective novels and short stories for over two decades without attracting any particular attention. Then chance, the sort of blind chance that figures in many of his stories, came into play. Ellery Queen came across a Vickers story about an imaginary branch of Scotland Yard devoted to collecting details on all unsolved murders and solving, eventually, some of them. The story had appeared originally in England in 1935. When it was reprinted in the November 1943 issue of Ellery Queen's Mystery Magazine, it garnered such "extravagant praise" that Queen asked Vickers for more. Vickers was inspired to resume writing about the Department. A collection of ten cases, with an introduction by Ellery Queen, appeared in 1949. And before Vickers' death in 1965 he had turned out a total of nearly forty Dead Ends cases.

In Twentieth Century Crime and Mystery Writers the stories in this series are called "the best detective stories of the 1940s." In them, Vickers mixed the police procedural approach with the inverted pattern introduced by R. Austin Freeman. "But he uses it," Julian Symons has said, "with more flexibility and sophistication than its inventor." Vickers possesses as well a strong sense of humor, also in evidence in novels like Murdering Mr. Velfrage and Gold and Wine, and in many of the Dead Ends investigations there is a feeling of deadpan farce that adds to the proceedings.

The following story is the first in the series, the one Ellery Queen chanced on nearly forty years ago.

The Rubber Trumpet
by Roy Vickers

1

If you were to enquire at Scotland Yard for the Department of Dead Ends you might be told, in all sincerity, that there is no such thing, because it is not called by that name nowadays. All the same, if it has no longer a room to itself, you may rest assured that its spirit hovers over the index files of which we are all so justly proud.

The Department came into existence in the spacious days of King Edward VII and it took everything that the other departments rejected. For instance, it noted and filed all those clues that had the exasperating effect of proving a palpably guilty man innocent. Its shelves were crowded with exhibits that might have been in the Black Museum—but were not. Its photographs were a perpetual irritation to all rising young detectives, who felt that they ought to have found the means of putting them in the Rogues' Gallery.

To the Department, too, were taken all those members of the public who insist on helping the police with obviously irrelevant information and preposterous theories. The one passport to the Department was a written statement by the senior officer in charge of the case that the information offered was absurd.

Judged by the standards of reason and common sense, its files were mines of misinformation. It proceeded largely by guess-work. On one occasion it hanged a murderer by accidentally punning on his name.

It was the function of the Department to connect persons and things that had no logical connexion. In short, it stood for the antithesis of scientific detection. It played always for a lucky fluke—to offset the lucky fluke by which the criminal so often eludes the police. Often it muddled one crime with another and arrived at the correct answer by wrong reasoning.

As in the case of George Muncey and the rubber trumpet.

And note, please, that the rubber trumpet had nothing logically to do with George Muncey, or the woman he murdered, or the circumstances in which he murdered her.

2

Until the age of twenty-six George Muncey lived with his widowed mother in Chichester, the family income being derived from a chemist's shop, efficiently controlled by Mrs Muncey with the aid of a manager and two assistants, of whom latterly George was one. Of his early youth we know only that he won a scholarship at a day-school, tenable for three years, which was cancelled at the end of a year, though not, apparently, for misconduct. He failed several times to obtain his pharmaceutical certificate, with the result that he was eventually put in charge of the fancy soaps, the hot-water bottles and the photographic accessories.

For this work he received two pounds per week. Every Saturday he handed the whole of it to his mother, who returned him fifteen shillings for pocket money. She had no need of the balance and only took it in order to nourish his self-respect. He did not notice that she bought his clothes and met all his other expenses.

George had no friends and very little of what an ordinary young man would regard as pleasure. He spent nearly all his spare time with his mother, to whom he was devoted. She was an amiable but very domineering woman and she does not seem to have noticed that her son's affection had in it a quality of childishness—that he liked her to form his opinions for him and curtail his liberties.

After his mother's death he did not resume his duties at the shop. For some eight months he mooned about Chichester. Then, the business having been sold and probate granted, he found himself in possession of some eight hundred pounds, with another two thousand pounds due to him in three months. He did not, apparently, understand this part of the transaction—for he made no application for the two thousand, and as the solicitors could not find him until his name came into the papers, the two thousand remained intact for his defence.

That he was a normal but rather backward young man is proved by the fact that the walls of his bedroom were liberally decorated with photographs of the actresses of the moment and pictures of anonymous beauties cut from the more sporting weeklies. Somewhat naïvely he bestowed this picture gallery as a parting gift on the elderly cook.

He drew the whole of the eight hundred pounds in notes and gold, said good-bye to his home and went up to London. He stumbled on cheap and respectable lodgings in Pimlico. Then, in a gauche, small-town way, he set out to see life.

It was the year when *The Merry Widow* was setting all London a-whistling. Probably on some chance recommendation, he drifted to Daly's Theatre, where he bought himself a seat in the dress-circle.

It was the beginning of the London season and we may assume that he would have felt extremely self-conscious sitting in the circle in his ready-made lounge suit, had there not happened to be a woman also in morning dress next to him.

The woman was a Miss Hilda Callermere. She was forty-three, and if she escaped positive ugliness she was certainly without any kind of physical attractiveness, though she was neat in her person and reasonably well-dressed, in an old-fashioned way.

Eventually to the Department of Dead Ends came the whole story of his strange courtship.

There is a curious quality in the manner in which these two slightly unusual human beings approached one another. They did not speak until after the show, when they were wedged together in the corridor. Their voices seem to come to us out of a fog of social shyness and vulgar gentility. And it was she who took the initiative.

"If you'll excuse me speaking to you without an introduction, we seem to be rather out of it, you and I, what with one thing and another."

His reply strikes us now as somewhat unusual.

"Yes, rather!" he said. "Are you coming here again?"

"Yes, rather! I sometimes come twice a week."

During the next fortnight they both went three times to *The Merry Widow*, but on the first two of these occasions they missed each other. On the third occasion, which was a Saturday night, Miss Callermere invited George Muncey to walk with her on the following morning in Battersea Park.

Here shyness dropped from them. They slipped quite suddenly on to an easy footing of friendship. George Muncey accepted her invitation to lunch. She took him to a comfortably furnished eight-roomed house—her own—in which she lived with an aunt whom she supported. For, in addition to the house, Miss Callermere owned an income of six hundred pounds derived from gilt-edged investments.

But these considerations weighed hardly at all with George Muncey—for he had not yet spent fifty pounds of his eight hundred, and at this stage he had certainly no thought of marriage with Miss Callermere.

3

Neither of them had any occupation, so they could meet whenever they chose. Miss Callermere undertook to show George London. Her father had been a cheery, beery jerry-builder with sporting interests and she had reacted from him into a parched severity of mind. She marched George round the Tower of London, the British Museum and the like, reading aloud extracts from a guide-book. They went neither to the theatres nor to the music-halls, for Miss Callermere thought these frivolous and empty-headed—with the exception of *The Merry Widow*, which she believed to be opera, and therefore cultural. And the extraordinary thing was that George Muncey liked it all.

There can be no doubt that this smug little spinster, some sixteen years older than himself, touched a chord of sympathy in his nature. But she was wholly unable to cater for that part of him that had plastered photographs of public beauties on the walls of his bedroom.

She never went to *The Merry Widow* again, but once or twice he would sneak off to Daly's by himself. *The Merry Widow*, in fact, provided him with a dream-life. We may infer that in his imagination he identified himself with Mr Joseph Coyne, who nightly, in the character of Prince Dannilo, would disdain the beautiful Sonia only to have her rush the more surely to his arms in the finale. Rather a dangerous fantasy for a backward young man from the provinces who was beginning to lose his shyness!

There was, indeed, very little shyness about him when, one evening after seeing Miss Callermere home, he was startled by the sight of a young parlourmaid, who had been sent out to post a letter, some fifty yards from Miss Callermere's house. If she bore little or no likeness to Miss Lily Elsie in the role of Sonia, she certainly looked quite lovely in her white cap and the streamers that were then worn. And she was smiling and friendly and natural.

She was, of course, Ethel Fairbrass. She lingered with George Muncey for over five minutes. And then comes another of those strange little dialogues.

"Funny a girl like you being a slavey! When's your evening off?"

"Six o'clock to-morrow. But what's it got to do with you?"

"I'll meet you at the corner of this road. Promise you I will."

"Takes two to make a promise. My name's Ethel Fairbrass, if you want to know. What's yours?"

"Dannilo."

"*Cool* Fancy calling you that! Dannilo What?"

George had not foreseen the necessity for inventing a surname and discovered that it is quite difficult. He couldn't very well say "Smith" or "Robinson," so he said:

"Prince."

George, it will be observed, was not an imaginative man. When she met him the following night he could think of nowhere to take her but to *The Merry Widow*. He was even foolish enough to let her have a programme, but she did not read the names of the characters. When the curtain went up she was too entranced with Miss Lily Elsie, whom (like every pretty girl at the time) she thought she resembled, to take any notice of Mr Joseph Coyne and his character name. If she had tumbled to the witless transposition of the names she might have become suspicious of him. In which case George Muncey might have lived to a ripe old age.

But she didn't.

4

Altogether, Ethel Fairbrass provided an extremely satisfactory substitute for the dream-woman of George's fantasy. Life was beginning to sweeten. In the daylight hours he would enjoy his friendship with Miss Callermere, the pleasure of which was in no way touched by his infatuation for the pretty parlourmaid.

In early September Ethel became entitled to her holiday. She spent the whole fortnight with George at Southend. And George wrote daily to Miss Callermere, telling her that he was filling the place of a chemist-friend of his mother's, while the latter took his holiday. He actually contrived to have the letters addressed to the care of a local chemist. The letters were addressed "George Muncey" while at the hotel the couple were registered as "Mr and Mrs D. Prince."

Now the fictional Prince Dannilo was notoriously an open-handed and free-living fellow—and Dannilo Prince proceeded to follow in his footsteps. Ethel Fairbrass undoubtedly had the time of her life. They occupied a suite. ("Coo! A bathroom all to our own two selves, and use it whenever we like!")

He hired a car for her, with chauffeur—which cost ten pounds a day at that time. He gave her champagne whenever he could induce her to drink it and bought her some quite expensive presents.

It is a little surprising that at the end of a fortnight of this kind of thing she went back to her occupation. But she did. There was nothing of the mercenary about Ethel.

On his return to London, George was very glad to see Miss Callermere. They resumed their interminable walks and he went almost daily to her house for lunch or dinner. A valuable arrangement, this, for the little diversion at Southend had made a sizeable hole in his eight hundred pounds.

It was a bit of a nuisance to have to leave early in order to snatch a few minutes with Ethel. After Southend, the few snatched minutes had somehow lost their charm. There were, too, Ethel's half-days and her Sundays, the latter involving him in a great many troublesome lies to Miss Callermere.

In the middle of October he started sneaking off to *The*

Merry Widow again. Which was a bad sign. For it meant that he was turning back again from reality to his dream-life. The Reality, in the meantime, had lost her high spirits and was inclined to weep unreasonably and to nag more than a little.

At the beginning of November Ethel presented him with certain very valid arguments in favour of fixing the date of their wedding, a matter which had hitherto been kept vaguely in the background.

George was by now heartily sick of her and contemplated leaving her in the lurch. Strangely enough, it was her final threat to tell Miss Callermere that turned the scale and decided George to make the best of a bad job and marry her.

5

As Dannilo Prince he married her one foggy morning at the registrar's office in Henrietta Street. Mr and Mrs Fairbrass came up from Banbury for the wedding. They were not very nice about it, although from the social point of view the marriage might be regarded as a step-up for Ethel.

"Where are you going for your honeymoon?" asked Mrs Fairbrass. "That is—if you're going to *have* a honeymoon."

"Southend," said the unimaginative George, and to Southend he took her for the second time. There was no need for a suite now, so they went to a small family-and-commercial hotel. Here George was unreasonably jealous of the commercial travellers, who were merely being polite to a rather forlorn bride. In wretched weather he insisted on taking her for walks, with the result that he himself caught a very bad cold. Eucalyptus and hot toddy became the dominant note in a town which was associated in the girl's mind with champagne and bath salts. But they had to stick it for the full fortnight, because George had told Miss Callermere that he was again acting as substitute for the chemist-friend of his mother's in Southend.

According to the files of the Department, they left Southend by the three-fifteen on the thirtieth of November. George had taken first-class returns. The three-fifteen was a popular non-stop, but on this occasion there were hardly a score of persons travelling to London. One of the first-class carriages was occupied by a man alone with a young baby wrapped in a red shawl. Ethel wanted to get into this compartment, perhaps having a sneaking hope that the man would require her assistance in dealing with the baby. But George did not intend to concern himself with babies one moment before he would be compelled to do so, and they went into another compartment.

Ethel, however, seems to have looked forward to her impending career with a certain pleasure. Before leaving Southend she had paid a visit to one of those shops that cater for summer visitors and miraculously remain open through the winter. She had a bulky parcel, which she opened in the rather pathetic belief that it would amuse George.

The parcel contained a large child's bucket, a disproportionately small wooden spade, a sailing-boat to the scale of the spade, a length of Southend rock, and a rubber trumpet, of which the stem was wrapped with red and blue wool. It was a baby's trumpet and of rubber so that it should not hurt the baby's gums. In the mouthpiece, shielded by the rubber, was a little metal contraption that made the noise.

Ethel put the trumpet to her mouth and blew through the metal contraption.

Perhaps, in fancy, she heard her baby doing it. Perhaps, after a honeymoon of neglect and misery, she was making a desperate snatch at the spirit of gaiety, hoping he would attend to her and perhaps indulge in a little horseplay. But for the facts we have to depend on George's version.

"I said 'Don't make that noise, Ethel—I'm trying to read' or something like that. And she said 'I feel like a bit of music to cheer me up' and she went on blowing the trumpet. So I caught hold of it and threw it out of the window. I didn't hurt her and she didn't seem to mind much. And we didn't have another quarrel over it and I went on reading my paper until we got to London."

At Fenchurch Street they claimed their luggage and left the station. Possibly Ethel abandoned the parcel containing the other toys, for they were never heard of again.

When the train was being cleaned, a dead baby was found under the seat of a first-class compartment, wrapped in a red shawl. It was subsequently ascertained that the baby had not been directly murdered but had died more or less naturally in convulsions.

But before this was known, Scotland Yard searched for the man who had been seen to enter the train with the baby, as if for a murderer. A platelayer found the rubber trumpet on the line and forwarded it. Detectives combed the shops of Southend and found that only one rubber trumpet had been sold—to a young woman whom the shopkeeper did not know. The trail ended here.

The rubber trumpet went to the Department of Dead Ends.

6

Of the eight hundred pounds there was a little over a hundred and fifty left by the time they returned from the official honeymoon at Southend. He took her to furnished rooms in Ladbroke Grove and a few days later to a tenement in the same district, which he furnished at a cost of thirty pounds.

She seems to have asked him no awkward questions about money. Every morning after breakfast he would leave the tenement, presumably in order to go to work. Actually he would loaf about the West End until it was time to meet Miss Callermere. He liked especially going to the house in Battersea for lunch on Sundays. And here, of course, the previous process reversed itself and it was Ethel who had to be told the troublesome lies that were so difficult to invent.

"You seem so different lately, George," said Miss Callermere one Sunday after lunch. "I believe you're living with a ballet girl."

George was not quite sure what a ballet girl was, but it sounded rather magnificently wicked. As he was anxious not to involve himself in further inventions, he said:

"She's not a ballet girl. She used to be a parlourmaid."

"I really only want to know one thing about her," said Miss Callermere. "And that is, whether you are fond of her."

"No, I'm not!" said George with complete truthfulness.

"It's a pity to have that kind of thing in your life—you are dedicated to science. For your own sake, George, why not get rid of her?"

Why not? George wondered why he had not thought of it before. He had only to move, to stop calling himself by the ridiculous name of Dannilo Prince, and the thing was as good as done. He would go back at once and pack.

When he got back to the tenement, Ethel gave him an unexpectedly warm reception.

"You told me you were going to the S.P.D. Sunday Brotherhood, you did! And you never went near them, because you met that there Miss Callermere in Battersea Park, because I followed you and saw you. And then you went back to her house, which is Number Fifteen, Laurel Road, which I didn't know before. And what you can see in a dried-up old maid like that beats me. It's time she knew that she's rolling her silly sheep's eyes at another woman's husband. And I'm going to tell her before I'm a day older."

She was whipping on hat and coat and George lurched forward to stop her. His foot caught on a gas-ring, useless now that he had installed a gas-range—a piece of lumber that Ethel ought to have removed weeks ago. But she used it as a stand for the iron.

George picked up the gas-ring. If she were to go to Miss Callermere and make a brawl, he himself would probably never be able to go there again. He pushed her quickly on to the bed, then swung the gas-ring—swung it several times.

He put all the towels, every soft absorbent thing he could find, under the bed. Then he washed himself, packed a suitcase and left the tenement.

He took the suitcase to his old lodgings, announced that he had come back there to live, and then presented himself at the house in Battersea in time for supper.

"I've done what you told me," he said to Miss Callermere. "Paid her off. Shan't hear from her any more."

The Monday morning papers carried the news of the murder, for the police had been called on Sunday evening by the tenants of the flat below. The hunt was started for Dannilo Prince.

By Tuesday the dead girl's parents had been interviewed and her life-story appeared on Wednesday morning.

"My daughter was married to Prince at the Henrietta Street registrar's office on November 16th, 1907. He took her straight away for a honeymoon at Southend, where they stayed a fortnight."

There was a small crowd at the bottom of Laurel Road to gape at the house where she had so recently worked as a parlourmaid. Fifty yards from Number Fifteen! But if Miss Callermere noticed the crowd she is not recorded as having made any comment upon it to anyone.

In a few days, Scotland Yard knew that they would never find Dannilo Prince. In fact, it had all been as simple as George had anticipated. He had just moved—and that was the end of his unlucky marriage. The addition of the murder had not complicated things, because he had left no clue behind him.

Now, as there was nothing whatever to connect George Muncey with Dannilo Prince, George's chances of arrest were limited to the chance of an accidental meeting between himself and someone who had known him as Prince. There was an hotel proprietor, a waiter and a chambermaid at Southend, and an estate agent at Ladbroke Grove. And, of course, Ethel's father and mother. Of these persons only the estate agent lived in London.

A barrister, who was also a statistician, entertained himself by working out the averages. He came to the conclusion that George Muncey's chance of being caught was equal to his chance of winning the first prize in the Calcutta Sweep *twenty-three times in succession*.

But the barrister did not calculate the chances of the illogical guesswork of the Department of Dead Ends hitting the bull's-eye by mistake.

7

While the hue and cry for Dannilo Prince passed over his head, George Muncey dedicated himself to science with such energy that in a fortnight he had obtained a post with a chemist in Walham. Here he presided over a counter devoted to fancy soaps, hot-water bottles, photographic apparatus and the like—for which he received two pounds a week and a minute commission that added zest to his work.

At Easter he married Miss Callermere in church. That lady had mobilized all her late father's associates and, to their inward amusement, arrayed herself in white satin and veil for the ceremony. As it would have been unreasonable to ask

George's employers for a holiday after so short a term of service, the newly married couple dispensed with a honeymoon. The aunt entered a home for indigent gentlewomen with an allowance of a hundred a year from her niece. George once again found himself in a spacious, well-run house.

During their brief married life, this oddly assorted couple seem to have been perfectly happy. The late Mr Callermere's friends were allowed to slip back into oblivion, because they showed a tendency to giggle whenever George absent-mindedly addressed his wife as "Miss Callermere."

His earnings of two pounds a week may have seemed insignificant beside his wife's unearned income. But in fact it was the basis of their married happiness. Every Saturday he handed her the whole of his wages. She would retain twenty-five shillings, because they both considered it essential to his self-respect that he should pay the cost of his food. She handed him back fifteen shillings for pocket-money. She read the papers and formed his opinions for him. She seemed to allow him little of what most men would regard as pleasure, but George had no complaint on this score.

Spring passed into summer and nearly everybody had forgotten the murder of Ethel Prince in a tenement in Ladbroke Grove. It is probably true to say that, in any real sense of the word, George Muncey had forgotten it too. He had read very little and did not know that murderers were popularly supposed to be haunted by their crime and to start guiltily at every chance mention of it.

He received no reaction whatever when his employer said to him one morning:

"There's this job-line of rubber trumpets. I took half a gross. We'll mark them at one-and-a-penny. Put one on your counter with the rubber teats and try them on women with babies."

George took one of the rubber trumpets from the cardboard case containing the half gross. It had red and blue wool wound about the stem. He put it next the rubber teats and forgot about it.

8

Wilkins, the other assistant, held his pharmaceutical certificate, but he was not stand-offish on that account. One day, to beguile the boredom of the slack hour after lunch, he picked up the rubber trumpet and blew it.

Instantly George was sitting in the train with Ethel, telling her "not to make that noise." When Wilkins put the trumpet down, George found himself noticing the trumpet and thought the red and blue wool very hideous. He picked it up—Ethel's had felt just like that when he had thrown it out of the window.

Now it cannot for one moment be held that George felt anything in the nature of remorse. The truth was that the rubber trumpet, by reminding him so vividly of Ethel, had stirred up dormant forces in his nature. Ethel had been very comely and jolly and playful when one was in the mood for it—as one often was, in spite of everything.

The trumpet, in short, produced little more than a sense of bewilderment. Why could not things have gone on as they began? It was only as a wife that Ethel was utterly intolerable, because she had no sense of order and did not really look after a chap. Now that he was married to Miss Callermere, if only Ethel had been available on, say, Wednesday evenings and alternate Sundays, life would have been full at once of colour and comfort. . . . He tried to sell the trumpet to a lady with a little girl and a probable baby at home, but without success.

On the next day he went as far as admitting to himself that the trumpet had got on his nerves. Between a quarter to one and a quarter past, when Wilkins was out to lunch, he picked up the trumpet and blew it. And just before closing-time he blew it again, when Wilkins was there.

George was not subtle enough to humbug himself. The trumpet stirred longings that were better suppressed. So the next day he wrote out a bill for one-and-a-penny, put one-and-a-penny of his pocket money into the cash register and stuffed the trumpet into his coat pocket. Before supper that night he put it in the hot-water furnace.

"There's a terrible smell in the house. What did you put in the furnace, George?"

"Nothing."

"Tell me the truth, dear."

"A rubber trumpet stuck on my counter. Fair got on my nerves, it did. I paid the one-and-a-penny and I burnt it."

"That was very silly, wasn't it? It'll make you short in your pocket money. And in the circumstances I don't feel inclined to make it up for you."

That would be all right, George assured her, and inwardly thought how lucky he was to have such a wife. She could keep a fellow steady and pull him up when he went one over the odds.

Three days later his employer looked through the stock.

"I see that rubber trumpet has gone. Put up another. It may be a good line."

And so the whole business began over again. George, it will be observed, for all his unimaginativeness, was a spiritually economical man. His happy contentment with his wife would, he knew, be jeopardized if he allowed himself to be reminded of that other disorderly, fascinating side of life that had been presided over by Ethel.

There were six dozen of the rubber trumpets, minus the one burnt at home, and his employer would expect one-and-a-penny for each of them. Thirteen shillings a dozen. But the dozens themselves were thirteen, which complicated the calculation, but in the end he got the sum right. He made sure of this by doing it backwards and "proving" it. He still had twenty-three pounds left out of the eight hundred.

Mrs Muncey had a rather nice crocodile dressing-case which she had bought for herself and quite falsely described as "gift of the bridegroom to the bride."

On the next day George borrowed the crocodile dressing-case on the plea that he wished to bring some goods from the shop home for Christmas. He brought it into the shop on the plea that it contained his dinner jacket and that he intended to change at the house of a friend without going home that night. As he was known to have married "an heiress" neither Wilkins nor his employer was particularly surprised that he should possess a dinner jacket and a crocodile dressing-case in which to carry it about.

At a quarter to one, when he was again alone in the shop,
he crammed half a gross (less one) of rubber trumpets into
the crocodile dressing-case. When his employer came back
from lunch he said:

"I've got rid of all those rubber trumpets, Mr Arrowsmith.
An old boy came in, said he was to do with an orphanage,
and I talked him into buying the lot."

Mr Arrowsmith was greatly astonished.

"Bought the lot, did you say? Didn't he ask for a discount?"

"No, Mr Arrowsmith. I think he was a bit loopy myself."

Mr Arrowsmith looked very hard at George and then at
the cash register. Six thirteens, less one, at one-and-a-
penny—four pounds, three and fivepence. It was certainly a
very funny thing. But then, the freak customer appears from
time to time and at the end of the day Mr Arrowsmith had
got over his surprise.

Journeying from Walham to Battersea, one goes on the
Underground to Victoria Station, and continues the journey
on the main line: From the fact that George Muncey that
evening took the crocodile case to Victoria Station, it has
been argued that he intended to take the rubber trumpets
home and perhaps bury them in the garden or deal with them
in some other way. But this ignores the fact that he told his
wife he intended to bring home some goods for Christmas.

The point is of minor importance, because the dressing-
case never reached home with him that night. At the top of
the steps leading from the Underground it was snatched from
him.

George's first sensation, on realizing that he had been
robbed, was one of relief. The rubber trumpets, he had already found, could not be burnt; they would certainly have
been a very great nuisance to him. The case, he knew, cost
fifteen guineas, and there was still enough left of the twenty-
three pounds to buy a new one on the following day.

9

At closing-time the next day, while George and Wilkins
were tidying up, Mr Arrowsmith was reading the evening paper.

"Here, Muncey! Listen to this. 'Jake Mendel, thirty-seven, of no fixed abode, was charged before Mr Ramsden this morning with the theft of a crocodile dressing-case from the precincts of Victoria Station. Mr Ramsden asked the police what was inside the bag. 'A number of toy trumpets, your worship, made of rubber. There were seventy-seven of 'em all told.' Mr Ramsden: 'Seventy-seven rubber trumpets! Well, *now* there really is no reason why the police should not have their own band.' (Laughter.)" Mr Arrowsmith laughed too and then: "Muncey, that looks like your lunatic."

"Yes, Mr Arrowsmith," said George indifferently, then went contentedly home to receive his wife's expostulations about a new crocodile dressing-case which had been delivered during the afternoon. It was not quite the same to look at, because the original one had been made to order. But it had been bought at the same shop and the manager had obliged George by charging the same price for it.

In the meantime, the police were relying on the newspaper paragraph to produce the owner of the crocodile case. When he failed to materialize on the following morning they looked at the name of the manufacturer and took the case round to him.

The manufacturer informed them that he had made that case the previous Spring to the order of a Miss Callermere—that the lady had since married and that, only the previous day, her husband, Mr Muncey, had ordered an exactly similar one but had accepted a substitute from stock.

"Ring up George Muncey and ask him to come up and identify the case—and take away these india-rubber trumpets!" ordered the Superintendent.

Mrs Muncey answered the telephone and from her they obtained George's business address.

"A chemist's assistant!" said the Superintendent. "Seems to me rather rum. Those trumpets may be his employer's stock. And he may have been pinching 'em. Don't ring him up—go down. And find out if the employer has anything to say about the stock. See him before you see Muncey."

At Walham the Sergeant was taken into the dispensary where he promptly enquired whether Mr Arrowsmith had missed seventy-seven rubber trumpets from his stock.

"I haven't missed them—but I sold them the day before

yesterday—seventy-seven, that's right! Or rather, my assistant, George Muncey, did. Here, Muncey!" And as George appeared:

"You sold the rest of the stock of those rubber trumpets to a gentleman who said he was connected with an orphanage—the day before yesterday it was—didn't you?"

"Yes, Mr Arrowsmith," said George.

"Bought the lot without asking for a discount," said Mr Arrowsmith proudly. "Four pounds, three shillings and fivepence. I could tell you of another case that happened years ago when a man came into this very shop and——"

The Sergeant felt his head whirling a little. The assistant had sold seventy-seven rubber trumpets to an eccentric gentleman. The goods had been duly paid for and taken away—and the goods were subsequently found in the assistant's wife's dressing-case.

"Did you happen to have a crocodile dressing-case stolen from you at Victoria Station the day before yesterday, Mr Muncey?" asked the Sergeant.

George was in a quandary. If he admitted that the crocodile case was his wife's—he would admit to Mr Arrowsmith that he had been lying when he had said that he had cleverly sold the whole of the seventy-seven rubber trumpets without even having to give away a discount. So:

"No," said George.

"Ah, I thought not! There's a mistake somewhere. I expect it's that manufacturer put us wrong. Sorry to have troubled you, gentlemen! Good morning!"

"Wait a minute," said Mr Arrowsmith. "You *did* have a crocodile dressing-case here that day, Muncey, with your evening clothes in it. And you *do* go home by Victoria. But what is that about the trumpets, Sergeant? They couldn't have been in Mr Muncey's case if he sold them over the counter."

"I don't know what they've got hold of, Mr Arrowsmith, and that's a fact," said George. "I think I'm wanted in the shop."

George was troubled, so he got leave to go home early. He told his wife how he had lied to the police, and confessed to her about the trumpets. Soon she had made him tell her the real reason for his dislike of the trumpets. The result was that when the police brought her the original crocodile case she flatly denied that it was hers.

In law, there was no means by which the ownership of the case could be foisted upon the Munceys against their will. Pending the trial of Jake Mendel, the bag-snatcher, the crocodile case, with its seventy-seven rubber trumpets, was deposited with the Department of Dead Ends.

A few feet above it on a shelf stood the identical trumpet which George Muncey had thrown out of the window on the three-fifteen, non-stop Southend to Fenchurch Street, some seven months ago.

The Department took one of the trumpets from the bag and set it beside the trumpet on the shelf. There was no logical connexion between them whatever. The Department simply guessed that there might be a connexion.

They tried to connect Walham with Southend and drew blank. They traced the history of the seventy-seven Walham trumpets and found it simple enough until the moment when George Muncey put them in the crocodile case.

They went back to the Southend trumpet and read in their files that it had not been bought by the man with the baby but by a young woman.

Then they tried a cross-reference to young women and Southend. They found that dead end, the Ethel Fairbrass murder. They found: *"My daughter was married to Prince at the Henrietta Street registrar's office on November the sixteenth, 1907. He took her straight away for a honeymoon at Southend where they stayed a fortnight."*

Fourteen days from November the sixteenth meant November the thirtieth, the day the rubber trumpet was found on the line.

One rubber trumpet is dropped on railway line by (possibly) a young woman. The young woman is subsequently murdered (but not with a rubber trumpet). A young man behaves in an eccentric way with seventy-seven rubber trumpets more than six months later.

The connexion was wholly illogical. But the Department specialized in illogical connexions. It communicated its wild guess—in the form of a guarded Minute—to Detective-Inspector Rason.

Rason went down to Banbury and brought the old Fairbrass couple to Walham.

He gave them five shillings and sent them into Arrowsmith's to buy a hot-water bottle.

INSPECTOR WEXFORD

The most recent of our Britannic investigators, Inspector Reginald Wexford, initially appeared in 1964 in From Doon with Death. This was Ruth Rendell's first published novel, although she had written several others. "I wrote many novels before my first was accepted," she has said. "The first novel I did submit to a publisher was a sort of drawing room comedy.... This was kept for a long time and then returned ... and they asked if I had done anything else. I had written a detective story just for my own entertainment...." And that was how Inspector Wexford came into the world. He soon became one of the most popular of current British detectives. Not quite the traditional police inspector, Wexford grows and changes from novel to novel. In her subsequent novels about him, Ruth Rendell has chosen to deal "with the psychological, emotional aspects of human nature rather than the puzzle, forensics...." In our story you'll find Wexford and his associate, Burden, dealing with both the psychological and the forensic.

Means of Evil
by Ruth Rendell

"Blewits," said Inspector Burden, "parasols, horns of plenty, morels and boletus. Mean anything to you?"

Chief Inspector Wexford shrugged. "Sounds like one of

those magazine quizzes. What have these in common? I'll make a guess and say they're crustacea. Or sea anemones. How about that?"

"They are edible fungi," said Burden.

"Are they now? And what have edible fungi to do with Mrs. Hannah Kingman throwing herself off, or being pushed off, a balcony?"

The two men were sitting in Wexford's office at the police station, Kingsmarkham, in the County of Sussex. The month was November, but Wexford had only just returned from his holiday. And while he had been away, enjoying in Cornwall an end of October that had been more summery than the summer, Hannah Kingman had committed suicide. Or so Burden had thought at first. Now he was in a dilemma, and as soon as Wexford had walked in that Monday morning, Burden had begun to tell the whole story to his chief.

Wexford, getting on for sixty, was a tall, ungainly, rather ugly man who had once been fat to the point of obesity but had slimmed to gauntness for reasons of health. Nearly twenty years his junior, Burden had the slenderness of a man who has always been thin. His face was ascetic, handsome in a frosty way. The older man, who had a good wife who looked after him devotedly, nevertheless always looked as if his clothes came off the peg from the War on Want Shop, while the younger, a widower, was sartorially immaculate. A tramp and a Beau Brummell, they seemed to be, but the dandy relied on the tramp, trusted him, understood his powers and his perception. In secret he almost worshipped him.

Without his chief he had felt a little at sea in this case. Everything had pointed at first to Hannah Kingman's having killed herself. She had been a manic-depressive, with a strong sense of her own inadequacy; apparently her marriage, though not of long duration, had been unhappy, and her previous marriage had failed. Even in the absence of a suicide note or suicide threats, Burden would have taken her death for self-destruction—if her brother hadn't come along and told him about the edible fungi. And Wexford hadn't been there to do what he always could do, sort out sheep from goats and wheat from chaff.

"The thing is," Burden said across the desk, "we're not looking for proof of murder so much as proof of *attempted* murder. Axel Kingman could have pushed his wife off that balcony—he has no alibi for the time in question—but I had no reason to think he had done so until I was told of an attempt to murder her some two weeks before."

"Which attempt has something to do with edible fungi?"

Burden nodded. "Say with administering to her some noxious substance in a stew made from edible fungi. Though if he did it, God knows how he did it, because three other people, including himself, ate the stew without ill effects. I think I'd better tell you about it from the beginning."

"I think you had," said Wexford.

"The facts," Burden began, very like a Prosecuting Counsel, "are as follows. Axel Kingman is thirty-five years old and he keeps a health-food shop here in the High Street called Harvest Home. Know it?" When Wexford signified by a nod that he did, Burden went on, "He used to be a teacher in Myringham, and for about seven years before he came here he'd been living with a woman named Corinne Last. He left her, gave up his job, put all the capital he had into this shop, and married a Mrs. Hannah Nicholson."

"He's some sort of food freak, I take it," said Wexford.

Burden wrinkled his nose. "Lot of affected nonsense," he said. "Have you ever noticed what thin pale weeds these health-food people are? While the folks who live on roast beef and suet and whisky and plum cake are full of beans and rarin' to go."

"Is Kingman a thin pale weed?"

"A feeble—what's the word?—aesthete, if you ask me. Anyway, he and Hannah opened this shop and took a flat in the high-rise tower our planning geniuses have been pleased to raise over the top of it. The fifth floor. Corinne Last, according to her and according to Kingman, accepted the situation after a while and they all remained friends."

"Tell me about them," Wexford said. "Leave the facts for a bit and tell me about them."

Burden never found this easy. He was inclined to describe people as "just ordinary" or "just like anyone else," a negative attitude which exasperated Wexford. So he made an effort. "Kingman looks the sort who wouldn't hurt a fly. The fact is, I'd apply the word gentle to him if I wasn't coming round to thinking he's a cold-blooded wife-killer. He's a total abstainer with a bee in his bonnet about drink. His father went bankrupt and finally died of alcoholism, and our Kingman is an anti-booze fanatic.

"The dead woman was twenty-nine. Her first husband left her after six months of marriage and went off with some girl friend of hers. Hannah went back to live with her parents 'and had a part-time job helping with the meals at the school where Kingman was a teacher. That was where they met."

"And the other woman?" said Wexford.

Burden's face took on a repressive expression. Sex outside marriage, however sanctioned by custom and general approval, was always distasteful to him. That, in the course of his work, he almost daily came across illicit sex had done nothing to mitigate his disapproval. As Wexford sometimes derisively put it, you would think that in Burden's eyes all the suffering in the world, and certainly all the crime, somehow derived from men and women going to bed together outside the bonds of wedlock. "God knows why he didn't marry her," Burden now said. "Personally I think things were a lot better in the days when education authorities put their foot down about immorality among teachers."

"Let's not have your views on that now, Mike," said Wexford. "Presumably Hannah Kingman didn't die because her husband didn't come to her a pure virgin."

Burden flushed slightly. "I'll tell you about this Corinne Last. She's very good-looking, if you like the dark sort of intense type. Her father left her some money and the house where she and Kingman lived, and she still lives in it. She's one of those women who seem to be good at everything they put their hands to. She paints and sells her paintings. She makes her own clothes, she's more or less the star in the local dramatic society, she's a violinist and plays in some string trio. Also she writes for health magazines and she's the author of a cookery book."

"It would look then," Wexford put in, "as if Kingman split up with her because all this was more than he could take. And hence he took up with the dull little school-meals lady. No competition from her, I fancy."

"I daresay you're right. As a matter of fact, that theory has already been put to me."

"By whom?" said Wexford. "Just where did you get all this information, Mike?"

"From an angry young man, the fourth member of the quartet, who happens to be Hannah's brother. His name is John Hood and I think he's got a lot more to tell. But it's time I left off describing the people and got on with the story.

"No one saw Hannah fall from the balcony. It happened last Thursday afternoon at about four. According to her husband, he was in a sort of office behind the shop doing what he always did on early-closing day—stock-taking and sticking labels on various bottles and packets.

"She fell onto a hard-top parking area at the back of the flats, and her body was found by a neighbour a couple of hours later between two parked cars. We were sent for, and Kingman seemed to be distraught. I asked him if he had had any idea that his wife might have wished to take her own life and he said she had never threatened to do so but had lately been very depressed and there had been quarrels, principally about money. Her doctor had put her on tranquillizers—of which, by the way, Kingman disapproved—and the doctor himself, old Dr. Castle, told me Mrs. Kingman had been to him for depression and because she felt her life wasn't worth living and she was a drag on her husband. He wasn't surprised that she had killed herself and neither, by that time, was I. We were all set for an inquest verdict of suicide while the balance of the mind was disturbed when John Hood walked in here and told me Kingman had attempted to murder his wife on a previous occasion."

"He told you just like that?"

"Pretty well. It's plain he doesn't like Kingman, and no doubt he was fond of his sister. He also seems to like and admire Corinne Last. He told me that on a Saturday night at the end of October the four of them had a meal together in the Kingmans' flat. It was a lot of vegetarian stuff cooked by Kingman—he always did the cooking—and one of the dishes was made out of what I'm old-fashioned enough, or narrow-minded enough, to call toadstools. They all ate it and they were all OK but for Hannah, who got up from the table, vomited for hours, and apparently was quite seriously ill."

Wexford's eyebrows went up. "Elucidate, please," he said.

Burden sat back, put his elbows on the arms of the chair,

and pressed the tips of his fingers together. "A few days before this meal was eaten, Kingman and Hood met at the squash club of which they are both members. Kingman told Hood that Corinne Last had promised to get him some edible fungi called shaggy caps from her own garden, the garden of the house which they had at one time shared. A crop of these things show themselves every autumn under a tree in this garden. I've seen them myself, but we'll come to that in a minute.

"Kingman's got a thing about using weeds and whatnot for cooking, makes salads out of dandelion and sorrel, and he swears by this fungi rubbish, says they've got far more flavour than mushrooms. Give me something that comes in a plastic bag from the supermarket every time, but no doubt it takes all sorts to make a world. By the way, this cookbook of Corinne Last's is called *Cooking for Nothing*, and all the recipes are for making dishes out of stuff you pull up by the wayside or pluck from the hedgerow."

"These warty blobs or spotted puffets or whatever, had he cooked them before?"

"Shaggy caps," said Burden, grinning, "or *coprinus comatus*. Oh, yes, every year, and every year he and Corinne had eaten the resulting stew. He told Hood he was going to cook them again this time, and Hood says he seemed very grateful to Corinne for being so—well, magnanimous."

"Yes, I can see it would have been a wrench for her. Like hearing 'our tune' in the company of your ex-lover and your supplanter." Wexford put on a vibrant growl. " 'Can you bear the sight of me eating our toadstools with another?' "

"As a matter of fact," said Burden seriously, "it could have been just like that. Anyway, the upshot of it was that Hood was invited round for the following Saturday to taste these delicacies and was told that Corinne would be there. Perhaps it was that fact which made him accept. Well, the day came. Hood looked in on his sister at lunchtime. She showed him the pot containing the stew which Kingman had already made and she said *she had tasted it* and it was delicious. She also showed Hood half a dozen specimens of shaggy caps which she said Kingman hadn't needed and which they would fry for their breakfast. This is what she showed him."

Burden opened a drawer in the desk and produced one of

those plastic bags which he had said so inspired him with confidence. But the contents of this one hadn't come from a supermarket. He removed the wire fastener and tipped out four whitish scaly objects. They were egg-shaped, or rather elongated ovals, each with a short fleshy stalk.

"I picked them myself this morning," he said, "from Corinne Last's garden. When they get bigger, the egg-shaped bit opens like an umbrella, or a pagoda really, and there are sort of black gills underneath. You're supposed to eat them when they're in the stage these are."

"I suppose you've got a book on fungi?" said Wexford.

"Here." This also was produced from the drawer. *British Fungi, Edible and Poisonous.* "And here we are—shaggy caps."

Burden had opened it at the *Edible* section and at a line and wash drawing of the species he held in his hand. He passed it to the chief inspector.

"*Coprinus Comatus,*" Wexford read aloud, "*a common species, attaining when full-grown a height of nine inches. The fungus is frequently to be found, during late summer and autumn, growing in fields, hedgerows and often in gardens. It should be eaten before the cap opens and disgorges its inky fluid, but is at all times quite harmless.*" He put the book down but didn't close it. "Go on, please, Mike," he said.

"Hood called for Corinne and they arrived together. They got there just after eight. At about eight-fifteen they all sat down to table and began the meal with avocado *vinaigrette*. The next course was to be the stew, followed by nut cutlets with a salad and then an applecake. Very obviously, there was no wine or liquor of any sort on account of Kingman's prejudice. They drank grape juice from the shop.

"The kitchen opens directly out of the living-dining room. Kingman brought in the stew in a large tureen and served it himself at the table, beginning, of course, with Corinne. Each one of those shaggy caps had been sliced in half lengthwise and the pieces were floating in a thickish gravy to which carrots, onions and other vegetables had been added. Now, ever since he had been invited to this meal, Hood had been feeling uneasy about eating fungi, but Corinne had reassured him, and once he began to eat it and saw the others were eating it quite happily, he stopped worrying for the time being. In fact, he had a second helping.

"Kingman took the plates out and the tureen and immediately *rinsed them under the tap*. Both Hood and Corinne Last have told me this, though Kingman says it was something he always did, being fastidious about things of that sort."

"Surely his ex-girl friend could confirm or deny that," Wexford put in, "since they lived together for so long."

"We must ask her. All traces of the stew were rinsed away. Kingman then brought in the nut concoction and the salad, but before he could begin to serve them Hannah jumped up, covered her mouth with her napkin, and rushed to the bathroom.

"After a while Corinne went to her. Hood could hear a violent vomiting from the bathroom. He remained in the living room while Kingman and Corinne were both in the bathroom with Hannah. No one ate any more. Kingman eventually came back, said that Hannah must have picked up some 'bug' and that he had put her to bed. Hood went into the bedroom where Hannah was lying on the bed with Corinne beside her. Hannah's face was greenish and covered with sweat and she was evidently in great pain because while he was there she doubled up and groaned. She had to go to the bathroom again and that time Kingman had to carry her back.

"Hood suggested Dr. Castle should be sent for, but this was strenuously opposed by Kingman who dislikes doctors and is one of those people who go in for herbal remedies—raspberry leaf tablets and camomile tea and that sort of thing. Also he told Hood rather absurdly that Hannah had had quite enough to do with doctors and that if this wasn't some gastric germ it was the result of her taking 'dangerous' tranquillizers.

"Hood thought Hannah was seriously ill and the argument got heated, with Hood trying to make Kingman either call a doctor or take her to a hospital. Kingman wouldn't and Corinne took his part. Hood is one of those angry but weak people who are all bluster, and although he might have called a doctor himself, he didn't. The effect on him of Corinne again, I suppose. What he did do was tell Kingman he was a fool to mess about cooking things everyone knew weren't safe, to which Kingman replied that if the shaggy caps were dangerous, how was it they weren't all ill? Eventually, at about midnight, Hannah stopped retching, seemed to have no more pain, and fell asleep. Hood drove Corinne home, returned to the Kingmans' and remained there for the rest of the night, sleeping on their sofa.

"In the morning Hannah seemed perfectly well, though weak, which rather upset Kingman's theory about the gastric bug. Relations between the brothers-in-law were strained. Kingman said he hadn't liked Hood's suggestions and that when he wanted to see his sister he, Kingman, would rather he came there when he was out or in the shop. Hood went off home, and since that day he hasn't seen Kingman.

"The day after his sister's death he stormed in here, told me what I've told you, and accused Kingman of trying to poison Hannah. He was wild and nearly hysterical, but I felt I couldn't dismiss this allegation as—well, the ravings of a bereaved person. There were too many peculiar circumstances, the unhappiness of the marriage, the fact of Kingman rinsing those plates, his refusal to call a doctor. Was I right?"

Burden stopped and sat waiting for approval. It came in the form of a not very enthusiastic nod.

After a moment Wexford spoke. "Could Kingman have pushed her off that balcony, Mike?"

"She was a small fragile woman. It was physically possible. The back of the flats isn't overlooked. There's nothing behind but the parking area and then open fields. Kingman could have gone up by the stairs instead of using the lift and come down by the stairs. Two of the flats on the lower floors are empty. Below the Kingmans lives a bedridden woman whose husband was at work. Below that the tenant, a young married woman, was in but she saw and heard nothing. The invalid says she thinks she heard a scream during the afternoon but she did nothing about it, and if she did hear it, so what? It seems to me that a suicide, in those circumstances, is as likely to cry out as a murder victim."

"OK," said Wexford. "Now to return to the curious business of this meal. The idea would presumably be that Kingman intended to kill her that night but that his plan misfired because whatever he gave her wasn't toxic enough. She was very ill but she didn't die. He chose those means and that company so that he would have witnesses to his innocence. They all ate the stew out of the same tureen, but only Hannah was affected by it. How then are you suggesting he gave her whatever poison he did give her?"

"I'm not," said Burden frankly, "but others are making suggestions. Hood's a bit of a fool, and first of all he would only keep on about all fungi being dangerous and the whole dish being poisonous. When I pointed out that this was obviously not so, he said Kingman must have slipped something into Hannah's plate, or else it was the salt."

"What salt?"

"He remembered that no one but Hannah took salt with the stew. But that's absurd because Kingman couldn't have known that would happen. And, incidentally, to another point we may as well clear up now—the avocados were quite innocuous. Kingman halved them *at the table* and the *vinaigrette* sauce was served in a jug. The bread was not in the form of rolls but a home-made wholemeal loaf. If there was anything there which shouldn't have been it was in the stew all right.

"Corinne Last refuses to consider the possibility that Kingman might be guilty. But when I pressed her she said she was not actually sitting at the table while the stew was served. She had got up and gone into the hall to fetch her handbag. So she didn't see Kingman serve Hannah." Burden reached across and picked up the book Wexford had left open at the description and drawing of the shaggy caps. He flicked over to the *Poisonous* section and pushed the book back to Wexford. "Have a look at some of these."

"Ah, yes," said Wexford. "Our old friend, the fly agaric. A nice-looking little red job with white spots, much favoured by illustrators of children's books. They usually stick a frog on top of it and a gnome underneath. I see that when ingested it causes nausea, vomiting, tetanic convulsions, coma and death. Lots of these agarics, aren't there? Purple, crested, warty, verdigris—all more or less lethal. Aha! The death cap, *amanita phalloides*. How very unpleasant. The most dangerous fungus known, it says here. Very small quantities will cause intense suffering and often death. So where does all that get us?"

"The death cap, according to Corinne Last, is quite common round here. What she doesn't say, but what I infer, is that Kingman could have got hold of it easily. Now suppose he cooked just one specimen separately and dropped it into the stew just before he brought it in from the kitchen? When he comes to serve Hannah he spoons up for her this specimen, or the pieces of it, in the same way as someone might select a special piece of chicken for someone out of a casserole. The gravy was thick, it wasn't like thin soup."

Wexford looked dubious. "Well, we won't dismiss it as a theory. If he had contaminated the rest of the stew and others had been ill, that would have made it look even more like an accident, which was presumably what he wanted. But there's one drawback to that, Mike. If he meant Hannah to die, and was unscrupulous enough not to mind about Corinne and Hood being made ill, why did he rinse the plates? To *prove* that it was an accident, he would have wanted above all to keep some of that stew for analysis when the time came, for analysis would have shown the presence of poisonous as well as non-poisonous fungi, and it would have seemed that he had merely been careless.

"But let's go and talk to these people, shall we?"

The shop called Harvest Home was closed. Wexford and Burden went down an alley at the side of the block, passed the glass-doored main entrance, and went to the back to a door that was labelled *Stairs and Emergency Exit*. They entered a small tiled vestibule and began to mount a steepish flight of stairs.

On each floor was a front door and a door to the lift. There was no one about. If there had been and they had had no wish to be seen, it would only have been necessary to wait behind the bend in the stairs until whoever it was had got into the lift. The bell by the front door on the fifth floor was marked *A. and H. Kingman*. Wexford rang it.

The man who admitted them was smallish and mild-looking and he looked sad. He showed Wexford the balcony from which his wife had fallen. It was one of two in the flat, the other being larger and extending outside the living-room windows. This one was outside a glazed kitchen door, a place for hanging washing or for gardening of the window-box variety. Herbs grew in pots, and in a long trough there still remained frost-bitten tomato vines. The wall surrounding the balcony

was about three feet high, the drop sheer to the hard-top below.

"Were you surprised that your wife committed suicide, Mr.
Kingman?" said Wexford.

Kingman didn't answer directly. "My wife set a very low
valuation on herself. When we got married I thought she was
like me, a simple sort of person who doesn't ask much from
life but has quite a capacity for contentment. It wasn't like
that. She expected more support and more comfort and en-
couragement than I could give. That was especially so for the
first three months of our marriage. Then she seemed to turn
against me. She was very moody, always up and down. My
business isn't doing very well and she was spending more
money than we could afford. I don't know where all the
money was going and we quarrelled about it. Then she'd become depressed and say she was no use to me, she'd be better
dead."

He had given, Wexford thought, rather a long explanation
for which he hadn't been asked. But it could be that these
thoughts, defensive yet self-reproachful, were at the moment
uppermost in his mind. "Mr. Kingman," he said, "we have
reason to believe, as you know, that foul play may have been
involved here. I should like to ask you a few questions about
a meal you cooked on October 29th, after which your wife
was ill."

"I can guess who's been telling you about that."

Wexford took no notice. "When did Miss Last bring you
these—er, shaggy caps?"

"On the evening of the 28th. I made the stew from them in
the morning, according to Miss Last's own recipe."

"Was there any other type of fungus in the flat at the
time?"

"Mushrooms, probably."

"Did you at any time add any noxious object or substance
to that stew, Mr. Kingman?"

Kingman said quietly, wearily, "Of course not. My
brother-in-law has a lot of ignorant prejudices. He refuses to
understand that that stew, which I have made dozens of times
before in exactly the same way, was as wholesome as, say, a
chicken casserole. More wholesome, in my view."

"Very well. Nevertheless, your wife was very ill. Why didn't you call a doctor?"

"Because my wife was not 'very' ill. She had pains and diarrhoea, that's all. Perhaps you aren't aware of what the symptoms of fungus poisoning are. The victim doesn't just have pain and sickness. His vision is impaired, he very likely blacks out or has convulsions of the kind associated with tetanus. There was nothing like that with Hannah."

"It was unfortunate that you rinsed those plates. Had you not done so and called a doctor, the remains of that stew would almost certainly have been sent for analysis, and if it was harmless as you say, all this investigation could have been avoided."

"It was harmless," Kingman said stonily.

Out in the car Wexford said, "I'm inclined to believe him, Mike. And unless Hood or Corinne Last has something really positive to tell us, I'd let it rest. Shall we go and see her next?"

The cottage Corinne had shared with Axel Kingman was on a lonely stretch of road outside the village of Myfleet. It was a stone cottage with a slate roof, surrounded by a well-tended pretty garden. A green Ford Escort stood on the drive in front of a weatherboard garage. Under a big old apple tree, from which the yellow leaves were falling, the shaggy caps, immediately recognisable, grew in three thick clumps.

She was a tall woman, the owner of this house, with a beautiful, square-jawed, high-cheekboned face and a mass of dark hair. Wexford was at once reminded of the Klimt painting of a languorous red-lipped woman, gold-necklaced, half covered in gold draperies, though Corinne Last wore a sweater and a denim smock. Her voice was low and measured. He had the impression she could never be flustered or caught off her guard.

"You're the author of a cookery book, I believe?" he said.

She made no answer but handed him a paperback which she took down from a bookshelf. *Cooking for Nothing. Dishes from Hedgerow and Pasture* by Corinne Last. He looked through the index and found the recipe he wanted. Opposite it was a coloured photograph of six people eating what looked like brown soup. The recipe included carrots, onions, herbs, cream, and a number of other harmless ingredients. The last lines read: *Stewed shaggy caps are best served piping hot with wholewheat bread. For drinkables, see page 171.* He glanced at page 171, then handed the book to Burden.

"This was the dish Mr. Kingman made that night?"

"Yes." She had a way of leaning back when she spoke and of half lowering her heavy glossy eyelids. It was serpentine and a little repellent. "I picked the shaggy caps myself out of this garden. I don't understand how they could have made Hannah ill, but they must have done because she was fine when we first arrived. She hadn't got any sort of gastric infection, that's nonsense."

Burden put the book aside. "But you were all served stew out of the same tureen."

"I didn't see Axel actually serve Hannah. I was out of the room." The eyelids flickered and almost closed.

"Was it usual for Mr. Kingman to rinse plates as soon as they were removed?"

"Don't ask me." She moved her shoulders. "I don't know. I do know that Hannah was very ill just after eating that stew. Axel doesn't like doctors, of course, and perhaps it would have—well, embarrassed him to call Dr. Castle in the circumstances. Hannah had black spots in front of her eyes, she was getting double vision. I was extremely concerned for her."

"But you didn't take it on yourself to get a doctor, Miss Last? Or even support Mr. Hood in his allegations?"

"Whatever John Hood said, I knew it couldn't be the shaggy caps." There was a note of scorn when she spoke Hood's name. "And I was rather frightened. I couldn't help thinking it would be terrible if Axel got into some sort of trouble, if there was an inquiry or something."

"There's an inquiry now, Miss Last."

"Well, it's different now, isn't it? Hannah's dead. I mean, it's not just suspicion or conjecture any more."

She saw them out and closed the front door before they had reached the garden gate. Farther along the roadside and under the hedges more shaggy caps could be seen as well as other kinds of fungi Wexford couldn't identify—little mushroom-like things with pinkish gills, a cluster of small yellow umbrellas, and on the trunk of an oak tree, bulbous smoke-coloured swellings that Burden said were oyster mushrooms.

"That woman," said Wexford, "is a mistress of the artless insinuation. She damned Kingman with almost every word, but she never came out with anything like an accusation." He shook his head. "I suppose Kingman's brother-in-law will be at work?"

"Presumably," said Burden, but John Hood was not at work. He was waiting for them at the police station, fuming at the delay, and threatening "if something wasn't done at once" to take his grievances to the Chief Constable, even to the Home Office.

"Something is being done," said Wexford quietly. "I'm glad you've come here, Mr. Hood. But try to keep calm, will you, please?"

It was apparent to Wexford from the first that John Hood was in a different category of intelligence from that of Kingman and Corinne Last. He was a thick-set man of perhaps no more than twenty-seven or twenty-eight, with bewildered, resentful blue eyes in a puffy flushed face. A man, Wexford thought, who would fling out rash accusations he couldn't substantiate, who would be driven to bombast and bluster in the company of the ex-teacher and that clever subtle woman.

He began to talk now, not wildly, but still without restraint, repeating what he had said to Burden, reiterating, without putting forward any real evidence, that his brother-in-law had meant to kill his sister that night. It was only by luck that she had survived. Kingman was a ruthless man who would have stopped at nothing to be rid of her. He, Hood, would never forgive himself that he hadn't made a stand and called the doctor.

"Yes, yes, Mr. Hood, but what exactly were your sister's symptoms?"

"Vomiting and stomach pains, violent pains," said Hood.

"She complained of nothing else?"

"Wasn't that enough? That's what you get when someone feeds you poisonous rubbish."

Wexford merely raised his eyebrows. Abruptly, he left the events of that evening and said, "What had gone wrong with your sister's marriage?"

Before Hood replied, Wexford could sense he was keeping

something back. A wariness came into his eyes and then was gone. "Axel wasn't the right person for her," he began. "She had problems, she needed understanding, she wasn't . . ." His voice trailed away.

"Wasn't what, Mr. Hood? What problems?"

"It's got nothing to do with all this," Hood muttered.

"I'll be the judge of that. You made this accusation, you started this business off. It's not for you now to keep anything back." On a sudden inspiration, Wexford said, "Had these problems anything to do with the money she was spending?"

Hood was silent and sullen. Wexford thought rapidly over the things he had been told—Axel Kingman's fanaticism on one particular subject, Hannah's desperate need of an unspecified kind of support during the early days of her marriage. Later on, her alternating moods, and then the money, the weekly sums of money spent and unaccounted for.

He looked up and said baldly, "Was your sister an alcoholic, Mr. Hood?"

Hood hadn't liked this directness. He flushed and looked affronted. He skirted round a frank answer. Well, yes, she drank. She was at pains to conceal her drinking. It had been going on more or less consistently since her first marriage broke up.

"In fact, she was an alcoholic," said Wexford.

"I suppose so."

"Your brother-in-law didn't know?"

"Good God, no. Axel would have killed her!" He realised what he had said. "Maybe that's why. Maybe he found out."

"I don't think so, Mr. Hood. Now I imagine that in the first few months of her marriage she made an effort to give up drinking. She needed a good deal of support during this time but she couldn't, or wouldn't, tell Mr. Kingman why she needed it. Her efforts failed, and slowly, because she couldn't manage without it, she began drinking again."

"She wasn't as bad as she used to be," Hood said with pathetic eagerness. "And only in the evenings. She told me she never had a drink before six, and after that she'd have a few more, gulping them down on the quiet so Axel wouldn't know."

Burden said suddenly, "Had your sister been drinking that evening?"

"I expect so. She wouldn't have been able to face company, not even just Corinne and me, without a drink."

"Did anyone besides yourself know that your sister drank?"

"My mother did. My mother and I had a sort of pact to keep it dark from everyone so that Axel wouldn't find out." He hesitated and then said rather defiantly, "I did tell Corinne. She's a wonderful person, she's very clever. I was worried about it and I didn't know what to do. She promised she wouldn't tell Axel."

"I see." Wexford had his own reasons for thinking she hadn't done so. Deep in thought, he got up and walked to the other end of the room where he stood gazing out of the window. Burden's continuing questions, Hood's answers, reached him only as a confused murmur of voices. Then he heard Burden say more loudly, "That's all for now, Mr. Hood, unless the chief inspector has anything more to ask you."

"No, no," said Wexford abstractedly, and when Hood had somewhat truculently departed, "Time for lunch. It's past two. Personally, I shall avoid any dish containing fungi, even *psalliota compestris.*"

After Burden had looked that one up and identified it as the common mushroom, they lunched and then made a round of such wineshops in Kingsmarkham as were open at that hour. At the Wine Basket they drew a blank, but the assistant in the Vineyard told them that a woman answering Hannah Kingman's description had been a regular customer, and that on the previous Wednesday, the day before her death, she had called in and bought a bottle of Courvoisier Cognac.

"There was no liquor of any kind in Kingman's flat," said Burden. "Might have been an empty bottle in the rubbish, I suppose." He made a rueful face. "We didn't look, didn't think we had any reason to. But she couldn't have drunk a whole bottleful on the Wednesday, could she?"

"Why are you so interested in this drinking business, Mike? You don't seriously see it as a motive for murder, do you? That Kingman killed her because he'd found out, or been told, that she was a secret drinker?"

"It was a means, not a motive," said Burden. "I know how it was done. I know how Kingman tried to kill her that first time." He grinned. "Makes a change for me to find the answer before you, doesn't it? I'm going to follow in your footsteps and make a mystery of it for the time being, if you don't mind. With your permission we'll go back to the station, pick up those shaggy caps and conduct a little experiment."

Michael Burden lived in a neat bungalow in Tabard Road. He had lived there with his wife until her untimely death and continued to live there with his sixteen-year-old daughter, his son being away at university. But that evening Pat Burden was out with her boy friend, and there was a note left for her father on the refrigerator. *Dad, I ate the cold beef from yesterday. Can you open a tin for yourself? Back by 10.30. Love, P.*

Burden read this note several times, his expression of consternation deepening with each perusal. And Wexford could precisely have defined the separate causes which brought that look of weariness into Burden's eyes, that frown, that drooping of the mouth. Because she was motherless his daughter had to eat not only cold but leftover food, she who should be carefree was obliged to worry about her father, loneliness drove her out of her home until the appallingly late hour of half-past ten. It was all nonsense, of course, the Burden children were happy and recovered from their loss, but how to make Burden see it that way? Widowhood was something he dragged about with him like a physical infirmity. He looked up from the note, screwed it up and eyed his surroundings vaguely and with a kind of despair. Wexford knew that look of desolation. He saw it on Burden's face each time he accompanied him home.

It evoked exasperation as well as pity. He wanted to tell Burden—once or twice he had done so—to stop treating John and Pat like retarded paranoiacs, but instead he said lightly, "I read somewhere the other day that it wouldn't do us a scrap of harm if we never ate another hot meal as long as we lived. In fact, the colder and rawer the better."

"You sound like the Axel Kingman brigade," said Burden, rallying and laughing which was what Wexford had meant him to do. "Anyway, I'm glad she didn't cook anything. I shouldn't have been able to eat it and I'd hate her to take it as criticism."

Wexford decided to ignore that one. "While you're deciding just how much I'm to be told about this experiment of yours, d'you mind if I phone my wife?"

"Be my guest."

It was nearly six. Wexford came back to find Burden peeling carrots and onions. The four specimens of *coprinus comatus*, beginning to look a little wizened, lay on a chopping board. On the stove a saucepanful of bone stock was heating up.

"What the hell are you doing?"

"Making shaggy cap stew. My theory is that the stew is harmless when eaten by non-drinkers, and toxic, or toxic to some extent, when taken by those with alcohol in the stomach. How about that? In a minute, when this lot's cooking, I'm going to take a moderate quantity of alcohol, then I'm going to eat the stew. Now say I'm a damned fool if you like."

Wexford shrugged. He grinned. "I'm overcome by so much courage and selfless devotion to the duty you owe the taxpayers. But wait a minute. Are you sure only Hannah had been drinking that night? We know Kingman hadn't. What about the other two?"

"I asked Hood that when you were off in your daydream. He called for Corinne Last at six, at her request. They picked some apples for his mother, then she made him coffee. He did suggest they call in at a pub for a drink on their way to the Kingmans', but apparently she took so long getting ready that they didn't have time."

"OK. Go ahead then. But wouldn't it be easier to call in an expert? There must be such people. Very likely someone holds a chair of fungology or whatever it's called at the University of the South."

"Very likely. We can do that after I've tried it. I want to know for sure *now*. Are you willing to?"

"Certainly not. I'm not your guest to that extent. Since I've told my wife I won't be home for dinner, I'll take it as a kindness if you'll make me some innocent scrambled eggs."

He followed Burden into the living room where the inspector opened a door in the sideboard. "What'll you drink?"

"White wine, if you've got any, or vermouth if you haven't. You know how abstemious I have to be."

Burden poured vermouth and soda. "Ice?"

"No, thanks. What are you going to have? Brandy? That was Hannah Kingman's favourite tipple apparently."

"Haven't got any," said Burden. "It'll have to be whisky. I think we can reckon she had two double brandies before that meal, don't you? I'm not so brave I want to be as ill as she was." He caught Wexford's eye. "You don't think some people could be more sensitive to it than others, do you?"

"Bound to be," said Wexford breezily. "Cheers!"

Burden sipped his heavily watered whisky, then tossed it down. "I'll just have a look at my stew. You sit down. Put the television on."

Wexford obeyed him. The big coloured picture was of a wood in autumn, pale blue sky, golden beech leaves. Then the camera closed in on a cluster of red-and-white-spotted fly agaric. Chuckling, Wexford turned it off as Burden put his head round the door.

"I think it's more or less ready."

"Better have another whisky."

"I suppose I had." Burden came in and re-filled his glass. "That ought to do it."

"What about my eggs?"

"Oh, God, I forgot. I'm not much of a cook, you know. Don't know how women manage to get a whole lot of different things brewing and make them synchronise."

"It is a mystery, isn't it? I'll get myself some bread and cheese, if I may."

The brownish mixture was in a soup bowl. In the gravy floated four shaggy caps, cut lengthwise. Burden finished his whisky at a gulp.

"What was it the Christians in the arena used to say to the Roman Emperor before they went to the lions?"

"*Morituri, te salutamus,*" said Wexford. " 'We who are about to die salute thee.' "

"Well . . ." Burden made an effort with the Latin he had culled from his son's homework. "*Moriturus, te saluto.* Would that be right?"

"I daresay. You won't die, though."

Burden made no answer. He picked up his spoon and began to eat. "Can I have some more soda?" said Wexford.

There are perhaps few stabs harder to bear than derision directed at one's heroism. Burden gave him a sour look. "Help yourself. I'm busy."

Wexford did so. "What's it like?" he said.

"All right. It's quite nice, like mushrooms."

Doggedly he ate. He didn't once gag on it. He finished the lot and wiped the bowl round with a piece of bread. Then he sat up, holding himself rather tensely.

"May as well have your telly on now," said Wexford. "Pass the time." He switched it on again. No fly agaric this time, but a dog fox moving across a meadow with Vivaldi playing. "How d'you feel?"

"Fine," said Burden gloomily.

"Cheer up. It may not last."

But it did. After fifteen minutes had passed, Burden still felt perfectly well. He looked bewildered. "I was so damned positive. I *knew* I was going to be retching and vomiting by now. I didn't put the car away because I was certain you'd have to run me down to the hospital."

Wexford only raised his eyebrows.

"You were pretty casual about it, I must say. Didn't say a word to stop me, did you? Didn't it occur to you it might have been a bit awkward for you if anything had happened to me?"

"I knew it wouldn't. I said to get a fungologist." And then Wexford, faced by Burden's aggrieved stare, burst out laughing. "Dear old Mike, you'll have to forgive me. But you know me, d'you honestly think I'd have let you risk your life eating that stuff? I knew you were safe."

"May one ask how?"

"One may. And you'd have known too if you'd bothered to take a proper look at that book of Corinne Last's. Under the recipe for shaggy cap stew it said, 'For drinkables, see page 171.' Well, I looked at page 171, and there Miss Last gave a recipe for cowslip wine and another for sloe gin, both highly intoxicating drinks. Would she have recommended a wine and a spirit to drink with those fungi if there'd been the slightest risk? Not if she wanted to sell her book she wouldn't. Not unless she was risking hundreds of furious letters and expensive lawsuits."

Burden had flushed a little. Then he too began to laugh.

After a little while they had coffee.

"A little logical thinking would be in order, I fancy," said Wexford. "You said this morning that we were not so much seeking to prove murder as attempted murder. Axel Kingman could have pushed her off that balcony, but no one saw her fall and no one heard him or anybody else go up to that flat during the afternoon. If, however, an attempt to murder her was made two weeks before, the presumption that she was eventually murdered is enormously strengthened."

Burden said impatiently, "We've been through all that. We know that."

"Wait a minute. The attempt failed. Now just how seriously ill was she? According to Kingman and Hood, she had severe stomach pains and she vomited. By midnight she was peacefully sleeping and by the following day she was all right."

"I don't see where all this is getting us."

"To a point which is very important and which may be the crux of the whole case. You say that Axel Kingman attempted to murder her. In order to do so he must have made very elaborate plans—the arranging of the meal, the inviting of the two witnesses, the ensuring that his wife tasted the stew earlier in the same day, and the preparation for some very nifty sleight of hand at the time the meal was served. Isn't it odd that the actual method used should so signally have failed? That Hannah's *life* never seemed to have been in danger? And what if the method had succeeded? At post-mortem some noxious agent would have been found in her body or the effects of such. How could he have hoped to get away with that since, as we know, neither of his witnesses actually watched him serve Hannah and one of them was even out of the room?

"So what I am postulating is that no one attempted to murder her, but someone *attempted* to make her ill so that, taken in conjunction with the sinister reputation of nonmushroom fungi and Hood's admitted suspicion of them, taken in conjunction with the known unhappiness of the marriage, *it would look as if there had been a murder attempt.*"

Burden stared at him. "Kingman would never have done that. He would either have wanted his attempt to succeed or not to have looked like an attempt at all."

"Exactly. And where does that get us?"

Instead of answering him, Burden said on a note of triumph, his humiliation still rankling, "You're wrong about one thing. She *was* seriously ill, she didn't just have nausea and vomiting. Kingman and Hood may not have mentioned it, but Corinne Last said she had double vision and black spots before her eyes and . . ." His voice faltered. "My God, you mean . . . ?"

Wexford nodded. "Corinne Last only of the three says she had those symptoms. Only Corinne Last is in a position to say, because she lived with him, if Kingman was in the habit of rinsing plates as soon as he removed them from the table. What does she say? That she doesn't know. Isn't that rather odd? Isn't it rather odd too that she chose that precise moment to leave the table and go out into the hall for her handbag?

"She knew that Hannah drank because Hood had told her so. On the evening that meal was eaten you say Hood called for her at her own request. Why? She has her own car, and I don't for a moment believe that a woman like her would feel anything much but contempt for Hood."

"She told him there was something wrong with the car."

"She asked him to come at six, although they were not due at the Kingmans' till eight. She gave him *coffee*. A funny thing to drink at that hour, wasn't it, and before a meal? So what happens when he suggests calling in at a pub on the way? She doesn't say no or say it isn't a good idea to drink and drive. She takes so long getting ready that they don't have time.

"She didn't want Hood to drink any alcohol, Mike, and she was determined to prevent it. She, of course, would take no alcohol and she knew Kingman never drank. But she also knew Hannah's habit of having her first drink of the day at about six.

"Now look at her motive, far stronger than Kingman's. She strikes me as a violent, passionate and determined woman.

Hannah had taken Kingman away from her. Kingman had rejected her. Why not revenge herself on both of them by killing Hannah and seeing to it that Kingman was convicted of the crime? If she simply killed Hannah, she had no way of ensuring that Kingman would come under suspicion. But if she made it look as if he had previously attempted her life, the case against him would become very strong indeed.

"Where was she last Thursday afternoon? She could just as easily have gone up those stairs as Kingman could. Hannah would have admitted her to the flat. If she, known to be interested in gardening, had suggested that Hannah take her on to that balcony and show her the pot herbs, Hannah would willingly have done so. And then we have the mystery of the missing brandy bottle with some of its contents surely remaining. If Kingman had killed her, he would have left that there as it would greatly have strengthened the case for suicide. Imagine how he might have used it. 'Heavy drinking made my wife ill that night. She knew I had lost respect for her because of her drinking. She killed herself because her mind was unbalanced by drink.'

"Corinne Last took that bottle away because she didn't want it known that Hannah drank, and she was banking on Hood's keeping it dark from us just as he had kept it from so many people in the past. And she didn't want it known because the fake murder attempt that *she* staged depended on her victim having alcohol present in her body."

Burden sighed, poured the last dregs of coffee into Wexford's cup. "But we tried that out," he said. "Or I tried it out, and it doesn't work. You knew it wouldn't work from her book. True, she brought the shaggy caps from her own garden, but she couldn't have mixed up poisonous fungi with them because Axel Kingman would have realised at once. Or if he hadn't, they'd all have been ill, alcohol or no alcohol. She was never alone with Hannah before the meal, and while the stew was served she was out of the room."

"I know. But we'll see her in the morning and ask her a few more questions." Wexford hesitated, then quoted softly, " 'Out of good still to find some means of evil.' "

"What?"

"That's what she did, isn't it? It was good for everyone but Hannah, you look as if it's done you a power of good, but it was evil for Hannah. I'm off now, Mike, it's been a long day. Don't forget to put your car away. You won't be making any emergency trips to hospital tonight."

They were unable to puncture her self-possession. The languorous Klimt face was carefully painted this morning, and she was dressed as befitted the violinist or the actress or the author. She had been forewarned of their coming and the gardener image had been laid aside. Her long smooth hands looked as if they had never touched the earth or pulled up a weed.

Where had she been on the afternoon of Hannah Kingman's death? Her thick shapely eyebrows went up. At home, indoors, painting. Alone?

"Painters don't work with an audience," she said rather insolently, and she leaned back, dropping her eyelids in that way of hers. She lit a cigarette and flicked her fingers at Burden for an ashtray as if he were a waiter.

Wexford said, "On Saturday, October 29th, Miss Last, I believe you had something wrong with your car?"

She nodded lazily.

In asking what was wrong with it, he thought he might catch her. He didn't.

"The glass in the offside front headlight was broken while the car was parked," she said, and although he thought how easily she could have broken that glass herself, he could hardly say so. In the same smooth voice she added, "Would you like to see the bill I had from the garage for repairing it?"

"That won't be necessary." She wouldn't have offered to show it to him if she hadn't possessed it. "You asked Mr. Hood to call for you here at six, I understand."

"Yes. He's not my idea of the best company in the world, but I'd promised him some apples for his mother and we had to pick them before it got dark."

"You gave him coffee but had no alcohol. You had no drinks on the way to Mr. and Mrs. Kingman's flat. Weren't you a little disconcerted at the idea of going out to dinner at a place where there wouldn't even be a glass of wine?"

"I was used to Mr. Kingman's ways." But not so used, thought Wexford, that you can tell me whether it was normal or abnormal for him to have rinsed those plates. Her mouth curled, betraying her a little. "It didn't bother me, I'm not a slave to liquor."

"I should like to return to these shaggy caps. You picked them from here on October 28th and took them to Mr. Kingman that evening. I think you said that?"

"I did. I picked them from this garden."

She enunciated the words precisely, her eyes wide open and gazing sincerely at him. The words, or perhaps her unusual straightforwardness, stirred in him the glimmer of an idea. But if she had said nothing more, that idea might have died as quickly as it had been born.

"If you want to have them analysed or examined or whatever, you're getting a bit late. Their season's practically over." She looked at Burden and gave him a gracious smile. "But you took the last of them yesterday, didn't you? So that's all right."

Wexford, of course, said nothing about Burden's experiment. "We'll have a look in your garden, if you don't mind."

She didn't seem to mind, but she had been wrong. Most of the fungi had grown into black-gilled pagodas in the twenty-four hours that had elapsed. Two new ones, however, had thrust their white oval caps up through the wet grass. Wexford picked them, and still she didn't seem to mind. Why, then, had she appeared to want their season to be over? He thanked her and she went back into the cottage. The door closed. Wexford and Burden walked out into the road.

The fungus season was far from over. From the abundant array by the roadside it looked as if the season would last weeks longer. Shaggy caps were everywhere, some of them smaller and greyer than the clump that grew out of Corinne Last's well-fed lawn. There were green and purple agarics, horn-shaped toadstools, and tiny mushrooms growing in fairy rings.

"She doesn't exactly mind our having them analysed," Wexford said thoughtfully, "but it seems she'd prefer the analysis to be done on the ones you picked yesterday than on those I picked today. Can that be so or am I just imagining it?"

"If you're imagining it, I'm imagining it too. But it's no

good, that line of reasoning. We know they're not potenti-
ated—or whatever the word is—by alcohol."

"I shall pick some more all the same," said Wexford.
"Haven't got a paper bag, have you?"

"I've got a clean handkerchief. Will that do?"

"Have to," said Wexford, who never had a clean one. He
picked a dozen more young shaggy caps, big and small, white
and grey, immature and fully grown. They got back into the
car and Wexford told the driver to stop at the public library.
He went in and emerged a few minutes later with three books
under his arm.

"When we get back," he said to Burden, "I want you to get
on to the university and see what they can offer us in the way
of an expert in fungilogy."

He closeted himself in his office with the three books and a
pot of coffee. When it was nearly lunchtime, Burden knocked
on the door.

"Come in," said Wexford. "How did you get on?"

"It's not fungologist or fungilogist," said Burden with tri-
umphant severity. "It's *mycologist* and they don't have one.
But there's a man on the faculty who's a toxicologist and
who's just published one of those popular science books. This
one's about poisoning by wild plants and fungi."

Wexford grinned. "What's it called? *Killing for Nothing?*
He sounds as if he'd do fine."

"I said we'd see him at six. Let's hope something will come
of it."

"No doubt it will." Wexford slammed shut the thickest of
his books. "We need confirmation," he said, "but I've found
the answer."

"For God's sake! Why didn't you say?"

"You didn't ask. Sit down." Wexford motioned him to the
chair on the other side of the desk. "I said you'd done your
homework, Mike, and so you had, only your textbook wasn't
quite comprehensive enough. It's got a section on edible fungi
and a section on poisonous fungi—*but nothing in between.*
What I mean by that is, there's nothing in your book about
fungi which aren't wholesome yet don't cause death or intense suffering. There's nothing about the kind that can make
people ill in certain circumstances."

"But we know they ate shaggy caps," Burden protested.

"And if by 'circumstances' you mean the intake of alcohol, we know shaggy caps aren't affected by alcohol."

"Mike," said Wexford quietly, *"do* we know they ate shaggy caps?" He spread out on the desk the haul he had made from the roadside and from Corinne Last's garden. "Look closely at these, will you?"

Quite bewildered now, Burden looked at and fingered the dozen or so specimens of fungi. "What am I to look *for?*"

"Differences," said Wexford laconically.

"Some of them are smaller than the others, and the smaller ones are greyish. Is that what you mean? But, look here, think of the differences between mushrooms. You get big flat ones and small button ones and . . ."

"Nevertheless, in this case it is that small difference that makes all the difference." Wexford sorted the fungi into two groups. "All the small greyer ones," he said, "came from the roadside. Some of the larger whiter ones came from Corinne Last's garden and some from the roadside."

He picked up between forefinger and thumb a specimen of the former. "This isn't a shaggy cap, it's an ink cap. Now listen." The thick book fell open where he had placed a marker. Slowly and clearly he read: *"The ink cap,* coprinus atramentarius, *is not to be confused with the shaggy cap,* coprinus comatus. *It is smaller and greyer in colour, but otherwise the resemblance between them is strong. While* coprinus atramentarius *is usually harmless when cooked, it contains, however, a chemical similar to the active principle in* Antabuse, *a drug used in the treatment of alcoholics, and if eaten in conjunction with alcohol will cause nausea and vomiting."*

"We'll never prove it."

"I don't know about that," said Wexford. "We can begin by concentrating on the one lie we know Corinne Last told when she said she picked the fungi she gave Axel Kingman *from her own garden."*

Suggestions for Further Reading

Our reading list, modestly annotated, will limit itself to books dealing with the English detectives who appear in this collection:

Sherlock Holmes (Arthur Conan Doyle)
The Great Detective's adventures are available in a multitude of editions (including several comic-book versions). Below are the basic titles.
NOVELS
A Study in Scarlet (1888)
The Sign of Four (1890)
The Hound of the Baskervilles (1902)
The Valley of Fear (1914)
SHORT STORY COLLECTIONS
The Adventures of Sherlock Holmes (1892)
The Memoirs of Sherlock Holmes (1894)
The Return of Sherlock Holmes (1905)
His Last Bow (1917)
The Case Book of Sherlock Holmes (1927)

Loveday Brooke (C. L. Pirkis)
As mentioned earlier, Miss Brooke stars in but a single volume: *The Experiences of Loveday Brooke, Lady Detective* (1894). Individual cases appear in several of the collections listed at the end of this reading list.

Sexton Blake
There are hundreds of Blake novels. Those interested in reading further about Baker Street's other Great Detective

can consult the Hubin bibliography listed in the Acknowledgments on pages vii–viii.

Martin Hewitt (Arthur Morrison)

SHORT STORY COLLECTIONS

Martin Hewitt, Investigator (1894)
The Chronicles of Martin Hewitt (1895)
The Adventures of Martin Hewitt (1896)
The Red Triangle (1903)
Best Martin Hewitt Detective Stories (1976)

The last title, edited and introduced by the dependable E. F. Bleiler, reprints the adventures exactly as they originally appeared in magazine form. The book remains in print from Dover.

Colonel Clay (Grant Allen)

The one and only title is *An African Millionaire* (1897). Arno Press issued a hardcover library edition in 1976. Dover came forth with a trade paperback in 1980. Only by reading all dozen stories can you fully appreciate the colonel's genius.

Eugène Valmont (Robert Barr)

Another detective who appears in but one book: *The Triumphs of Eugène Valmont* (1906). Valmont can also be found in some of the collections listed later on.

Barr's Holmes parody appears in his collection *The Face and the Mask* (1894).

Dr. Thorndyke (R. Austin Freeman)

NOVELS

The Red Thumb Mark (1907)
The Eye of Osiris (1911)
The Mystery of 31, New Inn (1912)
A Silent Witness (1914)
Helen Vardon's Confession (1922)
The Cat's Eye (1923)
The Mystery of Angelina Frood (1924)
    This is Freeman's solution to the Edwin Drood mystery.
The Shadow of the Wolf (1925)
The D'Arblay Mystery (1926)
A Certain Dr. Thorndyke (1927)

As a Thief in the Night (1928)
Mr. Pottermack's Oversight (1930)
   A novel-length use of the inverted formula.
Pontifex, Son and Thorndyke (1931)
When Rogues Fall Out (1932) (U.S. title: *Dr. Thorndyke's Discovery*)
Dr. Thorndyke Intervenes (1933)
For the Defence: Dr. Thorndyke (1934)
The Penrose Mystery (1936)
Felo De Se? (1937) (U.S. title: *Death at the Inn*)
The Stoneware Monkey (1938)
Mr. Polton Explains (1940)
The Jacob Street Mystery (1942) (U.S. title: *The Unconscious Witness*)

SHORT STORY COLLECTIONS
Dr. Thorndyke's Cases (1909)
The Singing Bone (1912)
The Great Portrait Mystery (1918)
Dr. Thorndyke's Case Book (1923) (U.S. Title: *The Blue Scarab*)
The Puzzle Lock (1925)
The Magic Casket (1927)
Dr. Thorndyke Omnibus (1932)
   Contains thirty-seven of the good doctor's investigations.

For the lighter side of Freeman, see *The Adventures of Romney Pringle* (1902, 1968) and *The Further Adventures of Romney Pringle* (1969). Oswald Train reprinted the original collection, giving credit not to the Clifford Ashdown penname but to Freeman and John J. Pitcairn. The second book brings together the rest of the stories and is a first edition.

Father Brown (G. K. Chesterton)
SHORT STORY COLLECTIONS
The Innocence of Father Brown (1911)
The Wisdom of Father Brown (1914)
The Incredulity of Father Brown (1926)
The Secret of Father Brown (1927)
The Scandal of Father Brown (1935)
The Father Brown Omnibus (1951)

Gives you all the stories, including the previously un-
collected "Vampire of the Village."

There is an assortment of other Chesterton collections of
detective and crime stories. My own particular favorite is *The
Club of Queer Trades* (1905).

Mr. Fortune (H. C. Bailey)

Novels

Shadow on the Wall (1934)
Black Land, White Land (1937)
The Great Game (1939)
The Bishop's Crime (1940)
The Apprehensive Dog (1942)
Mr. Fortune Finds a Pig (1943)
The Cat's Whiskers (1944)
The Life Sentence (1946)
Honour Among Thieves (1947)
Save A Rope (1948)

SHORT STORY COLLECTIONS

Call Mr. Fortune (1920)
Mr. Fortune's Practice (1923)
Mr. Fortune's Trials (1925)
Mr. Fortune, Please (1927)
Mr. Fortune Speaking (1929)
Mr. Fortune Explains (1930)
Case for Mr. Fortune (1932)
Mr. Fortune Wonders (1933)
Mr. Fortune Objects (1935)
A Clue for Mr. Fortune (1936)
Mr. Fortune Here (1940)

Hercule Poirot (Agatha Christie)

NOVELS

The Mysterious Affair at Styles (1920)
The Murder on the Links (1923)
The Murder of Roger Ackroyd (1926)
The Big Four (1927)
The Mystery of the Blue Train (1928)
Peril at End House (1932)
Thirteen At Dinner (1933)

Gaudy Night (1935)
Busman's Honeymoon (1937)
SHORT STORY COLLECTIONS
Lord Peter Views the Body (1928)
Hangman's Holiday (1933)
In The Teeth of the Evidence (1939)
Lord Peter (1972)
This one gives you all the Lord Peter short stories, including the "lost" one entitled "Tallboys."

Mr. Campion (Margery Allingham)
NOVELS
The Crime at Black Dudley (1929)
Mystery Mile (1930)
Look to the Lady (1931)
Police at the Funeral (1931)
The Fear Sign (1933)
Death of a Ghost (1934)
Flowers for the Judge (1936)
Dancers in Mourning (1937)
The Fashion in Shrouds (1938)
Traitor's Purse (1941)
Coroner's Pidgin (1945)
More Work for the Undertaker (1949)
The Tiger in the Smoke (1954)
Tether's End (1958)
The China Governess (1962)
The Mind Readers (1963)
Cargo Eagles (1968)
SHORT STORY COLLECTIONS
Mr. Campion, Criminologist (1937)
Mr. Campion and Others (1939)
The Case Book of Mr. Campion (1947)

Dr. Fell (John Dickson Carr)
NOVELS
Hag's Nook (1933)
The Mad Hatter Mystery (1933)
The Blind Barber (1934)
The Eight of Swords (1934)
Death Watch (1935)

The Three Coffins (1935)
The Arabian Nights Murder (1936)
To Wake the Dead (1938)
The Crooked Hinge (1938)
The Problem of the Green Capsule (1939)
The Problem of the Wire Cage (1939)
The Man Who Could Not Shudder (1940)
The Case of the Constant Suicides (1941)
Death Turns the Tables (1942)
Till Death Do Us Part (1944)
He Who Whispers (1946)
The Sleeping Sphinx (1947)
The Dead Man's Knock (1948)
Below Suspicion (1950)
In Spite of Thunder (1960)
The House at Satan's Elbow (1965)
Panic in Box C (1966)
Dark of the Moon (1968)

SHORT STORY COLLECTIONS
Dr. Fell, Detective (1947)
The Third Bullet (1954)

The Department of Dead Ends (Roy Vickers)
SHORT STORY COLLECTIONS
The Department of Dead Ends (1949)
Some Dead Ends yarns will also be found in the following compilations:
Murder Will Out (1954)
Seven Chose Murder (1959)
In America these appeared only as part of the three-decker volumes issued by the Detective Book Club.

Inspector Wexford (Ruth Rendell)
NOVELS
From Doon With Death (1964)
A New Lease of Death (1967)
Wolf to the Slaughter (1967)
The Best Man to Die (1970)
A Guilty Thing Surprised (1970)
No More Dying Then (1971)
Murder Being Once Done (1972)

Some Lie and Some Die (1973)
Shake Hands Forever (1975)
A Sleeping Life (1978)
Make Death Love Me (1979)
Death Notes (1981)
SHORT STORY COLLECTION
Means of Evil (1979)

Now a list of collections which include stories about British detectives.

Sleuths (1931) edited by Kenneth MacGowan

This venerable collection includes fifteen English tecs among its twenty-three entrants. There are also biographical notes on each detective, many written by the authors themselves.

The Rivals of Sherlock Holmes (1970) edited by Hugh Greene

Crime On Her Mind (1975) edited by Michele B. Slung

Ladies only, including Loveday Brooke.

A Treasury of Victorian Detective Stories (1979) edited by Everett F. Bleiler

Bleiler writes just about the best introductions in the business.

Rivals of Sherlock Holmes (1978) edited by Alan K. Russell

The Rivals of Sherlock Holmes 2 (1979) edited by Alan K. Russell

Not to be confused with the Hugh Greene books, these are enormous hardcovers. All of the stories are photo-offset from the original magazine pages. I've only seen them on sale in discount bookshops.

SIGNET Thrillers by Mickey Spillane

(0451)

- [ ] **THE BIG KILL** (114418—$1.95)
- [ ] **BLOODY SUNRISE** (114035—$1.95)
- [ ] **THE BODY LOVERS** (096983—$1.95)
- [ ] **THE BY-PASS CONTROL** (092260—$1.75)
- [ ] **THE DAY OF THE GUNS** (096533—$1.95)
- [ ] **THE DEATH DEALERS** (096509—$1.95)
- [ ] **THE DEEP** (114027—$1.95)
- [ ] **THE DELTA FACTOR** (114019—$1.95)
- [ ] **THE ERECTION SET** (118081—$2.95)
- [ ] **THE GIRL HUNTERS** (195588—$1.95)
- [ ] **I, THE JURY** (113969—$2.95)
- [ ] **KILLER MINE** (117972—$1.50)
- [ ] **KISS ME DEADLY** (064925—95¢)
- [ ] **THE LAST COP OUT** (095928—$1.95)
- [ ] **THE LONG WAIT** (096517—$1.95)
- [ ] **ME, HOOD** (116798—$1.95)
- [ ] **MY GUN IS QUICK** (097912—$1.95)
- [ ] **ONE LONELY NIGHT** (096975—$1.95)
- [ ] **THE SNAKE** (114043—$1.95)
- [ ] **SURVIVAL . . . ZERO** (114051—$1.95)
- [ ] **THE TOUGH GUYS** (092252—$1.75)
- [ ] **THE TWISTED THING** (114000—$1.95)
- [ ] **VENGEANCE IS MINE** (117344—$1.95)

Buy them at your local bookstore or use this convenient coupon for ordering.

THE NEW AMERICAN LIBRARY, INC.,
P.O. Box 999, Bergenfield, New Jersey 07621

Please send me the books I have checked above. I am enclosing $_____
(please add $1.00 to this order to cover postage and handling). Send check
or money order—no cash or C.O.D.'s. Prices and numbers are subject to change
without notice.

Name_____

Address_____

City _____ State _____ Zip Code _____
Allow 4-6 weeks for delivery.
This offer is subject to withdrawal without notice.